Marianne a

Juliette Benzoni was b
the Collège d'Hulet,
she obtained a BA de
and a Licentiate in I
Gallois in 1941 and had tw
moved to Casablanca and lived there for two y
Paris she married Count André Benzoni di Costa in March 1953. Juliette Benzoni is the author of the famous 'Catherine' series of historical romances, set in medieval France, and of the successful 'Marianne' series, set in Napoleonic France.

Previously published by Juliette Benzoni in Pan Books

Marianne series

Marianne Book I: The Bride of Selton Hall
Marianne Book II: The Eagle and the Nightingale
Marianne and the Masked Prince
Marianne and the Privateer
Marianne and the Rebels
Marianne and the Lords of the East

Catherine series

One Love is Enough
Catherine
Belle Catherine
Catherine and Arnaud
Catherine and a Time for Love
A Snare for Catherine

Juliette Benzoni

Marianne and the Crown of Fire

Translated by Anne Carter

Pan Books in association with
Heinemann

First published in French as *Les Lauriers de Flammes* Vol II

First published in Great Britain 1976 by William Heinemann Ltd
This edition published 1979 by Pan Books Ltd,
Cavaye Place, London SW10 9PG
in association with William Heinemann Ltd

ISBN 0 330 25588 6
Printed in Great Britain by
Cox & Wyman Ltd, London, Reading and Fakenham

Contents

Principal Characters

Marianne Elisabeth d'Asselnat, now Princess Sant'Anna. The daughter of a French marquis and his English wife, both of whom perished in the French Revolution. She was rescued as a baby by her godfather, Gauthier de Chazay, and taken to England to be brought up by her spinster aunt, Ellis Selton. In 1809 she married Francis Cranmere who, on her wedding night, gambled away both her fortune and her virginity to an American privateer, Jason Beaufort, with whom, in the course of many subsequent adventures, Marianne became involved in a tempestuous love affair. But it was as the ambassadress of her former lover, the Emperor Napoleon, that she made the journey to Constantinople which brought her, indirectly, to Odessa, to rescue the man she loved from a Tsarist prison. Now, with the *Sea Witch* burned behind them and a vital warning to Napoleon sewn into the bosom of her dress, Marianne has turned her back on her husband and the small son born to her in his Turkish palace, and sets out with Jason to cross the endless Russian steppe.

Adelaide d'Asselnat. A French cousin of Marianne's, an elderly spinster and devoted companion.

Jason Beaufort. The man to whom Francis Cranmere lost Marianne's fortune and virginity. He generously failed to claim the second but reappeared later in Paris to become first her friend and then her lover, although not until he himself was unhappily married to the cruel and vindictive Pilar. Still fate, and Napoleon, seem determined to come between them. After a brief reunion in Venice at the start of the ill-fated voyage to Constantinople, Jason fell victim, in mind and body, to the evil Dr

Leighton whose attempts to take possession of the brig, *Sea Witch*, ended in her capture by the Turks. Jason seemed lost, but reappeared, thanks to the good offices of Prince Corrado, in time to see the birth of Marianne's son and persuade her to accept the baby. Then, attempting to return to America, now on the verge of war with England, he seized the brig, once more impounded by the Turks, and endeavouring to fly, was driven into the arms of the Russian fleet, his ship captured and himself made prisoner.

Gauthier de Chazay, a French Abbé, later Cardinal San Lorenzo, Marianne's much-loved godfather, who rescued her as a baby and was responsible for arranging her marriage to Prince Sant'Anna.

Francis, Lord Cranmere. Marianne's dastardly first husband. She fought a duel with him and left him for dead in the blazing wreck of Selton Hall, but he reappeared in Paris as an English spy, and was executed by Napoleon.

Matteo Damiani. Illegitimate son of Corrado's grandfather and steward of the Sant'Anna estates. A gross and sinister figure, given to the practice of black magic, he abducted Marianne and, boasting that he had murdered her husband, forced upon her the child she bore in Constantinople. Prince Corrado killed him in Venice.

Arcadius, Vicomte de Jolival. A French aristocrat and one of Marianne's staunchest friends. Formerly her theatrical manager, now her business agent.

Craig O'Flaherty. An Irishman, Jason's friend and first officer aboard the *Sea Witch*.

Gracchus-Hannibal Pioche. A former Paris errand-boy and now Marianne's faithful coachman, factotum and self-appointed guardian.

Prince Corrado Sant'Anna. Marianne's second husband. Corrado lived the life of a recluse and the marriage was one in name only. Marianne had never seen his face until the Prince revealed himself as the merchant Turhan Bey in Constantinople and also as the 'Ethiopian', Caleb, whom she had known aboard the *Sea Witch.* Corrado's longing for a son to bear his name caused him to insist on Marianne bearing the baby fathered by Matteo Damiani. At last, reluctantly, she agreed and the boy was born in 'Turhan Bey's' palace at Humayunabad, on the Bosphorus. Believing that Marianne had rejected her child, Corrado then spirited him away to an unknown destination.

Sebastiano Sant'Anna. Marianne's baby son by the evil Matteo Damiani.

Part One
Will Moscow Burn?

Chapter One

The Banks of the Kodyma

The plain stretched endlessly in all directions. Its silvery surface rippled gently in the summer sunshine as the light wind sent it rolling in long waves to the horizon. It was as if some fabulous goddess had let down her floating mane of silken hair after a party. Here and there gleamed the red flower of the wild thistle or the plumed heads of feather-grass.

The heat grew more intense the farther they advanced and by midday was often suffocating, yet Marianne had never been so happy.

In the week or more since she had been travelling with her companions over this vast sea of grass she had experienced a happiness so deep and piercing that it was almost painful. But she knew that this time of grace could not last and that at the end of the long, northward journey was the war that must shatter her present happiness, and so she snatched at it like a starving man, obsessively searching out the smallest crumb and savouring it to the last.

By day, they journeyed across the steppe from one stage to the next. The posting houses lay at intervals of some fifteen versts, or roughly ten miles, and thanks to Gracchus's miraculously acquired permits they were able to change horses, and drivers also, without finding themselves fleeced. The drivers thought themselves well paid at two kopecks a verst and sang all day long.

In theory they covered two stages a day, stopping at night to rest, and the posting houses doubled also as inns, which were otherwise non-existent in the great steppes. The travellers found rooms right enough, but for the most part they were unfurnished, except for the inevitable icons on the walls, hence the necessity for the mattresses with which Gracchus had provided them. Sometimes it was possible to obtain food as well but this varied according to the wealth and generosity of the landowner on whose estates the inn was situated.

The inns, in fact, were a charge on the local nobility, who in the Ukraine and the ancient region of Podolia were mostly Polish. These maintained both horses and staff and for the most part got little enough in return, since paying travellers were few, owing to the ease with which the celebrated permits could be procured.

In her character as an English lady, Marianne might easily have claimed the hospitality of the nobles themselves and have found in their houses, though few and far between, a degree of comfort and even luxury unknown to the imperial post roads. But these mansions, situated in the midst of vast cornfields which in the rich black earth of the steppes grew as rampantly as weeds in a wilderness, often lay a long way from the road. Besides, she had grown to like the bare rooms, with their clean-smelling wooden walls, where they put down their mattresses and she passed passionate nights in Jason's arms, nights that would have been impossible in a private house where the 'manservant' would have been relegated to the servants' quarters.

Both of them had suffered too much and had been parted for too long to have a thought to spare for keeping up appearances or for making any sort of pretence to their companions. Jason had laid his cards on the table the very first night, in Count Hanski's posting house. They had no sooner finished their meagre dinner of duck stuffed with mince and sour milk than he had risen to his feet and silently held out his hand to Marianne. With a deep 'good night' to the assembled company, he had borne her off to her bedchamber.

There, still without a word, they faced one another and, not touching but with their eyes locked in each other's, they had proceeded methodically to undress. As two hands meet and clasp, they came together and together they remained, as one, oblivious of the world around them, until morning light.

Every night after that the lovers lost themselves in their shared ecstasy. By day they abandoned themselves to the endless rocking of the kibitka as it travelled over the highroad. For the most part they slept, despite the jolting and the heat, which both shortened the journey and left them fresher for the night. Twilight falling and the scent of wormwood rising from the steppe would reawaken their desires and from then on they lived only for the magic moment that would lift them out of time, to become once again the first man and woman, naked together in the first night of the world.

Jason's thirst for this woman was insatiable. With her, he could forget his lost ship, the war that lay ahead and all past bitterness and misunderstanding. While in his arms Marianne forgot the child she had lost, her mysterious husband, the perilous secret she carried and all her past sufferings. Above all, for both of them, came forgetfulness that each day was carrying them deeper into a country rent by invasion, bringing them nearer to the blazing heart of the volcano and to the inevitable moment of parting. For with the feel of the imperial letter moving lightly against her skin under her dress Marianne sensed even then that she would never go with Jason to St Petersburg, that the time would come when she must make the choice that would divide their paths once more, for how long she could not tell.

Her task was to reach the Emperor and speak to him. And after that she must return to Paris to await the Cardinal's messenger and give into his hand the diamond she carried at her breast, in a little wash-leather bag sewn to her chemise. It was not in her power to go straight to America. Later, yes, but for the present there were things she still had to do in Europe. Even if it were only to make one more attempt at a last sight of her baby, Sebastiano.

On the evening of the ninth day, the road came to a river. It lay in a shallow valley lined with bushes and small trees, bent by the wind that blew off the steppes, and planted with a patchwork of crops that ranged from grain to melons, and water melons too. The wide blue stream flowed between reedy banks where fishing boats bobbed lazily at their moorings, along with what appeared to be some kind of ferry boat. This was the Kodyma, a tributary of the Bug. A village had grown up on the bank and it was here the travellers came just as the sun was setting.

It was not a large place, consisting only of a group of whitewashed, reed-thatched houses, each with its vegetable patch and cluster of outbuildings, scattered about an open space facing the church. This too was whitewashed and built in the shape of a cross with equal arms, each with its small pediment, facing to the four cardinal points, so that the priest in charge might look eastward while saying mass. In the centre was a gilded onion dome surmounted by a Greek cross that caught the light of the setting sun. Ducks and chickens wandered at will and rose-coloured kingfishers were swooping low over the river.

The posting house stood at the roadside some little distance from the centre of the village. The kibitka drew up before it, startling a pair of fat bustards into cumbrous flight. The driver, reining in his horses, said something only Gracchus, who, far from wasting his time in Odessa, had acquired a fair smattering of the difficult Russian language, was able to understand.

'He says this place is called Velikaia Stanitsa,' he translated now. 'It's a Cossack village.'

'Cossack?' exclaimed Jolival, in whom the word had roused a passion for history that was never very far below the surface. 'How can that be? I thought this was the territory of the old Zaporogi, suppressed by Catherine the Great in the last century.'

'Well, she can't have suppressed all of them,' Craig suggested. 'There must have been some left over.'

Gracchus essayed a question or two, to which the driver responded with a lengthy speech that came as something of a surprise from one who had so far done little more than sing.

'What is he saying?' Marianne asked, stunned by this sudden eloquence.

'I couldn't understand it all by a long way, but I think the gist of it, setting aside a good many appeals to the Little Mother of all the Russias, is that a number of survivors gathered into a few villages. The only thing is, they aren't Zaporogi any more but Black Sea Cossacks.'

The driver, in the meantime, had jumped down from his seat and was pointing with his whip to the church square. He called out something and this time Jolival needed no translation.

'He's right,' he cried. 'Look there!'

The sound of a bell had brought men out from the little gardens, leading horses saddled for a journey. The men were armed to the teeth and wore long tunics of black woollen stuff, caught in at the waist, over baggy trousers of some sort, with tall hats of shaggy fur on their heads. Their weapons consisted of a gun barrel slung over their shoulders, a curved sword, pistol and dagger thrust through their belts and a long lance. Their small, wiry horses carried high, sheepskin-covered saddles.

All the men wore long beards and their appearance was so alarming that Marianne asked uneasily: 'What are they doing? Why are they all coming out together?'

'That's not hard to guess,' Jolival said gloomily. 'Remember what was happening at Odessa. The Cossacks live quietly in their villages, tilling their fields and minding their flocks, until their Ataman sends out his summons over the steppes. Then they put away their ploughs and get out their weapons and set out for the mustering place. That is what these are doing. We've no need to ask what enemy they are going to fight.'

Marianne shivered. It was the first time since leaving Odessa that she had been reminded so clearly of the conflict taking place so far away on the borders of Lithuania that no news of it had yet come to their ears. Sobered by the sight, she would have liked to retreat at once into the posting house but her companions seemed fascinated by the spectacle.

The Cossacks were gathering before the church, in the doorway of which now stood a priest in full canonicals. After the men came the women, clothed, or rather bundled up, in a kind of woollen shift, tied at the waist and worn over a long skirt. They were barefoot and their heads were covered with red or blue scarves. Last of all came the old women and children. The whole population formed up in a half circle in front of the church, as though waiting for something.

At that point the last of the warriors appeared. He was clothed and bearded like his fellows but distinguished from them by the expression of brutal rage that disfigured his flat features and by one thing more. Instead of his horse, he was dragging after him, by her long, tangled black hair, a screaming woman clad only in her shift. Behind these again came an old, grey-haired woman of impassive countenance, carrying a large sack made of heavy canvas.

The woman being so roughly used was young and might have been pretty had her face not been distorted by weeping and screaming. She was doing her utmost to wriggle free from the man's ruthless hand that was dragging her in the dust. When he came in front of the church, the man released the handful of hair in his grasp and sent her sprawling in the centre of the circle of villagers.

There was a murmur of appreciation from the men and a chorus of abuse from the women which the priest silenced with a gesture of his hand. Then the man stepped forward and, in a voice that sounded curiously calm in contrast to his recent behaviour, delivered himself of a short speech which the driver did his best to translate for the benefit of his passengers.

'What is he saying?' Jason asked.

'Well, all I can say is that these people here have some peculiar habits,' Gracchus answered. 'As far as I can gather, the man speaking is the husband of the woman on the ground. She has been unfaithful and he is casting her off before he leaves for the war so that she shall not soil his hearth with the fruit of her misdeeds.'

'He need not cast her off so brutally,' Marianne said indignantly.

'That's not the half of it,' Gracchus went on. 'If there's another man in the village willing to take her, she may live. If not, she'll be tied up in that sack that the old woman, her mother-in-law, is carrying and be thrown into the river.'

'But that's scandalous!' Marianne exclaimed fiercely. 'Why, it's nothing more than criminal! Where is the man who was her lover?'

'It seems he was some vagabond, a wandering fellow of the steppes belonging to the woman's own people. She is a gipsy and she'll not have many friends in this village.'

Certainly a deep silence had fallen. The woman still lay on the ground. She tossed her head to throw back a lock of long hair that trailed across her face. Her anguished black eyes searched the faces that stared back at her body, barely hidden by the torn shift, and at the weals and the darkening bruises showing on the brown skin. The husband had folded his arms and he too was staring about him, as though defying his fellows to take up what he had cast off. At his back a group of women clustered about the mother-in-law, who, like some avenging fury, was already busying herself shaking out the sack.

'Surely there must be one,' Marianne breathed, aghast, 'a very young one, perhaps, or else an old man for whom such a girl would be a gift . . .?'

But there was neither old man nor young boy not yet of an age to bear arms who was willing to buy himself endless trouble for the sake of a guilty woman not of his own people. The woman's doom was clear in every glance. The priest, standing like a glittering statue at the entrance to his church, seemed to understand it, for he traced the sign of the cross in the air a number of times with the cross he carried and began intoning a prayer. The husband uttered a short, harsh laugh and turned away while the women advanced with a horrid eagerness. Another moment and the condemned woman, who was howling now like a wolf in pain, would have been seized and tied into the sack and thrown into the river which, for all its beauty, was to be the instrument of her death.

Then it was that Gracchus leapt forward and without a second's thought rushed at the group, crying out '*Stoi! Stoi!* Stop! Stop!' with the full force of his lungs.

'Good God!' Marianne gasped with horror. 'He'll get himself lynched! Go after him!'

She had no need to ask. Already Jason, Craig and Jolival were running, dragging with them the driver, more dead than alive, and lurching grotesquely in the American's strong grip.

For a moment the situation was fraught with danger. In their fury at seeing their victim snatched from them, the women fell upon Gracchus, shrieking like hyenas over their prey, and the men, at this unexpected intervention, were on the point of joining in when the priest plunged in to the young man's rescue, brandishing his cross. This had the effect of instantly arresting the Cossacks. The women reluctantly released their hold on Gracchus and his friends gathered round him with the air of men determined not to be browbeaten.

With the priest as mediator, the long, laborious argument

began. There were shouts and threatening gestures, especially on the part of the wronged husband, who evidently meant to witness the death of the woman who had betrayed him. Marianne, who had not moved from her place by the coach, wondered what she ought to do. If the danger began to look urgent, the best thing might be to drive the kibitka full tilt into the crowd and try to use its weight and the effects of surprise to snatch the four men from certain death. For not one of them had thought of such weapons as there were inside it.

She had climbed into the driver's seat and was already grasping the reins, preparatory to turning the vehicle, when the hubbub subsided suddenly. The women, the old men and the children, began to drift back to the houses. The men returned to their horses. The only people left in the middle of the square were the condemned woman, whom Gracchus had helped to her feet, the priest and the foreigners. The priest raised his cross again to point the way going down to the river. Gracchus took the woman by the hand and, followed by the three others and the coachman, still more dead than alive, came back to the posting house and their coach.

The generous impulse which had prompted the young man's action had cooled somewhat during the discussion and he approached Marianne with a faintly shamefaced air.

'The priest says that she is now my wife! Her name is Shankala,' he muttered, sounding so downcast that Marianne smiled at him comfortingly.

'Why are you looking so miserable, Gracchus? You could not have stood by and seen the poor creature murdered,' she said gently. 'You acted splendidly and for my part I am proud of you.'

'And so am I! From a humanitarian point of view, at any rate,' Jolival agreed. 'But I am wondering what we are going to do with her?'

'I can't see that the question arises,' the Irishman said cheerfully. 'The woman should go with her husband and since this wild cat is now Madame Gracchus . . .'

'Oh, as to that, I didn't take the holy man too seriously.' The bridegroom broke in with an air of would-be carelessness. 'I'm not really married, of course. Besides, I'm for liberty. I don't go much for priests and if you want the truth I've more faith in the Goddess of Reason than in God the Father. Not that she wasn't a handsome wench—'

'Well, Gracchus,' Marianne exclaimed in amazement; 'this is certainly a profession of faith! I've always known you for a child of the Revolution but I wonder what the cardinal would say if he could hear you?'

Gracchus hung his head and fidgeted a little.

'Forgive me, Mademoiselle Marianne. I said more than I meant. This business has me in a proper whirl. But after all, surely the girl could always make a maid for you. She'd never be as good as Agathe, of course, but still better than nothing.'

Jason, so far, had said nothing. He was gazing at the rescued woman with a curious expression, as though she were some strange animal. At last he gave a shrug.

'A ladies' maid? That girl? You don't know what you're saying, Gracchus. It seems to me that she'll be more trouble to tame than a she-wolf. Nor do I think she will show us much gratitude for saving her.'

Marianne was inclined to agree with him. Even in her present wretched state, with her torn shift and her bruises and covered in dust, the gipsy girl was not an object for pity. Her black eyes gleamed under their heavy brows with a savage fire that was more than a little disturbing. Seen from close to, she was in fact quite beautiful, in spite of a rather flattened nose and high cheekbones. Her rather slanting eyes betrayed traces of mongol blood. Her skin was smooth and her hair a deep blue-black, but the wide mouth with its full, red lips betrayed a latent sensuality.

She stared insolently from one to another of her rescuers and when Marianne smiled kindly at her and held out her hand, she pretended not to see it and turned away quickly to snatch away the bundle wrapped in red cloth which her mother-in-law had tossed at the driver out of her doorway and which probably contained the girl's belongings.

Craig laughed softly. 'Well now, to be sure, it's a pleasant journey we'll be having with this colleen—'

'Bah!' Jolival said. 'I'll be surprised if she stays with us long. She'll be off at the first opportunity as soon as she's put sufficient distance between herself and her friends in the village here. You heard what Gracchus said? She's a gipsy, a born traveller.'

'Oh, let her do as she likes,' Marianne said with a sigh, nettled by the girl's contemptuous attitude. 'Gracchus is the only one of us who can talk to her. Let him try what he can do.'

She had had more than enough of the business and if she was not precisely sorry they had saved the gipsy girl from drowning, she certainly wanted to put her out of her mind as far as possible. After all, Gracchus was a grown man and old enough to be responsible.

She turned her steps towards the doorway of the inn where the familiar figure of the postmaster stood cap in hand to greet them. Jason followed her but when Gracchus took Shankala by the arm to lead her inside she twisted out of his grasp like a snake and, running after Jason, took his hand and pressed it to her lips with fierce intensity. As she released it she spoke some words in a low, guttural voice.

'What does she say?' Marianne cried with rising irritation.

Gracchus had turned scarlet to the roots of his carroty hair and his blue eyes flashed.

'She says that – that if she must have a master she will choose him for herself. The hussy! I've a good mind to call back her husband and hand her over to the women again.'

'It's too late now,' Jolival said.

Indeed, the Cossacks, after a final blessing from their priest, were already beginning to cross the river. Heedless of wetting themselves, they rode into the water at a place known to them which must have been a ford because the horses, guided by their sure hands, were never more than breast deep in the stream. The leaders were already mounting the farther bank. The rest followed in their turn and before very long they were all forming up again in perfect order on the other side. Two by two, the black-clad riders vanished into the gathering darkness.

That night, in the little boarded room beneath the icon of the Virgin and Child, both of them sporting the most atrocious squints, Marianne failed to recover the perfect happiness of earlier nights. She was nervous and irritable and unable to respond wholeheartedly to her lover's caresses. Her mind still dwelled on the woman who was sleeping somewhere beneath their common roof. In vain she told herself that she was little more than a wild animal, a creature of no importance who could never affect her own life; still she could not rid herself of the notion that the gipsy was a danger, a threat that was the more formidable because she could not tell what form it would take.

Tired of clasping an unresponsive body and of kissing lips that did not take fire from his, Jason got up suddenly and, fetching the candle that burned before the icon, brought it close to Marianne's face. In the light her eyes were wide open and shining, with no hint of amorous softness in them.

'What is it?' he murmured, laying a finger softly on her lips. 'You look as if you'd seen a ghost. Don't you feel like making love tonight?'

She did not move her head but her eyes, as they looked at him, were full of sadness.

'I'm frightened,' she said.

'Frightened? What of? Are you afraid those village harpies will come and sit down outside our windows to get Shankala back?'

'No. I think it is Shankala I am afraid of.'

Jason laughed. 'What an idea! She's no very friendly look about her, I'll agree, but then she doesn't know us and from what we've seen she's had no cause so far to love the human race. Those old witches would have torn her to pieces if they could. Her beauty can't have helped her there.'

Marianne was conscious of a nasty little tug somewhere in the region of her heart. She did not at all like to hear Jason speak of the woman's beauty.

'Have you forgotten she deceived her husband? She's an adulteress—'

The sudden harshness that came into her voice made her feel as if the words had been a scream. Or perhaps it was the silence that followed them. For a moment Jason studied the sharpened lines of his beloved's face. Then he blew out the candle and drew her hard against him, holding her so close that it was as if he would have crept inside her very skin. He kissed her, a long kiss that sought to warm her cold lips and instil into them something of his own passion, but in vain. His lips moved to her cheek, then nibbled at her ear before he whispered at last: 'But you, too, are an adulteress, my love. Yet no one has suggested drowning you . . .'

Marianne leapt as if a serpent had stung her and struggled to draw away but he held her firmly and, the better to immobilize her, imprisoned both her legs between his hard thighs, while she cried out: 'You are mad! I, an adulteress? Don't you know that I am free? That my husband is dead?'

She was panic-stricken, seized with a terror she could not control. Guessing that she was on the point of screaming aloud, Jason spoke more tenderly than ever.

'Hush! Be quiet,' he murmured against her lips. 'Don't you think it's time you told me the truth? Don't you know yet that I love you – and that you can safely trust me?'

'But – what do you want me to tell?'

'What I have a right to know. I know I may not have given you much cause to think that I will understand. I have been brutal, cruel, violent and unjust. But I have been sorry for it, Marianne! All through those days when I lay like a corpse in the sunshine at Monemvasia, waiting for the recovery that seemed to elude me, I thought only of you, of us two – and of all that I had so wantonly destroyed. If I had helped and understood you then, we would not be here now. You would have carried out your mission and at this moment we would be sailing back to my country, instead of journeying endlessly over these barbarous steppes. So let us have no more foolishness, no more lies and pretence! Let us cast off everything but ourselves, as we cast off our clothes to love one another. I want to see your naked soul, my love . . . Tell me the truth. It is more than time if we want to be able ever to build up a true happiness—'

'The truth?'

'Yes. I will help you. Where is your child, Marianne?'

Her heart missed a beat. She had always known that, sooner or later, Jason would ask her that question but until that moment she had tried to ward off all the possible answers, perhaps from an unconscious weariness at all the lies she had been forced to tell.

She knew that he was right, that they must make an end, once and for all, of all misunderstandings, and that only then would all things become possible. Yet she still shrank, unaccountably, from uttering the words, like a little girl trembling on the brink of a deep ditch.

'My child . . .' she began slowly, halting over the words, 'he is . . .'

'With his father, is he not? Or at least with the man who would be a father to him? He is with Turhan Bey, or rather, with your permission, with the Prince Sant'Anna.'

Once again, there was silence but this time there was a different quality in the air. A sudden relief, a clear note of release rang in Marianne's voice as she asked, almost timidly: 'How did you find out? Who told you?'

'No one – and everyone. He, most of all, I think, a man who could choose slavery by going aboard my ship. He had no reason to bear what he did from me and from others unless it was to protect some other person, and that someone you. To be sure, I did not guess it all at once. But the thick web that was woven so closely about you became amazingly clear one morning at the palace of Humayunabad, when I met the Sant'Annas' faithful servant bearing the last of those princes with such triumphant joy and pride to be presented to a simple merchant, of no very certain nationality, who, in the ordinary way, could not have had so pressing an interest in the child that all else must make way for it. But you, Marianne? When did you learn the truth?'

She told him then. Eager to complete the tale he had already heard from Jolival, she told him everything, emptying her heart and her memory once and for all with an inexpressible feeling of release. She told him all about the nocturnal visit to Rebecca's house, about the Prince's demand and her stay at the Morousi palace, about the bargain she had made with her husband, the peril she had been in from the English ambassador and her installation in the palace by the Bosphorus, culminating in the Prince's sudden departure with the child, believing that its mother had rejected it, at the very moment when she had come to know her own heart. Last of all, she told him of her fears as to his own reactions when he should learn that she had been married to a black.

'We had agreed to part,' she said, 'so what was the good of telling you all this at the risk of making you angry again?'

He uttered a mirthless little laugh.

'Making me angry? So, in your eyes, I am nothing more than some kind of slave trader?' he said bitterly. 'I suppose you'll never understand that I grew up among black people, that I owe some of the best parts of my childhood to them, and that to me it seems quite natural that I should be their master and love them just the same? As for him—'

'Yes, tell me. How do you think of him?'

He thought for a moment and she heard him sigh.

'I don't really know. With liking, certainly, and respect for his courage and his selflessness. But with anger, too – and jealousy. He is altogether too great a man. Too noble, too remote from other men, from common or garden adventurers like me! And a darn sight too good-looking also! What's more, in spite of everything, he is your husband. You bear his name in the sight of God and men. And then he has your child, flesh of your flesh – something of you! So you see, there are times when I think that for all his willing sacrifice, he has the luck . . .'

All at once there had come into the privateer's voice a sadness so deep and bitter that Marianne was overwhelmed. Instinctively, she clung more closely to him. Never before had she felt herself so close to him, felt how much she loved him. She belonged to him utterly and not for anything in the world, in spite of all the suffering he had caused her, would she have had it any other way, for tears and suffering were the strongest mortar of love.

Pressing her lips against the firm muscles of his neck, she whispered fiercely: 'Don't think of it, not any more, I beg you. Forget all that . . . I have told you, I shall not remain the Prince's wife. There will be a divorce. He is in full agreement and there is nothing now stands between me and my freedom, thanks to the Emperor's new laws, but a simple formality. When that is done I can be yours entirely and for ever. All this part of my life will be wiped out, like a bad dream—'

'And the child? Will that be wiped out too?'

She jerked away from him as though he had struck her and remained staring. He had a sudden feeling that beneath the soft skin every muscle in the girl's body had tensed. But it was only for a moment. Then, with a sigh that might have been unconscious, she was back in his arms again, hugging him to her with all her might, in a primitive need to assure herself that both of them were really there. At the end of one long kiss and then another, she gave a sigh.

'I think I've always known that there is no true joy or happiness on earth that does not have to be paid for sooner or later. Old Dobbs, the head groom at Selton, taught me that when I was very small.'

'Your head groom was a philosopher, then?'

'Philospher is too strong a word. He was a strange old man, though, full of wisdom and good sense. He never spoke much and what he said was mostly in proverbs and old sayings he had picked up here and there all over the world, for he had been a sailor in his youth, under Admiral Cornwallis. One day when I was determined to ride Firebird, the finest and most mettlesome of all our horses, and was beginning to throw a tantrum because he would not let me, Dobbs took his pipe out of his mouth – he was always smoking a pipe – and said, quite calmly: "Very well, then, Miss Marianne. If you're set on breaking a leg, or maybe two, let alone your head into the bargain, that's your business. As to that, there's a saying I once heard somewhere comes to my mind. There's God, you see, a-showing man all the pleasures of the world and 'Take all you want,' says He, 'take it and pay!' " '

'And did you ride Firebird?'

'Indeed I did not! But I never forgot what Dobbs had said and I've had cause to test the truth of it more than once. I've even come to think that the child is the price I have to pay for the right to be with you. Because, I can confess it to you, ever since he was born I have been longing to ask the Prince to give him to me. So much that I actually considered taking him back without his permission. But that would be wrong, cruel even, because it was he who wanted him, much more than I. I was rejecting him with all my might. He is the one hope, the one happiness in a life of complete self-sacrifice—'

'And aren't you going to suffer?'

She gave a sad little laugh. 'I'm suffering already. But I shall try and think that I have lost him, that he did not live. And besides,' she added with a sudden warmth, filled with all the intensity of her secret hopes, 'besides, I shall have other children, your children. They will be both yours and mine and I know that the first time I bear you a son my pain will be eased. Love me, now. We have talked and thought too much. Let us forget everything but ourselves . . . I love you . . . You will never know how much I love you.'

'Marianne! My love! My brave, foolish darling!'

The words died as their lips joined and after that the only sounds in the small room were the plaintive sighs and moans of a woman in the throes of love.

Next morning, as Jason, Craig and Gracchus helped the innkeeper and the driver to manoeuvre the kibitka on to the ferry boat for the crossing of the Kodyma, everyone could see that Gracchus seemed to be in a remarkably bad temper and that he bore the marks of fresh scratches on his cheek.

'I wonder,' Jolival whispered in Marianne's ear, 'Whether our friend did not, after all, take the village priest a lot more seriously than he made out.'

She could not help smiling.

'You think—?'

'That he tried to assert his marital rights and got short shrift? I'd go bail he did. And I can't say I'm surprised. She's a fine-looking wench.'

'You think so?' Marianne remarked primly.

'Good Lord, yes! To anyone who has a fancy for that type of noble savage. Though she's no very accommodating air about her, to be sure.'

Dressed once more in her proper clothes which consisted of a full skirt and a red bodice with barbaric stripes, with a voluminous black shawl draped over all, Shankala presented an even wilder and more enigmatic figure than she had done in her torn shift the day before. Enveloped in quantities of funereal black woollen stuff as in a Roman toga, with her hair falling in thick braids on either side of her face, she stood apart from the rest at the forward end of the boat, her small bundle wrapped in red cloth lying by her bare feet, watching the farther shore as it approached.

Her refusal to cast even one single glance backwards at the village she was leaving, probably for ever, was a thing almost palpable in its intensity. Nor was it, all in all, in any way hard to understand, especially since her last action before embarking had been to spit savagely on the ground, like a wild cat, and then, thrusting out her hand with first and fourth fingers extended towards the little cluster of cottages lying white and peaceful under the rising sun, she had hurled some imprecation in a harsh, fierce voice so full of hate that it could only have contained a curse.

Marianne reflected that she for one would be only too pleased if Jolival's prediction came true and their new companion were to take the first opportunity of parting from them.

Once across the river, Jolival paid off the ferryman and they all resumed their places in the kibitka. But when Gracchus took Shankala by the arm to help her up into the seat between himself and the driver the girl tore herself free, with the same fierce, angry gesture as on the night before, and springing lightly up under the hood settled herself on the boards at Jason's feet, looking up at him with a smile that was an open invitation.

'Is there no way,' Marianne said in a voice throbbing with anger, 'of making that woman understand that she is not mistress here?'

'I'm with you there, Ma— milady,' Gracchus agreed. 'I've a good mind to toss her into the river after all and be rid of her. I'm beginning to see her husband's point, and her mother-in-law's.'

'Not so loud,' Jason said. 'You only have to know how to deal with her.'

He bent down and, taking the woman's arm, calmly but firmly obliged her to take her seat on the box, taking no notice at all of the poisonous look she darted at Marianne.

'There,' he said. 'Now that we are all settled, you may tell the driver to drive on, Gracchus.'

The man gave vent to a guttural cry to set his horses in motion and the vehicle resumed its northward journey over the same road the Cossack horsemen had taken the night before.

Day after day, week after week, the occupants of the kibitka pursued their way from one posting house to the next, never departing from the main road which would bring them, by way of Uman, Kiev, Bryansk and Moscow, to St Petersburg.

They could in fact have shortened their journey considerably by going by way of Smolensk, but when they reached the venerable and ancient princely city of Kiev, generally regarded by the Russians as the cradle of their country, the travellers found the place in something like a ferment. The packed churches were reverberating to the sound of public prayers and a perfect forest of candles blazed in front of every glittering iconostasis.

The reason for it was the grave news brought to the holy city by exhausted messengers galloping weary horses. A few days earlier General Barclay de Tolly and his army had been beaten at Smolensk and had abandoned the city after setting fire to it. The chief city of the Borysthenes, one of the greatest of the Tsar's empire, had been virtually destroyed and was now in the hands of Napoleon's *Grande Armée*, that vast horde of four hundred thousand armed men, speaking several languages, in which Wurtembergers, Bavarians and Danes fought side by side with Schwartzenberg's Austrians, the troops belonging to the Confederation of the Rhine and the Italians under Prince Eugene. And Kiev, the holy city of St Vladimir, mourned for its dead and prayed to heaven to punish the barbarian who had dared to set foot on the sacred soil.

This news brought about the beginnings of an argument between Jason and Marianne. She was filled with joy at Napoleon's capture of Smolensk and saw no reason, now, to continue her journey to Moscow.

'If the French hold Smolensk,' she pointed out, 'we can save time and make directly for St Petersburg. We can even beg assistance—'

Jason's reply was curt and to the point.

'Assistance? For Lady Selton? Unlikely, surely? Unless you mean to make your presence known to Napoleon? Well, I mean to have nothing to do with him. We had decided to go by way of Moscow and by Moscow we shall go.'

'But he may be in Moscow before us!' Marianne cried, suddenly defensive. 'At the rate his army is advancing, it is more than likely. What is the distance from Smolensk to Moscow?' she demanded, turning to Gracchus.

'About a hundred versts,' he told her, after a rapid consultation with the driver. 'Whereas for us it is about three hundred.'

'You see?' Marianne concluded triumphantly. 'It's no use deceiving yourself. Short of making an enormous detour by the Volga, perhaps, we can't avoid Napoleon's army. Besides, how do we know Napoleon himself won't take the road to St Petersburg?'

'You'd like that, wouldn't you, eh? Go on, admit you're longing to set eyes on your beloved emperor again!'

'He's not my beloved emperor,' Marianne retorted sharply. 'But he is my emperor and Jolival's and Gracchus's too! Whether you like it or not, we are all French and we've no cause to be ashamed of it.'

'Indeed? That's not what's written on your *podaroshna*, my lady! You had better make up your mind. For my part, it's the Russians I need and I've no intention of making enemies of them by falling into the arms of their invaders. From now on, we travel twice or even three times as fast. I want to get to Moscow before Napoleon.'

'You want, you want! What right have you to dictate what we do? But for us you would still be held a prisoner by your dear friends the Russians! You seem very ready to forget that they are even more closely allied to England and that your own country is just now at war with your friends' friends. How do you know that these Krilovs you put such faith in are going to befriend you? You are expecting them to help you? Give you a ship? What if they slam the door in your face and will have nothing to say to you? What will you do then?'

He cast her a fulminating glance, annoyed that she should cast doubts on what seemed to him so certain.

'I don't know. But it will never happen.'

'But suppose it did?'

'Oh, you make me lose all patience. We shall see. There are always ways of finding a ship. If the worst comes to the worst—'

'You can always steal one? It's becoming a habit with you. Well, it's not always possible, let me tell you. Not even for such an intrepid seaman as yourself. Be sensible for once, Jason, and listen to me. We have nothing to fear from Napoleon and everything to gain. Let us go straight to meet him. I promise you I've no ulterior motive in suggesting it. And indeed,' she gave a bitter little laugh, 'indeed I thought that we had finished once for all with all that, that it was old history—'

'It won't be old history until you have rid yourself of this overriding obsession to go to him at any cost.'

Marianne sighed distressfully. 'But I have no obsession, except to get away and go with you, as soon as possible! The only thing is that I have it in my power to do the Emperor a service, a very great service in return for which he will gladly provide me with the best and fastest ship in Danzig – not just a passage, or even a loan, but as a gift! You see—'

There was no holding her now. In spite of all Jolival's anxious glances, warning her not to show all her hand, Marianne was carried away by her own anger, and by an almost physical need to convince Jason. She was beyond stopping and by the time she saw that she had given too much away it was too late. The inevitable question had been asked.

'A service?' Jason demanded suspiciously. 'What kind of service?'

It was said to hurt and she was on the point of snapping back that it was none of his business but she controlled herself and merely reminded him that the question might have been more courteously phrased. 'However, I will answer it all the same, as politely as I can,' she said. 'Naturally, considering the state of your feelings towards the Emperor, I cannot tell you the precise nature of the information I am carrying. I will only tell you that I learned by chance of a grave danger threatening not just the Emperor himself but his whole army and—' She broke off, for Jason had begun to laugh but it was a laughter with no trace of amusement in it.

'I will follow you to Siberia if you will, you said! And all the time your one object was to reach Napoleon! And I believed you!'

'And you should believe me still, for I meant what I said, and so I do still. But that does not mean that when fate puts into my hand the means of warning my friends of a danger threatening them that I should do nothing and maybe let them walk into a trap.'

Jason's brow was set in obstinate lines and he was clearly about to make a sharp rejoinder when Jolival came to his friend's aid.

'Don't be a fool, Beaufort,' he cried impatiently. 'And don't start behaving again in a way you will be sorry for afterwards! None of us forgets that you have little to be grateful for in the Emperor's treatment of you but you will not remember that Napoleon is not a private person to be dealt with as an equal by us or by you.'

'I'd have expected you to agree with Marianne,' the American remarked.

'I see no cause to disagree with her. Far from it. And, if I may say so, this seems to me to be a singularly pointless argument. You want to reach St Petersburg and our way there, whether you like it or not, is almost bound to bring us into contact with Napoleon's army. That being so, Marianne would be betraying her country if she failed to deliver the information she has. In any case, to put your mind at rest, I can tell you, if it will satisfy you, that she will not see Napoleon. I will go to him myself when the time comes. I shall leave you and we will meet again later. If you are willing to wait for me, I may even be able to bring you an order for a vessel, in which case there will be no further problem. Does that satisfy you?'

Jason made no answer. He was standing with folded arms staring down with a grim expression into the blue waters of the Dnieper, which the Greeks had called Boysthenes, as it flowed southwards in a broad, majestic stream at his feet. The travellers had descended from their vehicle and strolled a little way along the river, past the painted wooden houses of the lower town, newly rebuilt after the disastrous fire which had destroyed the commercial district of Podil, with its church and warehouses, in the preceding year. Above them, on a kind of cliff overhanging the river harbour, which occupied the narrow strip of land between it and the stream, was the old town, enclosed within its medieval walls, with its blue and gold onion domes, its rich religious houses and old-fashioned, brightly-painted wooden palaces.

Outside the inn built of undressed logs which did duty as a posting house, the driver was unhitching the horses.

Still Jason said nothing and in the end it was Craig O'Flaherty who lost patience and answered for him. Clapping his captain on the back with a force sufficient to have knocked him into the river, he beamed at Jolival with cheerful approval.

'He'll be a churl if he's not satisfied. Sure, you talk like a book, Vicomte. And you've a knack of hitting on a solution that suits everyone. And now, if you please, let's be making for that hen-house they call an inn and see if they can find us some dinner. I could eat a horse.'

Jason followed the others without a word but Marianne had a feeling he was still not convinced. She was sure of it when, after what was certainly the best meal they had eaten since setting out, consisting as it did of a vegetable bortsch to start with, followed by a thick, twisted sausage called *kolbassa* and *vareniki*, light, sugared tarts, the privateer got up from the table and announced curtly that they had better get to bed since they would be leaving the city at four the next morning. This was tantamount to a declaration that he intended to do his utmost to beat Napoleon's army to it, and no one made any mistake about it.

Marianne least of all, for that night she waited in vain for her lover beneath the inevitable icon which, this time, depicted, no less inevitably, St Vladimir. The door of the tiny room with its lingering odours of cooking fat and cabbage never opened to admit Jason.

In the end, tired of turning over and over on her mattress like St Lawrence on his gridiron, she got up but remained undecided what to do next. She hated the idea of letting a fresh misunderstanding grow between them. This quarrel was a stupid one, like so many lovers' tiffs in which both parties seemed determined to vie with one another in selfishness and unfairness. But with a man as stubborn as Jason, who could carry obstinacy to the point of blind stupidity, it could become protracted. And that, too, was something Marianne could not endure. Their journey was painful enough as it was.

For a minute or two she prowled to and fro between the door of her room and its small window, set wide open because of the heat which, even at this time of night, was stifling. She was consumed with longing to go to Jason. After all, it was her idea of going straight on to Smolensk which had started the argument and it might be for her to make the first move towards a reconciliation. But to do that she would have to overcome her pride which revolted at the picture of herself going humbly to seek out her lover in the room which he was no doubt sharing with Jolival (which would not be too bad) or, much more awkward, with Craig, and dragging him from his bed to her own, like a she-cat on heat come looking for a tom.

Still struggling with herself, she lingered at her window which framed a view of the river and the low, flat outline of its eastern shore. The Dnieper ran like a stream of quicksilver in the moonlight and the reeds upon its banks stood out like fine, black strokes brushed in Indian ink. The big freight barges slumbered side by side, waiting for their next voyage and dreaming perhaps of fabulous, distant seas that they would never see, even as Marianne herself dreamed of America which at that moment seemed to her to be retreating farther and farther into the mists of the unattainable.

She was making up her mind to go down to the water's edge in search of a little freshness to cool the fever that burned in her and had actually begun to reach for her clothes, although still without taking her eyes from the river, when she saw walking by the very man who filled her thoughts.

Jason was strolling down towards the gleaming water, his hands clasped behind his back in that familiar attitude of his as he paced his quarterdeck. And Marianne smiled suddenly, relieved to know that he too had been unable to sleep. It filled her with tenderness to think that he had been fighting the same battle with his pride as she had with hers. Jason had never found it easy to extricate himself from a situation of this kind. She had only to humble herself a very little and she would have no trouble in bringing him back to her.

She was on the point of rushing from the room when, all at once, she saw Shankala.

The gipsy girl was evidently following Jason. Making no more sound than a cat in her bare feet, she was running as lightly as a ghost after the man who drew her and who had clearly no suspicion of her presence there.

Marianne, in the darkness of her room, felt her cheeks flush with sudden anger. She had had more than enough of this woman. She had not yet exchanged a single word with her and yet her silent presence oppressed her like a nightmare. Through all the long miles they had travelled together in the enforced proximity of the kibitka, the gipsy's black eyes had remained fixed on one of two points: on the white ribbon of the road ahead, at which she would gaze tirelessly for hours on end as though searching for something, or on Jason to whom she would turn from time to time with a smile lurking in her eyes. The look on her face as she moistened her red lips with the tip of a pointed tongue made Marianne long to hit her.

Jason strolled on slowly until he was hidden behind one of the piles of logs which lined the waterside beyond the narrow strip of quay. At Kiev, the steppes came to a sudden end and gave way to the great forests whose produce was piled beside the waterway that would carry it south.

Shankala, however, instead of following Jason, had turned aside and was taking a parallel path on the nearer side of the heaped-up logs. Marianne, observing her eagerly, saw her set off at a run towards the rising ground which marked the end of the river harbour. The gipsy's intention was clear. She meant to meet Jason coming the other way.

Unable to stay where she was a moment longer and impelled by a curiosity she could not control, Marianne left the inn in her turn and hurried down to the river. Jealousy, a primitive instinct, drove her after Jason, a jealousy she could not have justified or explained. She only knew that she wanted to see what Jason would do when he came face to face alone with the woman who had made no secret of her intentions towards him.

Rounding the first log pile and coming to the river she saw nothing at all, for a curve in its course hid everything beyond. Her feet made no sound on the close-packed sand and she began to run. But when she reached the bend she clapped a hand to her mouth to stifle an exclamation and shrank back into the deep shadows between two piles of logs.

Jason was there, a few yards away from her. He had his back to her and standing facing him was Shankala. She had let fall her dress and was standing naked before him in the moonlight.

Marianne's throat felt dry. The witch was beautiful beyond a doubt. With the moon's rays silvering her brown skin she looked like a water sprite emerging from the shining river and born of its substance. Her arms hung loose at her slender sides, palms outward, her head was flung slightly backward, the eyes half-closed, and she stood quite still, allowing a sensuality so powerful as to be an almost palpable thing to work its own magic. Only the slight quickening of her breath, the rhythmic heaving of her heavy, round yet perfect breasts, betrayed her desire for the man before her. Her attitude was precisely that of the statue of Dona Lucinda in the temple at the Villa Sant'Anna and Marianne almost cried out at the resemblance.

Jason, too, seemed turned to stone. From her hiding place, Marianne could not see the expression on his face but the total stillness of his body clearly betrayed a kind of fascination. Marianne felt weak and red lights danced before her eyes. She was forced to lean back against the rough tree trunks, incapable of taking her eyes from the scene that held them yet longing desperately to sink into the water if Jason yielded to temptation. The silence and the stillness seemed to last for ever.

Suddenly Shankala moved. She took a step towards Jason, then another. Her eyes were gleaming and Marianne, in torment, dug her nails into the palms of her hands. The woman's panting breath filled her ears like a rushing wind. She was moving closer to the man who even now had not moved. One step . . . and one more. She was about to touch him, to cling to him with that form whose very walk was vibrant with desire.

Her lips were slightly parted, showing the small, sharp, carnivorous teeth. Marianne wanted to cry out in terror but no sound came from her throat, she was paralysed with shock. In another instant the love of her life would crumble at her feet, like a god with feet of clay.

But Jason had stepped back. His outstretched arm touched the woman's shoulder and held her at a distance.

'No,' he said.

Then, with a shrug of his shoulders, he turned away and strode swiftly in the direction of the inn, unaware of Marianne still clinging to the piled logs in her shadowed corner, weak and spent, yet filled with a relief so shattering that she almost swooned with it. For a long moment she stayed where she was, her forehead drenched with sweat, her eyes closed, listening to the frantic drumming of her heart return to normal.

When she opened her eyes again the river bank was deserted so that for a moment she wondered if she had not dreamed it all, but when she looked more closely she could just make out a running figure moving away towards the point where the bank became a cliff. Then she too turned back towards the inn. Her legs were trembling so that she could barely climb the steep wooden stair that led up to the bedrooms and at the top she had to pause for a moment to get back her breath before she dragged herself to her own door and pushed it open.

'Where have you been?' Jason's voice said curtly.

He was there, standing in the broad, white swathe of moonlight. She thought that he looked huge and reassuring, like a lighthouse in a storm. Never had she needed him so much and giving a little moan she threw herself into his arms, shaken by a paroxysm of sobbing that swept away all the dreadful fear that had overwhelmed her.

He let her cry for a little without speaking, only petting her like a child and stroking her tumbled hair with a gentle hand. Then, as the violence abated, he put his hand under her chin and tilted up her tear-stained face.

'Idiot,' was all he said. 'As if I could want any woman but you.'

An hour later Marianne was asleep, tired out and lulled by the happy thought that Shankala, having failed, would give up the attempt and must already have made up her mind to part from her travelling companions. She had seen her running off towards the cliff . . . Perhaps she meant never to return . . .

But when, at daybreak, they all gathered by the kibitka, into the shafts of which their new driver was engaged in putting fresh horses, the gipsy was there, as cool and distant as if nothing at all had happened. Without a word she took her place by Gracchus on the box and Marianne, smothering a sigh of disappointment, could only comfort herself with the thought that Shankala had not so much as glanced at Jason as she passed him.

This was such slender consolation that when they drew up that evening at Darnitsa, in the midst of resin-scented pine-woods, she could not resist taking Gracchus aside. His relations with the gipsy had not notably improved since the village on the Kodyma but at least the extraordinary girl had condescended to exchange a few words with her so-called husband.

'How long are we to be forced to endure this Shankala?' Marianne asked him. 'Why does she stay with us? It's clear she doesn't do it because she likes us. So why does she persist in staying?'

'She is not staying with us, Mademoiselle Marianne, or not in the way you mean.'

'No? Then what is she doing?'

'She's hunting!'

'Hunting?'

'I can't imagine what kind of game – apart from Monsieur Beaufort, of course.' Marianne could not resist that jibe at least.

She had expected him to agree with her in that, but Gracchus shook his head, frowning.

'I thought so too, at first, but it's not that. Oh, she'd have got him if she could, of course, combining pleasure with business—'

'Business? I understand less and less.'

'You'll soon see. What Shankala is after is revenge. She's not coming with us, she's following the man who cast her off and delivered her up to the hatred of the village women. She has sworn to kill him and I think she hoped, by seducing Captain

Beaufort, to make him the instrument of her revenge by persuading him to kill her former husband.'

Marianne shrugged impatiently. 'This is madness. How does she hope to find the man again in a country this size?'

'That may not be as difficult as you might think. The Cossack, whose name, by the way, is Nikita, has gone off to fight the French. We are going the same way, and so she knows. Don't worry, she asks about the Cossack troop at every posting house. Not only that, but she knows precisely what her Nikita is after.'

'And what is he after?'

'To win the prize. Become rich and famous, noble and powerful—'

'Gracchus,' Marianne interrupted him with a good deal of impatience, 'if you can't bring yourself to talk more clearly you and I are going to fall out. What is all this nonsense?'

Then Gracchus embarked on what sounded like the wildest fairy-tale. He explained how, a short time before, a fantastic story had blazed through steppes and forests like wildfire. Count Platov, the almost legendary Ataman of the Don Cossacks and now the acknowledged leader of all the companies, or *sotnias*, of other regions, had promised, just as in the chivalrous tales of old, to give his daughter's hand in marriage to any Cossack, whoever he might be, who should bring him Napoleon's head.

At that the fever had mounted in every Cossack village, or *stanitsa*, and every man who did not own a wife had risen up in answer to the great chief's call, and in the hope of winning the fabulous prize. They had polished up their weapons, saddled their horses with the high wooden saddles covered with sheepskins, and pulled on their boots. Some of them in their frenzy had even contrived, more or less discreetly, to do away with wives who had suddenly become an embarrassment.

'Shankala's husband was one of those,' Gracchus concluded. 'He claims to be certain of winning the Ataman's daughter, but where he gets his certainty, don't ask me. Even Shankala doesn't know.'

'Out of an even greater conceit than the rest of his fellows!'

Marianne exclaimed indignantly. 'These savages have no idea! The Emperor's head indeed! I ask you!' Then, with an abrupt change of tone, she added: 'But Gracchus, does this mean the woman was innocent when they tried to drown her? I must say I find it hard to believe.'

Evidently Gracchus did too. He pushed back his cap and scratched his red thatch, shifting from foot to foot, then letting his fingers stray to the still visible marks of the gipsy's fingernails.

'That,' he said, 'is a matter we did not touch on. With a woman like that you never know. All she told me was that once his first passion died down Nikita had neglected her and relegated her to the position of a servant to his mother. All things considered, if that's true and she did deceive him, he'd no one but himself to blame. It seems to me he was a poor enough fellow.'

'Indeed? Well, that's no reason to go and find out. And if you want us to remain friends, Gracchus-Hannibal Pioche, I'd advise you not to let Shankala use you to obtain her revenge either. Supposing you were to come out of it alive, I wonder how your grandmother, the laundress in the rue de la Révolte, would welcome such a daughter-in-law?'

'I know well enough. She'd stick out two fingers in the sign against the evil eye and then she'd be off to the curé to sprinkle her with holy water. Then she'd show both of us the door. Don't worry, Mademoiselle Marianne, I've no wish to reduce still further what little chance we have of ever seeing the rue Montorgueil and your house in the rue de Lille again.'

He touched his cap and was moving away to help the driver unhitch the horses when Marianne, struck by the cynicism of his last words, called him back.

'Gracchus! Do you really think that in trying to reach the Emperor we are running into serious danger?'

'It's not so much because we are trying to reach him, it's just that when the Little Corporal goes to war he doesn't do things by halves and we're likely to find ourselves, as they say, caught between the hammer and the anvil. And random shots aren't always as random as all that! But we'll do the best we can, won't we?'

And, whistling his favourite marching song more furiously out of tune than ever, Gracchus went off cheerfully to attend to his everyday duties as groom, leaving Marianne to her thoughts.

Chapter Two

The Duel

On the eleventh of September they came to the outskirts of Moscow. It was a fine, bright day and the earth basked in the sunshine of late summer. But the warm light and the beauty of the countryside could not dispel the sense of tragedy that loomed in the air.

The road passed through the pretty, picturesque village of Kolomenskoy, with its old, brightly painted wooden cottages, large pond with several families of ducks upon it and clumps of trees in which the pale trunks of birches mingled with slender, fragrant pines and rowans borne down with great bunches of crimson fruit.

But farther west the guns were firing and there was an endless procession of vehicles of every kind, from tradesmen's carts to gentlemen's carriages, driven by rigid, sleepwalking figures with set faces and haunted eyes. Plants and buildings alike had their freshness smothered in a choking pall of dust.

In this crowd of refugees the kibitka's progress was like that of a swimmer struggling against the current of a mighty river. For three days they had been unable to obtain a change of horses. All those that could be found were already between the shafts. The stables were empty.

Jason might fret and fume in his impatience to travel day and night until they had put Moscow behind them but they were still obliged to halt every day at nightfall to rest the horses, although the men took turns to stand guard to prevent them being stolen.

They had lost their driver. The last man had refused to proceed beyond the posting house at Toula and had run away, helped on by Jason's belt laid about his shoulders for trying to take the horses with him. That night they had been forced to quit the posting house in a hurry and seek refuge in the nearby forest because the man had gone for help to the estate of Prince Volkonski and had returned to his erstwhile employers reinforced by a gang of men armed with staves. The firearms with which Gracchus had prudently provided them had sufficed to hold them off for long enough for the party to make good its escape but they had supped that day off whortleberries and spring water only.

The crowds they passed were strangely silent, showing no sign of panic. The crested broughams and barouches of the nobility, built in London or Paris, waited patiently among the assortment of Russian conveyances, from the travelling *telega* to the urban *droshky* with its driver in his long robe with a brass plate on his back, including kibitkas of every size and even common-or-garden tree trunks slung on four wheels.

In the midst of all these, old men, women and children trudged uncomplainingly through the dust, their bundles on their backs and their eyes on the road ahead. The only sounds were the shuffle of feet and the creaking of wheels and this silence was the most impressive thing of all for it was heavy with resignation.

Now and then a priest appeared, accompanied by a deacon or two and sheltering some precious relic under the folds of his black robe, before which the peasants would kneel piously. The gates of the big estates were guarded by *karaoulny*, old soldiers with white hair who had lost an arm or a leg in Catherine the Great's wars. And all the time, like a knell, the distant menace of the guns.

No one took any notice of the dusty, travel-worn kibitka forcing its way against the current of refugees. Once or twice someone would glance up indifferently for a moment, too preoccupied with their own troubles to betray much curiosity.

But when they came to the end of the village, Jason, who had taken over the reins from Gracchus, brought the vehicle to a standstill beside the impressive entrance to a large monastery whose dull blue domes rose close beside an ancient wooden mansion.

'It's madness to go on,' he said with conviction. 'We'll turn back and make a detour round the city to join the road to St Petersburg.'

Marianne had been dozing against Jolival's shoulder but she sat up at once.

'Why should we avoid the city? It's not easy, I grant you, but we are making progress. There's no reason to change direction now and risk losing ourselves.'

'And I'm telling you it's madness,' Jason repeated. 'Can't you see what's happening, all these people running away?'

'What they are running from holds no terrors for me. The very fact that we can hear the guns means that the French are not far off, especially if the exodus from Moscow has already begun.'

'Marianne,' he said wearily, 'we are not going over all that again. I've told you time and again that I don't want to meet Napoleon. I thought we had agreed that if we came within reach of the invading army Jolival should take charge of this mysterious warning you want to send to your Emperor and then catch up with us later on the road.'

'And you thought I'd agree to that?' Marianne cried indignantly. 'You talk of sending Jolival to Napoleon as if it were no more than going to post a letter. Well, let me tell you something. Look at all these people round us. The roads must be packed like this in all directions and we have absolutely no idea where to look for the army, or for the Russian army either. If we separate we're lost. Jolival would never find us again. And you know it.'

Arcadius, alarmed at the angry turn the argument was taking, made an effort to intervene but Marianne silenced him with an imperious gesture. Then, as Jason still sat hunched in his seat, remaining obstinately silent, she snatched up her valise and sprang down into the road.

'Come, Arcadius,' she said imperatively to her old friend. 'Captain Beaufort would rather part from us than involve himself in any way with the army of a man he so dislikes. He has done with France.'

'After what I suffered there it would be stranger still if I hadn't. I think I have good cause,' the American said sulkily.

'Oh yes, most certainly. Very well, then, go and join your good friends the Russians, and your old friends the English – but when all this is over, for all wars have an end, you had better forget all about Madame Veuve Clicquot-Ponsardin and her champagne, and about the bordeaux wines and chambertins in which you once drove such a thriving contraband trade. And you can forget me, too, while you are at it! Because all these things are France!'

With that Marianne put up her little chin in a gesture of superb defiance and contempt and, still shaking with anger, picked up her valise and tramped off up the dusty road, which here took a slight turn uphill, without looking back. She had thought, after the quarrel at Kiev, that Jason had been finally convinced and she was seething with rage at finding him still fixed in his stubborn resentment. He was nothing but a deceiver, a hypocrite without a heart.

'Let him go to the Devil!' she muttered through clenched teeth.

She heard him behind her, swearing and cursing in the approved manner of the coachman whose role he had adopted. But there was another sound too, the creaking of the kibitka getting under way. For an instant she was horribly tempted to look round and see if he were turning back but that would have been an admission of weakness amounting almost to giving in and she would not allow herself even to slacken her pace. A moment later he had caught up with her.

Tossing the reins to Gracchus, he sprang to the ground and went after her. He caught her by the arm and forced her to stop and face him.

'Not only are we in a scrape you don't appear to have the least idea of,' he raged, 'but now we have to put up with your tantrums as well!'

'My tantrums?' she threw back at him indignantly. 'And what about yours? Who is it who won't listen to a word anyone says? Who won't hear of anything but his own selfish obsessions? I won't let Arcadius sacrifice himself, do you hear? I will not! Is that clear?'

'No one is asking him to sacrifice himself. You have a talent for twisting people's words.'

'Have I indeed? Well, listen to this, Jason Beaufort. One evening at Humayunabad, when I reproached you for wanting to leave me and go back to your own country to fight, you said to me: "I come of a free people and I must fight with them", or something of the kind. Well, I wish you would remember sometimes that I belong to the French people who had done more than any for the sake of freedom, beginning with the freedom of some others I could name.'

'That's not true. You're half English.'

'I can't think why that seems to give you so much pleasure. You must be out of your mind. Whose are the guns that at this very moment may be sending to the bottom any number of ships like your *Sea Witch* – flying the same flag, at least?'

He glared at her as if he could have struck her. Then, abruptly, he shrugged and turned away, striving to repress a grin of apology.

'Touché!' he growled. 'Very well. You win. We'll go on.'

In an instant all her anger was forgotten. Like a schoolgirl she flung her arms round the American's neck, regardless of what the refugees might think, seeing a woman dressed in such a comparatively ladylike fashion eagerly embracing a bearded moujik. He returned her kiss and they might have remained lost to the world around them if Craig O'Flaherty's jovial voice had not come to their ears.

'Come and see!' he called. 'It's well worth looking at!'

All the others had climbed down from the wagon and walked over to a terrace terminating in a balustraded wall. Marianne and Jason joined them, hand in hand, and saw Moscow lying at their feet.

The view which met their eyes was both grand and romantic, and with something fascinating about it also. It took in the whole extent of the great city, enclosed within its red walls, twelve leagues in extent and very ancient. At their feet the Moskva looped itself in snakelike coils round islands studded with palaces and gardens. Most of the houses were built of wood plastered over. Only the public buildings and the huge mansions of the nobility were constructed of brick of a dark, velvety softness. Numerous parks and gardens could be seen, their greenery forming a harmonious background to the buildings.

The sun shone on a thousand and one church steeples and was reflected brilliantly from their gilded or sky blue domes and from rooftops of metal painted black or green. And in the midst of the city, set upon a raised hillock and ringed about by lofty walls and battlemented towers was a vast citadel, a veritable bouquet of palaces and churches: the Kremlin, the proud symbol of the ancient glory of Holy Russia. While all around it Europe and Asia met and mingled like the warp and weft of some fabulous material.

'It's beautiful!' Marianne breathed. 'I never saw anything like it!'

'Nor I,' said Jolival, adding, as he turned to his companions: 'It was certainly worth the journey.'

Clearly he spoke for all of them, even Shankala who, since Kiev, had seemed to lose all interest in her companions. Occasionally, at the staging posts or when the kibitka slowed down on the road, she would speak to a passing peasant or to a stable lad, always asking the same question. The man would wave his arm and answer her briefly and then the gipsy would return to her place without a word and resume her scrutiny of the road ahead.

But now she was leaning on the balustrade, gazing down with blazing eyes upon the fabulous city spread out at her feet, while her nostrils quivered as though seeking out one single scent from all the many odours that rose to meet her. For the trail of the man she followed must end here, before this city over whose beauty war hung like a menacing cloud.

For the war was a presence to be breathed and felt. The wind carried a smell of burnt powder and, except for an occasional outburst of noise here and there, the silence in the city seemed to grow more disquietingly complete with every moment that passed. None of the ordinary, everyday sounds could be heard, no bells, no cheerful bustle of men at work, no music hovering about the smokeless rooftops. It was as though the harsh voices of the distant guns had silenced every other.

Jolival was the first to break the spell which seemed to hold them all enthralled. He sighed and turning from the balustrade remarked: 'If we want to be inside the city by nightfall, I think it's time that we were on our way. We can try and get news of what's happening down there. All the people of the better sort speak French and there always used to be a large French colony in Moscow.'

Enchantment gave way to something more like horror as they descended the hill and approached the city gates. The confusion here was unbelievable. The tide of refugees came up against a solid mass of women and old men, all kneeling in the dust before the doors of the Danilovski monastery, staring up with clasped hands at the great cross on the principal dome as though expecting some miraculous apparition. The sound of their prayers was a ceaseless murmur.

At the same time a large convoy of wounded men emerging from a side street was endeavouring to enter by the gates which were already jammed with the press of vehicles. The people in the crowd did their best to make way for it and indeed showed to the wounded men a pious awe almost as great as that with which they gazed upon the monastery cross. Some of the women even fell on their knees and attempted to kiss the blood-stained rags binding an arm or leg.

These wounded soldiers, filthy and ragged, were a sight both pathetic and terrible, an army of spectres with hollow eyes burning in faces parched by the sun.

People ran out from those few shops which had remained open and from the houses near the gate with offerings of fruit and wine and food of all sorts, while some of those who were leaving actually turned back to give up their carriages to them, or to offer the use of houses left empty in the care of a few servants. Indeed, it all seemed so natural that it did not occur to Marianne and her companions to protest when a pair of tall fellows wearing aprons, who could have been in charge of the wounded, requisitioned their kibitka.

'We'll probably be torn to pieces if we refuse,' Jolival whispered. 'It'll be a poor look-out if in all this confusion we can't find a vehicle of some sort to continue our journey! Besides, I must confess these people have surprised me. They show a remarkable example of unity in the face of disaster.'

'Unity?' Craig muttered. 'Yet it seems to me that there is one great difference between those leaving and those staying. For the most part the carriages we've met have been smart and well-upholstered. The rich are going, the poor are left behind.'

'Well, naturally, only those who have some property to go to outside the city can go away. What's more, I think it's chiefly their property that they are trying to protect. The others have nowhere to go. Besides, the Russian soul is essentially fatalistic. They believe that everything happens by God's will.'

'I'm coming to very much the same view of things myself,' Jason said grimly. 'The exercise of free will seems to have become increasingly difficult for some time past.'

However, after some delay and considerable effort on their part, they did manage to pass through the gate and found themselves in a long street, equally jammed with traffic, leading towards the centre of the city. But as they went on they passed the entrances to broad, deserted boulevards and empty streets that showed no sign of life, in vivid contrast to the one they were following. Many of the houses had their shutters up and presented blind faces to the world.

Before long they came to the Moskva and saw men in barges busy sinking casks and boxes in the river. The Kremlin walls towered redder than ever in the setting sun. But the travellers' eyes were already growing accustomed to the almost asiatic splendours of the Holy City and they spared no more than a passing glance for the ancient citadel of the Tsars. What was taking place outside its walls was far more interesting.

There were still crowds of people all along the river and on the bridges across it, and in the huge square outside the Kremlin wall. But these crowds were of a different kind from those outside the city. Young gentlemen in frock coats, armed with swords, were hurrying to meet the convoys of wounded, which seemed to be arriving from all directions, and greeting them with eager cries. Their youth, the elegance of their dress and, in many cases, their extreme good looks formed a striking contrast to the dirt and suffering among which they moved and attempted in a clumsy and often ill-judged fashion to relieve.

Trapped in the bottle-neck of one of the bridges, Marianne

and her friends were caught up and carried along almost in spite of themselves in an irresistible tide, so that they had crossed the river almost without noticing and found themselves deposited, with more or less freedom of movement, in the vast square in front of an enormous, glittering church whose vivid colours made it look like some gigantic jewel.

On its eastern side, the square was bounded by a line of large and splendid private palaces which, with their elegant, white stuccoed classical façades and green, spreading gardens formed a barrier between it and Kitaigorod, the chief commercial district of Moscow. And outside these palaces a crowd had gathered and was roaring with excitement at what, Marianne soon realized with horror, could only be a public execution.

A ladder had been placed upon a platform built against the palace wall and bound to it by his wrists dragged up above his head was a man, naked to the waist, and being beaten with the knout.

The whip, which was made of fine thongs of plaited white leather which it was the habit to steep in milk the night before an execution in order to stiffen them, left a bloody weal across the victim's back at every stroke and drew a groan of agony from him.

Standing on the dais a step or two away from the ladder, observing the proceedings, was a giant of a man with a *nagaika*, or horse-whip, thrust through his belt. His arms were folded on his chest and he was dressed in a coat of military cut, blue and high-collared, with gilt epaulettes. His strong, arrogant features showed traces of Turcoman blood, but it was nevertheless an expressive face, animated by a pair of very large eyes of some indeterminate colour, although at the moment it reflected nothing but a cold cruelty.

The crowd had fallen silent, manifesting neither pleasure nor any other emotion at the torture of a fellow being. Yet as she mingled with them, Marianne was struck by the look on the people's faces. All, without exception, expressed a total, absolute and, as it were, concentrated hatred. The sight of it appalled her.

'What are these people made of?' she muttered under her

breath. 'The enemy is at their gates and they stand here watching a poor devil being flogged to death.'

A sharp jab from an elbow in her side silenced her abruptly. Looking round, she saw that it had come, not from one of her companions, but from an elderly man of pleasant and distinguished appearance, dressed in old-fashioned style but with a simplicity that did not preclude a certain elegance. Far from it, for while he wore his hair long, no trace of powder marred the gleaming surface of the black satin ribbon that confined it and showed off its fine, silvery hue.

Seeing Marianne gazing at him in astonishment, he smiled faintly.

'You should be more careful, Madame,' he murmured. 'French is not an unfamiliar language in these parts.'

'I speak no Russian, but if you would rather we conversed in some other tongue – English, for instance, or German—'

This time the old gentleman, for such he clearly was, smiled openly, an action which detracted somewhat from his charm by revealing some regrettable deficiencies in his teeth.

'As to English, it is rare enough to arouse some curiosity. German, on the other hand, is known and, ever since the time of Peter III, cordially detested.'

'Very well then,' Marianne said. 'Let us continue in French. That is, Monsieur, if you will be kind enough to satisfy my curiosity. What has the wretched man done?'

Her new friend shrugged his shoulders.

'His crime is twofold. He is a Frenchman and he dared to rejoice openly at the approach of Bonaparte's armies. Before this he was a man much valued and even respected for his culinary talents, but that was enough to ruin him.'

'Culinary?'

'Yes indeed. His name is Tournais and he was head cook to the Governor of Moscow, Count Rostopchin whom you see there, personally overseeing his punishment. Unfortunately for his back, Tournais allowed his tongue to run away with him.'

Marianne clenched her fists, feeling herself overcome with helpless rage. Must she stand there in the sunset watching a fellow-countryman flayed alive for nothing more than loyalty to his emperor? Fortunately, she had not long to wonder for the beating was coming to an end.

At an order from Rostopchin, the unfortunate chef was cut down, unconscious and covered in blood, and carried inside the palace.

'What will become of him?' asked Jolival, who had joined Marianne and overheard her conversation.

'The governor has given out that tomorrow he is to be sent to Orenburg to work in the mines.'

'But he has no right to do that!' Marianne burst out, once more forgetting all caution. 'The man is not a Russian. It's horrible to treat him like a guilty moujik!'

'So he is also being treated as a spy. Ultimately, poor Tournais, for whom I am sincerely sorry, for he is a true artist, is merely a scapegoat. Now that the great battle is over Rostopchin is not sorry to show the people that he means to have no mercy on all who have the slightest connection with Bonaparte.'

It was the second time the old gentleman had used that name and it gave Marianne the clue she needed. Evidently he was one of those unyielding emigrés who were sworn never to return to France as long as the scourge of God, Napoleon, reigned there. A little circumspection would therefore be wise. Nevertheless, Marianne could not resist her thirst for information.

'A great battle, did you say?'

The old gentleman stared and, reaching for the lorgnettes suspended on a velvet ribbon round his neck, set them on his nose and considered the young woman with astonishment.

'Well, well! My dear young lady, where have you been, if I may make so bold?'

'In the south, Monsieur, more precisely at Odessa, where I had the privilege of meeting his grace the Duc de Richelieu.' She added a few more vague words of explanation but her new friend was no longer listening. The name of Richelieu had quite won him to her and now that he felt sure that this young woman was one of his own kind he heartily approved of her. From then on there was no stopping him and once Jolival also had been introduced, the others being relegated to the obscurity of servants, he seemed prepared to hold forth endlessly.

And so it was in the pleasant, educated tones of the man they learned to call Monsieur de Beauchamp that the travellers heard of what had taken place five days earlier on the plain of Borodino, on the right bank of the river Kologha, a tributary of the Moskva, and some thirty-five leagues from Moscow itself. The Russian army, which up to that point had seemed to melt into the landscape as the French advanced had decided to make a stand and attempt to bar the way to the capital. The fighting for the redoubts on the road was fierce and the casualties on both sides appalling,[1] if the reports of the wounded who were even now being brought into the city were to be believed.

'But who won?' Jolival demanded, beside himself with impatience.

The old gentleman gave a sad little smile.

'We were told it was the Russians. The Tsar had replaced Barclay de Tolly with old Kutuzov, the darling child of victory, and no one ever imagined it could be otherwise. There was even a *Te Deum* sung in this very place. But the wounded tell a different story. They say that the army is retreating hard on her heels and that Bonaparte is marching on Moscow, Tomorrow or the day after, he will be here. As soon as that became known, all those who could began to leave Moscow. Hence the dreadful confusion throughout the city. Even Rostopchin is going, he has just said so, but for the present he is staying to await Kutuzov whose army must pass through the city to fall back on Kazan.'

With Jason's stern eye upon her, Marianne succeeded in maintaining her supposed character and remained calm in the face of news which filled her with joy. Jolival, meanwhile, was thanking the old gentleman with exquisite, courtly politeness for his recital and begging him to set the seal on his kindness by recommending an inn, that was, if there were any left open, which would provide them with a roof. This request produced an immediate protest from Jason.

'There's no call for us to stay here, least of all if Bonaparte is coming! We'd better be gone before nightfall and find ourselves a hostelry of some kind on the road to Petersburg.'

[1] Fifty thousand Russians and 28,000 of Napoleon's troops were left dead on the field.

Monsieur de Beauchamp directed his lorgnette at him and stared for a moment with a mixture of outrage and astonishment at this bearded moujik, evidently a servant, who had the impertinence not merely to venture an opinion but actually to do so in French. Then, apparently considering it beneath his dignity to give the fellow a set-down, the old gentleman merely shrugged his shoulders and, turning his back on him, addressed himself to Jolival.

'You will never get out of the city tonight. Every street is packed solid with carts and carriages, with the exception of those leading westwards. But there is a chance that you will still find a lodging in Kitaigorod, the walls of which you see before you over there, even if only with—'

But Marianne was fated never to hear the name of the innkeeper who might have offered them a bed because at that moment something like a huge tidal wave swept into the square and drove like a bullet from a gun straight for the dais on which the governor was still standing, engaged in giving orders to a number of underlings. Several thousand men and women armed with picks and axes and pitchforks and shrieking like famished wolves bore down on the Rostopchin palace. The massive wave broke against its walls with a shuddering impact that swept apart the little group gathered round the old gentleman.

In an instant Marianne found herself torn from her friends, half submerged in a welter of waving arms, and borne irresistibly back towards the river. Convinced that she had been caught up in a revolt and believing that her last hour had come, she uttered a shrill scream: 'Jason! Help!'

He heard her. Kicking and fighting his way he managed to get to her and grabbed her wrist and together they tried to fight their way against the fierce, undisciplined tide. But it was impossible. Better to let themselves be carried along if they did not want to be thrown down and trampled underfoot, which would have been certain death.

Without knowing how it happened, the two of them found themselves swept back across the Kremlin bridge and into a small square where a few houses and a church, painted like a theatre backdrop, huddled up against the high walls of a large building with a bright green leaded roof that occupied the river frontage and turned out to be the Foundling Hospital.

Here there were far fewer people than on the bridge, for the overflow had been diverted along the quays beside the Moskva, and Marianne, gasping and half-suffocated, sank down on a convenient mounting block to get her breath. It was only then that she realized that she was alone with Jason and Shankala. One of the girl's hands, still clutching the privateer's belt, showed clearly how it was that she had been able to keep up with them.

'Where are the others?' Marianne asked.

Jason shrugged and waved his arm to take in the square, which was like the crater of a volcano on the point of eruption.

'In there somewhere!'

'But we must try and find them—'

Tired as she was, she was already struggling to her feet ready to launch herself again into the seething mass had he not held her back by main force.

'Don't be insane! You'd only get yourself killed to no purpose. Think yourself lucky to have got out of that in one piece.' Seeing her eyes begin to fill with tears, he added more gently: 'Craig and Gracchus are well able to look after themselves. As for Jolival, he's no fool. I'd be very much surprised if he came to grief in there.'

'But what are we going to do? How shall we ever find them?'

'The best thing is to simply hang around this damned square and wait for them. This little spot of trouble won't last for ever. These people will either leave the city like the rest or go back to their homes. Then all we have to do is to head back to the place where we were separated. The others are certain to do the same. It'd be crazy to go wandering about a strange city at random.'

What he said made sense, as Marianne readily admitted. She would even have enjoyed the fact of being alone with him, in whatever hysterical circumstances, had it not been for Shankala who was still clinging tightly to Jason and staring fixedly at her without saying a word and with an enigmatic expression in her black eyes. It was as if she had abandoned her own personality and turned herself into a kind of familiar animal, silent but persistent, sticking close to her master's heels.

'You are quite right,' Marianne said with a sigh. 'We will stay here, then, and wait for things to clear, if they ever do.'

Certainly, although the crowd in Red Square seemed to be growing calmer and thinning out, access to the bridge was still practically impossible on account of the packed convoys of wounded which had emerged simultaneously from three different side streets. If they had all been on foot the bridge could have absorbed them easily but those able to walk were far outnumbered by the ones being carried on improvised stretchers and there were also a fair number of carts moving along amid the pitiful train from which came a continual groaning intermingled with cries of pain as the injured were jostled by the crowd.

Here and there a house which happened to be still inhabited opened its door to the wounded but the majority went on towards the military hospital and the two private hospitals on the other side of the river, not far from the Kremlin.

'We'll never get through,' Marianne said impatiently. 'The riverside is black with people.'

'Especially since the people in question are soldiers. Look! I can see horsemen over there. Cossacks!'

His seaman's eyes, accustomed to peering through the worst weather at sea, had picked out the soldiers while Marianne's could still perceive nothing more than a kind of red haze beyond the distant head of the convoy.

'The Russians must be in full retreat,' Jason went on. 'They must be falling back to defend the city. We can't stay here. We're in danger of being trampled underfoot by the horses.'

'Well, where do you want to go? I'm not leaving here until we've found the others.'

'I caught sight of an inn in that little square over there. Let's try and get to it. You still have some money on you?'

Marianne nodded. She had lost her valise, of course. It had been torn from her in the rush. But she had got into the habit of carrying her money and the invaluable *podaroshna* in an inner pocket of her dress. Even so, she felt reluctant to leave her perch. The inn did not look particularly easy to reach. A man and two aproned women were standing at the door, washing a filthy wound here and offering a cup of wine there to men who paused briefly and went on. The man and his womenfolk were labouring unsparingly, with a warmth and generosity that compelled admiration. Anyone could see that they were ready to give the poor soldiers everything in their house, but Marianne wondered whether their welcome would extend equally to foreign travellers.

A flung stone, narrowly missing her and breaking a window at her back, made up her mind for her. She jumped up with a cry, but not quickly enough to avoid a splinter of glass which cut her on the forehead just below the hairline. Jason caught her to him and took out his handkerchief to staunch the little trickle of blood.

'Damned savages!' he fumed. 'Have they nothing better to do than go about breaking their own windows?'

Marianne had turned round to observe the damage and she pointed wordlessly to the gaily painted signboard, depicting a magnificent cream cake, which announced that at the sign of the *Puits d'Amour* the brothers Lalonde could be relied upon to supply their clients with the finest pastries in all Moscow, as well as every kind of French sweetmeat from *bêtises* of Cambrai to *bergamotes* of Nancy, not forgetting the marzipans of Aix and Agen plums.

'The surprising thing is that the house is still standing at all,' Marianne said. 'You are right. We'll try the inn. Another minute and it will be too late.'

They set off again, Shankala still at their heels, and endeavoured to force a passage through to the doorway. A lucky thinning of the stream moving towards the bridge at last allowed them to reach the three outside the inn, whose white aprons were stained by now with wine and blood.

Marianne spoke to the man.

'We are travellers from the south. We have come a long way. Can you give us lodging?' she asked, speaking in French but with an attempt to recover her former English accent.

For an innkeeper, the man did not appear to be very partial to strangers, because he regarded her suspiciously.

'Where have you come from?' he asked in the same language

but with an accent so thick as to be almost incomprehensible.

'From Odessa.'

'That's a fair way. What are you? Italian? French?'

'No, no, English!' she told him quickly, smarting at the necessity for the lie, and also at her lack of success so far. 'I am Lady Selton and these – these people are my servants.'

The man's attitude relaxed. He was clearly convinced, perhaps less by the title she claimed than by the note of authority in her voice. As an Englishwoman she was entitled to a consideration he would not have granted to a member of any other nation, although he could not find it in him to approve of the passion for travel which seemed to afflict the females of that country. He even managed an apologetic smile as he explained that such few rooms as he had were all taken up with wounded but that if she would be satisfied with a corner of his coffee room he would be delighted to provide her with a fitting meal.

'Tomorrow,' he said, 'I'll see what I can do to find a more suitable lodging for milady but at least you'll be out of the cold for tonight, and out of the way of the troops coming back into Moscow, who won't be at all fit company for a young lady of quality.'

'Are they falling back to defend the city?'

'Why, to be sure they are, milady! Who could ever imagine our little father the Tsar allowing Antichrist to lay his wicked hands on our holy city? I, Ivan Borisovitch, I tell you that great things are going to be happening here and your ladyship will soon see what Russians can do in defence of their sacred soil.' And he added on a note of happy confidence that he had had it from a Chasseur that Kutuzov, old Marshal 'Forwards' as they called him, would be in the city before nightfall.

'But then what was the cause of the uprising in the square just now?'

'Uprising? What uprising?'

'I saw it with my own eyes. Just about sunset I was standing outside the governor's palace where a man was being flogged when all at once a crowd of people waving weapons and screaming came rushing this way.'

Ivan Borisovitch laughed. 'That was no uprising, milady.

Simply, news came this morning that the accursed French had reached the monastery of Mojaisk, some twenty leagues from here—'

Marianne lifted an eyebrow. 'Yet another holy place?' she inquired sardonically. But the good man was equally impervious to French irony and to the English sense of humour. He merely crossed himself earnestly several times.

'Extremely holy, your ladyship! Our good people wanted to go out and meet the enemy and began assembling this morning at the Dorogomilov gate, waiting for the governor to lead them. But they waited all day in vain and then came back to see what could be keeping him. In any case, the arrival of the army would have forced them to turn back.'

Marianne was careful not to give expression to her thoughts, which were that Count Rostopchin had other fish to fry, his unfortunate chef amongst them, than to put himself at the head of a wild, undisciplined band and ride out with it to meet Napoleon's army.

Without further comment she allowed him to lead her to a corner of a large, low room without very much light in it. Ivan Borisovitch piled the settles in a corner between two windows with all the pillows and eiderdowns that he could spare and announced that supper would be served immediately.

The meal, washed down by a wine from the Crimea, was respectable but the night seemed to Marianne the longest she had ever lived through for, despite the cushions, she was unable to get a wink of sleep. Only Shankala, accustomed to lying on the bare ground, slept soundly. Even Jason managed to doze for an hour or two. But Marianne, seated at the window, spent the whole night watching what was happening outside. If she had been in a feather bed she would probably have slept no more because the noise was almost unbearable. All night long, the Russian armies marched past.

They came in two columns, on either side of the river, the uniforms of chasseurs, grenadiers, hussars and troops of the line alternating with the red and blue tunics of the Cossacks and the goatskin caps of the Kalmuks, all advancing in the light of torches. Mounted regiments followed those on foot without undue confusion and the rumble of the guns echoed throughout the city.

In the smoky light of the torches that flickered over everything, even over the summit of the red walls of the Kremlin, the men's faces looked haggard and weary. Marianne found herself wondering if they had really come to take up a position in the city or whether they would pass right through, for they all went on along the river as though making for the eastern gates, the very ones by which the enemy would not come.

All night long, too, Ivan Borisovitch, with his sister and his wife, stood at the door of their house tirelessly offering flasks of wine and mugs of kvass, only as the time went on the fine confidence and eagerness that he had displayed earlier in the evening seemed to crumble and melt away. From time to time he would ask some question of the soldier he was serving and each time the answer left him looking more anxious, with his head sunk a little lower between his shoulders.

At about four o'clock in the morning, just as the sky was growing light, there was a tremendous explosion somewhere down the river, and a flash so bright that it was as if the rising sun itself had blown up. But it was only the great bridge at the south-eastern corner of the Kremlin exploding in a blinding shower of sparks. It was then that Ivan Borisovitch, his face now grey and drawn, came over and shook Jason where he slept, then spoke to Marianne.

'I'm very sorry, milady, I am indeed,' he said awkwardly, 'but I'm afraid you'll have to go.'

'Go?' Jason echoed, once again forgetting his part as the respectable serving man. But the unhappy innkeeper was past the stage of noticing such niceties. He only nodded wretchedly and Marianne could see that there were tears in his eyes.

'Yes, you must go,' he repeated heavily. 'You must quit Moscow within the hour, milady. You are English and the Corsican ogre is coming. You will be in peril if you stay. Go! Go at once! Such a pretty lady as you are, you must not fall into their filthy hands.'

'But – but I thought the soldiers were coming to defend Moscow?'

'No – they are only marching through. They are running away ... one of the soldiers told me they are going towards Riazan—' His voice choked suddenly. 'Our army is beaten – beaten! Our city is lost. We are all going, all of us! But you should be gone! We will only put a few things together and be gone also. I've a brother at Kaluga. I shall go to him.'

'You are abandoning your house?' Jason said. 'But what about the wounded men in your bedchambers?'

'They will have to trust in God. It will not help them much if I get myself killed defending them. I've a family to consider.'

It was no use arguing. The three travellers left and found themselves walking along the riverside, where a state of indescribable confusion reigned. The troops were still passing but now, in amongst them, were all those Muscovites who had stayed at home until that moment but were now leaving precipitately. As they passed the doorway to the Foundling Hospital they caught sight of a group of children about ten years of age, wearing some kind of green uniform, gathered in the porch about a tall fair man dressed like a superior officer but whose round, pleasant face was running with tears and his fists clenched in helpless rage.

The anguish of all these people was so real and poignant that Marianne could not help but be touched by it. However you looked at it and whichever side you were on, war was a dreadful thing, a calamity that people might endure but never really wanted, for even such enthusiasm as patriotism engendered was snuffed out like a light at the first real hardship.

To her awareness of taking part in a tragedy which was not her own was added the anxiety she felt at the thought of her lost friends. If she and Jason went on allowing themselves to be borne along on this flood of humanity they would find themselves outside Moscow, having lost all hope of ever finding Jolival, O'Flaherty and Gracchus again. Possessed by the idea of reaching Red Square and the Rostopchin palace at all costs, they infiltrated a stream of people making for the first bridge across the Moskva in order to be at least on the right side of the river.

'It must be possible to get to the square by cutting down a

side street and going round a little way,' Jason said. 'The first thing is to get free of this mass of soldiers.'

But the chaos on the other side of the river was even worse and Marianne and Beaufort found themselves suddenly trapped at the corner of another bridge, or rather in the angle between two bridges, because a tributary, the Yaouza, ran into the Moskva at this point and there were bridges across both. The struggling mass of people was equally thick on each. The first rays of the morning sun shining on the Yaouza bridge showed them the figure of Count Rostopchin. Wearing a military greatcoat with huge gilt epaulettes, he was standing with his horsewhip in his hand flailing indiscriminately at all who came within his reach and shouting at them like one possessed to move along. He was doing his best to clear the way and Marianne soon saw why. Coming towards her, surrounded by the cheers and acclamations of the crowd, was a group of generals mounted on magnificent horses.

Dressed in white or dark green uniform coats and enormous black cocked hats adorned with nodding white plumes or black cocks' feathers, they were grouped about a very stout old gentleman on a little grey horse and might almost have been guarding him like some precious relic, or like a prisoner. The old man had a kindly face, although it looked very sad, and he was modestly attired in an old black military coat, quite free of decorations, with a long scarf wound round his neck and a laced cap on his grey hair. All around the excited crowds were shouting frantically: 'Kutuzov! Kutuzov!'

Then Marianne knew that she was looking at the famous field-marshal, ancient enemy of the young Bonaparte and the man whom the Tsar Alexander, who did not like him, had recalled from his provincial exile a bare two weeks before but in whom all Russia saw a man of destiny and their last hope.

All Russia? Perhaps not, for as the headquarters staff drew near to the narrow bridge on which Rostopchin stood the Count charged like a bull and began hurling a stream of abuse at the marshal, in spite of all that two of the plumed generals could do to restrain him. He had to be hustled away by main force, still roaring that Kutuzov was nothing but a traitor, running like a coward and abandoning the city he had sworn to defend. Kutuzov himself merely shrugged his heavy shoulders, mouthed a brief command and then went on his way, surrounded by his glittering staff.

Jason, whose great height gave him a partial view over the heads of the crowd, caught sight of an empty space behind them and grasping Marianne by the wrist drew her after him.

'Come on,' he cried. 'Now is the time to cross! We'll be able to reach the street just over there.'

They ran for it, still dragging the gipsy after them. The gap turned out to be caused by a troop of Cossacks who had drawn rein at the door of a large monastery, where an officer had dismounted and was talking to an old, bearded priest in crow-black, funereal robes.

As ill-luck would have it, just as they reached the other side a sudden movement in the crowd, which was still coming on, jostled the Cossacks and Marianne, jerked forward by Jason to avoid being crushed beneath their hooves, crashed hard against the priest and trod on his foot.

He uttered a squawk of shock and displeasure and, seeing that his assailant was a woman, pushed her away sharply but not before the officer had grabbed her roughly by the arm and, shouting at her in words she did not understand, was evidently trying to force her to her knees in order to beg the man's pardon. Jason would have sprung to her assistance but two of the Cossacks forcibly restrained him, while Marianne, still struggling furiously in the officer's grip, found herself suddenly staring into his face. It was no more than an instant, but they knew one another.

'Chernychev!' Marianne gasped.

It was none other. As blond and handsome as ever, and as exquisite also, in spite of the blood and dust that marred the dark green dolman, from which the Legion of Honour had disappeared, and in spite of the lines of fatigue on his pale face. His eyes, too, were the same, the same cruel, cat-like gaze, the green eyes slanting slightly upwards and the high cheekbones hinting at mongol blood. Oh yes, he was the same man, the same attractive, disturbing Count Alexander Chernychev, the Tsar's spy and the lover of half the ladies in Paris, although it was not easy to recognize the nonchalant seducer, so skilled at gathering the secrets of the Empire from the Princess Borghese's arms, in this hard-bitten warrior. But the recollection of their last meeting was enough to make Marianne try desperately to wrench herself from his grasp and escape.

She was wasting her time. She knew already that the slim, white fingers clenched about her arm could be as hard as steel. Besides, he too had leaped at once to the name that went with that passionate face and the huge eyes just then dilated with terror.

'Why, it's my princess!' he cried in French. 'The most precious of all my possessions. The fabulous emerald of the poor camel-driver on the road to Samarkand. By Our Lady of Kazan, this meeting was the very thing I needed to make me believe that God is still a Russian!'

Before Marianne could recover from the shock of this unexpected encounter, he had swept her into his arms and was kissing her in a way that drew a roar of approval from his own men and a shout of fury from Jason.

'Let her go!' he bellowed, casting prudence to the winds. 'Damn you, you filthy Cossack! How dare you lay a hand on her!'

Against all expectation, Chernychev released Marianne and turned towards the other man still struggling in the grip of his Cossacks.

'I think I have the right to handle my own property,' he said arrogantly. 'As for you, moujik, how dare you even speak to me? Are you jealous? Are you her lover also? Then here is something to make you change your tone!'

He raised the whip he held in his hand and slashed it viciously across Jason's face, so that the trace of the lash stood out in a red weal. The American strained frantically to break free of his captors but only succeeded in provoking their mirth.

'Coward!' he roared. 'You're nothing but a coward, Count Chernychev, who strikes only when he can do so with impunity and bandies insults in the same way! You don't hesitate to defame a woman who is a defenceless stranger here!'

'Defame the Princess Sant'Anna? How do I do that by speaking the truth? In the name of my patron St Alexander, may I die if I lied when I said that she is mine! As for you, I've a good-mind to make you pay for your insolence under the knout. It's the only proper treatment for your kind.'

'Look closer! I'm not one of your moujiks. I'm a man who already has one account to settle with you. Have you forgotten the night they played *Britannicus* at the Comédie Française?'

The Russian's arm, already raised to strike again, fell slowly. He took another step towards Jason and scrutinized him closely. Then he broke into a shout of laughter.

'By God, it's true? The American! Captain – Captain Lefort, is it not?'

'Beaufort, if you please. Now that you know who I am, I am waiting for an explanation, not to say an apology, for what you have just said.'

'So be it! You have my apology – but only for mispronouncing your name.' He favoured Jason with a mocking grin. 'I've always had the greatest difficulty with foreign names. As for this lady—'

Unable to bear any more, Marianne ran to Jason.

'Don't listen to him! He's nothing but a mischief-maker. A spy – a wretch who uses friendship and love alike to serve his own interests—'

'My master's interests, madame! And Russia's!'

He snapped out an order to the men who were still holding Jason and they loosed their grip immediately. The American found his arms free once more and promptly used them gently to put aside Marianne who was trying to cling to him.

'Let be. I want to hear what he has to say for himself. And I must ask you not to interfere. This is a matter between gentlemen. Now, Monsieur,' he went on, turning to Chernychev. 'I am still waiting. Are you going to admit that you lied?'

The Count gave a shrug. 'If I were not afraid of shocking your sensibilities and exhibiting the worst of bad taste, I would have my men strip her clothes off here and now and you would then see that she bears a small scar on her side – my crest imprinted on her flesh after a night of love.'

'A night of love?' Marianne cried, beside herself. 'You dare to call it a night of love? The barbarous way you treated me? He got into my bedchamber, Jason, by breaking the window. He knocked me half-unconscious and tied me to my bed with the cords from the curtains and then raped me! Do you hear? He raped me as if he were putting a city to the sack! And as if that were not enough, he wanted to leave some permanent mark upon me and so – and so he – he heated up the seal ring that he wears and pressed it, red hot, into my flesh. That is what he calls a night of love!'

With a cry of wrath, Jason sprang at the Russian with clenched fists raised to strike but Chernychev sidestepped quickly and, drawing his sword, pressed its point against his attacker's chest.

'Not so fast . . .! I may have been a trifle hasty that night and I acknowledge that "night of love" was a slight exaggeration – at least where I was concerned. It would have been better applied to the man who came after me – the one with whom I fought a duel, my charmer, in your garden . . .'

Marianne shut her eyes. She felt sick with anger and despair. She seemed to be caught in a web of half-truths more damaging than any insults. Jason's face had taken on a grey tinge. Even his eyes, strangely emptied of expression, seemed to have lost their colour and become as grey as steel.

'Chernychev,' she murmured faintly, 'you are a villain!'

'I don't see why. You can scarcely accuse me of lying, my sweet. Unhappily I'd not have very far to go to call the man himself to be my witness. He can't be more than a day's march away at this moment. He is with Marshal Victor's corps which is pursuing Wittgenstein. But with your permission, we will finish this interesting conversation at another time. My men are blocking the way for those coming up behind. I'll order up mounts for you and—'

'Indeed you will not,' Jason interrupted him with ominous coolness. 'I am not going one step in your company, nor have I any reason to do so.'

The Russian half-closed his eyes so that they gleamed like bright green slits. Still smiling, he slowly lowered his sword.

'You think not? I can think of an excellent reason, and that is that you have no choice! Either you come with me and we settle our differences when we make camp tonight, or I have you shot as a spy. Because I am sure there are other reasons for your presence here than simply to bring my fair conquest to me. As to the lady herself, I have only to say the word – tell this crowd of people here precisely who she is – and she would be torn to pieces in five minutes. So choose – but choose fast.'

'Then say the word!' Marianne cried. 'Say it and be done, for no power on earth will induce me to go with you. You are the most despicable person of my acquaintance. Make them kill me! I hate you—'

'Be quiet!' Jason ordered her roughly. 'I've already told you this is a matter between men. And you, sir, I'll have you know that I propose a third course. We will fight here and now. You seem very ready to forget that you left Paris within a few hours of calling me out and that I have every right to call you a coward.'

'When the Tsar commands, I obey. I am a soldier first and foremost. I was obliged to leave, much to my regret, but I repeat, sir, you shall have your satisfaction tonight.'

'No, I will have it now. Damnation, Count Chernychev, it's no easy task to get you to fight. But perhaps this will do it.' And with that Jason struck the Russian two swift, glancing blows across the face. Chernychev went very pale.

'Now,' Jason asked, almost pleasantly, 'will you fight?'

The Count's face was waxen white against the dark green of his uniform. His nostrils were pinched and he seemed to have difficulty with his breathing. He looked as if he were about to be sick.

'Yes,' he hissed at last through clenched teeth. 'Give me time to get my troop on its way and then we'll fight!'

In another moment the road was cleared and the Cossacks had ridden off, with thunderous cries of encouragement, leaving only a dozen of their number and a youthful, beardless captain remaining. Chernychev turned to take his leave of the priest with whom he had been talking when Marianne bumped into him but he had already gone inside, shocked either by the violent turn events seemed to be taking or by his fellow-countryman's behaviour towards the unknown woman, and the monastery doors had closed silently behind him. The Count shrugged with an air of annoyance and muttered something under his breath. Then he turned back to his adversary.

'Come,' he said. 'At the end of that side street you see there is a small square in between the monastery wall and the gardens of two large private houses. It is very quiet and will serve our purpose admirably. Prince Aksakov will see to the lady.' The youthful captain thus indicated lapsed momentarily from the military rigidity of his stance and hurriedly ordered his arm to the half-fainting Marianne.

'If you please, Madame,' he said in fluent, virtually accentless French, bowing with unexpected grace. This drew a bark of laughter from Chernychev.

'You may address the lady as Serene Highness, my dear Boris,' he said sardonically. 'It is no less than her due.' Then, indicating Shankala who was still standing silently by. 'And who is this? She appears to belong to you also.'

'The Princess's maid,' Jason put in quickly, before Marianne had time to find her voice.

'She looks more like a gipsy than a respectable servant but then your tastes were always a trifle bizarre, Marianne, my dear. Well then, I think we may make a move.'

They set off, the two parties to the projected duel leading, followed by Marianne leaning heavily on the young officer's arm and cudgelling her brains desperately for some way of stopping this duel which could only end in tragedy. For if Jason did manage to save his own life running the Russian through, who could say what the Cossacks would do to them in their rage at the loss of their leader? At the moment they were pressing close on all sides and indeed serving a useful purpose in keeping back the press of armed men which had once more overtaken them.

But in another second or two they had reached the shady square and found it as silent and deserted as if it had been the middle of the night. With its blind walls and closely shuttered windows it was like something from a dead world and at its entrance the clamour of the nearby street fell oddly silent. The long, leafy branches of a gigantic sycamore, dark green on one side, soft and silvery beneath, stretched over the gilded railings of a garden wall and the ground below them was quite flat.

'This seems a good enough place,' Jason observed. 'I trust that your – er – kindness will extend to the loan of a weapon?'

But the captain was already freeing his sword from its silken knot and tossing it over to him. Jason caught it and drew it from the sheath and, after resting the blade against his thumb, tried a few passes with it. The sun glittered on the flashing steel.

Chernychev, meanwhile, had thrown off his cloak and unbuttoned his jacket, which he threw to one of his men. Then, after a moment's hesitation, he ripped off his shirt of fine lawn. Jason smiled grimly and did the same with his blouse.

Stripped to the waist, the two men looked about equally matched for strength but they might indeed have belonged to two different races so great was the contrast between the white skin of the one and the reddish hair on his chest, with the body of the other, deeply tanned by long exposure to the sea air. Without so much as a glance at the woman for whose sake they were about to fight, the pair took up their stations facing one another underneath the sycamore where the shadow was thickest and where the sun was least likely to bother them.

Chernychev, having tested the edge of his own sword, saluted his opponent with a sardonic smile.

'I regret that I have no better weapon to offer you. I fear you may not be familiar with the sabre.'

Jason grinned back at him wolfishly.

'I'm touched by your solicitude but have no fear. I shall do very well with this. A naval cutlass is far heavier.' He returned the salute with an ironical swish of his blade.

Chernychev glanced briefly at the girl clinging, pale as death, to his junior officer's arm and murmured softly: 'Do you not desire to say farewell to the Princess? It is unlikely that both of us will emerge from this encounter alive.'

'No, for I expect to live. But I have a word to say to you before we engage. If I should die, will you give me your word to let her go? I want her taken to within reach of the French lines. No doubt once there she will be able to claim the protection of the man with whom you fought that night in the garden.'

A hideous stab of pain shot though Marianne, for Jason's tone left no doubt as to his feelings towards her at that moment. Jealousy, reawakened, had brought with it scorn and contempt. At that moment she even feared that in his revulsion he might court death deliberately.

'It's not true! I swear to you by my father's honour, by my mother's memory that General Fournier – for he is the man in question – is nothing more to me than a friend who came to my rescue at a moment when I stood in dire need of help. He loves my dearest friend, Fortunée Hamelin and for her sake defended me! He called on me that night to thank me for interceding for him to get him restored to his command. May I drop dead this instant if that is not the whole truth! It was his generosity which enabled this dastard here, who had done nothing to deserve it, to make good his escape when the law officers discovered them, while Fournier himself left the house under armed escort. Dare you deny it, Chernychev?'

'How can I, after all I was not there to see! But you may well be right. It – it was certainly the arrival of the officers which prompted my own flight.'

'Ah! There you are!'

Marianne felt suddenly weak with relief, so that she was obliged to sink down on to the low wall at the base of the railings, giving thanks with all her heart that the Russian had shrunk at that moment, when he might be about to meet his Maker, from adding one more lie to the burden on his soul.

Jason threw a quick glance at her and within the forest of his beard his teeth flashed in a suggestion of a smile.

'We can discuss that later. *En garde*, sir!'

The two blades engaged with a violence born of the hatred that burned in each man's breast, while Marianne, leaning heavily on Aksakov, could only put her trust in God and embark on a long, tremulous prayer. Chernychev fought like a man with no time to lose, tight-lipped, his face a mask of fury. He was constantly on the attack and his curved blade hissed through the air as fiercely as if he were mowing an invisible field of corn.

Jason, on his side, was content at first merely to parry his strokes without taking the initiative. He had spoken confidently enough but even so the strange weapon took some getting used to, for although somewhat lighter than the seaman's cutlass it was also without a guard. Moreover, he was studying his opponent's swordplay. Feet planted firmly on the ground, the upper part of his body almost motionless and the sword blade whistling about him, he looked like nothing so much as one of those Hindu idols with a multiplicity of arms.

But then, as Chernychev pressed home his attack with renewed vigour, he fell back a pace and in doing so caught his foot against a stone. Marianne cried out sharply and the Russian, taking instant advantage of the momentary mishap, followed up with a lunge that would have pierced the American right through if he had not made a lightning recovery and parried the thrust. As it was the sabre merely glanced across his chest leaving a few bright drops of blood in its wake.

This narrow escape roused afresh all the anger which had seemed momentarily to have deserted Jason. Now it was he who began pressing his adversary who gave ground but not quickly enough to avoid a stab in the fleshy part of the arm. Jason pressed home his advantage and a second, more determined stroke wounded Chernychev in the shoulder. He cursed softly and despite the pain attempted a riposte but the American's sword flashed out a third time and caught him in the chest.

He staggered and dropped to his knees as Jason sprang back. His lips writhed in a brave attempt to smile.

'I have it, I think . . .' he whispered and fainted.

There was a moment's shocked silence. The Cossacks stared down at the tall white figure lying on the ground as if they could not believe their eyes. But it lasted no more than a second. As Marianne sped to Jason with a sobbing moan of relief and he let fall the weapon he had just used with such deadly effect, Aksakov ran to his superior officer.

'Come away,' Marianne gasped breathlessly. 'Come away quickly! It was a fair fight and you won but you must not stay here—'

The young captain finished his examination of the wound

and turned to look up at them with a combination of anger and relief.

'He is not dead,' he said. 'And it's as well for you he's not, for I would have had you shot without delay.'

Jason was putting on his blouse but at these words he stiffened and, turning slowly, subjected the officer to a haughty stare.

'Is that your conception of honour in an affair between gentlemen? I was the victor, therefore I am free.'

'The laws governing the duel do not hold in time of war. I shall not kill you because you have not killed him but I am taking you with me. You are my prisoner. The Ataman must decide what is to be done with you. Only the lady may go free.'

'But I don't want to!' Marianne protested. 'Either you free us both or you take us both. I will not leave him.'

She clung round Jason's neck but at a word from the Prince two men stepped forward and detached her forcibly while others overpowered Jason and tied him by the wrists to one of their saddlebows.

When she realized that she was being left alone in the panic-stricken city while Jason was led away to an unknown fate, perhaps even to his death, Marianne burst into uncontrollable weeping. She forgot everything, her reason for being in that place, her desire to reach the Emperor and warn him, even the need to find Arcadius and the others. All she knew was that these wild-looking men, hardly one of whom understood a word she said, were like an unyielding wall about to divide her for ever from the man she loved.

When the men restraining her released their hold to mount their horses again, she ran to Aksakov, who was supervising the removal of his captain, and cast herself at his feet.

'I implore you, take me too! What harm can it do? You will have two prisoners instead of one and I demand to share my friend's fate!'

'That may be so, Madame. But it was expressly stated as a condition of the fight that you, and you alone, should be set free. My duty demands it.'

'And what is freedom to me? You make great play with your

duty, sir, yet by arresting the victor in an affair of honour you are contravening its first rule! Oh, I beg of you – you cannot know how much this means to me—'

Jason's voice, sounding strangely cold and distant, interrupted her.

'Be quiet, Marianne! I will not have you humble yourself for my sake. I forbid you to entreat him further. If this officer insists on behaving dishonourably I am not going to make one move to prevent him. Nor will I permit you to do so.'

'But don't you understand, he means to separate us? We are going to be parted, here and now, and they may be taking you to face a firing squad.'

The corner of his mouth lifted a little in his familiar, mocking smile. Then he shrugged.

'That is in God's hands. Think of yourself. You know quite well that you'll come through. You won't be friendless in the city for very long.'

'But I don't want to! I don't want to! I want to stay with you, to share your fate whatever it may be.'

She was striving desperately to reach him and cling to him, even at the risk of being trampled by the horses, but already the squad of mounted men had closed in on him. She uttered a piercing cry, like a wounded animal: 'Jason! Don't leave me!'

Aksakov, too, was lifting himself into the saddle as she turned to him.

'Don't you understand that I love him?'

It was his turn to shrug and he made a derisory little bow.

'I dare say. But we must abide by the conditions. Your Serene Highness is free – free even to follow us if you wish, although at the risk of being trampled by the crowd and lost without trace.'

With that, paying no further attention to her, the little troop formed up about the wounded man who had been hoisted as comfortably as possible on to his own horse until a conveyance could be found for him and, with the prisoner in their midst, rode off down a side street which, in due course, would bring them up with the body of the retreating army.

Marianne watched them go. In her wretchedness it was even some time before the significance of Aksakov's last words sank in. Not until the last horse had vanished round the corner of the street did her brain grasp the fact that nothing, as the captain had said, prevented her from following, whatever the dangers involved. As he had just told her, she was free.

The thought of her friends whom she was abandoning with little hope of ever seeing them again crossed her mind briefly but she dismissed it. Her fate was bound to Jason's. She could not and would not have it otherwise. She had to follow him to the last moment, even if that last moment were very close now. After all that she had been through to find and keep him, anything else would be senseless desertion and a betrayal of herself.

She threw back her head and took a deep breath, then set off in her turn along the same way that the Cossacks had taken. She had crossed the square and was just entering the street when she saw Shankala.

The gipsy was standing in the middle of the narrow thoroughfare with her arms spread wide as though to bar the way. All through the fight Marianne had not thought of her once, for the girl had an incomparable talent for vanishing into the tiniest patch of shadow and remaining there unseen and unheard. But now she had shown herself and Marianne knew by the grin of hatred and triumph that distorted her brown features that if she wanted to go after her lover it would not be without a fight. Too late, she understood that by pretending, against all probability, to be pursuing the man who had cast her off, the half-wild gipsy girl had all the time been aiming at nothing but the conquest of the master she had chosen for herself and taking him from the woman who might consider him her own rightful property.

Marianne stepped out boldly towards the other woman who, in her blood-red garments, looked like nothing so much as one of those crosses that were once drawn on the doors of houses where the plague had struck. Throwing out her arm in a commanding gesture, Marianne ordered her to let her pass.

'Begone!' she said sternly.

The other gave a shrill, high laugh and then, before Marianne could lay a hand on her to put her out of the way, she had drawn a dagger from her belt. The short blade gleamed for a moment in the sun and then she struck.

With a sound like a groan, Marianne collapsed on to the earth, already trampled by the horses' hooves. Shankala was bending over her, her weapon already lifted again to deliver one final stroke, when a sudden outcry made her look quickly back towards the farther end of the square. Instantly she abandoned her intention and instead ran swiftly after the Cossacks.

Chapter Three
The Player Queen

Pain bit sharply through the cocoon of thick mist which for Marianne had replaced the world of reality. It was like a persistent burning sensation and she tried to shake it off but her invisible tormentor refused to be dismissed.

A voice was speaking, a feminine voice with a lilting Italian accent.

'It's better than I feared. *Madre mia*, but she was lucky! I quite thought she was dead.'

'I too,' agreed a second voice, this time without an accent. 'But her assailant did not. She was just about to strike again when you shouted out and banged the shutters, Vania dear. Luckily we frightened her.'

The voices belonged definitely to the real world. Marianne opened her eyes and nearly closed them again at once at the strange picture made by the two women bending over her in the light of a candle. She who held the light was a handsome woman, no longer in her first youth, with red hair, a pale complexion and golden-brown eyes, dressed in the velvet farthingale, starched ruff and peaked head-dress of a renaissance princess, while the other, who was clad in the dark red draperies of a Roman matron, bent over the injured girl energetically sponging the wound, with such an expression of concentration on her fine, regular features below the piled-up hair and Roman diadem adorned with flame-coloured plumes that her black brows met in a frown above her dark eyes and the tip of a pointed tongue protruded from between shapely red lips.

She was dressing Marianne's wound with the aid of a bottle of brandy and a wad of lint with a thoroughness that drew a moan of protest from her patient.

'You're hurting me,' she protested.

The wearer of the plumes paused in her work and addressed a beaming smile to her companion.

'She speaks French! And without a trace of accent,' she cried, giving full range to a magnificent contralto voice. 'How strange that we do not know her!'

'I am French,' Marianne said. 'And I gather that you are also. But, please, you are hurting me.'

The other lady laughed, revealing small, pointed teeth, irregular but of a flawless whiteness.

'Be glad that you can still feel pain,' she observed. 'In any case, we cannot help it. The girl's knife may have been dirty. The wound must be cleaned.'

'Besides, it is finished,' the Roman lady said cheerfully. 'The wound is not very deep. I've probed it and by good fortune I have with me a quite miraculous ointment. I am going to bandage you up and, with a little rest, I think you will do very well.'

She was doing so as she spoke, anointing the wound with a kind of thick cream that smelled agreeably of balsam and concocting a makeshift bandage out of a pad and a long strip which the renaissance princess had ripped from the bottom of what had once been a white petticoat. This done, she reached for the brandy bottle again, poured a little into a glass and, placing two or three cushions under Marianne's head, obliged her to drink it.

Now that she was sitting up, Marianne could see that she was lying on a large sofa in a fair-sized room but the shutters, drawn tightly across the windows, made it too dark for her to make out many details. However, the candle in the princess's hand enabled her to make out strange shapes of stacked-up and dilapidated furniture.

She felt stronger after the brandy and made an effort to smile at the two women who were regarding her with some anxiety.

'Thank you,' she said. 'I think I owe you a great deal. But how did you find me?'

The Roman lady stood up, displaying a queenly yet graceful form, and moved to a window, her dark red robes swishing dramatically around her.

'We saw it all from this window. Not very clearly, of course, because you were at the far end of the square.'

'You saw it all?'

'Everything. The Cossacks and that splendid duel . . . not that we understood much of what it was about, or of what happened afterwards. It was quite thrilling, and most mysterious. But we should never have interfered if it had not been for the last moment when that woman went for you with the knife. Then we threw back the shutters and shouted so that she ran away and we went down and fetched you up here. And that is all about it.'

'Not quite. Won't you tell me where I am?'

The woman in the ruff burst out laughing.

'That is the first thing you should have asked. Where am I? What's happening? What is that noise? That is the sort of thing heroines always say in plays when they come round after a faint. There is some excuse for you, though, because we must have looked very strange to you so I will put your mind at rest. You are in a room over the stables in the Dolgorouki Palace. The place is left empty for the best part of the time and the porter, who is a friend of ours, let us in. I might go on to puzzle you still further by introducing myself as Mary Stuart and this lady as Dido, but I will rather tell you that I am Madame Bursay, director of the Théâtre Français in Moscow. And I daresay you will feel more honoured by the attentions of your temporary doctor when I tell you that she is none other than that celebrated singer Vania di Lorenzo, of La Scala, Milan—'

'And of the Théâtre des Italiens in Paris! Admirer and personal friend of our great Emperor Napoleon himself!' Dido concluded with a triumphant air.

In spite of the pain in her shoulder and the misery which had returned with the return of consciousness, Marianne could not help smiling.

'You too?' she said. 'I have heard much praise of your voice and talents, Signora. I myself am Princess Sant'Anna and I—'

Before she could finish, Vania de Lorenzo had snatched the candle impetuously out of her friend's hand and was holding it so that its light fell on her face.

'Sant'Anna?' she exclaimed. 'I knew I had seen you somewhere! Princess Sant'Anna you may be but to me you are the singer, Maria Stella, the Emperor's nightingale and the woman who preferred a titled husband to a brilliant career. I know, for I was at the Théâtre Feydeau on the night of your début. What a voice! What a talent! And what a crime to let it all go!'

The effect of this outburst was almost magical because, notwithstanding Vania's genuine disapproval, it completely broke the ice between the three women by reason of that amazing sense of fellowship which exists between all theatre people under any circumstances, however bizarre.

To Madame Bursay, as to Signora de Lorenzo, Marianne had ceased to be a great lady, or even a lady of quality, she was simply one of their own kind, no more – and certainly no less.

While they made a meal of smoked pork and dried apricots washed down with beer – the diet of the refugees in the Dolgorouki Palace was distinctly unorthodox, being derived almost exclusively from the contents of the palace cellars – the actress and the prima donna explained to their new friend how they came to be there.

Madame Bursay and her company had been holding a dress rehearsal of Schiller's *Maria Stuart* in the city's Grand Theatre the previous evening and Vania had been trying on the costume in which she was to sing Dido in a few days' time, when the theatre had been invaded by a furious mob. The arrival of the first of the wounded from Borodino and the disastrous news they brought with them had driven the people of Moscow wild with rage. A wave of hatred against the French had arisen and spread like wildfire. The people had turned on everything in the city that had any connection with the hated nation. Shops had been broken into and plundered, private dwellings ravaged and even some French *émigrés* with no love for Napoleon had suffered.

'We were the best known,' Madame Bursay sighed, 'and the best loved also, until this unhappy day.'

'Unhappy!' Marianne cried. 'When the Emperor is victorious and will soon be in Moscow?'

'I too am a loyal subject of His Majesty,' the tragedienne said, smiling a little, 'but if you had lived through what we did yesterday— It was horrible! At one time we thought we were going to be burned to death in our own theatre. We had barely time to escape by way of the cellars, just as we were, and then we had to wait for nightfall before we could leave our underground refuge. It was impossible to reach our hotel. Lekain, one of our company who was not rehearsing, did manage to get there unobserved and saw our rooms ransacked and all our belongings thrown into the street and burned. And what was worse, while we women were escaping, our stage manager, Domergue, was caught by the mob and nearly torn to pieces. Fortunately, a company of police coming to prevent the theatre from being burned down was able to intervene and he was taken into custody. It seems that Count Rostopchin has announced his intention of sending him to Siberia!'

'Along with his own cook,' Marianne said, sighing. 'It seems to be a passion with him. But what became of the rest of your company?'

Vania made a helpless gesture. 'We don't know. Apart from Louise Fusil and Mademoiselle Anthony who are here with us, living across the courtyard, and young Lekain, who has gone out to try and get news, we know nothing of the others' whereabouts. It seemed wiser to separate – being in costume we looked strange enough on our own, but all together! Well, imagine Mary Queen of Scots and all her followers, her guards and ladies in waiting and so forth all walking about the streets of Moscow! We can only hope that they have been as lucky as we are and have found somewhere where they can hide in comparative safety until the Emperor enters Moscow.'

'You took a very great risk in coming out to rescue me,' Marianne said quietly. 'God knows what might have happened to you if you had been seen.'

Vania laughed. 'What was happening in the square was so exciting that we never thought of that,' she said. 'It was like a scene from a play! And we had been so bored. So of course we never hesitated. But in any case I don't believe that there is anyone still living in this part of the city.'

Inevitably, after hearing from the other two, Marianne had

to tell something of her own story. She did it as briefly as possible because she was beginning to feel extraordinarily sleepy, as well as slightly feverish from her wound. She dwelt especially on her fears for Jason and her sorrow at having failed to find her friends again. Then, overcome by emotion, she broke down and cried and Vania came and sat on the edge of the sofa and, throwing back the folds of her robe, laid a cool hand on her new friend's brow.

'That's enough of that kind of talk. You are feverish and should rest. When the porter comes up this evening, we will try and persuade him to let us have a better room so that you may have a bed at least. Until then, you must try to forget about your friends because there is nothing you can do to help them. When the French have entered the city – then I expect all those who are hiding will come out again—'

'If there is still a city at all,' said a cavernous voice from the depths of the room. The two women turned towards it.

'Ah, Lekain! Here you are at last,' Madame Bursay exclaimed. 'What is the news?'

A young man of about thirty, fair-haired with a weak but not unattractive face and graceful in a rather effeminate fashion, stepped out of the shadows. His clothes would have been fashionably elegant but for the dust which covered them and he seemed on the point of exhaustion. His blue eyes rested on the faces of all three women in turn and he summoned up a grin.

'The longer I live abroad, the more I love my own country,' he declaimed, adding in a more ordinary tone: 'Things are going from bad to worse. I don't know if the Emperor will reach Moscow in time to save us. My compliments, Madame,' he went on, turning to Marianne. 'I've no idea who you are but you look as pale as you are beautiful.'

'This is a friend I came upon by chance,' Vania announced. 'Signora Maria Stella of the Théâtre Feydeau. But tell us quickly, young man, what is the latest threat?'

'Give me a drink first. My tongue feels like a dry sponge. It's too big for my mouth.'

'It will be bigger still after a good soaking then,' Madame Bursay retorted but she poured him a full mug of beer which he swallowed down with eyes half-closed and an expression of utter bliss upon his face. Disdaining such trifling matters as good manners, he smacked his lips and bolted down a slice of ham, helping it on its way with a second draught of beer, then threw himself down bodily upon a decrepit armchair which groaned under his weight, and fetched a deep, lugubrious sigh.

'Even when one's body may be doomed to extinction at any minute,' he remarked, 'there is still a great deal of comfort to be found in feeding it.'

'Well, you're a cheerful one, I must say,' Vania scolded him. 'What makes you think we may be doomed to imminent extinction, as you call it?'

'The things that are happening in the city. The rumour is spreading that Murat's cavalry is hard on Kutuzov's heels. The civilian population is in full flight.'

'That's no news. They've been fleeing for three days.'

'Maybe, but this is somewhat different. Yesterday it was the rich, the nobility and gentry. Today, it's anyone who has anything to lose. Only beggars, the bedridden and the dying will be left. And by this time all of them are in despair because they are taking away the sacred images from all the churches and monasteries to keep them from falling into the hands of Antichrist and his marauding hordes. Near the church of Peter and Paul I saw the people escorting the wounded to the Lefort Hospital, throw themselves down in the dust at the feet of the priests, stretching out their arms to the icons and pleading for them to remain, crying that the wounded would surely die, and then move on before the priests so much as lifted a hand to ask them, such is the habit of submission among these people. But there is worse to come—'

'What now?' Madame Bursay said irritably. 'Why must you always save everything for dramatic effect, Lekain?'

'It's you I'm trying to save! Before leaving Moscow, that damned Rostopchin threw open all the prisons, letting all the rogues and thieves and murderers they contained loose upon the city. And they'll not leave it without filling their pockets. I saw a gang of them getting into the Kremlin by the Saviour's Gate – and I can tell you, none of them were stopping to bow to the icon there, nor was there anyone to remind them of the law! I think they'll probably break into every house of any size.'

'And you stand there moralizing!' Vania cried indignantly. 'We must warn the caretaker, tell him to barricade the doors and windows and – and – I don't know what else?'

Lekain laughed grimly. 'The caretaker? He's a long way off by now and probably still running. I saw him going off with a cartload of stuff as I came back. If we have to put up a fight, there'll be none but ourselves to do it. Besides, I shouldn't think we'd much to fear up here—'

Marianne had been following her new friends' conversation in silence, but now she voiced her own opinion.

'But this store room is near the main gate, isn't it? And surely they'll try to break the first doors and windows they come to? We'd be more likely to escape them in the servants' quarters.'

The young actor had been gazing at her with evident pleasure but now he smiled with evident intent to captivate.

'I said a moment ago that you were as pale as you were beautiful, Madame, and now I say that you are as wise as you are both. The servants' rooms in the attics seem to me an admirable refuge – unless the mob should see fit to fire the house, in which case we shall undoubtedly be roasted, or if—'

'If, if, if,' Vania broke in impatiently. 'You can prove anything with *if!* For myself,' she added nobly, tossing the folds of her antique robe over one shoulder, 'I'd rather be roasted than ravished!'

'You have the oddest tastes, then,' Lekain said with a grimace. 'That's what comes of singing Dido. It gives you a fancy for a funeral pyre. At all events, I think the lady is right. We had better move. Since the caretaker has absconded, we should be able to break into the palace itself and get upstairs. We may not be troubled at all. Moscow is very large and there are many palaces. But in any case we shall be safer there, and it may enable us to hold out until the French enter Moscow. I'd better go and fetch the others.'

Suiting the action to the words, he left the store room and made his way across the courtyard to knock on the door of the little chamber where the other two actresses had taken up residence. Meanwhile, Vania crossed over to where Marianne was pushing back her cushions and struggling to rise and bent over her.

'How are you feeling? Do you think that you can walk – enough to climb up three flights of stairs? We will help you all we can.'

The younger woman looked up at the Italian with a washed-out smile.

'I must. I do feel a little faint still, but I think I can manage. Have I lost a great deal of blood?'

'A certain amount. But you must have an excellent constitution for it stopped flowing quite quickly. Come, I will support you.'

Slipping an arm under Marianne's sound shoulder, she gripped her round the waist and helped her to stand. There followed a bad moment for the sufferer who felt as if the walls were revolving round her and all the blood she had left had drained into her feet.

'Have a little more brandy,' Madame Bursay suggested, surveying her blanched cheeks with some anxiety.

'It will make me drunk—'

'As if that mattered! Once we are upstairs you can be put to bed and sleep. The thing is to get there.'

Marianne meekly swallowed a thimbleful of the aromatic spirit. A trace of colour came into her cheeks but it was at Vania that she smiled gratefully.

'Very well then,' she said simply.

While Madame Bursay made a bundle of their provisions in the remains of the torn-up petticoat and added as many cushions as she could carry, Marianne and Vania made their way with slow, cautious steps towards the door. The Florentine singer's arm was firm and steady and with her help Marianne was able to walk better than she had feared. However, she found that she had an odd, instinctive confidence in her new friend, and with it a feeling of having known her all her life. It may have been something to do with the scent of roses that clung about the dark red robe, reminding her of Fortunée Hamelin.

In the courtyard they found Lekain struggling, with the

assistance of two young women, one dressed as an *ingénue*, the other in a page's costume, to lift into place the heavy iron bar which secured the palace against intruders at night. By the time they had finished, they were all three very red and out of breath but this did not prevent them throwing themselves enthusiastically at the main doorway of the palace itself, consisting of an imposing pair of oak leaves framed by a colonnade. Lekain got the better of it without much difficulty with the aid of some tools he had picked up in the store room and, without pausing for introductions, the little band of fugitives swept inside. Their voices rang through the huge and splendid vestibule as though in a cathedral.

Impressed despite herself, by the grandeur of the place, Madame Bursay chuckled and said softly: 'We must look a weird sight in our stage finery against all this marble and gilt.'

'Indeed?' Vania took her up at once. 'For myself, I feel perfectly at home here. One has only to know the right way to go about it.' And she proceeded to demonstrate how perfectly at ease she found herself in her surroundings by embarking on a spirited rendering of Don Alfonso's aria from *Cosi fan Tutte*:

'Fortunato l'uom che prende
O gni cosa per buon verso . . .'

all the while continuing to support Marianne up the length of the monumental staircase.

Louise Fusil, the girl dressed as a page, who had been nicknamed Rossignolette, or Little Nightingale, by her companions, joined her sweet voice to the Italian's for the fun of it and in a moment all the others had been carried away by one of those moods of collective hilarity which beset theatre people sometimes at the gravest moments, almost like a need for reassurance, and were playing away at imaginary instruments to accompany them. Marianne tried to join in but her injured shoulder hurt her too badly and she was forced to give up.

All the same, it was on the whole a gay little procession which made its way up to the attics and the servants' bedrooms. These, naturally, did not compare with the splendour of the rooms below and they found only plain deal furniture, straw mattresses and common earthenware ewers and basins. Even so it was a relief to Marianne to be able to stretch herself on a bed which, although unmade, was at least clean, which was not the case with all of those they found.

Vania remained with her and the others took possession of rooms nearby, while Lekain went downstairs again and took it upon himself to explore the cellars of the palace, which he had been unable to do while the caretaker remained in residence, and procure food for the uninvited guests.

He came back bowed down with the weight of two enormous baskets, one of which contained the wherewithal to make a fire and an assortment of kitchen utensils, and the other a supply of food. From this second basket protruded the necks of a number of venerable, dusty bottles boasting some noble waxen seals.

'I have found marvels,' he proclaimed triumphantly. 'Look here! Champagne, caviar, smoked fish, sugar – and coffee!'

The word and its associations were enough to rouse Marianne who, overcome with pain and weariness, had been on the point of falling asleep.

'Coffee?' she cried, raising herself on one elbow. 'Is it true?'

'True? Only smell this, fair dame,' Lekain told her, waving the little canvas bag he had been opening under her nose. 'And I've brought everything we need to roast it and make enough for everyone. You shall have a cup of it upon the instant. Only trust me and you'll see that when it comes to coffee I am something of a genius.'

Marianne smiled, in amusement and gratitude.

'You are certainly a wonderful man. I don't know if this will be my last night on earth but at least I shall have you to thank for being able to face it with a cup of coffee inside me. There's nothing I like better.'

She drank, indeed, a second and even a third cup, for Lekain had not exaggerated his skill, disregarding Vania's not unreasonable warnings that it would keep her from closing her eyes all night. But Marianne had already passed one sleepless night in Ivan Borisovitch's inn and she fell asleep almost as soon as the third cup was empty.

She woke to a sustained noise and a strong sense of danger in the blackest part of the night, with the feeling of terror that comes of waking in a strange place. She could not remember in the least where she was, but then she made out Vania di Lorenzo's figure etched, with its diadem and plumes, against the lighter square of the window.

'What's happening?' she asked, instinctively keeping her voice low.

'We have visitors. It was only to be expected. This is one of the richest and most beautiful houses in the city.'

'What time is it?'

'One o'clock, or a little after.'

Marianne slipped out of bed, finding it less painful than she had feared, and joined the singer at the window but there was little to be seen beyond lights from below shining out over the trees in the garden. The noise, however, was growing louder all the time: shouts, laughter, a good deal of drunken singing and now and then the crash of breaking glass or a heavier thud announcing that some large piece of furniture had been overturned.

'How did they get in?' Marianne asked, for their window looked out over the garden and not towards the main courtyard and she had no means of telling.

'Over the stable roof,' came Lekain's voice from behind her. He sounded worried. 'I saw how they did it. There were two of them with ropes and grapnels and once inside they lifted the bar and let in the rest.'

'What are we going to do?' This from Louise Fusil who had followed him into the room. 'I wonder if we were wise to hide up here. How do we know they won't come up to look at the servants' quarters when they've finished plundering downstairs? We might have done better to hide in the garden—'

'In the garden? Look—'

A fresh mob had appeared on the lawn which lay below the terrace giving on to the main salons. In the light of the torches they carried, the watchers above could make out men with fierce, bearded faces clad in ragged blouses and bits of blankets tied with string. They were armed with pitchforks, knives and guns and they were advancing silently, like hunting cats, upon the palace which must have been shining like a vast lantern in the night.

'They must have climbed over the railings or over a wall somewhere,' Lekain said gloomily. 'That's cut off our retreat.'

'Not necessarily,' Vania answered him. 'There are two sets of back stairs, one at each end of this passage. I will stand by one and you by the other and if either of us hears anyone coming up we will try to escape by the other and out into the garden.'

'Very well. We can only hope that if they do come it won't occur to them to do it by both stairs at once.'

'Always the optimist, I see,' Vania retorted, and she swept off, as regally imperturbable as ever, to take up the post she had assigned to herself.

The four women who were left separated also. Madame Bursay and Mademoiselle Anthony went into one of the rooms facing the front of the building while Marianne and Louise Fusil stayed where they were, listening with thudding hearts.

Before long, the uproar had swelled to infernal proportions. The yells and screams reached fever pitch and were punctuated by loud, rumbling crashes that shook the whole solidly built edifice as though the earth had moved beneath it.

'Anyone would think they were tearing down the walls,' Marianne said faintly.

'Perhaps they are. But I think they have started fighting amongst themselves,' Louise Fusil answered quietly.

It was true that the cries from below had altered. The drunken bellowing and the yells of joy and triumph were mingled now with groans and shrieks of pain. Apparently the robbers who had entered by way of the park were endeavouring to persuade their fellows inside to part with a share of the plunder. To the listeners, suspended, as it were, above the tumult, the murderous orgy had something horrible about it, for it told them all too clearly that the moment when these human fiends in their blind fury should discover their refuge, would be their last.

Marianne's heart thudded in her chest. Her hands felt icy cold and she had forgotten the pain in her shoulder. She slipped out quietly into the passage which ran down the centre of the house, illuminated at either end by a round window above the stairhead. Vania and Lekain stood motionless beside the stairways, straining their ears to catch the sounds from below.

'Still nothing?' Marianne whispered.

Both shook their heads silently. Then, all at once, there came a sound of running footsteps and the clamour rose and swept outside as though the house had suddenly burst its bounds.

'I think they're going!' It was Mademoiselle Anthony who spoke, struggling to contain the joy that leaped in her voice. 'I can see a crowd of men pouring out into the street.'

'There's no one in the garden that I can see,' echoed Madame Fusil. 'They won't bother to climb out by the same way. Come and see.'

The two sentries came running back and everyone crowded into the room where Marianne had slept. The palace was spewing out the ragged, hairy groups of gesticulating demons, dyed red with the wine they had been wallowing in, and probably with blood also, as a draining ulcer casts out pus. But the actors' rejoicings as they watched this dangerous rabble departing were short-lived. Louise Fusil brought them to an end a moment later with a strangled cry:

'Fire! They have set fire to the house!'

It was true. A ruddy glow was spreading out from the downstairs rooms and the clamour of seconds before had given place to an ominous roaring. The last of the looters could even be seen turning as they left and hurling the torches they carried back inside the palace, uttering savage cries.

'Back!' Lekain cried. 'Downstairs, quickly! We must get to the garden—'

They sped towards the staircase which seemed to be farthest from the principal seat of the fire. Vania would have supported Marianne as before but the girl would not have it.

'The coffee and the sleep have done me good. Only give me your arm. But we must hurry—'

They groped their way down the dark stairway, built in the thickness of the wall, bumping against the sides and terrified as they felt the heat increasing moment by moment. By the time they reached the first floor the narrow space was so suffocatingly hot that it was like entering an oven.

'The fire must be very close,' Vania said, coughing. 'Lucky for us – this place – built of stone. If it were wood – like so many of them – we'd be cooked by now—'

'It's only a matter of time,' Lekain answered, swearing like a trooper. 'The stairs are beginning to burn.'

Even as he spoke, there was a red glow in the darkness and they rounded the last corner to see that the bottom steps were already well alight and a dense pall of smoke, almost as deadly, billowing up to meet them.

'We – we'll never get through,' Louise wailed. 'We'll all be killed—'

'Not on your life,' Vania shrieked. 'Hold your dress tight round you and run! We've a second or two yet. If your clothes catch, roll yourselves on the grass or on the gravel as soon as you get outside. Come on! Follow me!'

Giving Marianne no time to think, she caught her round the waist with one arm and clutching her robe around her with the other launched them both at the flames.

Marianne shut her eyes. She felt for a moment as if her lungs were on fire and held her breath. But Vania was half-carrying her forward in an irresistible rush and she scarcely felt the lick of the flames, even when her skirt caught alight. The scream that broke from her was caused more by the pain of her injured shoulder when her companion ran with her down the terrace steps and rolled with her on the grass to extinguish the fire in their clothes.

Seconds later they were joined by the others. Their clothes, too, were smouldering and they flung themselves down on the grass in turn, uttering shrieks of pain but fortunately without suffering any very serious injury. When they realized that they were all there, scorched, breathless and almost overcome by smoke but alive, they sat for a minute or two, staring at one another with a kind of incredulity, unable to believe their luck.

'Well,' Madame Bursay gasped, 'that was a narrow escape! We are all here and in one piece, so it seems.'

'Then let's see if we can stay that way,' Lekain said. 'Which we won't if we stay here. We must move away before the building falls in.'

Prince Dolgorouki's handsome mansion was blazing, now, from top to bottom in a great sheet of flame. The heat was unbearable. The building was like a fierce, roaring cascade of fire and the blinding light of it illumined every corner of the garden.

'Madona!' Vania groaned. 'Are there no fire-engines in the city? If nothing is done to stop it, it will set the whole district on fire.'

Her words might have been a signal. Almost as she finished speaking, the heavens opened. Volumes of water poured down on Moscow with an apocalyptic roar, drenching in an instant the Dolgorouki gardens and those within them who fled precipitately to escape the clouds of boiling steam that rose from the burning building. In a short time the blaze had been transformed under the pelting rain to something more resembling a gigantic steam boiler.

Soaked to the skin, Marianne and the actors tried to find somewhere to shelter but the gardens contained none of the small summer-houses often found in other places and trees saturated with water, soon ceased to offer any protection at all.

'We must get out of here,' Mademoiselle Anthony called out, 'before we catch our deaths of cold!'

'Never mind that,' Vania complained. 'But I could be in danger of losing my voice. I'm a creature of the sun and I hate damp like the plague. If I take cold I cannot sing!'

'I'm amazed that you can think of singing at all at this moment,' Lekain said with a chuckle. 'But I agree with you when you say that we ought to quit this inhospitable place forthwith. The question is, how?'

It proved, indeed, to be easier said than done. The garden was surrounded by walls and railings, except for one small door, bolted and barred as heavily as a strong room, which it was clearly impossible to open.

'Well, the looters got in somewhere,' Louise Fusil said. 'Why can't we get out?'

'They got in over the wall,' Lekain answered. 'I'm very willing to make a back for you to climb up if you will only help me up after you. Although I confess I don't see how.'

Vania had been tugging off her diadem and the snapped and sodden plumes which draggled over her face. Now, in answer, she unwound the length of red silk which constituted her Roman robe and held it out to him, sublimely disregarding the appearance she presented in her sleeveless petticoat.

'We'll drop this down to you once we are up. It's very strong. Then we can use it to climb down the other side.'

Thus armed, they proceeded almost gaily to the assault of the wall. Vania, as the supplier of the idea and the means, went first. She settled herself firmly astride the wall and leaned down to catch Marianne as the other women assisted her to climb painfully on to Lekain's back. From there, Vania's grip on her good arm was enough to hoist her up to the top. The rest followed and pulled Lekain up after them.

The descent was effected in the same order, using Dido's robe twisted into rope. But once safely on the other side Marianne's small strength was exhausted and she found herself close to fainting. While Vania helped the others to scramble down, she was obliged to lean against the wall, her heart thudding violently and her head swimming, scarcely even aware of the rain which was still pelting down.

'Not feeling quite the thing, eh?' Vania said sympathetically, seeing her wan looks.

'Not quite. Where are we going now?'

'I don't honestly know. We had so many friends but there can be none left now.'

'No,' Madame Bursay said, 'but we should be able to find an empty house to shelter in. There are plenty of those.'

'Empty houses can contain unpleasant surprises,' Lekain said without enthusiasm, trying to put up his coat collar to keep some of the rain off his neck.

'Why not try to find the rest of the company?' Louise Fusil suggested. 'I've been thinking of them ever since we parted company and wondering whether they might not have sought refuge in the Naryshkin Palace. The Prince was being very particular to little Lamiral—'

'It's one thing to make up to a dancer and another to take in a whole company,' Lekain expostulated. 'But I suppose it's possible. The good prince seemed very much taken with her. We could always go and see.'

'*Santa Madona!* Think for a moment,' Vania broke in. 'The Naryshkin Palace is on the other side of the city, and this poor child could never walk so far! I have a better idea. The priest of St Louis-des-Français—'

'The Abbé Surugue?' Lekain spoke with evident distaste. 'What a notion!'

'Why not? He is a Frenchman and a man of God. He will take us in. I know him. He is generosity itself.'

'Maybe, but he is still a priest and I do not care for priests. Relations between the Church and the stage may not be as bad as they were in Molière's time, but they are not so good even now. I'm not going.'

'Nor I,' said Madame Bursay. 'I don't know whether—'

'Well I am,' Vania interrupted her, slipping an arm round Marianne's waist. 'You go where you like. You'll know where to find me. Besides, you may be right. Not to distrust the Abbé Surugue, but to spare him an invasion. He may be overwhelmed with refugees already.'

'But I don't want to be the cause of separating you,' Marianne exclaimed miserably. 'Take me to this priest's house and then go with your friends. It's stupid to break up your party for the sake of a stranger.'

'You're not a stranger. You're a singer like myself. And what is more you are a princess of Tuscany and I am a Tuscan myself. So let us have no more words but be on our way. God keep you all until we meet again.'

'We may as well go with you as far as St Louis,' Madame Bursay said. 'We can go on from there. It's not far and we can take shelter in the church until the rain stops.'

This being agreed upon, they made their way through the empty streets as far as the chapel which had been dignified with the name of St Louis-des-Français, in imitation of that in Rome. It stood on the outskirts of Kitaigorod and adjoining it was a house of modest size, built of wood like nearly all those in the neighbourhood, but with a small garden bounded by a brick wall on its leftward side. The front door was up two steps and above it, well protected from the weather, a thick glass lantern illumined a small Roman cross carved in the stone. This was the presbytery.

With Lekain's help, Vania got Marianne up the two steps and, lifting the brass knocker, rained a series of loud bangs upon the door. The others, meanwhile, had discovered that the church door was locked and drifted off.

The door was opened by a little man dressed in black like a sacristan, with a skull cap over his grey hair. He carried a candle.

'You must be the verger,' Vania said in French, with her colourful Italian accent. 'This lady is hurt and we came to ask the Abbé Surugue if she and I might—'

The sight of a woman clad in a soaking wet petticoat did not appear to cause the verger of St Louis any particular surprise. He held the door open wide.

'Come in quickly, Madame,' was all he said. 'I will inform Monsieur the Curé.'

Marianne's head had drooped, exhausted, on to her companion's shoulder but at the sound of that voice she lifted it at once and their eyes met, not without amazement on both sides. For the verger of St Louis was Gauthier de Chazay.

Chapter Four
The Fire

The glance held for no more than an instant. Marianne's mouth opened. She was on the point of saying something, making some exclamation, but the strange verger had turned away quickly, murmuring something about fetching the Abbé, and vanished with his candle, leaving the two women in almost total darkness in a narrow entrance hall smelling of incense and yesterday's cabbage soup.

Marianne pulled herself together. Her godfather, she realized, did not want to be recognized, either because of Vania's presence there or for some other reason. There was never any shortage of mysterious reasons where he was concerned, as befitted the head of a religious order which, although underground, was none the less powerful for that. Clearly, he was here incognito, perhaps in hiding – but from whom? Or what?

Exhausted as she was, Marianne's persistent, insatiable curiosity was wide awake now and, in some curious way, seemed to revive her. What object could a cardinal of the Roman Church, and General of the Jesuits no less, which was to say the most powerful man in the Church after the Pope, and possibly even before him, since Napoleon had been holding him a prisoner, what object could such a man possibly have for disguising himself in the modest garb of a verger of a parish church?

It was true that, ever since she had known him, Gauthier de Chazay had always shown a superb disregard for splendid attire. It was clad in a simple suit of black that his goddaughter would always remember him. The magnificent red robe which he had worn that epoch-making day at the Tuileries had struck her as some fantastic disguise. But on this occasion, the black garments were not simply modest but not even very clean.

'God forgive me,' Marianne thought, 'but I don't believe my

godfather has shaved for days! He looks like a real moujik!'

She had no opportunity to verify this because it was not he who came back to them but a middle-aged priest wearing a soutane whose kindly face was surmounted by a few grey locks of hair shielding a balding crown. He flung up his arms to heaven at the sight of the two women sitting in their wet clothes on the bench in his hall.

'My poor children!' he cried, and the touch of the south in his voice brought a hint of sunshine into the dank passage. 'Have you, too, come to seek refuge here? But my house is full. Half the French residents of Moscow are here already. Where can I put you?'

'We don't need much room, *padre*,' Vania pleaded. 'Just a tiny corner in the church, perhaps?'

'It is packed to bursting. I was forced to shut the door into the street to keep more people from entering. One more and they will suffocate!'

'Here, then. If it were for myself alone, I should do very well on this bench, but my friend is hurt and exhausted . . . Only a simple mattress . . .'

The priest spread out his hands despairingly.

'I should not have said what I have if I had a mattress to offer you. But I have just given that belonging to Guillaume, my sacristan, to Madame Aubert's chief *vendeuse*, who is expecting a baby, and my own—'

'I understand. That was gone long ago,' Marianne said, trying to smile. 'If you had only a little straw we might lie down on, that would be more than enough. We belong to the stage and do not look for comfort—'

'To be sure! At all events I cannot turn you from my door on such a night – and in such a storm. Come with me.'

They followed him along the passage. From behind the closed doors on either side came a variety of sounds, whisperings, muttered prayers and snores, all telling how the priest's house was fulfilling its role of sanctuary that night. At the very far end the priest opened a small door beside the kitchen.

'There is a cupboard here where we keep tools and things. But I will fetch you some straw and I think there may be just room for the two of you to lie down. Then I'll bring you some means to dry yourselves and a warm drink.'

In a few minutes, Vania and Marianne found themselves installed in comparative luxury among the brooms and buckets and garden tools, with a truss of straw spread on the floor, a towel to dry themselves, tablecloths to wrap round them while they hung their wet clothes over the heads of the rakes to dry, and a steaming jug of hot spiced wine which they drank with infinite enjoyment by candlelight after their host had bidden them good night.

Before putting out the light, Vania made a careful examination of Marianne's bandaged shoulder. It was very wet but the thick layer of ointment she had spread on the wound had protected it from the rain. A strip torn from the towel made a fresh bandage. Then the singer laid her hand on her patient's brow.

'You will heal fast,' she said, with satisfaction. 'You have no sign of fever, even after all you have been through. *Santa Madona*, you must have a wonderfully sound constitution!'

'What's more, I'm very lucky – most of all in meeting you.'

'Bah!' Vania sang softly under her breath: ' "Luck is a woman . . ." And I might say the same. I have long wanted to meet you.'

Neither woman was long in falling asleep but Marianne's was restless and uneasy. The day had been a long and trying one for her: the panic-stricken streets, the meeting with Chernychev, the duel, Jason's arrest, then the gipsy's murderous attack and her own wound, all culminating in their escape from the blazing building and the flight through the pouring rain, had given her a terrible battering. While her body slept, her mind, freed from its control, beat about like a frantic bird, finding no rest. She was still a prey to all the terrors which had assailed her but had been temporarily set at a distance by a warm-hearted, picturesque angel in a fiery robe and an absurd head-dress of feathers.

Strangely enough, she found herself caught up once more in the old dream which had so often haunted her. The sea – the sea rising in angry waves and making a foam-flecked barrier between her and the ship that was sailing away from her with all sails set. Despite the fury of the waves, she was fighting desperately to reach it, struggling with every ounce of strength and willpower until, just as she was about to sink, a vast hand came out over the sea and descended to pluck her from the abyss. But tonight the sea was red and no hand appeared. What came was something else, something that touched and shook her lightly. Marianne started awake to see her godfather bending over her and gently shaking her.

'Come,' he whispered. 'Out into the passage. I must speak to you.'

Marianne glanced quickly at her companion but Vania, curled up in the Abbé Surugue's tablecloth, was sleeping like a child and showed no signs of waking when her friend rustled the straw in rising.

The passage was in darkness. Only the lamp burning at the street door lightened the gloom a little, enough at least to show that the place was deserted. Even so, Marianne and the cardinal stayed in the archway of the door.

'I'm sorry I had to wake you,' the cardinal said. 'I see that you are hurt?'

'It's nothing. I was hit – in the crowd,' Marianne lied, feeling herself unequal to the business of a long explanation.

'Good, because you must be gone from this house first thing in the morning, and from Moscow as well. From Moscow most of all. I can't understand how you come to be here at all. I thought you at sea, on your way to France.'

He spoke shortly, as though he had been running, and his breath smelled sour and feverish, nor was there the least tenderness in his tone, but rather a kind of querulous irritation.

'I might say the same to you,' Marianne retorted. 'What is Cardinal San Lorenzo doing in Moscow, disguised as a verger, just when the Emperor is about to enter the city?'

In that dim light, she caught the flash of anger in the churchman's eyes.

'That is no concern of yours. And I have no time now for explanations. Go, I tell you. Fly this city, for it is doomed.'

'By whom? And to what fate? Do you think Napoleon is mad enough to destroy it? That is not his way. He hates plunder and destruction. If he takes Moscow, Moscow has nothing to fear.'

'Ask me no questions, Marianne. Do as I tell you. Your safety, your very life depends on it. Who is this woman with you?'

'Vania di Lorenzo. She is a famous singer – and a very good-hearted person.'

'I know of the singer, but nothing of her heart. Never mind. She must know something of the city and I am glad that you are not alone. You will leave here in the morning – almost at once, indeed, for it will soon be light. Ask her to show you the road taken by those travelling to Siberia. At Kuskovo, you will find the house of Count Sheremetiev. It is not far, not more than a league and a half. The Count is a friend. Tell him you are my goddaughter. He will give you a welcome and you may wait there until I come to you.'

'Should I tell him also that I am Princess Sant'Anna, the friend of the Emperor? I think that might serve to cool his welcome somewhat,' Marianne said ironically. Then, speaking very firmly, she went on: 'No, Godfather. I am not going to Kuskovo. I am sorry to go against your wishes. It is the first time in my life that I have ever done so intentionally. But I have no business there and I mean to stay in Moscow.'

She felt the cardinal's cold, dry hand clasp hers suddenly in the darkness.

'How stubborn you are,' he said crossly. 'Why do you insist on staying? It is to see him, is it not? Admit that you are waiting for Bonaparte!'

'There is no reason for me not to admit it, if you must put it so. Yes, I am waiting for the Emperor. I wish to speak to him.'

'What about?'

Marianne recognized that she was on slippery ground. In another moment she would forget that Gauthier de Chazay was one of the Corsican's most deadly enemies and allow him to guess something of the information she carried. She caught herself just in time and answered, after only the slightest hesitation: 'About my friends who are lost. I came here with Jolival and Jason Beaufort and his lieutenant, an Irishman named O'Flaherty, but I have lost them all. Jolival and O'Flaherty yesterday, in the crowd in Red Square, while Jason was made prisoner by the Russians after wounding Count Chernychev in a duel.'

She thought the cardinal would burst with rage at that.

'Fool! Three times fool! A duel! In a city in a state of total uproar and with one of the Tsar's favourites into the bargain! And what was this duel all about?'

'About me,' Marianne snapped back at him, no longer troubling to keep her voice down. 'It's about time you stopped regarding all my friends as rogues and vagabonds and your own as saints. I'm not likely to find Jolival or Craig O'Flaherty at Count Sheremetiev's house. Nor even my poor Jason. Heaven knows what the Cossacks will have done with him! He may not even be still alive!'

The cardinal heard the break in her voice and his own softened perceptibly.

'Of course he is – unless his opponent has died, in which case . . . well, Sheremetiev may still be able to help you find him. He has a great deal of influence and any number of friends with the army. Go to him, I beg you.'

But after a short struggle with herself, she shook her head. 'Not until I have found Jolival. After that, yes, I may do so. There is not much else I can do. In return – you seem to have such powerful connections, to have so much influence yourself, please, won't you try to find out what has become of Jason? If you will do that, then I will go to Kuskovo.'

What she did not say was that she needed Jolival to help her carry out her self-imposed mission to Napoleon, without which she would not sail for America.

Now it was the cardinal's turn to hesitate. At last he shrugged.

'Tell me how and where this idiotic duel took place. Where do you think the Cossacks were taking this American of yours?'

'I don't know. They only said the Ataman should decide what was to be done with him. As to the duel . . .' She described it briefly, mentioning the part played by Prince Aksakov, and waited for what her godfather should say.

He was silent for a moment, then he muttered: 'I think I know where Ataman Platov is to be found. I will see what I can do. But you must do as I tell you. Try to find your friends if you must, but be sure you are out of Moscow by tomorrow evening. Your life depends on it.'

'But won't you tell me why?'

'That I cannot do. It is out of my power. But I implore you to listen to me. By the evening of tomorrow, the fifteenth of September, you must be at Kuskovo. I will see you there.'

Without another word, Gauthier de Chazay turned and left her, his small, dark shape seeming to melt into the shadows of the passage.

Marianne went back to her cupboard where Vania was still sleeping soundly. She lay down beside her and, feeling somewhat comforted by the thought that she had entrusted the search for Jason to someone qualified to undertake it, did her best to forget the mysterious danger hanging over her. In any case, she had nearly thirty-six hours before her. And so, this time, when she fell asleep she did not dream.

She was woken by a sound of trumpet calls and, opening her eyes, saw in the light of the candle, for no daylight penetrated their retreat, Vania struggling into a black dress which, although a trifle tight for her, was nevertheless more suitable to the occasion, and certainly less conspicuous than Dido's flowing robes. She was, however, experiencing a good deal of difficulty, having omitted to undo the sash, and was swearing freely in several languages at once.

Marianne made haste to extricate her by unfastening the knot and pulling the dress down over her head.

'Thank you!' Vania gasped, emerging red-faced and dishevelled, from the suffocating folds of cloth. 'I have our host's generosity to thank for this elegant garment. He brought it a minute ago. I suppose he had it as a donation from some charitable lady – but I could wish her charity had gone so far as to make it a new one,' she added, with a grimace. 'I don't care for her scent at all – or for the smell it's meant to cover up!'

Sleep and Vania's ointment had worked wonders. Marianne's shoulder was stiff but much less painful and she was sure she had no fever at all.

'What time is it?' she asked.

'Goodness, I don't know. I left my watch at the theatre and

there is no way of telling the time in this cubby hole. And I never thought to ask the abbé.'

He reappeared at that moment, bringing a tray with two steaming cups of milkless tea, some sour cream and slices of dark brown bread.

'It's close on noon,' he said, 'and this, I fear, is all I have to offer to you. You must excuse me.'

'With all our hearts, *padre*. Even the prettiest girl can't give more than she has,' Vania said boldly.

But the abbé gave no sign of being shocked by the comparison and the singer said no more but instead changed the subject by asking the reason for the trumpet calls that had been making themselves heard for some minutes.

'What do you think?' the abbé sighed, shrugging his shoulders. 'Bonaparte's army is entering Moscow.'

That one word Bonaparte told Marianne more than a long speech could have done. Here was yet another who had no love for Napoleon. Indeed, since that indefatigable conspirator, Gauthier de Chazay, was staying in the house— Even so, she smiled at him gratefully.

'We shan't trouble you for much longer, Monsieur le Curé,' she said. 'If the French are here, we will no longer be in danger.'

They made haste to swallow their breakfast and, after thanking the abbé for his hospitality, left the presbytery. Nor did he show much inclination to detain them. Without quite knowing why, Marianne was in a hurry to be gone now from what, in spite of everything, she could not help seeing as a nest of conspirators.

They saw no one else on their way out and she concluded that none of the refugees within had any desire to witness the arrival of their countrymen. Vania had much the same idea.

'The Abbé Surugue is a fine man,' she observed, 'but I suspect him of having a hand in politics. I should like to have got a sight of the people in his house. I didn't fancy his verger's looks at all.'

Marianne was obliged to laugh.

'Nor I,' she said sincerely. 'I'm sure I never saw a verger like him before.'

When they emerged into the street, bright sunshine had replaced the downpour of the night before, traces of which still showed in broken branches and shattered flower pots and the large puddles of water that lay everywhere. But in the region of the church there was not a soul to be seen.

'Let's go towards Red Square,' Vania proposed. 'That is the heart of Moscow and the place the troops will make for. I should think the Emperor will want to take up his quarters in the Kremlin.'

With the exception of an occasional figure glimpsed in a doorway or at a window, the streets were all equally deserted as the two women made their way to the river Moskva and then along its embankment towards the square. There they saw that only two bridges remained. Eight others must have been destroyed during the night and the bed of the river was littered with the debris.

It was strange to be walking through the abandoned city, so drained of all signs of activity as to be almost dead. The only sounds were the trumpet calls, growing nearer all the time, and the distant rumble of cannon and drums. The effect was both painful and oppressive and although the two friends were glad to be in the open air again, and Marianne, especially, relieved to be able to walk again without too much discomfort, it was not long before they ceased to exchange any comments and lapsed into silence.

The expanse of Red Square opened before them, empty but for a couple of stragglers from the Russian army kneeling before the amazing red, blue and gold pile of St Basil's Cathedral, and some cattle from the slaughterhouse roaming about at random, still unaccustomed to their unexpected freedom.

But on the battlements of the Kremlin there were figures to be seen which reminded Marianne unpleasantly of those she had seen the night before.

'I can't see much evidence of the French as yet,' she murmured. 'Where are they? We can hear them but not see them.'

'Why yes!' exclaimed the singer, who had moved closer to the river. 'Look! They are fording the river.'

At a point near the western corner of the Kremlin, a regiment of cavalry was indeed engaged in quietly crossing the Moskva, which at that place appeared to be no deeper than the horses' withers.

Marianne leaned over the parapet and stared.

'French? Are you sure? I can't tell.'

Vania laughed merrily. 'Not French, no! But part of the *Grande Armée*, most certainly! Lord, don't tell me you can't recognize the Emperor's soldiers! Why, I know all their uniforms and every division! The army is a passion with me. I've never seen a more handsome set of men!'

Marianne, greatly entertained by her eagerness, reflected privately that Vania and her dear Fortunée appeared to have a good deal more in common than a fondness for attar of roses. Evidently they shared a passion for soldiers.

'Look!' Vania cried. 'Here come the first of them! It's the Polish hussars, the Tenth, Colonel Uminski's! And after them I can see the Prussians, Major von Werther's Uhlans, and then – I think it's Württemberg's Chasseurs and behind them several regiments of French hussars! Yes, it's them! I can tell by their plumes. Oh, it's so wonderful to see them again! I know that they have put us all in an impossible situation by coming but, truly, it was worth it and I, for one, can't be sorry . . .'

Caught up in her companion's infectious enthusiasm, Marianne watched with equal fascination as the mounted columns forded the river in good order. Vania, at her side, leaning over and clutching at the parapet, was almost shaking with excitement. Her eyes were wide and her nostrils quivering. Suddenly, she uttered a cry and threw out an arm.

'Oh, look! Look there! The man riding up the column and crossing the river at full gallop!'

'The one in green with the white plumes almost as tall as himself?'

'Yes! Oh, I'd know him in a thousand! It's the King of Naples! It's Murat – the finest horseman in the Empire!'

Vania's excitement had reached fever pitch and Marianne suppressed a smile. She had long known of Napoleon's brother-in-law's penchant for exotic, not to say fantastic costumes, but this time he seemed to have gone his length. Only he could have had the effrontery to appear in his present extravagant dress of dark green velvet polonaise with massive gold frogs, worn with a sash of gold threadwork and bonnet of the same colour surmounted by a white ostrich plume not less than three feet high. And, strangest of all, was the way he managed not to appear ridiculous in such an outfit.

Vania was suddenly so flushed with happiness that Marianne shot her a glance half-envious, half-amused.

'You seem to have a great admiration for the King of Naples?' she said with a smile.

The singer turned and looked her straight in the eyes, then, with a pride that was not without its greatness, she said simply: 'He is my lover. I would go through fire for him.'

'It would be a pity if you did. No man, however brilliant, deserves to have such a woman as you destroy herself for his sake. Live and if your love is returned, enjoy your happiness.'

'Oh, I do believe he loves me! But there are so many women running after him—'

'Beginning with his wife. Are you not afraid of the formidable Caroline?'

'Why should I be? She is all very well, but had her brother not been an emperor she would never have been a queen and no one would have paid very much attention to her at all. She cannot even sing. Besides, even as wives go, she's not the most faithful.'

Evidently this, to the prima donna, was a fatal flaw, and her argument was not without its logic. Marianne preferred to leave Caroline Murat to her own fate, which was a matter of some indifference to her, for she had never held Napoleon's youngest sister in affection. She had known her for too long for a devious and ill-natured woman.

Consequently, she was able to look on indulgently at Vania's meeting with her royal lover. As the King's white horse burst into the square, the Italian sprang forward almost under its hooves and might easily have been trampled but for Murat's presence of mind. He leaned down with a yell of delight and, grasping her round the waist, swept her up into the saddle. Whereupon, regardless of who might be looking on, the King and the singer embraced passionately, spoke briefly and then embraced once more. Then, as easily as he had caught her up, Murat lowered his mistress to the ground.

'Until tomorrow!' he cried. 'Go to the Kremlin and ask for General Durosnel. He will tell you where my headquarters are.'

He was about to ride on when Marianne ran forward.

'Sire!' she called. 'Can you tell me if the Emperor is coming?'

Murat reined in his mount and stared at her with some astonishment. Then he burst out laughing.

'What? Are you here too? Here's a pleasant surprise for the Emperor! I hope he appreciates it as he should!'

'But will I see him, Sire? Is he following you? I have to speak to him.'

'I hope, for his sake, that you'll do no more than speak. He is at a place called Bird Hill at this moment but I don't expect him to enter Moscow tonight. I must take a look at the city before he comes and gives chase to that old fox, Kutusov. Has he much of a start, do you know?'

'He went through yesterday morning, but his army was passing all night, going towards Riazan. There are some stragglers left even now.'

'Good. Forward, gentlemen! It's for us to catch them up. As for you, Madame, do not try to reach the Emperor today. Tomorrow, he will be in the Kremlin, for they will be making his quarters ready for him tonight. Be patient a little longer. He will be delighted to see you.'

Pulling off his magnificent, if ridiculous hat, Murat swept them a low bow and, handling his horse with consummate skill, set off at a gallop along the Moskva, followed by several troops of horse and Vania's eyes, which were shining like twin stars.

'Tomorrow,' she sighed. 'How long it seems! What shall we do until then? I don't suppose you want to go back to St Louis-des-Français?'

'By no means! I mean to try to find my friends. Would you mind if we went over to the governor's palace? It was there we became separated, two days since.'

As they strolled slowly, arm in arm, in the direction of Rostopchin's mansion, the two women were able to watch Napoleon's troops gradually taking possession of Red Square. Not a moment was wasted as the artillery and the foot batteries moved in and established a park. A few shots were fired from the Kremlin ramparts, whereupon guns were trained on the massive Saviour's Gate while a group of officers, accompanied by a platoon of Polish lancers shouting orders in Russian, set about effecting an entry.

'They'll not have much trouble,' Vania remarked. 'There's only a rabble inside. They won't make it a regular siege. They couldn't.'

Temporarily losing interest in the matter, she drew her companion off in the direction of the governor's palace, where a few people had gathered to watch the entry of the invaders. A smartly dressed female, accompanied by a number of much younger ladies attired in a much simpler style, detached herself from them and began hurrying towards a group of horsemen, seen by their plumes to be senior officers of some kind, who were dismounting before the doors of St Basil's cathedral.

'Come, Mesdemoiselles!' she called. 'Do not be afraid. These are our own people. They will surely be able to restore my poor husband whom these savages have taken away!'

'It seems to me that the Russians took more hostages than we thought,' Vania remarked. 'That is Madame Aubert, the celebrated French dressmaker. She has been too careless recently and made no effort to conceal her joy at the news of the war. Rostopchin must have paid her by taking her husband.'

But Marianne was no longer listening. Among the people outside the palace, she had just caught sight of Craig O'Flaherty. He was strolling slowly up and down, with head bent, hands clasped behind his back and a dejected expression, like a man waiting for something but who had almost given up hope.

Uttering a joyful cry, Marianne literally threw herself into his arms, quite forgetting her wound. She was reminded of it brutally enough and her cry of joy ended in a squeak of anguish which O'Flaherty scarcely seemed to notice.

'Here you are at last!' he cried, lifting her at arms' length as if she had been a doll. 'By St Patrick, I was beginning to think that you were gone for good. Where's Beaufort?'

Marianne gave him a rapid account of her adventures since they had last seen one another and presented Vania, who seemed to make a considerable impression on the Irishman. Then, without pausing for breath, she went on: 'Now you know as much as I do. I hope to get news of Jason very soon. But do you know anything of Gracchus and Jolival?'

'Gracchus is scouring the town for you. As to Jolival, he's in there.' He jerked his thumb in the direction of the Rostopchin house behind him. 'After the mob had passed the other day, some of those young fellows practising their swordplay here recognized him for a Frenchman and gave chase. In running from them he had the ill-luck to fall and break his leg.'

'Is he – oh, my God! They did not kill him?'

'No. I managed to disarm one of them and get his weapon and so brought our friend off safe enough. Sure, he was a trifle under the weather but the luck was ours in that we fell in with a medical man, another Frenchman and the governor's personal physician, which gave him the more reason for making himself scarce, for fear of what might be coming to him from that quarter. He saw Jolival fall and by the mercy of God his Hippocratic oath proved stronger than his fears. He came to our assistance and we carried the poor fellow into the palace stables where he had been hiding. The horses had all gone by that time. Then, when Rostopchin and his people departed some hours later, we were able to move quietly into the house itself.' He laughed. 'At this very moment our dear Vicomte is probably lolling in the governor's own bed. Come in and see him. The sight of you will be the best medicine he can possibly have.'

They found Arcadius ensconced like a king in a vast wing armchair full of cushions, set in the window of a large, luxuriously appointed bedchamber, with his splinted leg propped up before him on a stool, supported by a pillow. There was gilding everywhere but the fact that the decorations consisted almost exclusively of battle scenes and military trophies, together with a complete absence of carpets, combined to make the place about as cosy as a throne room.

Clearly, it had been getting the Vicomte down. That much

was evident from the way he welcomed them, hailing Marianne's arrival with cries of joy and treating Vania to an almost princely courtesy. As a result of his instructions and the more practical endeavours of Dr Davrigny, now left sole master of the house, the two women found themselves in possession of a fine apartment adjoining his which had formerly belonged to the Countess Rostopchin.

After that Vania departed with Davrigny in search of news, tactfully announcing that she wished to try and locate her companions from the theatre, and Marianne was left alone with Craig and Jolival.

Seated on either side of the Vicomte's chair, they held a council of war. The time for secrecy was past and in any case the Irishman had given sufficient proof of his friendship and loyalty to be trusted with anything that concerned his friends.

Marianne described in detail all that had befallen her and Jason and went on to tell of the night she had spent in the Abbé Surugue's house and her strange encounter there.

'I still cannot understand this danger which is supposed to threaten us and which made the cardinal insist on my promising to leave Moscow before tomorrow night,' she finished with a sigh. 'On the contrary, it seems to me that once the Emperor is here we should have nothing more to fear.'

It was clear, however, that Jolival did not share her optimism. Indeed, the more Marianne said, the deeper grew the frown between his brows.

'The cardinal is better informed than any man of my acquaintance,' he said darkly. 'And with good reason. If he tells you to go, then go you should. Moreover, Dr Davrigny has heard some strange rumours also, although it's fair to say that he paid scant attention to them, knowing the Russian love of high drama. But added to what you have just told us . . .'

'What are these rumours?'

'They say that the chief men of the city, including, of course, the governor, have determined, in their patriotic fervour, to sacrifice Moscow for the sake of the Empire.'

'Sacrifice Moscow?'

'Yes. In the Biblical meaning of the word. Moscow is to be the pyre on which Napoleon's army will be offered up as a holocaust to the Tsar's injured pride. People are saying that for several weeks past a kind of arsenal has been set up on Prince Repnin's estate at Vorontsovo, some six versts from Moscow, where they are manufacturing rockets and bombs and such to be placed in an enormous balloon, like that of the Montgolfier brothers, which is to be exploded over the city.'

'But that is madness!' Marianne exclaimed impatiently. 'Only a few days ago, the Russians believed they had won the battle at Borodino, and even yesterday, when they knew they were beaten, they were still insisting that Kutuzov was falling back on the city to defend it.'

'I know. That is why Davrigny paid no heed to the rumours – nor I, either. But a warning from the cardinal is something we must take seriously. It would be best if you were to go tonight, my dear.'

'Absolutely not. Your leg changes everything. You cannot be moved, so I will stay with you and, if there should be any danger – well, we will face it together. Besides, you are forgetting the Emperor. I understand that he is to make his entry into the city tomorrow and at all costs I must speak to him.'

'Can't you trust that confounded letter to O'Flaherty? He can hand it over just as well as yourself.'

'Sure,' put in the Irishman. 'It's entirely at your service I am.'

But Marianne would not hear of it.

'Thank you, Craig, but I cannot accept your offer. You would never get near Napoleon, whereas I can go straight to him, and if there really is some grave danger threatening the city tomorrow night, then I must warn him. That is a much more serious trap than the one I came to tell him about, because if the Russians truly mean to burn Moscow it may be that neither Napoleon nor his troops will ever see France again.'

Jolival was not the man to admit defeat without a struggle, especially where Marianne's safety was concerned. He was getting ready to defend his viewpoint energetically when O'Flaherty put an end to the argument by remarking that since there were still twenty-four hours to elapse before the danger, if danger there was, was due to make itself felt, Marianne had plenty of time to see the Emperor and then set out with her friends for Count Sheremetiev's country house.

'I'll drum up some sort of a carriage for you to travel in, Vicomte,' he asserted with his usual optimism, 'and if there are no more horses to be had in Moscow, then Gracchus and I will pull you ourselves! Now, suppose we all settle down to a pleasant evening listening to the gentle music of the King of Naples' trumpeters. After that, a good night's sleep will do us all the good in the world.'

The others had barely time to agree to this sensible proposal when the aforesaid gentle music of the cavalry's trumpeters was drowned by the tramp of marching feet, the roar of commands and the clatter of men standing at ease.

'Now what are we in for?' Jolival said testily, leaning forward as far as he could to try and catch a glimpse of what was happening below.

'Nothing much,' Craig answered him. 'Just an entire regiment, no less! Grenadiers, I think. I can see a whole lot of bearskins. We are about to be subjected to an army of occupation.'

A moment later, a tall, fair, blue-eyed young man, smartly turned out in a well-brushed uniform, carrying his hat under his arm, made his way up to Jolival's bedchamber. He saluted smartly and then, realizing that there was a lady in the room, favoured her with a beaming smile and a flash of firm, white teeth under a reddish-brown moustache.

'Adrien Jean-Baptiste-François Bourgogne,' he introduced himself in ringing tones, 'formerly of Condé-sur-Escaut, now grenadier-sergeant of the Guard. Good evening, everyone.'

'The Guard!' Marianne cried. 'Does that mean Napoleon is in Moscow?'

'No, Madame. It means only that we are here, to take possession of the district surrounding the old castle. The Emperor is still outside the walls. I did hear that he was waiting to receive a delegation of boyars.'

'Boyars?' Jolival laughed. 'We're not living in the Middle Ages, you know! There aren't any boyars any more. What's more, I think His Majesty will wait a long time before he sees any delegation at all. The city is as empty as my pockets.'

Sergeant Bourgogne shrugged philosophically. 'So we saw,' he agreed. 'All we met was a handful of sorry-looking ragamuffins who fired a few shots at us. Anyone would think these Russians were afraid of us! Yet we mean them no harm. We're full of goodwill. Besides, we have strict orders . . .'

'Setting that aside for a moment,' Jolival inquired, 'what brings you here, sergeant? Are you going to billet yourselves here?'

'Yes, if that's all right with you. This is the Governor's palace.'

'Yes, but I'm not the Governor. We are merely French people who have sought refuge here.'

'I guessed as much. Well, Messieurs and Madame, we don't mean to trouble you. We'll be camping downstairs and in the courtyard and we'll try not to keep you awake. I'll wish you good night, then. And you may sleep sound because we're here to protect you, so you've nothing more to fear from the rabble still left in the city.'

But the night was by no means as restful as the worthy sergeant had hoped. Not only did Vania not return, which made Marianne uneasy, but a number of explosions were heard, all of them very close.

They learned from Gracchus, who reappeared at daybreak, having spent part of the night on patrol with the sergeant's men, for the two had struck up an immediate friendship, that a house in the Yaouza quarter had been blown up, that fire had broken out in a part of the bazaar of Kitaigorod and a large brandy warehouse near the Stone Bridge, which was one of the few that remained standing, the property of the crown, had burned to the ground but that nothing could be done to put out the flames because, as Gracchus said: 'there was not a single working fire-engine left in the city. The only two there were completely useless.'

This last piece of information did nothing to allay the fears of the occupants of the Rostopchin palace. The disappearance of the fire engines seemed to fit in ominously with the rumours overheard by Dr Davrigny (who had also failed to return) and with the cardinal's warning.

'I don't like it,' Jolival said. 'We must be out of Moscow before tonight. See what you can do to find a conveyance, Craig, there's a good fellow. And you, Marianne, try to see the Emperor as soon as he arrives.'

'According to the sergeant, that will be quite early,' Gracchus put in. 'Six or seven o'clock, perhaps.'

'All the better. Your task will be over all the sooner, my dear, and Napoleon can make whatever dispositions he thinks fit. When you have done, come back here as quickly as you can. Gracchus will go with you. There's no saying what might happen to a young and personable female going unprotected amongst this mass of troops.'

At six o'clock, Marianne crossed the courtyard with Gracchus at her side and received a cheerful but not unrespectful greeting from the sergeant who was in his shirtsleeves supervising the cooking of the men's breakfast over the campfires. He pointed proudly to a corner where four men lay sulkily, bound hand and foot, upon the ground.

'We've done a good night's work, M'dame. Caught those four beauties setting fire to a house back there. There were ladies there and we were able to save them, though we lost one of our own men, I'm sorry to say.'

'What will you do with them?' Gracchus asked.

'Why, shoot them, to be sure! Would you believe it, from all we can discover, these lads belong to the police—'

'Sergeant,' Marianne interrupted him, 'you would do well to make sure there are no more of their kind still at liberty. There is a rumour that the governor has left orders for the burning of Moscow.'

'We know that. They've even begun to try and carry it out. But we soon dealt with that. Never you trouble your pretty head for that, M'dame. Our Father of Victories knows what he's about.'

'Ah, have you any news? Is he here yet?'

'The Emperor? Not yet. But he won't be long now. Listen! I

can hear them playing "Victory is Ours". That tune means he's not far off.'

Marianne picked up her skirts and ran.

The square outside the palace presented a remarkable sight. The troops bivouacked there might have been preparing for a masquerade, for most of them seemed to be engaged in trying on a variety of strange and exotic costumes. There were men so covered in furs that they could have been mistaken for bears, and others dressed as Kalmuks, Tartars, Chinamen, Turks, Persians and even as gentlemen of the time of Catherine the Great. Heaped all about them was such an assortment of every kind of foodstuff, sausages, hams, broached casks, fish, flour and sugar, that the scene resembled nothing so much as a vast, unlikely carnival. Like children, the soldiers were trying to compensate themselves in this way for the weeks of misery and wretchedness that they had endured on the interminable march. It was like the market place of Samarkand after the passing of Genghis Khan.

Then, all at once, everything stopped. The roll of drums and bellowed commands rose at last above the din. Slowly, the men began tugging off their finery and assumed a more military demeanour, lining up in such a way as to conceal the litter of supplies cluttering the square. The marching tune of the guards could still be heard for a moment or two longer, then that, too, died away and once again there was the deathly silence that had hung over Moscow twenty-four hours before. There was the clash of arms, a brief command or two, then, suddenly, a loud burst of cheering. The Emperor had arrived.

In spite of herself, Marianne held her breath and raised herself on tiptoe to get a better view. He was riding slowly, walking the Emir, one of his favourite mounts, dressed as he often was in the uniform of the Chasseurs, with a thoughtful expression on his face and one hand thrust into the front of his waistcoat. He had eyes for nothing but the great red fortress he was about to enter and which glowed redder than ever in the light of the rising sun. Only now and then he let his gaze flicker for an instant towards the Bazaar, from which a black column of smoke was still rising.

'He's put on weight,' Gracchus whispered. 'He doesn't look well.'

He was right. Napoleon's face had a bilious yellow tinge and his figure had undoubtedly thickened. Curvetting around him were Berthier, Caulaincourt, Duroc, the Mameluke, Ali, and others whose identity Marianne was unable to make out. He lifted his hand in acknowledgment of the men's frenzied cheers and then the whole cavalcade, with a company of the 1st Chasseurs bringing up the rear, swept through the Saviour's Gate, where the Chasseurs instantly took up guard duties.

'Do you think they will let us in, Mademoiselle Marianne?' Gracchus asked uneasily. 'We don't look very respectable, with our clothes all dirty and everything.'

'There's no reason why they shouldn't. I saw the Grand Marshal there. I shall go and ask for him. Come on.'

Without more ado, she made her own way up to the great tower which housed the Saviour's Gate. But as Gracchus had predicted, the sentries refused to let her pass, although she stated her name and titles clearly.

'We've had no orders as yet,' she was told by a young lieutenant who could barely have dismounted from his horse. 'Wait a minute.'

'But I am only asking you to let Grand Marshal Duroc know that I am here. He is a friend of mine.'

'I daresay. But you must give him time to find his way about, and us to get our orders.'

Marianne waited patiently for a minute or two and then, as the officer seemed to have forgotten all about her, she returned to the attack. But with no more success than at first. The argument was threatening to become protracted when, by good fortune, a figure smothered in a good deal of gold lace appeared in the huge archway.

Marianne recognized him at once.

'There is Captain de Trobriant,' she said. 'Bring him to me.'

'You are out of date, Madame. He is a major now and our commanding officer. But I do not see— Here, you! Come back!'

But Marianne was tired of arguing and she had slipped under his arm, outstretched to bar her way, and was running towards his superior officer. Trobriant was, in fact, an old acquaintance. She had met him first on that memorable evening at Malmaison when she and Jason had succeeded in warning Napoleon of the attempt on his life planned by the Chevalier de Bruslart. Since then, the handsome officer of Chasseurs had been a frequent visitor in the drawing-rooms of the Hôtel d'Asselnat and it did not take him a second to know the pale, quietly dressed woman who came running towards him.

'You? But what are you doing here? On my oath, I'd no idea you were in Russia and I do not think the Emperor himself—'

'It is the Emperor I am here to see. Please, Trobriant, get me inside. You know me. I am not mad or hysterical but I must speak to His Majesty at once. What I have to tell him is of the greatest importance. It concerns the safety of all—'

He stared into her eyes for a moment and what he saw there must have convinced him for he drew her arm through his without another word.

'Come,' he said.

Then, turning to the subaltern, he added: 'Let in the young man with the Princess Sant'Anna, Breguet. He is her coachman.'

'How was I to guess that?' Breguet muttered. 'How can a man tell a coachman without coach or horses – any more than a princess dressed like a chambermaid.'

'No one expects it of you.' Trobriant smiled at Marianne. 'I trust I shall be able to find my way about this barracks of a palace. Perhaps you know it better than I do?'

'By no means. I have only just come here myself.'

In the officer's company, she passed through courts and gardens dotted with churches and palace buildings, making for the largest of them all, an amazing mixture of gothic and modern styles the bulk of which had been erected by the Tsarina Elizabeth. Soldiers were settling in all around them and the Emperor's servants were already making themselves at home in their new quarters.

'Is the Emperor pleased?' Marianne asked as they climbed a broad marble staircase.

'You mean is he in a good temper?' the officer said, laughing. 'Yes, I think so. As he rode into the courtyard just now, I heard him exclaim: "So at last I am in Moscow, in the Kremlin, the ancient palace of the Tsars!" I'm glad he took it like that because when we entered the city and saw it so deserted we feared the disappointment would be too great. But no – the Emperor thinks the people are afraid and will come out of hiding when they see that he means them no harm.'

Marianne shook her head sadly. 'They are not going to come out, my friend. This whole city is one enormous trap.'

She said no more because just then they came into a huge gallery in the midst of which the Master of Ceremonies, the Comte de Ségur, and the Prefect of the Palace, the Marquis de Bausset, both of whom had arrived the previous evening to prepare quarters for the staff, were busy explaining the billeting arrangements to the people crowding the room.

All of them were far too busy to take any notice of the new arrivals and Trobriant, catching sight of the impassive figure of the Mameluke, Ali, standing with folded arms before a great inlaid door, steered a course towards him.

'Is the Emperor within?'

Ali nodded, indicating that Napoleon was in his bedchamber in the company of his valet.

'Constant?' Marianne cried. 'He is just the man I need! Go and fetch him, for the love of heaven! Tell him the Princess Sant'Anna is here and wishes to see His Majesty upon the instant.'

A minute later, Napoleon's Flemish valet came hurrying through the door and literally fell upon Marianne, for whom he had always had a particularly soft spot. He was almost in tears.

'Mademoi— Princess, I should say! Your Serene Highness! This is an unexpected pleasure! But by what happy chance—?'

'Later, my dear Constant, later. I want to see the Emperor. Is it possible?'

'But of course! There has been no time yet to establish protocol. And he will be so happy. Come! Come quickly!'

Several doors, a succession of rooms, another door and Marianne found herself precipitated into a large chamber, littered with an assortment of baggage, with Constant's voice announcing her in ringing tones, as if she had been another victory.

Beside the great tented bed, surmounted by the double-headed eagle and an imperial crown, Napoleon was engaged, with Duroc's assistance, in hanging up the portrait of a fair-haired child.

Both men turned and Marianne dropped into her curtsy.

There was a moment's astonished silence, so profound that Marianne, almost on her knees, could not even bring herself to raise her head. Then she heard Napoleon's voice.

'What? Is it you?'

'Yes, Sire, it is I! Forgive me for bursting in on you like this, but I have travelled a long road to come to you.'

Once again there was silence, but this time she gathered the courage to look up. And as she looked at him she was suddenly conscious of a wave of disappointment, and even of a vague disquiet. After what Murat had told her, after Trobriant's warm welcome and Constant's ecstatic one, she had expected him to show pleasure, to be really glad to see her. But that seemed to be very far from the case. The Emperor's face had set in its most forbidding expression. He was frowning at her grimly, kneading his hands behind his back, and since he showed no disposition to give her leave to rise she repeated softly: 'I ventured to tell Your Majesty that I had travelled a long road. I am very weary, Sire.'

'You are – oh, yes, very well. You may get up. Off with you, Duroc. Leave us, and see that I am not disturbed.'

The smile which the Grand Marshal of the Palace bestowed on her in passing was some comfort to Marianne as she rose, not without effort for it was some time since she had been obliged to perform a full court curtsy.

Meanwhile Napoleon, falling naturally, in this strange palace, into his old habits of Saint-Cloud and the Tuileries, had begun pacing up and down the thickly carpeted floor, glancing now and then out of the windows which commanded a view of the Moskva and of the whole of the southern part of the city beyond. Not until the soft click of the latch told him that he was alone with Marianne did he pause for a moment in his pacing and look at her.

'You seem to be got up very oddly for a court lady,' he observed drily. 'Upon my word, your dress is full of holes. And dirty into the bargain. And if your hair is not too bad, no one could say that you were looking your best. What do you want?'

Stung by the harshness of this address, Marianne felt the blood rush to her face.

'My dress is like myself, Sire! It has travelled three-quarters of the way across Russia, all the way from Odessa, to reach you! There may be holes in it, but it has served at least to keep this safe!'

From its inner pocket, she drew out the letter and the Tsar's note which she had managed to preserve unharmed through so many vicissitudes, as she had also the diamond still sewn inside her chemise.

'What's this?' Napoleon asked gruffly.

'A letter from the Swedish crown prince to his good friend the Tsar,' Marianne said, speaking very clearly so that he could not possibly seem to misunderstand her. 'For a one-time general of the Republic, Your Majesty will see that he has some strange counsel to give. You will see also, Sire, a note from the same source, making clear the prince's ambitions and the price he is willing to pay for their fulfilment.'

He almost snatched the letter from her hand and, after a sharp glance at her, began to read it. As he read, Marianne saw his nostrils tighten and a little vein swelled in his forehead. Knowing his temper, she expected him to give vent to an angry outburst, but he did nothing of the kind. Instead he tossed both papers on to the bed, as if unwilling to soil his hands with them.

'Where did you get these?' was all he asked.

'From the Duc de Richelieu's desk, Sire – after seeing him suitably drugged, and shortly before setting fire to a number of vessels in the port of Odessa.'

Now he was looking at her in frank amazement, an eyebrow lifted alarmingly.

'Drugged?' he said faintly. 'Setting fire to—' Then, without warning, he gave a shout of laughter and held out his hand to her. 'Come and sit here by me, Princess, and tell me all about it. Truly, you are the most astonishing woman I have ever met! I send you off on one mission in which you fail magnificently and then you carry off another on your own initiative and make an unbelievable success of it.'

He was just sitting down beside her when a timid knock at the door made him start up again.

'I said I did not wish to be disturbed,' he shouted.

Constant's head peered cautiously round the door.

'It's General Durosnel, Sire. He insists that you must see him. He says it is a matter of the utmost importance.'

'Another of 'em! Everything seems to be vitally important this morning. Very well, send him in.'

The general entered and saluted. Then, remaining stiffly at attention, he said: 'Sire, I ask your forgiveness. But it is right that your Majesty should know at once that I have insufficient men to keep order in a city of this size. Fires have broken out during the night and everywhere we find desperate-looking fellows with weapons who fire upon my men—'

'Well, what do you suggest?'

'Appoint a governor at once, Sire. The Gendarmerie is not enough. With your Majesty's permission, I should advise giving the post to the Duc de Trévise—'

'Marshal Mortier?'

'Yes, Sire. The Young Guard under his command have already taken up positions in and around the Kremlin. It is vital that he should be given overall control of Moscow.'

Napoleon thought for a moment, then: 'Very well. Send Berthier to me. I will instruct him accordingly. You may go.' The Emperor turned back to Marianne. 'To come back to you, my dear. Tell me the story of your adventures. I shall enjoy hearing it.'

'Sire,' Marianne cried, beseechingly, 'I beg you, let that wait, for I have something much more serious to tell you.'

'More serious? Good Lord, what's that?'

'You are in danger in this city, Sire – in very great danger. Believe me, you should not stay another hour in this palace – or in Moscow! For by tomorrow there may be nothing left of Moscow, or of your army either—'

Napleon rose so abruptly that he almost toppled the sofa, and Marianne with it.

'What is this nonsense? Upon my word, you must be out of your mind!'

'I wish I were, Sire. Alas, I fear that I am all too sane.'

Then, since he made no answer, she went on hurriedly to tell him all that she had learned in the Rostopchin palace, of the arsenal at Vorontsovo, the balloon, the emptying of the prisons and the dangerous felons at large and of the abandoned city.

'They will not return, Sire. Already, last night, fires have broken out. It will happen again tonight, at any moment, perhaps, and since there is not a single fire engine left in Moscow you are in deadly danger. Listen to me, Sire, I implore you! Leave this place! Leave before it is too late! I know that all those who value their lives must have left the city before tonight.'

'You *know*, you say? How do you know?'

She did not answer immediately and when at last she spoke it was slowly, choosing her words carefully so as not to risk involving her godfather.

'The night before last, I was obliged to seek shelter in the house of a catholic priest. There were refugees there – *émigrés*, I suppose, for I overheard one of them pressing his companions to quit Moscow before tonight at all costs.'

'The names of these people?'

'I do not know, Sire. I have only been here for three days. I know no one.'

He was silent for a moment, evidently thinking, then he turned back to her and sat down again with a shrug.

'Don't take what you overheard too seriously. It came, as you quite rightly thought, from *émigrés*, I am sure of that. They hate me but they have always taken the wish for the fact. The Russians have more sense than to burn their holy city on my account. Besides, I shall be writing to the Tsar tonight with an offer of peace. Yet, if it will make you happier, I will give orders for Moscow to be searched with a fine toothcomb. But I am not alarmed. To burn this fine city would be more than a crime, it would be a mistake, as your friend Talleyrand might say. And now, tell me your story. I long to hear it.'

'It may take some time.'

'Never mind. I have earned a little rest. Constant! Bring us some coffee! A great deal of coffee and some cakes if you can find them.'

As clearly and concisely as she could, Marianne described the incredible sequence of events which had happened to her since Florence. She suppressed nothing, not even those details most painful to her modesty. To her the man who listened so attentively had ceased to be the Emperor, or even her former lover. He was only a man whom she had once loved with all her heart and for whom, in spite of all his faults, his temper and the set-downs he could deliver so freely, she still retained a very deep affection, respect, admiration and a real trust. She knew that he could be cruel and even ruthless, but she knew, too, that inside this small man of genius, on whose shoulders rested the weight of an empire, there beat the heart of a true gentleman, whatever his inveterate enemies might say of him.

And so it was that she had no hesitation in revealing Prince Sant'Anna's secret and the reason why that great aristocrat had desired the blood of an emperor for his son. Yet, for all that, as she told him she did experience a momentary fear of what Napoleon might say. She need not have worried.

She was on the point of taking up her narrative again after a brief pause when she felt the Emperor's hand on her arm.

'I was angry with you once for marrying without my consent, Marianne,' he said, with the rare but very real tenderness which belonged to him alone. 'Now, I ask you to forgive me. I could never have found you such a husband.'

'What? You are not shocked? Do you really think—'

'That you have married a most exceptional man, and one of rare quality. You realize that, I hope?'

'Certainly. I could hardly fail to do so. But—'

He got up then and, putting one knee on the sofa, took her chin in his hand so that she was obliged to meet his eyes.

'But what?' he said, and there was that steely note in his voice which boded no good. 'Are you, by any chance, going to talk to me again about that American of yours? Take care, Marianne. I have always believed that you, too, were no ordinary woman. I should not like to have to change my opinion.'

'Sire!' she exclaimed in some alarm. 'I beg of you! I – I have not finished yet.'

He let her go and walked away from her.

'Go on then. I am listening.'

There had been a subtle change in the atmosphere which, for a moment, had become what it had been in earlier days. Napoleon had resumed his pacing of the room but he was walking very slowly, his head sunk on his chest, listening and pondering at once. And when at last Marianne fell silent he turned towards her slowly and his grey eyes looked consideringly at her for a long time, and once again the anger had gone from them.

'What do you mean to do now?' he asked her gravely.

She hesitated a little. She had, naturally enough, omitted all reference to Cardinal de Chazay's presence in Moscow and it was therefore impossible to declare her intention of proceeding to Count Sheremetiev's country estate. Moreover, if she had done so, Napoleon might very well have taken exception to this trafficking with the enemy.

Dropping her head to avoid his searching eyes, she said in a low voice: 'I thought – I thought to leave Moscow tonight. My friend Jolival is lying in the Rostopchin Palace with a broken leg and if there should be trouble it would be difficult for him to escape.'

'Where will you go?'

'I – I don't know.'

'You're lying.'

'Sire!' she protested indignantly, furious to feel herself blushing.

'No protests. I tell you you are lying, as you very well know. What you want is to go running after the Cossacks, isn't it? Come hell or high water, you want to find this Beaufort because you are so besotted about him that it has addled your wits. Don't you see that he is destroying you?'

'That's not true! I love him—'

'What has that to say to anything? I loved Josephine but I divorced her because I wanted an heir. I loved you – oh, yes, you may smile, but I loved you truly and perhaps I love you still. Yet I married another because she was the daughter of an emperor and the foundation of a dynasty demanded it.'

'It's not the same—'

'Why not? Because you think you have invented love? Because you think that he is the one love of your life? Come now, Marianne – not to me! When you married him, did you not love the man I sent to the guillotine at Vincennes?'

'He killed my love. Besides, I was a child, infatuated—'

'Come, come! If he had not been the wretch he was but the man that you had pictured him, you would have adored him your whole life through and never looked at another. Yet you had already met Monsieur Beaufort— And myself?'

'You?'

'Yes, me. Did you love me, yes or no? Or were you playing with me at the Trianon? And at the Tuileries?'

She gazed at him in terror, knowing that in the face of this remorseless logic she was lost.

'I hope,' she murmured softly, 'that you don't believe that. Yes, I loved you – loved you so much that I was mad with jealousy on your wedding day.'

'And if I had married you, I should have had no more faithful empress. And yet you knew Jason Beaufort then! Tell me, Marianne, can you recall the precise moment when you knew you loved him?'

'I don't know. It's all so vague . . . These things don't happen all at once. But I think that when I really knew it was – at the Austrian ambassador's ball.'

The Emperor nodded. 'When you saw him with another woman. When you learned that he was married and so lost to you. Just as I thought.'

'What do you mean?'

He smiled at her fleetingly, with that smile that brought back all his vanished youth, and very tenderly he put his arm round her and drew her to him.

'You are like a child, Marianne. Children always want what they cannot have, and the more it eludes them, the more they want it. They will spurn the prettiest toys, the greatest treasures even, for the sake of a thing of no value at all that lies beyond their reach. They are even capable of dying in the effort to grasp a star that glitters in the darkness of a well. You are like that. You would throw away the world for a reflection in the water – for something you will never reach and which will destroy you.'

She protested again, but with less conviction.

'He loves me too.'

'You do not say it quite so loudly – because you are not really sure. And you are right. What he loves is, above all, the image of himself which he sees in your eyes. Oh, to be sure, he may love you in his fashion. You are lovely enough. But admit that he has done little enough to prove it. Believe me, Marianne, and give up this idea. Relinquish this love for no good will come of it. You must not go on living a life that is not for you, living for another and through another—'

'I cannot! I cannot!'

He moved away without answering and left her to her tears. Going quickly to the wall, he took down the portrait which he had hung there so carefully a little while before, and put it in her hands.

'See! That is my son. The portrait is by Gérard. Bausset brought it to me from Paris on the eve of the Moskva. It is my most precious possession. See how beautiful he is.'

'Very beautiful, Sire.'

Filled with a despair she could not comprehend, she stared down through her tears at the picture of a fine, fair-haired baby boy who looked back gravely, in spite of the muslins and the garlands of flowers which were his scanty clothing. The Emperor's voice had dropped to a confidential murmur, yet there was an urgency in his words:

'You too have a son. You told me what a fine boy he was. You say you cannot help loving Beaufort but what of your son, Marianne? Is it so easy to cease loving him? You know it is not. If you persist in this mad quest for an impossible happiness, in running after a man who already has a wife – for the Señora Beaufort still exists, you know, however much you may seek to forget her – so, if you persist, the day will come when the longing to see your child again will be more than you can bear, even, indeed especially, if you have other children by then, for he will be the one whose love you have never known.'

Marianne could bear no more. She let go of the portrait and threw herself at full length on the sofa, torn by shattering sobs that made her whole body tremble. She scarcely heard the Emperor when he murmured: 'Weep! It will do you good. Stay here. I will come back soon.'

And weep she did, for how long she did not know, nor was she even very sure what she was weeping for. For the life of her, she could not have said who was the cause of the despair that racked her, whether it was the man she so persistently adored or the child so suddenly recalled to her mind.

At last she felt herself being lifted up and a gentle hand wiping her face with a cloth drenched in eau de Cologne, which made her sneeze.

She opened her eyes and saw Constant bending over her with such an anxious expression that, for all her wretchedness, she had to smile.

'It's a long time since you last had to take care of me, Constant, my friend.'

'It is indeed, Princess. I have often thought so with regret. Do you feel better now? I have made some more coffee.'

She took the scalding cup and drank the contents almost at a gulp, conscious only that she felt better almost at once. Then, realizing that the room was empty but for the faithful valet, she asked: 'Where is the Emperor?'

'In the next room which he has made his office. It appears that fresh fires have broken out along a smaller river which is called the Yaouza, in the vicinity of a mansion of the name of Balachov where the King of Naples has established his headquarters.'

Marianne was on her feet at once and running to the windows, but these did not look in the right direction and she saw nothing beyond a slight haze of smoke to the east.

'I told him there would be more,' she said tensely. 'Perhaps this new outbreak will make him decide to pull out.'

'I hardly think so,' Constant observed. 'Withdraw is not a word known to His Majesty. Any more than the word retreat. He does not know the meaning of it. And that in spite of any danger. See,' he added, showing her a fat, green portfolio which he had just extracted from a travelling trunk, 'look at this folder. Do you see the laurel crown that is stamped on it in gold leaf?'

Marianne nodded. Constant sighed and his finger traced, almost tenderly, the design stamped on the leather.

'That crown is the same as the one he placed on his own head in Notre Dame on the day of his coronation. Look at the design of the leaves. They are pointed like the arrows of our old archers and, like them, go straight for their goal.'

'But they may be destroyed. What will become of your laurels in the midst of the fire, my poor Constant?'

'A halo, your Highness, and shining all the brighter in time of trouble. A flaming crown, as you might say.'

He broke off as the Emperor's quick footsteps sounded outside and withdrew, with a deep bow, to the far end of the room, just as Napoleon came in. His face was clouded now and his frowning brows were drawn down like a bar above his steely-grey eyes.

Thinking that she must be in the way, Marianne sketched a curtsy.

'With your permission, your Majesty—'

He glared at her frostily.

'Save your curtsy, Princess. There is no question of your leaving. I wish you to stay. You have a recent wound, let me remind you, and I've no intention of letting you go running off to be a prey to all the hazards of war.'

'But Sire – I can't!'

'Why not? Because of your – forebodings? Are you afraid?'

She shrugged her shoulders faintly, more from weariness than disrespect.

'Your Majesty must know that I am not. But I left my young coachman outside and there are old friends waiting for me at the Rostopchin Palace who may be anxious—'

'Then they need not be. You are in no danger with me, so far as I know. As to the Rostopchin Palace, Trévise's grenadiers are billeted there, so your friends are not without protection. Never mind. I won't have you worrying, or making some foolhardy attempt to escape. Who brought you here?'

'Major Trobriant.'

'Another old friend,' the Emperor commented sardonically. 'There seems to be no end of them. Well, I will have him sent for to go and pick up your Jolival and the – Irishman, I think you said he was? They should be brought here. There's room in this place to lodge an army, thank God! Constant will see to you and tonight we will sup together. That is not an invitation, Madame,' he added, seeing Marianne about to beg him to excuse her. 'It is an order.'

There was nothing for it but to obey. Marianne swept a low curtsy and then followed the valet who, with the confidence of a man long used to finding his way about the most extensive palaces, led her by way of two corridors and a small staircase to a comfortable room with windows almost directly above the Emperor's, only rather more dusty.

'We'll see what we can do by way of chambermaids tomorrow,' he told her with a reassuring smile. 'For tonight, if your Highness would kindly make allowances . . .'

Left to herself, Marianne did her best to calm her agitated spirits and to shake off the misery that oppressed her. She felt lost and abandoned, in spite of the undoubted concern Napoleon had shown for her, and that at a time when he must have had other things to do than trouble himself with a woman's private emotions. What was it he had said? That perhaps he still loved her? No, that must be impossible. He had said it only to comfort her. The one he loved was his little blonde Austrian. Besides, what did it matter now? What was more serious, and more disturbing also, was that bold, categorical declaration of his. With what remorseless logic he had demonstrated that she was not a woman dedicated to a single love, that she might be susceptible to the attractions of other men besides Jason. How could he fail to see that that was false, that she loved him, had never loved anyone else but him, not even after Corfu when—

She clasped her hands together tightly and a shiver ran down her spine. Corfu! Why had that name come to her mind just then? Was it because, unconsciously, something in her mind was trying to prove the Emperor right? Corfu – the cave – and the fisherman, that mysterious lover whom she had never seen but in whose arms she had experienced total fulfilment, an intoxication such as no other man had ever given her, not even Jason. That night she had behaved like a wanton, and yet she had not regretted it, not once. Far from it. The memory of that invisible lover, whom she privately thought of as Zeus, remained to charm and trouble her.

'I must be mad!' she exclaimed wildly, clutching her head in her hands as though she would tear out such sacrilegious thoughts. But that she could not do. Everything Napoleon had said went on going round and round in her head, driving agonizing furrows through her brain and raising a thousand questions which she knew she could not answer, yet which resolved themselves at last into one single question: could she really know herself so little?

Confronted with the most difficult problem she had ever had to face, Marianne lost all consciousness of time. Hours must have passed while she sat deep in thought, for the sun was long past its zenith when there was a tap at the door and Constant reappeared. Finding her still seated bolt upright on a low, straight-backed chair, he exclaimed: 'There, I don't believe your Highness has rested at all, and you looked so tired . . .'

Marianne tried to smile at him and, failing, drew an ice-cold hand across her brow.

'Yes, I am tired. What time is it?'

'Gone six o'clock, Madame. And the Emperor is asking for you.'

'Good God! And I've not even combed my hair—'

'That is of no account. His Majesty has something he wishes you to see – something very serious.'

Her heart missed a beat.

'Serious? My friends—'

'Have arrived – quite safely, never fear. But come quickly.'

This time he took her to a kind of antechamber where an extraordinary scene met her eyes. A number of men were grouped about a stretcher on which lay a figure draped in red.

The Emperor was standing beside the stretcher and next to him was a distinguished-looking man whom Marianne had never seen before. Reclining on a bench a little way off, enveloped in a dressing-gown several sizes too big for him, was Jolival, a pale-faced Gracchus at his side.

Marianne felt a wave of relief at the sight of them.

'Thank God, you are here—' she was beginning, when Napoleon beckoned her to him.

'They tell me you know this woman. That it was she who tried to kill you. Is this true?'

Marianne's eyes widened. The figure wrapped in red cloth was Shankala, but a Shankala so changed that Marianne could not help feeling a rush of pity. The gipsy's face was very white and there was a trickle of blood at one corner of her mouth. She seemed to have great difficulty in breathing.

'Her chest is crushed,' the Emperor said. 'She will not last an hour, and well for her. It will spare her a hanging. Do you want to hear what she had to say?'

Marianne stared in stunned amazement from Napoleon's stern face to the waxen features of the dying girl.

'Yes, of course . . . But how does she come to be here?'

Gracchus spoke up timidly from his corner.

'It was Monsieur Craig who found her when he was coming back with a carriage, along by the Yaouza, just as the fire was taking hold. She was still living, so he brought her with him in the hope of learning something about Monsieur Beaufort. He arrived just as the major and I came to fetch them and Monsieur le Vicomte said that we should bring her to you because – because it seemed to be important.'

Understanding came to Marianne and she uttered a strangled cry and clapped her hand to her mouth.

'Jason! Oh, my God! They've killed him—'

'Unfortunately not,' Napoleon said irritably. 'He is alive. Now stop tormenting yourself about him and listen to what they have to tell you. This is my interpreter, Baron d'Ideville. He managed to speak with the woman and make out rather more than this young man here was able to catch. Well, Baron.'

'No, sire!' Jolival spoke up on a note of entreaty. 'I beg you will let me tell her. It will be less painful. I am most grateful to the baron for his help, but we are strangers to him.'

Baron d'Ideville bowed, indicating that he perfectly understood, and moved away a little. Napoleon went with him and took his arm.

Marianne turned to her old friend.

'Well, Jolival? What is it you have to tell me that is so terrible?'

'Oh, nothing tragic after all,' he said, with a little shrug. 'It is not so very terrible – except for you, alas!'

'Explain, please! What is this all about? They said that Jason has not been shot?'

'No. He is in perfect health and at this moment is no doubt travelling serenely on his way to Petersburg. The Cossacks took him to Kutuzov's camp outside Moscow and there he was brought before an officer of the staff – a Colonel Krilov.'

'Krilov? But that was the name of the friends he was trying to reach!'

'He was undoubtedly a member of that family. Shankala could not tell us very much about him but she remembered the name and she saw Jason come out arm in arm with a Russian officer. The two seemed on the best of good terms. At that, thinking the danger was past, the gipsy went to Jason. He would have driven her away at first but then he changed his mind and called her back and had this Krilov question her. He asked where you were and why you were not with her.'

'What did she say?'

'That she did not know. That she had lost sight of you. That you had vanished round the corner of the street.'

'And he believed her?' Marianne cried, stunned.

'So it seems. He asked no more questions. He simply shrugged and went off with his new friend, after telling Shankala that he had had enough of her, or words to that effect. But she's a stubborn creature. She stayed in the camp, which was not difficult because there were other women with the army. No one took any notice of her and she was able to learn a little more because the affair naturally caused something of a stir in the camp – an American dressed as a moujik dropping, as it were, out of the blue. Well, she discovered that Colonel Krilov had obtained permission to escort him to St Petersburg himself to introduce him to his family and she hoped to be able to to follow them. But when Kutuzov resumed his march, he got rid of all the women and sent them back to the city. Shankala was caught up in the crowd and obliged to return here, willy nilly. There, that's the sum of it.'

'But it's not possible!' Marianne cried, unable to believe her ears. 'Jason will try to find me. He can't have gone already—'

'Shankala saw him mounted before she left the camp. By this time he must be well on his way.'

'It's not true. It can't be. The woman is lying—'

A groan from the stretcher made her turn and she saw that the gipsy's eyes were open. There was even, she thought, a faint trace of a smile on the pallid lips.

'I tell you she is lying!' she cried.

'Those as close to death as she is do not lie,' Jolival said gravely, while Gracchus bent quickly over the woman who was evidently trying to say something.

They heard a murmur ending in a low groan. The bloodless hand which Gracchus clasped in his relaxed suddenly. The face turned to stone.

'She's dead,' Gracchus whispered.

'What did she say? Did you catch any of it?'

He nodded, then looked away.

'She said: "Forgive me, Mademoiselle Marianne." Then she said: "Mad – as mad as I!"'

A few minutes later, when Marianne, with a heavy heart and mind a blank, had allowed the Emperor to lead her out on to the terrace and was sitting down to dine with him, Duroc came to say that fires had broken out again in various quarters of the city. Napoleon threw down the napkin he had been on the point of unfolding, got up from the table and made his way to the steps, along with all those present at the meal. What he saw brought an oath to his lips.

Clouds of black smoke, carrying a horrible reek of sulphur and pitch, were being driven before the wind. Eastwards, a long street was spouting flames, while down by the Moskva a huge warehouse was beginning to burn.

Someone said: 'That's the reserves of grain, and there's another outbreak over towards the Bazaar. I think that's where the shops are that sell oil and cooking fat. It's as well there's not much wind, or I doubt whether we could have got them under control.'

'Damned idiocy!' the Emperor growled. 'I see a whole regiment down there running about with buckets and casks. There may be no fire engines left but there's still plenty of water in the river—' He bellowed out some orders and then made his way to where Marianne was standing a little way apart, hugging her arms across her chest and staring unseeingly at the ominous spectacle.

'I'm beginning to think you may have been right – at least in part. These fools are trying to cut off our food supplies.'

She turned sightless eyes to him and shook her head.

'They won't be satisfied with that, Sire, you may be sure. But it doesn't matter about me. It's you we have to think of.'

'Little fool,' he murmured through clenched teeth. 'Do you think I'd leave you to perish? You're a good little soldier, Marianne, even when you talk nonsense, and I love my soldiers like my own children. Either we die here together, both of us, or we both come out of it alive. But we're not going to die just yet.' He saw that she was looking at him with a smile too sad for tears and added, more softly still: 'Trust me. Your life is not over yet. It is only just beginning. A long and happy life. I know you are unhappy now. I know you think I'm rambling, but the time will come when you will know that I was right. Forget about this Beaufort. He does not deserve you. Think of your child, waking to life without you. He can give you so much happiness. And think, too, of the man whose name you bear. He is worthy of you . . . and he loves you very much.'

'Are you a magician, Sire? Who can have told you that?'

'No one – unless it is my own knowledge of men. All that he has done, he can only have done for love. Stop trying to catch the star in the bottom of the well. There are roses close beside you. Do not let them fade. Promise me—'

He drew away, but still without taking his eyes from her. Then, with a brief glance at the city, he rejoined the rest. The flames seemed to be dying down now and the smoke was thinning. This had been no more than a warning.

The Emperor paused and turned.

'Well,' he said. 'I'm waiting!'

Marianne sank slowly into a deep curtsy.

'I will try, Sire. You have my word.'

Part Two
Winter

Chapter Five
Cassandra

The bed was as hard as a board and the blankets smelled faintly of mould. Marianne tossed and turned for a long time without finding sleep. Yet she was very tired and when the Emperor had retired early, immediately after a somewhat frugal and unconventional meal, she had been really glad to seek her own room. She had gone to ground there, as to a refuge, after first assuring herself that Jolival was comfortably installed in the room next door. The day had been an emotional one for her and it had ended so painfully that she could not help a feeling of relief at escaping from even the pale shadow of court etiquette which the Comte de Ségur had managed to inaugurate in the Kremlin.

Asking nothing better than to go to sleep and put off until tomorrow the consideration of problems which were becoming warped and magnified by weariness, Marianne went to bed at once, thinking that her brain would be clearer and her reactions sharper after a good night's rest. But the discomfort of her bed and the remorseless treadmill of her thoughts had given her no rest and the blessed oblivion of slumber still eluded her.

Her mind refused to be put off but went roaming along the road to St Petersburg after the man who had so callously and selfishly abandoned her, without troubling himself to discover what had become of the woman he professed to love. Yet even then she could not find it in her heart to blame him, so great and so blind was her love. She knew the fierce obstinacy of his nature, in its rancours and desires alike, too well not to have started finding excuses for him, even if only in his determined resentment of Napoleon and the passionate urge he felt to get back to his own country now that she was at war. Both sentiments were, after all, quite comprehensible, and wholly masculine.

Moreover, Marianne could not hide from herself that, but for the promise extracted from her by Napoleon, a promise she was already beginning secretly to regret, she would have made every effort to escape from the palace in which she felt herself to some extent a prisoner. How gladly would she have followed the example of Craig O'Flaherty! For the Irishman had not remained with Jolival and Gracchus in the Kremlin. On learning what had become of Jason, through the few words that Gracchus had been able to get from Shankala, he had made his decision at once.

'Now that you are safely back with your own people,' he had said to Jolival, 'I will ask leave to resume my own journey to the sea, in other words, to St Petersburg. I can't breathe on these interminable inland roads. I need the open sea! Once I get there I'll have no trouble at all in finding Beaufort. I'll only have to ask for his friends, the Krilovs. And even if he travels on horseback while I'm obliged to go on foot, I'll catch him up because it's bound to be some days before he can sail.'

The understanding Jolival had released him very readily and so Craig had departed, begging the Vicomte to make his farewells to Marianne, having first paid his respects to the Emperor who had generously presented him with a horse, a royal gift considering the circumstances.

His departure was a perilous temptation for Marianne. The word she had given seemed a fragile thing when every demon of disingenuousness was ranged against it. And, after all, she had not actually given her promise to Napoleon. She had only promised to try. But to try what? To give up once and for all the dream of happiness that she had carried with her for years?

Of course, if one were honest, Napoleon was right. Marianne acknowledged that he had been both kind and clear-sighted. She even admitted that in his place she might have said the same. More than that, she was prepared to concede that Jason's behaviour, in contrast, had been less than gentlemanly. But all the time her brain was trying to think sensibly, her heart was shouting aloud rebelliously that it had the right to beat as it listed and to follow blindly after the flight of a self-centred sea bird called Jason Beaufort.

But now the heart's stubborn cries seemed to be growing more vehement, as if, deep in Marianne's being, another voice was beginning, timidly, to make itself heard. It was the voice that had uttered its first murmur as she looked at the portrait of the little fair-haired boy. Suddenly, superimposed upon the face of the baby king, Marianne had seemed to see another, darker child, and she had felt again the weight of a small, silky head against her breast and the soft grip of a tiny hand curled briefly round her finger. Sebastiano! For the first time since the dreadful night when he had been taken from her, Marianne found herself able to say his name. Where was he now, while his mother was struggling to find herself? To what secret place had Prince Corrado spirited him away?

Marianne shook herself fiercely, as though to shake off a cloud of wasps that buzzed about her, and fell to castigating herself.

'Just you stop romanticizing, my girl,' she told herself, aloud. 'At this moment your son is not hidden away in any secret place. He is fast asleep, like a fairy princeling, in a palace in Tuscany set in the middle of a great garden, guarded by snow-white peacocks. He is very well and quite safe there. He is king of a wonderful world and very soon he will be running and playing—'

Her voice choked and was drowned in a sudden flood of tears, and then Marianne was crying into the musty pillow as if her heart would break. Carried along on the tide of events and sustained by the emotional demands of the endless journey, divided between fatiguing days and passionate nights, she had managed hitherto to keep the memory of her son at a distance. But now the Emperor's dire warning had ripped away the flimsy barriers she had so painfully erected and left her cruelly exposed to the real meaning of her voluntary renunciation. The truth was that the baby was going to begin his life without her, that she would not be there when he learned to laugh and to talk and that the word 'mother' would mean nothing to his baby ears. In a little while he would be discovering the use of his little legs but the hands that reached out tenderly to catch him would be Dona Lavinia's – or those of the man who, though he was none of his, had yet pledged himself to give him all his love, and even to love him for two.

The agony was coming to the surface now, overcoming the temptation to run away, and in her misery Marianne could not have said which torment was the greater at that moment: the thought of the lover going ever farther away from her or that of the child whose love she would never know.

She might easily have allowed herself to sink into one of the familiar troughs of despair which had so often caused her sleepless nights but for a sudden conviction that all was not well which roused her from her own unhappiness. She opened her eyes and sat up, and for a moment wondered vaguely at the light that filled her room.

Jumping out of bed, she ran to the window and uttered a startled cry. The unwonted brightness, lighting the place like daylight, was the city of Moscow burning. Two huge fires, out of all proportion to what had been seen so far, had broken out to the west and south and, driven by the wind, were spreading rapidly, eating up the wooden houses like so much chaff.

At that moment, her godfather's warning came back to her. How could she have forgotten it? Marianne dressed quickly, slipped on her shoes and hurried from the room. The darkness and silence of the palace were oppressive. A single lamp burned on the landing and all was quiet and peaceful, except for the loud, regular snoring from the door next to her own which told that Jolival was sleeping soundly. The city was burning but no one seemed aware of it.

Determined to raise the alarm, Marianne flung herself down the stairs and along the great gallery where sentries stood on guard. She ran towards the door of the imperial suite and had almost reached it when she saw Caulaincourt also, it seemed, making for the Emperor.

'Thank God you are here, Duke! I was beginning to fear that no one in the palace was awake. The city is burning and—'

'I know, Princess. I have seen it. My man woke me five minutes since.'

'We must warn the Emperor!'

'There is no hurry. The fire looks serious but it is not threatening the Kremlin. I have sent my servant to rouse the Grand Marshal. We will consult with him what is best to be done.'

The Grand Ecuyer's calmness was reassuring. Marianne had met him for the first time the previous evening, for at the time when she had been much in the Emperor's company Caulaincourt had been ambassador to Russia, where he had remained until 1811. But she had felt an instant liking for the courteous, intelligent aristocrat who, with his intellectual good looks and perfect manners, was somewhat different from the usual run of the Emperor's associates. Moreover she was sorry for his grief over the death of his brother, killed at Borodino, and respected the courage which prevented him from showing it.

With a sigh of resignation, she sank down on a seat covered in Genoa velvet and raised to his a face so tragic that he was forced to smile.

'You are very pale, Madame, and I know that you are barely recovered from a recent injury. You should go back to bed.'

She shook her head. The great wall of fire that she had glimpsed from her window was still before her eyes and her throat felt stiff with terror.

'I can't. Oh, warn the Emperor, I implore you! The whole city is going to burn, I know it is. I am quite certain – I have been told so.'

'Who could have told you such a thing, Marianne, my dear?' Duroc's voice spoke sleepily behind her. He had evidently been dragged ruthlessly out of his first sleep.

'A priest – a priest I met the day before yesterday at St Louis-des-Français when I sought refuge there. He warned me – he warned all of us there, to fly and leave the city! It is doomed! Rostopchin threw open all the prisons and let out the dregs of the city. They have been given drink and money to set Moscow on fire!'

'But this is absurd!' Caulaincourt broke in. 'I know the Russians—'

'You know the diplomats, Duke. You know men like yourself. You do not know the Russian people. They have been leaving for days past, abandoning the city, their holy city. And the

Governor has sworn that Moscow will not remain in your hands, and that he will use any means to prevent it.'

The eyes of the two officials met over Marianne's head.

'Why did you not tell us this before?' The Grand Marshal asked at last.

She shrugged. 'I tried to. I tried to warn the Emperor but he would not listen. You know how he is. But now we must save him. I swear to you that he is in danger. Wake him! Wake him, or I will do so myself!'

She rose and was already making for the closed door when Caulaincourt caught her arm.

'Calm yourself, Princess, I beg of you. Things have not reached such a pass yet. The Emperor is exhausted. For three nights he has not slept and the days have been hard. Let him rest a little longer, and you try to do the same. Listen, this is what we will do. You, Duroc, send to the Governor for news and have the Guard stood to arms. I am going to obtain a horse and ride out to see how matters stand, get together such help as I can. Something must certainly be done without delay. All available troops shall be mobilized to fight the fire.'

'Very well. Only don't ask me to go back to bed, for I could not. I could never sleep.'

'Come in here, then,' Duroc said, opening the door leading to the imperial antechamber. 'I'll leave you in Constant's care while I give the necessary orders and then I'll come back to you.'

'This is ridiculous,' Caulaincourt said. 'The lady—'

'I know the lady,' Duroc interrupted him. 'She is an old friend and I can promise you, my dear duke, that, with the exception of the Emperor himself, I know of no one more generally level-headed. Go and do what you have to do, and so will I.'

In the antechamber, they found the Mameluke, Ali, with two or three of his fellows, engaged in a fierce argument with Constant. Napoleon's valet was doing his best to calm them but they, like Marianne, appeared to be intent on waking the Emperor.

Duroc, with a few words, despatched them to their beds again, assuring them that they would be sent for at need.

'We will not wake His Majesty just yet,' he added firmly. 'He needs his sleep. And you are making noise enough to wake the dead.'

Constant lifted his shoulders philosophically and permitted himself a smile.

'The Grand Marshal knows that the court and the army are all alike. As soon as anything happens, they are lost unless the Emperor is there in person to assure them that all is well.'

'He can scarcely tell them so tonight,' Marianne said sharply. 'And if I were you, my good Constant, I would begin packing up His Majesty's belongings. You never know. And things might move faster than you think. What time is it?'

'A little before eleven, your Highness. May I suggest that your Highness should wait in the saloon until the Grand Marshal returns? It is a trifle damp, I fear, but there is a fire and the chairs are quite comfortable, and I will bring you a nice cup of coffee.'

Marianne smiled at him, marvelling at the way in which he managed to be invariably calm and efficient and as point-device as if he had just spent an hour getting dressed. He was, beyond all doubt, the perfect servant.

'A fire's the last thing I want to see tonight, Constant,' she said, 'but the coffee will be welcome,'

The saloon in question was an enormous room, divided into two halves by a massively pillared arch, the space between the walls and the pillars being filled by a pair of bronze tripods. The lavish gilding on both walls and pillars was dulled and tarnished with age. Sofas and armchairs were scattered about the floor and in one corner hung the inevitable icon in red and gold, depicting an emaciated Virgin with enormous eyes. Great, dusty carpets formed a pattern of islands on the black marble floor.

Marianne wasted little time in contemplation of the furnishings. While she waited for the promised coffee, she went to the windows and pressed her face against the glass and stared out at the threatened Russian capital. The wind was gusting strongly between north and west, driving the flames towards the centre of the city and sending showers of sparks blazing down on those houses that were still intact, so that they very soon became a source of fresh fires. The demon of fire had Moscow in its grip and none could say whether that grip could be prised loose.

The coffee arrived at the same time as Duroc and the two friends drank it in silence, each locked in their own thoughts and doing their best to hide their uneasiness. Although they did not know it, the thoughts of the Princess and the Grand Marshal were identical. The city on which, in their different ways, each had pinned such great hopes, now seemed to them like a pair of jaws closing inexorably on the fragile human figures within.

At about half past twelve, another fire broke out in a district which had been dark until that moment. It was followed by another.

'The fires are spreading,' Duroc remarked, and his voice was strangely hoarse.

'The circle is closing. Oh, I beg you, my friend, wake the Emperor while there is still time. I am frightened, terribly frightened. These people have made up their minds to leave no stone of Moscow standing.'

Duroc jerked his head angrily. 'No, it's not possible! You can't set fire to a whole city, not a city the size of this one! You are afraid because a few outlying districts are on fire but our soldiers are dealing with it. They will soon catch the incendiaries, if such there are.'

'Don't you believe it even now? You are all blind! I have been trying for hours to make you understand your danger and still you are half inclined to think I must be mad! I feel like Cassandra trying to make the Trojans see sense.'

But at the sight of Duroc's dubious expression she abandoned her classical similes. Obviously Troy was a long way from his thoughts and Cassandra the last person he wished to talk about. In any case, Caulaincourt's return turned the conversation into other channels.

The Duke of Vicenza's person was liberally adorned with soot and his uniform was pockmarked with tiny burns from flying sparks. Under his frowning brows, his eyes were very grave.

'It's a bad business,' he admitted. 'I've taken a good look all round the Kremlin and I think we are in for some unexpected excitement. The fire is gaining on all sides. There are fresh outbreaks to the north and the wind is rising steadily. But worse than that—'

'Worse,' Duroc said glumly. 'I don't see that there can be much worse!'

'The fire engines. There aren't any to speak of. And those we have found are unusable.'

'And doesn't that convince you that what I heard is true?' Marianne cried frantically. 'Good God, what more do you need? I've told you again and again that all this has been planned, deliberately organized down to the smallest detail. The Russians themselves are setting fire to Moscow on the orders of their governor. But you still won't listen to me! Why won't you escape? Wake the Emperor and—'

'And run?' Caulaincourt finished for her. 'No! We have not been at such trouble and sacrifice to come here, only to run like rabbits on account of a bit of a fire. It's not the first time we've had houses burned in our path—'

'But I daresay it's the first time they've been burned over your heads. I'm sorry, though, if I have said anything to open painful wounds. I am thinking only of the Emperor's safety and that of his army, Duke.'

'I know, and believe me I bear you no ill will.'

Repressing the movement of her shoulders which would too clearly have betrayed her irritation, Marianne moved away. She thought gloomily that this was just one more instance of the impossibility of preventing men from running headlong on their fate. Duroc, meanwhile, was seeking more information.

'How are things in the city?' he asked.

'The troops are standing to. As to the civilian population, for incendiaries they are behaving very oddly, abandoning their homes and crowding, weeping, into the churches which are packed to overflowing.'

'And here?'

'Everyone but the Emperor is awake. The gallery is filled with people in a state of great alarm. There is general anxiety and, if you ask me, panic is not far away. Little as I wish to, I fear it may be time I woke His Majesty.'

'So I should hope!' Marianne could not refrain from exclaiming.

Caulaincourt turned to her severely.

'The situation demands it, Madame. But we do not go to the Emperor in order to persuade him to fly. It is merely that, as it has done before, his presence may reassure all those in the palace who are allowing their fears to get the better of them – you, most of all, Princess.'

'I am not giving way to panic, Duke, whatever you may think. Simply that when disaster threatens I think it best to inform the master of the house. What time is it now?'

'Almost four o'clock. Go, then, Duroc.'

The Grand Marshal approached the imperial bedchamber, the door of which was already being held open for him by Constant. Meanwhile Marianne, reluctant to remain with Caulaincourt, who was quite clearly out of sympathy with her, decided to go in search of Jolival and Gracchus. The noise was now such that they could not be still asleep and, since neither of them was an emperor, they were probably wide awake and worrying about her.

But she had no need to return to the floor above. She had no sooner entered the gallery, which was crowded with officials, soldiers and servants of the imperial household, when she saw Jolival. He was sitting on a bench against the wall and standing on tiptoe on the seat beside him was Gracchus, staring over the heads of the crowd as though looking for someone. At the sight of Marianne both of them gave vent to exclamations of relief.

'And where the devil have you been?' Jolival fumed, his fear transforming itself into bad temper. 'We were beginning to wonder if you weren't somewhere in that sea of flames trying to—'

'Trying to run away? To reach the road to St Petersburg? Leaving you here, of course? Surely you know me better than that, my friend?' Marianne said reproachfully.

'You would have every excuse for it, especially as you knew Gracchus was with me. You might have chosen your freedom and a flight to the sea.'

She gave him a small, sad smile and, slipping her arm round his neck, kissed her old friend impulsively.

'Come now, Jolival! You know quite well that you and Gracchus are all I have left now. What should I do on the road to Petersburg? I am not even wanted. At this moment, Jason is thinking only of the ship which will take him back to his beloved America, and to the war and – and everything that stands between us. Do you really expect me to go running after him?'

'Was there no temptation to? Not even for a moment?'

Marianne answered him unhesitatingly.

'Yes,' she said, 'to tell the truth there was. But I thought better of it. If Jason wanted me as much as I want him, he would be here, in Moscow, at this very minute, looking for me, calling my name at the top of his voice.'

'How do you know he isn't?'

'You need not play the devil's advocate, my friend. You know as well as I that he is not. Jason is riding away from us, you may be sure. Really, it's nothing more than I deserve. I was a fool. Why did I have to get him out of prison in Odessa and follow him here? If I had left him with Richelieu, he would have stayed quietly where he was all through his country's wretched war with England, unless of course, he managed to escape. But I opened the cage door myself and, like any wild bird, he flew away and left me. It serves me right.'

'Marianne, Marianne, you are very bitter,' the Vicomte said gently. 'I am not the man to defend him, but it's possible that you are painting him blacker than he is.'

'No, Jolival. I ought to have understood long ago. He is what he is – and I have only got my deserts. There is a limit to how stupid—'

Her torrent of self-criticism and disillusionment was broken into suddenly by a loud babble of voices among which Marianne had no difficulty in picking out the Emperor's metallic tones. A moment later, the doors of the imperial suite were flung open and Napoleon himself swept through them. He was in his dressing-gown, his hair on end and the nightcap he had just snatched off still in his hand.

There was instant silence. The hubbub of conversation died

away as the Emperor's fulminating eye travelled over the assembled company.

'Why are you all standing here chattering like a flock of old women? Why was I not called? Why are you none of you at your posts? Fires are breaking out everywhere on account of the indiscipline of my troops and the careless way the inhabitants of this city are leaving their houses—'

'Sire!' The protest came from a handsome blond giant whose Nordic features were framed in a pair of luxuriant golden whiskers. 'Sire, the men are no more to blame for the fires than we ourselves! It is the Muscovites themselves—'

'Come, come! They tell me the city is given over to pillage. The soldiers are breaking down doors, bursting into cellars, carrying off tea, coffee, furs, wines and spirits. Well, I will not have it! You, Marshal, are Governor of Moscow. Put an end to this disorder!'

Marshal Mortier, at whom this censure was directed, made a movement of protest which doubled as a gesture of helplessness, then turned and vanished down the stairs, followed by two officers of his staff.

Meanwhile, Napoleon was declaiming: 'The Muscovites! The Muscovites! It's easy to blame the Muscovites! I cannot believe these people would set fire to their own houses to deprive us of a night's lodging!'

Courageously, Marianne made her way towards him.

'And yet, Sire, it is true. I beg you to believe me! Your troops are not responsible for this tragedy. Rostopchin alone—'

The imperial gaze fell wrathfully on her.

'Are you still here, Madame? At this hour a respectable woman should be in her bed. Return to yours!'

'And there wait patiently until my blankets are on fire and I may burn to death proclaiming my loyalty to the Emperor who is always right? No, thank you, Sire. If you will not listen to me, I would rather be gone from here.'

'And where to, if I may ask?'

'Anywhere, as long as it is out of here! I've no desire to wait until it is no longer possible to get out of this accursed palace! Or to form part of the holocaust Rostopchin has prepared to the memory of the Russian troops slain at the Moskva! You may do so if you like, Sire, but I am young and I still wish to live. And so, with your permission—' She swept a curtsy. But the reminder of his recent victory had calmed the Emperor. Bending forward suddenly he took the tip of her ear between his fingers and pulled it, with a force that drew a yelp from her.

'Calm yourself, Princess,' he said, smiling. 'You will not persuade me that you are afraid. Not you! As to your departure hence, we forbid it. If it becomes necessary to leave, we shall do so together. But for the present, let me tell you, there is no such necessity. You have my permission only to withdraw and rest yourself. We breakfast at eight.'

But Marianne was not fated to return to her room just yet. As the uneasy crowd which had filled the gallery began to disperse, a platoon of soldiers entered briskly, led by General Durosnel, escorting a number of men dressed in a species of green uniform and several long-haired moujiks, apparently prisoners. Lelorgne d'Ideville, the Emperor's interpreter, came hurrying after them. The Emperor, who had been about to return to his own apartments, turned frowning.

'Now what is it? Who are these men?'

Durosnel told him.

'They are called *boutechniks*, Sire. They are the law officers whose duty it is to keep order in the streets. They were caught with lighted torches in the act of setting fire to a shop selling wines and spirits. These beggars were with them, assisting them.'

Napoleon started and his glowering gaze went, automatically, to Marianne's.

'Are you sure of this?'

'Quite sure, Sire. Furthmore there are witnesses, in addition to these men who apprehended them – some Polish shopkeepers of the neighbourhood who are coming after us.'

Silence followed this. Napoleon began pacing up and down slowly in front of the group of frightened prisoners, his hands clasped behind his back, throwing occasional glances at the men, who held their breath instinctively. Suddenly, he stopped.

'What have they to say for themselves?'

Baron d'Ideville stepped forward.

'They claim that they were ordered to set fire to the whole city by Governor Rostopchin before—'

'That is not true!' the Emperor cried. 'It cannot be true because it does not make sense. The men are lying. They are simply trying to shuffle off responsibility for their crimes, hoping it may earn them a measure of leniency.'

'Then they must be in collusion, Sire, for here come some more of them and I'll wager we will hear the same tale from them.'

It was true, another group had appeared, in charge of Marianne's old acquaintance, Sergeant Bourgogne. This time, however, they were followed by an elderly Jew with scorchmarks on his gown. It was he who, with a great many bows and signs, explained how, but for the providential arrival of the sergeant and his men, he would have been burned, along with the entire contents of a grocer's shop.

'It's impossible!' Napoleon repeated several times. 'Impossible!' But his voice was losing some of its assurance. It was as if the repetition was intended, above all, to convince himself.

'Sire,' Marianne intervened quietly, 'these men would rather destroy Moscow than see you enjoy it. That may be a primitive emotion, but it is a facet of love. You yourself, if Paris were in question—'

'Paris? Burn Paris if the enemy took it? Now indeed you have run mad! I am not one to bury myself in ruins. A primitive emotion, say you? These people may be Scythians but they have no right to sacrifice the work of many generations to the pride of one. And what is more—'

But Marianne had ceased to listen to him. Instead, she was staring in horrified fascination at two men standing, deep in argument, at the entrance to the gallery. One was the court's master of ceremonies, the Comte de Ségur. The other was a diminutive priest in a black soutane whom she recognized without difficulty but with great uneasiness. What was Cardinal de Chazay doing here, in the presence of the man he had consistently opposed? What was his business? Why did he want to see the Emperor, for his arrival at the Kremlin in the middle of the night could have no other meaning?

Before she could so much as hazard a guess, Ségur and his companion had joined the group. Napoleon was already giving out fresh orders, saying that he wanted patrols sent out to every district where the fires had not yet struck and a thorough house-to-house search for more men of the same kind as those still standing sheepishly before him.

'What is to be done with these?' Durosnel asked.

The sentence was quick and merciless.

'We cannot take prisoners. Hang them or shoot them, as you will. They are felons in any case.'

'But Sire, they are mere tools—'

'A spy is likewise a tool and yet he can look for no mercy. There is nothing to prevent you from running Rostopchin to earth and hanging him too. Away!'

Their departure left the way open for the master of ceremonies and his companion. Ségur advanced to meet the Emperor.

'Sire,' he said, 'here is the Abbé Gauthier, a French priest, who is most anxious to speak to you regarding the present disturbances. He claims to possess reliable information.'

For no ascertainable reason, Marianne's heart missed a beat and she felt as if an iron hand had suddenly clamped down on her windpipe. While Ségur was speaking, she had caught her godfather's eye and read in it such a hardness of purpose that it sent a chill up her spine. Never before had she seen in him this icy calm, this authority, wordlessly forbidding her to interfere in what might come. But it was only for a moment. Then the priest was bowing with the assumed awkwardness of one unused to consorting with the great ones of the world.

Napoleon, meanwhile was observing him closely.

'You are a Frenchman, Monsieur l'Abbé? An *émigré* perhaps?'

'No, Sire. A humble priest but, owing to my knowledge of Latin, I was engaged some years since to tutor the children of Count Rostopchin in that noble language, and also in French.'

'A language no less noble, Monsieur l'Abbé. So you were a member of the household of one who, I am told, although I cannot believe it, is an incendiary?'

'And yet you must believe it, Sire. I am in a position to assure your Majesty that those were indeed the governor's orders. The city was to be razed to the ground, and the Kremlin also.'

'But this is absurd? It is pure madness!'

'No, Sire. It is the Russian way. There is only one way for your Majesty to save this ancient and renowned city.'

'And what is that?'

'Leave it. Withdraw from it immediately. There is still time. Abandon your intention to remain here and go back to France, and then the fires will stop.'

'How can you be sure of this?'

'I heard the Count give his orders. He has left certain trusted men who know where to find the fire-engines. It could all be over in an hour ... if your Majesty were to announce your immediate withdrawal.'

Clasping her hands tightly together, Marianne listened breathlessly to this exchange which, to her, was totally incomprehensible. She could not imagine why her godfather should be trying to save the imperial army on pretence of saving Moscow. At the same time something which the Duc de Richelieu had said in Odessa recurred unbidden to her mind: 'He is going to Moscow where a great task awaits him, should the wretched Corsican ever get so far ...'

The Corsican was here. And here, facing him, the man whose secret power he could not know, a man sworn to a great task, and a man who had vowed to bring about his ruin. And now it was the cardinal's calm, quiet voice that filled Marianne with foreboding, far more than the Emperor's curt, incisive tones, although it was he who was speaking now, and with a note of menace.

'My immediate withdrawal? Announce it to whom?'

'To the night, Sire. A simple command or two from the Kremlin walls would be enough. It would be understood.'

The silence that followed was so absolute that it seemed to Marianne that her own heartbeats must be heard by everyone.

'Monsieur l'Abbé, you seem to me to be remarkably well-informed for a humble priest. You are a Frenchman, surrounded by Frenchmen. We have conquered and you should be proud. Yet you talk shamefully of flight.'

'There is no shame in a flight from the elements, Sire, even for a conqueror. I am a Frenchman, yes, but I am also a man of God and I am thinking of how many men of yours will perish if you persist in opposing God.'

'Are you going to tell me God is a Russian?'

'God is the God of all nations. You have defeated the armies of this one but there are still the people, and the people reject you with all their might, even to destroying themselves with you. Believe me and go!'

The last word rang out so imperiously that Marianne trembled. Gauthier de Chazay must have taken leave of his senses to address the Emperor of the French in such a tone, nor could she imagine what he hoped to achieve by it. Did he really believe that Napoleon would abandon Moscow just because he told him to? One look at that pale face, with its pinched nostrils and hard jaw-line, was enough to show that the situation was becoming dangerous.

Sure enough, Napoleon jerked up his chin and spoke suddenly, with great vehemence.

'I respect your cloth, Monsieur, but you are mad! Get out of my sight before I lose patience with you.'

'No. I will not go. Not until I have made you understand, for once in your life, before your pride leads you into the abyss, and all your followers with you. Once, in time past, you took France, soiled and bleeding from the excesses of the Revolution, eaten away by the leprosy of jobbery and profiteering under the Directorate, and you stood her on her feet, swept and garnished, and you grew in stature with her. Yes, even I, who was never of your faction, I tell you you were great.'

'And am I so no longer?' the Emperor asked haughtily.

'You ceased to be so on the day you ceased to serve France and made her serve you. You had yourself made by a crime and since then to establish your sacrilegious power on a firmer footing you have taken from her, year by year, the best of her children and sent them to perish on every battlefield in Europe.'

'It is to Europe, Monsieur, that you should address your complaint. It is Europe who could never bear to see France become France again, but greater and more powerful than before.'

'Europe would have borne it had France remained France as you say. But you have swollen her belly with a host of kingdoms and annexations she had no need of. But you had to have thrones for your brothers, did you not, and fortunes for those who followed you? And to set up these paper kings you have ruined and destroyed the oldest families in Europe.'

'You have said it! Old, dead, worn-out, finished! What is it about my crown that irks you? Are you one of those who would have had me seek the foolish glory of a Monk? Who want to see the decrepit line of the Bourbons restored to the throne?'

'No!'

That one, emphatic cry left Marianne if anything more bewildered than before. What was happening? Was Gauthier de Chazay, secret agent of the Comte de Provence, who called himself Louis XVIII now denying his master? She had not long to wonder.

'No,' the cardinal said again. 'I do not deny that I wished it once. That I do so no longer is a matter for myself alone. I might even have come to accept you. But you have ceased to do your country good. You think only of your conquests and if you were allowed to do so would unpeople France for the glory of doing as Alexander the Great and reaching for the Indies to place the crown of Akbar on your head! No! It is enough! Go! Go, while there is yet time! Before God wearies of you!'

'Leave God out of it! I have heard enough! You are a mad old man. Get out before I have you put under guard!'

'Arrest me if you will. You will not arrest the wrath of God Look, all of you!'

Such was the passion that inhabited the frail body that all those present turned, automatically, and followed the direction of his pointing hand.

'See! The fire from heaven is upon you. Unless you quit this city by tonight there will be no stone left upon another and you will all be buried in the ruins! Truly, I say unto you—'

'Enough!'

Napoleon, white-faced, bore down on his antagonist with clenched fists.

'Your impudence is equalled only by your folly. Who sent you here? What is your purpose?'

'No one sent me – no one but God! And I have spoken for your good–'

'Indeed? Who do you expect will believe that tale? You were with Rostopchin, were you not? You must know a great deal more than you have told. And you thought, you and those who paid you, that you had only to come here and pour your curses into my ears and I would pick up my skirts and run, like some foolish old woman, and make myself a laughing-stock for you? Well, abbé, I am not an old woman and the terrors you may rouse in simple souls in the darkness of your confessionals cannot touch me. I am not going. I have conquered Moscow and I mean to keep it.'

'Then you will lose your Empire. And your son, the son you fathered, sacrilegiously, upon that unhappy princess who thinks herself your wife but who is nothing but your concubine, will never reign. And so much the better, for if he ever reigned it would be over a desert.'

'Duroc!'

The stunned and obscurely frightened onlookers gave way automatically to allow the Grand Marshal of the Palace to approach.

'Sire?'

'Arrest this man! Lock him up well! He is a spy in Russian pay. Let him be locked up to await my orders. He shall die before I leave this palace.'

'No!'

Marianne's cry of anguish was lost in the general hubbub. Immediately, the cardinal was surrounded by guards and his hands tied behind his back. He was led away, still shouting.

'You are on the edge of an abyss, Napoleon Bonaparte! Fly before it opens under your feet and drags you down, you and all those with you!'

Napoleon, cursing furiously, made for his own apartments,

accompanied by various members of his suite expressing shock and indignation at what had passed. Marianne hurried after them and caught up with the Emperor just as he was entering his bedchamber. She slipped in after him before the door closed on them both.

'Sire,' she cried, 'I must speak to you!'

Halfway across the room, he swung round and Marianne found herself shivering at the blackness of the look he bent on her.

'I have heard a great deal of speech this morning, Madame. A deal too much, indeed! I had thought my command to you was to go back to your bed. Do as I bid you and leave me in peace.'

She half knelt, as if she would have thrown herself at his feet, and clasped her hands in an instinctive gesture of supplication.

'Sire! I beseech you! Do as the priest bade you and begone from here!'

'Ha! Not you too? Will no one give me any peace? I wish to be alone, do you hear me? Alone!'

Seizing the first object which came to hand, which happened to be a Chinese vase, he hurled it violently across the room. As ill luck would have it, Marianne was just that instant rising. The vase caught her on the temple and with a little moan she subsided on to the carpet.

The bitter reek of sal volatile and a shattering headache were Marianne's first indications of returning consciousness. They were followed almost immediately by the voice of the invaluable Constant, speaking in soft and deferential reassurance.

'Ah, we are coming round. May I inquire how your Serene Highness feels now?'

'Dreadfully ill – and not very serene, I am afraid, Constant. Very far from it, in fact.' Then, as recollection flooded back, she added: 'The Emperor? Who would have thought that he— Was he trying to kill me?'

'No indeed, your Highness! But you were most imprudent. When his Majesty's temper has been tried to such an extent, it is unwise to attempt to approach him, much less to reason with him, and after what had just passed—'

'I know, Constant, I know . . . but it is so desperately serious!

What the – the priest said sounded insane, but there was truth in it. You know that as well as I do.'

'His Majesty's personal attendant cannot indulge in private opinions,' Constant said wryly. 'I will say, however, that on seeing your Highness fall insensibly at his feet, the Emperor appeared somewhat alarmed and – er – distressed. He sent for me at once and commanded me to do my utmost for his – victim.'

'That word I am very sure he did not use. He probably said presumptuous wretch or ninny or something of that kind.'

'Poor lunatic was the expression, if your Highness will forgive me,' the valet corrected her with the shadow of a smile. 'To some extent the exercise of violence has calmed the Emperor. His temper is somewhat improved.'

'I am delighted to hear it. It is gratifying to have been of use. And – the man – the spy, do you know what was done with him?'

'The Grand Marshal has just reported that, for want of a better place, he has been incarcerated in one of the outlying towers, the one known as the Secret Tower. You may see it from the window.'

Disregarding the agonizing pain in her head, Marianne got up from the day-bed on which she had been laid and, driven by an irresistible impulse, hastened to the window, followed by Constant's protesting adjurations to her to take care.

The windows commanded a view of the whole area of the Kremlin. The *tainitskie Bachnia,* the Tower of the Secret, was the oldest, going back to the fifteenth century, and also the nearest of the towers, a menacing pile of brickwork, black with age, its squat shape like the figure of a crouching man blocking the way to the river. But from the tower, Marianne's eyes travelled on to the city and she gave a gasp of fear. The fire was gaining ground.

Beyond the slender ribbon of the Moskva was a sea of fire advancing like an irresistible tide and sweeping nearer with every minute. Whole regiments of troops were at work along the river banks, forming long human chains to carry buckets of water from the river to the fire. The buckets were no more use than thimbles and the men were like Lilliputians striving with their tiny casks to slake the thirst of a giant Gulliver. More men were standing on the roofs of houses not yet invaded by the fire, trying with the help of brooms and wet cloths to deal with the continual shower of flaming debris that fell from above, while one by one they were engulfed in the billowing black smoke that, driven before the high wind, was gradually blotting out the whole landscape.

'What is the sense,' Marianne said at last in a colourless voice, 'of locking a man up when we are all in danger? How long will it be before we are overtaken by this cataclysm?'

Constant shrugged. 'The rogue will not have time to weary of his prison,' he said, and there was a note of anger in his voice; unusual for the big, placid Fleming. 'The Emperor has decreed that he be brought to trial this very evening, before the Duc de Trévise, the Governor of Moscow. He will be tried and before nightfall will have paid the penalty for his unthinkable temerity.'

'Why unthinkable?'

'Why, because he is a Frenchman and a person of no great account. That insane abuse he hurled at the Emperor might have been understandable on the part of a Russian, a defeated enemy, or even coming from one of the irreconcilable *émigrés* for whom his Majesty represents something between Cromwell and Antichrist. But for a miserable parish priest to utter such insults, to curse him in that prophetic fashion, and at such a time, that is unforgivable. Moreover, the man may not live even until tonight.'

Marianne's heart stopped beating.

'Why not? It is not like the Emperor to execute even a guilty man without fair trial—'

'No, no. But circumstances may make it necessary to dispatch the matter sooner. The Kremlin walls are old and stout and we stand on a hill, but the ring of fire is getting perilously close. His Majesty is on the point of going out to inspect our resources for combating the fire and to see for himself the gravity of the danger. If, by any chance, we should be obliged to evacuate the palace, then the man's fate will of course be decided before we leave. You heard the Emperor: he will die before we leave the palace.'

Marianne felt terror taking hold of her. A moment ago, when Constant had told her where the 'Abbé Gauthier' was imprisoned, she had been conscious of something like relief, for she had feared those about the Emperor might have killed him on the spot. But her relief had been short lived and now it seemed to her that things were moving with terrifying speed. A few hours! A few hours at most – perhaps only a few minutes, who could tell? And then the sentence would fall, inexorably as the blade of the guillotine, and there would be no more Gauthier de Chazay, ever again! To Marianne, the thought was as unbearable as a red-hot iron set to her flesh. She loved him. He was her godfather, almost a father to her, and their two lives were so intermingled, bound together by such invisible ties of mutual tenderness, that if one perished something would die also in the other.

Even now Marianne could still not understand what could have brought him, a man of wisdom and prudence, a great prince of the Church possessed of powers which, though unsuspected, were wide enough to compare with those of any crown, to that mad, fanatical exit. For all his dedicated hatred of Napoleon, it was not like him. The secret weapons of diplomacy were far more in tune with his temperament than grandiloquent speeches, especially ones doomed to failure. But now how could she snatch from death the good man who had always been there to rescue her from dangers and difficulties?

Her meditations were interrupted by the sound of a quick step in the adjoining room and she knew that Napoleon was coming. The next moment he was there, pausing in the doorway and then, catching sight of the girl standing in the window, coming quickly towards her. Before she could even begin to curtsy, he had laid his hands on her shoulders and kissed her with unexpected gentleness.

'Forgive me, little Marianne! I did not mean to hurt you. I was not aiming at you but at – oh, I don't know – at fate, perhaps, or the stupidity of mankind. That wretched madman had put me out of all patience. I think I could have strangled anyone who came near me. Does it hurt very badly?'

She shook her head, lying heroically, and managed to smile.

'If this little bump,' she touched the throbbing spot where the vase had hit her, 'has helped to ease your Majesty's nerves, then I am more than glad. I am – your servant always.'

'Don't be solemn. If you mean you're fond of me, then say so straight out, not with all these courtly circumlocutions! But you'd do better to tell me what you really think – which is that I'm a brute. We've both of us known it for long enough. And now tell me what I can do to make you forgive me. As anything you like, even my permission to – to commit follies you please! Is it horses you want? An escort to go with you to Petersburg? Do you want a ship? You can set out at once for Danzig, I will see that you have money, and there wait until your privateer drops anchor, as he is bound to do—'

'Why, can it be that you have changed your mind, Sire? Do you believe that, after all, I may have some chance of happiness with Jason Beaufort?'

'Not at all! I think the same as ever I did. Only I fear that I have asked too much of you – and perhaps exposed you to too great a danger. I am not unaware of the risks involved, but I and my troops are men and bred to risks. You are not. You have braved too many perils already to come to me. I have no right to demand more of you.'

As often happens at dramatic moments, a fantastic thought suddenly popped into Marianne's head. Could it be that, in offering her her freedom, Napoleon was also thinking to get rid of her? He did not seem to like Cassandra any more than his marshals did. But his motive was unimportant in the end. The fact that he had suggested it was so wonderful and so unexpected that for a moment she was dazzled. She knew that at that moment she held the keys to her life and liberty in her hands. One word and, in a matter of minutes, the gates of the Kremlin would open and let her out. A carriage with a strong escort would carry her, with Gracchus and Jolival, happily away to the seaport where the broken thread would be joined once more and whence, turning her back to Europe once and for all, she could fly away to a new life where all would be love ... But love was a word she could not, must not utter, for it would mean a double sentence of death for her godfather.

The little spark died away. Slowly, she slipped from the Emperor's hold and fell at his feet. Then, bowing her head, she murmured: 'Forgive me, Sire! One thing only I would ask of you and that is – the Abbé Gauthier's life!'

'What?'

He had started back as sharply as if he had been struck and stood staring at her as she knelt before him in her simple brown dress, with her face a mask of grief and her green eyes filled with tears, her hands clasped, trembling, before her in an attitude of prayer.

'Are you mad?' he breathed. 'The life of a spy – of that miserable fanatic of a priest? When he has called down the curses of his vengeful God on me and mine?'

'I know, Sire, and yet I ask for nothing but his life.'

He came to her then and, taking her by the arms, forced her to rise. The lines of his face had hardened and his grey eyes were the exact colour of steel.

'Come, get up! Explain yourself! Why do you want to save his life? What is this Abbé Gauthier to you? Tell me! I want to know!'

'He is my godfather, Sire!'

'What! What's this you're saying?'

'I say that the Abbé Gauthier is really Gauthier de Chazay, Cardinal San Lorenzo – and my godfather, the man who has always stood to me in place of a father. Forgive me, Sire, I beg of you, but I cannot help pleading for one who, in spite of his rash words, is still very dear to me.'

There followed a silence so profound that both parties to the painful scene were able to hear the sound of their own breathing. Napoleon's hands dropped slowly to his sides. Then, turning from Marianne, he thrust one inside his waistcoat and, holding the other behind his back, began pacing up and down with bowed head, in the familiar way he did when he was deep in thought.

He continued his pacing for a minute or two and Marianne, her heart in her mouth, made no move to interrupt him. Suddenly, the Emperor paused and rounded on her.

'Why? Why did he do it?'

'I don't know, Sire. I give you my word. I have been turning the question over and over in my mind ever since and I can find no answer that makes sense. He is a quiet man, of great intelligence and self-control, and a faithful servant of God. Only a sudden madness, possibly.'

'I don't think so. There was some other reason. He did not look like a madman. Myself, I think you do not know him, you are blinded by your affection. He hates me. I saw it in his eyes.'

'It is true, Sire, that he hates you. But it is possible, perhaps, that in speaking as he did – however insolently – he was simply seeking to save your life?'

'Come, come! Was he not one of the rebellious cardinals I sent packing when they refused to solemnize my marriage? San Lorenzo ... the name means something to me. And not only that I have heard of him somewhat too frequently on your account. Your marriage was his doing, was it not?'

Marianne's heart sank. Once more, slowly and inexorably, the gulf was widening between her and the Emperor. Soon, perhaps, he would see her, not as the girl he had almost killed, but simply as the near connection of a rebel spy.

'All that your Majesty says is true,' she answered with an effort, 'yet still I beseech you to be merciful. You did promise me—'

'Not that! How could I have guessed? Mad! All women are mad! Free that dangerous plotter! And what then? Why not give him weapons and the key to my bedchamber?'

'Sire, your Majesty is mistaken. I do not ask for his liberty, only for his life. After that your Majesty would be free to imprison him for life in whatever place you chose.'

'A simple matter, to be sure! Here we are a thousand leagues from Paris, surrounded by a ring of fire. What can I do but put him to death? Besides – I cannot grant a reprieve. No one would understand. If he were a Russian, the thing might be possible. But a Frenchman! No, a thousand times no! I cannot do it. What is more, he dared to speak of my son and that I will never forgive. Villain, to call a curse down on the child!'

'Sire!' Marianne begged.

'I said no! Cease your importunities and be done! Ask me something else.'

Despairingly, she saw that she was losing the battle, that he was in haste to be done with the subject. Already, the Mameluke, Ali, was there, to announce that the Emperor's horse was waiting. After him came Duroc, bringing a budget full of bad news: the fire had reached the palace kitchens, debris was beginning to fall on the Arsenal, the wind was strengthening . . .

Napoleon turned to Marianne, a frown between his brows.

'Well, Madame, I am waiting.'

Beaten she made her curtsy, her shoulders sagging in defeat.

'Let me see him for a moment, Sire, to say farewell. I ask nothing more.'

'Very well.'

He went quickly to a small writing desk which stood open in a corner and scribbled a few words on a sheet of paper. The pen squeaked and spluttered as he signed it. Then he handed it to Marianne.

'You may have half an hour, Madame, and not one moment longer, for it may be that we shall have to bring the matter to a conclusion sooner than we thought. I will see you later.'

He went out swiftly to where his escort waited in the antechamber. Marianne was left alone in the imperial bedchamber which, now that its owner had left it, had taken on the deserted and uncared-for look of an empty hotel room.

For a little while, like Napoleon himself, she paced up and down, deep in thought, the paper he had given her clutched in one hand. Then, having come to a decision, she went out in her turn. She went in search of Gracchus and Jolival, for she had some instructions to give them.

Chapter Six
Monsieur de Beyle

Outside the palace, the atmosphere was stifling. Billows of acrid smoke filled the courtyards and terraces. Partly as a protection against the choking fumes and the sparks and hot ashes borne on the wind, and partly from another, less straightforward motive, Marianne had taken care to wrap herself, despite the heat, in her great travelling cloak, pulling the hood well down over her eyes and holding a handkerchief, soaked in water and eau de Cologne, which she had borrowed from the Emperor's wardrobe, up to her face. Thus attired, she hurried down the grassy slope leading from the level of the palace itself down to the outer purlieus of the Kremlin, which were built at river level.

Seen from close at hand, the Tower of the Secret lost much of its impressiveness. Only half the height of its fellows, owing to an order for its demolition, along with the rest, in the time of the Empress Catherine II, enough of it had remained when the work was discontinued on grounds of expense to provide an exceedingly useful prison.

Two grenadiers were on guard, ensconced in a dark niche at the foot of the stairs. The sight of the imperial signature at the foot of the written order had them saluting respecfully and one of them undertook to guide her up to the floor above, where he paused below a low, arched doorway garnished with enough locks and bolts to have defended a town. Still with the same deferential attitude, he drew proudly from his pocket an enormous turnip watch, which could not have been long in his possession, and declared solemnly: 'I'll be back to let your ladyship out in half an hour, according to his Majesty's orders.'

Marianne nodded to show that she understood. From the moment of her entry into the tower, she had taken care not to let them hear the sound of her voice, merely holding out her permit silently and praying that the men would be able to read. But for the moment, luck was with her.

The cell, an ancient casemate pierced by a single embrasure, was very dark but it did not take her many seconds to make out its occupant. He was seated on a wide stone sill below the narrow window, trying to peer out through the drifts of smoke that penetrated through the slit. His face was very pale and there was a large bruise on one temple where someone must have struck him after his attack on the Emperor. He barely turned his head at Marianne's entry.

They looked at one another for a moment, on his side with a kind of bored indifference and on hers with a choking misery that she could not control. Then the cardinal sighed and asked: 'Why have you come? If it is a reprieve you bring – for I don't doubt you have been begging for one – understand that I don't want it. It will have been bought at too high a price.'

'I bring no reprieve. The Emperor would not listen to my pleas. Moreover, we have long ceased to be on such terms as you imply.'

The prisoner's only reply was a faint shrug and a mirthless laugh.

'Yet I did ask him to spare your life,' Marianne continued. 'God knows I pleaded with him! But it seems that people would not understand if he were to show mercy in a case of such gravity, and in the present circumstances.'

'He is quite right. The last thing he can afford is to be accused of weakness. Besides, I have told you, I prefer death to clemency from him.'

Marianne walked slowly towards him, conscious of a sharp pang, now that she saw him from close to, at the realization of how tired he looked, and how much older than he had done a few nights before, in the passage of St Louis-des-Français. Abruptly, she sank to her knees and, clasping his cold hands, pressed her lips to them.

'Godfather!' she begged. 'Dear Godfather, why did you do it? Why did you say such things to his face? What sort of impulse—'

'An idiotic impulse, isn't that what you mean?'

'It has done you no good! What did you hope to gain by speaking to Napoleon like that? To make him leave Moscow, depart from Russia?'

'Yes, I did. I wanted it with all my heart. You cannot conceive how much I wanted him to be gone from this place, to go back to his own country while there was still time to avert disaster.'

'He cannot! Even if he would, he is not alone. There are others – all those who stand to gain from his conquests. The men for whom Moscow has become a kind of Golconda. The marshals—'

'Them? They ask nothing better than to be gone! Most of them are dreaming all the time of going home. They have never really believed in this war, their hearts have not been in it and, above all, they have not needed it. All of them have grand titles, vast possessions and fortunes they want freedom to enjoy. It's human enough. As to the King of Naples, that glittering centaur, as vain as a peacock and just about as intelligent, at this present moment he is cavorting about in front of Platov's Cossacks who are guarding the Russian rear, and doing everything but fraternize with them! The Cossacks are swearing that the Russian army is at its last gasp, that more men are deserting every day, and assuring him that he's the most wonderful thing they've ever seen and he, the fool, believes them.'

'It can't be true!'

'Don't tell me you've met him and you don't believe it. He's so delighted with them that he's stripping all his staff officers of their watches and jewels to make presents of them – having parted with everything of his own already! Oh yes, if I had managed to convince Napoleon, the army would have been off in the morning.'

'That's all very well, but why do it yourself? I should think there must be plenty of persuasive men ready to face the risk – among all those millions at your command.'

He started and looked at her with a mixture of suprise and curiosity.

'What do you mean?'

'That I know who you are, and the power you possess in this world. You are the man they call the Black Pope.'

Instantly he gripped her hands hard to silence her and shot a furtive glance around him.

'Hush! There are some things which should not be said aloud. How did you guess?'

'It was Jolival. He realized it at Odessa, when you showed your ring to the Duc de Richelieu.'

A faint smile touched the cardinal's lips.

'I should have been more wary of your friend's sharp eyes. He is a good man, and no fool. I am happy to leave you in his care.'

Marianne was suddenly angry with him.

'Leave Jolival out of it. We are not talking about him. What I want to know is why you suddenly transformed yourself into a prophet of vengeance! You can't have had the faintest idea of Napoleon's character. To have done what you did was to condemn yourself to death without a doubt. He was bound to react as he did. He took you for an enemy spy.'

'And what makes you think that I am not? An enemy, I have always been, and if I do not care for the word spy I am very willing to admit that my life has been passed in serving secretly, in the shadows.'

'That is why I cannot understand what made you choose to step out into the limelight like that.'

He thought for a moment, then shrugged lightly.

'I admit that I was mistaken in the Corsican's character. I was counting on the Latin, the Mediterranean side of his nature. He is superstitious, I know. I could not have found a more dramatic setting, or a more auspicious moment to try and make an impression on him – and to bring him to reason.'

'You must have had a hand in the fire. Certainly you knew all about it.'

'Yes, I did know, and I was afraid for you when I found you here. That was the reason I did my best to save you. And then, when I saw such vast numbers of men – this huge army – and recognized some of our own among them—'

'Men of the old nobility, you mean?'

'Yes. Ségurs and Monatsquioux, even a Mortemart, I tell you, my heart bled. It was these, also, that I was trying to save, these men who had followed the star of this madman – a madman of genius, but still doomed. I'll not conceal from you that my object in coming here was to destroy him at all costs, he and his. God forgive me, I even contemplated assassination—'

'Oh no! Not that! Not you—'

'Why not? The society of which I am the head has not, in the course of its history, always shrunk from committing that sin when it seemed that the good of the Church demanded it. There was – Henri IV, and others. But I give you my word that I had changed my mind. I was sincere, most desperately sincere, when I begged him to turn back, return to France, abandon his needless wars and reign in peace at last.'

Marianne's great eyes had opened very wide and she was staring at the priest as if he had taken leave of his senses.

'Reign in peace. Napoleon? Godfather, you can't be serious? How can you possibly wish him to reign in peace when you have always served Louis XVIII?'

Gauthier de Chazay gave a faint smile with no touch of humour in it. He closed his eyes for an instant and then opened them and in the gaze that met her own his goddaughter read, for the first time, a grim despair.

'I serve only God now, Marianne, and God hates war. I was wagering everything, you see. Either I would succeed, or else leave here what has become to me a worthless life.'

Marianne's anguished cry held an element of disbelief.

'You cannot mean what you are saying? You, a prince of the church, heaped with honours and power – truly wish to die?'

'Perhaps. You see, Marianne, in the position to which I have been called I have learned many things. Above all, I have become the repository of the Order's secrets. The most terrible of these I learned only recently and it came as a bitter shock to me, worse than anything I had ever known. The true king of France is not the man I have served for so long, blindly as you said. It is another, closely concealed, a close kinsman of this man and yet indebted to him for a cruel, unjust and wicked fate!'

At that moment, Marianne had a feeling that he was no longer with her, that his mind and heart were somewhere else, caught up in a dreadful nightmare that oppressed him. It was as much to bring him back to reality as because she really wanted to know the meaning of what he hinted at, that she asked quietly: 'Do you mean that – that even if he ever came to the throne, Louis XVIII would be only an usurper – worse even than Napoleon? But that would mean that the boy Louis XVII, the son of Louis XVI and Marie-Antoinette, who was supposed to have perished in the Temple—'

The cardinal rose quickly and laid his finger on her lips.

'Say no more,' he said sternly. 'There are some secrets it is death to know and this is one you have no need to know. If I have told you something of it, it is because you are the child of my heart and so have some right to try to understand me. Know only this, that I found that among the papers of my predecessor – who died not long ago – which showed me that my whole life had been in error. I had made myself, without knowing it, the accessory to a crime, and it is that which I can no longer endure. But for my religion, and the cloth I wear, I might perhaps have put a period to my existence. Then it seemed to me that I might sacrifice my life and at the same time perform a singular service to the world. In making Napoleon turn back, snatching him from his deadly course, I could die in peace – gladly even, for at least he would cease to bleed white with her perpetual wars the country I love as much as God Himself, and yet have served so ill. I have failed, but I shall die none the less.'

Marianne stood up quickly.

'Yes,' she agreed, 'and very soon, unless you agree to what I have to propose.'

'And that is?'

'Your freedom. No,' she added, seeing him about to protest, 'I did not say anything about a reprieve. You are to be tried this evening and before nightfall you will be dead – unless you do as I say.'

'What is the good? I have failed, I tell you.'

'Precisely, and let me tell you that it is stupid to die for nothing. God did not make Napoleon listen to you but He cannot wish your death, since I am here.'

Something softened in the prisoner's strained face. For the

first time, he smiled at her with a hint of his old mischievous gaiety.

'How do you think you can help me elude the firing squad? Have you brought me a pair of wings?'

'No, you will walk out of here on your two feet, and the guards will salute you.'

Swiftly, she outlined her plan, which was of the simplest. The cardinal was to put on her cloak, drawing the hood down as far as possible and keeping his head bent, like a person in great grief. The handkerchief which had been displayed so prominently on Marianne's arrival would again be in evidence. And then when the guard came back, as he would do any minute, to tell her that the half-hour was up— But here the cardinal interrupted her indignantly.

'You mean to stay here in my place? And you believed that I would agree to it.'

'Why not? I am in no danger from a firing squad. To be sure, the Emperor won't be very pleased with me – but that does not matter very much now. We are a long away from Paris and, well, we French must hang together to some extent.'

'This is ridiculous! It can never work.'

'Why not? We are very much of a height, when I am wearing low heels. You are no fatter than I am and it is so dark in here that underneath the cloak no one will tell the difference between your black soutane and my dark dress. Godfather, I beg you, do as I say! Change clothes with me and go! You have still so much to do.'

'To do? But I have told you—'

'If I have understood you rightly, what you have to do is to repair a great injustice. You have to succour misfortune. And there is none but you to do it. That is what state secrets are for! They give life – or they take it! Go! They will be here in a moment. I swear to you that I am in no danger. Surely you know that for yourself. Believe me. Do as I tell you – or else – or else I will stay here with you and proclaim myself your accomplice!'

'No one would believe you,' he told her, laughing. 'You forget that you saved him—'

'Oh, do stop quibbling! Your life is at stake and you know that there is none dearer in the world to me.'

She had her cloak off already and with a quick movement she threw it round her godfather's shoulders, covering him completely. She was reaching up to pull the hood down over his eyes when he stopped her and caught her in his arms, kissing her very tenderly. She felt the tears wet on his cheeks.

'God bless you, my child! This day you have saved both my life and my soul. Take care of yourself. We shall meet again, for I will find you – even in America.'

She helped him hide his face under the hood of the cloak, then gave him the handkerchief and showed him how to hold it up before him. Indeed, the smoke was already beginning to thicken inside the cell and some such protection was becoming almost essential.

'Above all, remember to disguise your voice if anyone should speak to you. They did not hear mine. And pretend to be dreadfully upset. That will make a good impression. Oh—' Suddenly, she had remembered the precious trust she carried in the little wash-leather bag close to her breast. 'Would you like me to give you back the diamond?'

'No. Keep it. And do exactly as I told you. It belongs to the one of whom I spoke. In four months' time, a man will come to the rue de Lille and ask you for it. You have not forgotten?'

She shook her head, then pushed him gently towards the door, on the far side of which the heavy, nailed boots of the guard could already be heard climbing the stairs.

'Take care!' she whispered again, then ran to throw herself down on the heap of straw which had been strewn for a bed in the darkest corner of the cell. She burrowed down in it as far as she could, hiding her head in it and in her folded arms, like someone in the depths of despair. There, with her heart thudding anxiously, she waited.

There was the clang of bolts being shot back. The door creaked. Then came the rough voice of the grenadier.

'Sorry m'lady – time's up.'

He was answered by a high-pitched sob which did credit to the cardinal's dramatic talents. Then the door shut again and the footsteps died away. Even then, Marianne dared not move. Her whole being was strained, listening while she counted the interminable seconds in time to the laboured beating of her heart. At every moment she expected to hear an angry shout, sounds of a struggle, of voices calling for the guard. In her mind's eyes, she followed the progress of the prisoner and his guide. Down the stairs to the first landing, the second flight and then the guard-room – and the door itself.

She breathed more easily when she heard the heavy boom as it swung to, echoing up from below. Gauthier de Chazay was outside now, but he still had to reach one of the three gates of the Kremlin unrecognized. Fortunately, to judge by the increasing gloom inside the prison, it must be even darker than before outside. It was as well the cell itself was spacious and high-ceilinged or there would have been a real risk of death by suffocation.

Marianne got up at last and paced a few steps up and down her prison. A puff of acrid smoke caught her throat and made her cough. At that she tore a piece out of her petticoat and, dipping it in the traditional pitcher of water which stood in a corner of the cell, applied it to her burning face. Her heart had been beating so wildly that she felt quite feverish but she forced herself to think calmly.

It would not be long before they came for the prisoner. What would happen then? They would scarcely do her any actual injury, being a woman, but she would be taken before the Emperor without delay and, for all her courage, she could not help shivering a little at the thought of what lay before her. It was certainly not going to be pleasant. But a man's life, Gauthier de Chazay's above all, was surely worth a little unpleasantness, even if it were to end in prison. It was as well that Jolival had made few difficulties when she disclosed her intention to him. He had even agreed to do as she asked him.

'You had better be out of the way of the Emperor's wrath,' she had told him. 'Gracchus can arrange to get you out of the Kremlin. You might go back to the Rostopchin Palace – unless the fire spreads so much that you are obliged to quit Moscow. In that case, let us agree to foregather at the first posting house on the road to Paris.'

With her mind at rest on that score she had paid scant attention to Gracchus's disapproving sniffs, merely remarking that if people could not obey her orders, they had no business in her service. Then, with the matter of her companions satisfactorily dealt with, she had been free to concentrate on the plan of escape which now seemed in a fair way to success.

The hardest part was going to be the waiting, how to get through the time that must elapse before the escape was discovered. She calculated that the time must be about midday so that, unless the Emperor should decide to evacuate the Kremlin, it might be six or seven hours before anyone entered the cell. Six or seven hours! Six or seven times eternity!

A lump settled in Marianne's throat and she felt herself a prey to the panic of a small girl locked in a dark cupboard. She wanted desperately to get it over and yet she knew that the longer she was left to endure her torment, the greater the cardinal's chances of escape. She must be patient and, if she could, keep calm.

Remembering suddenly that she had eaten nothing since the previous night, she went to the niche in the wall where stood the pitcher of water and a crust of bread. But it was her will more than her appetite that forced down a little of the dark, rock-hard bread. She knew that she must keep up her strength, yet she was not conscious of the slightest hunger. On the other hand, the smoke that was creeping into the room rasped her throat and she swallowed half the contents of the pitcher at a draught.

The heat was becoming uncomfortable and when she approached the narrow slit which did duty as a window she was horrified to see nothing but a mass of flame. The whole southern part of the city must have been on fire. The Kremlin itself might be entirly surrounded. The fire was reflected in the river so that even that seemed to be on fire.

Still nibbling her piece of bread, she had begun walking slowly back and forth across her prison, partly as a cure for impatience and partly to calm her nerves. But all at once she stopped dead, listening with all her might, while her heart beat a little faster. They were coming. There were men coming up the stairs, making all the characteristic noises of soldiers carrying weapons. Marianne's mind leapt to the conclusion that the hour of the trial had been put forward and they were coming for the prisoner. The Emperor must have decided to abandon the Kremlin.

She tried feverishly to reconstruct the route the prisoner would have to follow. He must have succeeded in negotiating the fortified perimeter. But she had been so anxious that her estimate of time could have gone very much awry. Had he really had time to reach safety?

There was a grating of bolts and Marianne stiffened, clasping her hands tightly together until the bones cracked in the way she had when striving to control her feelings. She heard people enter. Then a voice spoke, a very youthful voice but stern and carrying.

'The court awaits you, Sir. If you will come with me—'

In such time for thought as her brief imprisonment had allowed her, Marianne had not managed to decide on the right course to pursue when her substitution should be discovered. She was relying wholly upon instinct but, determined to gain as much time as she could, she had withdrawn, at the sound of approaching footsteps, to the darkest corner of her cell, keeping her back to the door.

Not until she was spoken to did she turn to see, framed in the doorway, a young captain, a stranger to her, and two grenadiers. The captain was slim and fair, straight as a ramrod and rather touching in his dignity. It was clear that he was immensely proud of the mission entrusted to him. It was his moment of glory and he was going to be cruelly disappointed.

Marianne advanced a few steps into the light that entered from the staircase. Three separate gasps of astonishment greeted her appearance. But by that time Marianne had made her decision. Gathering up her skirts, she darted through the gap between the two soldiers and plunged down the stairs, descending them like lightning before the men could recover from their surprise. She had reached the guardroom before she heard the young captain shouting: 'What the devil! Well, after her, damn you! Don't stand there gawping! Catch her!'

It was too late. Luckily for Marianne, the tower door had been left open. She was outside before the guards had even started after her. With a triumphant gasp, she plunged into the smoke as though into a protecting fog and ran straight ahead, regardless of possible obstructions, spurred on by the one thought of all escaping prisoners: to put as much ground between herself and her pursuers as possible. But the way sloped steeply uphill to the terrace and behind her she could hear shouts and yells that sounded horribly near.

She did not know the Kremlin or its exits and those portions of the upper terrace that she could see through the smoke looked hopelessly full of people. She had to find some way or other of concealing her identity if she did not want to be caught between two fires.

She was still wondering where to go when she caught sight of a tree not far from the top of the grassy slope, close up against one corner of the palace. It was an old tree, several hundred years old certain, and its branches dropped wearily down to the ground. It was twisted with age but the mass of its foliage looked impenetrable. The noise of the wind in the leaves was like a rookery in full voice.

Running before the wind, which was now gusting strongly from the south, Marianne found herself at the top of the slope, right up against the trunk. She measured the distance with her eye and decided that in the ordinary way it should not prove too difficult to climb. But would her injured shoulder allow her to do what would have been easy for her before?

It is a well-known fact that the love of liberty can lend wings to the least able and, all things considered, Marianne had no wish to confront the anger of Napoleon. What she wanted more than anything in the world at that moment was to find her friends and be gone from that accursed city as soon as possible. Gasping with pain, but spurred on by the desperate longing to escape, she managed it. After what seemed an age but could not have been more than a few seconds, she found herself seated astride one of the great branches and completely hidden from below. She was only just in time. A bare half-minute later she saw her young captain pass directly beneath her. He was running like a hare and shouting 'Guards! Guards!' at the top of his voice, regardless of the blazing debris falling all about him.

The fugitive's respite was brief. Her situation was less urgent but no less perilous, for the conflagration raging in the city had grown to terrifying proportions since her entry into the tower. Driven by the equinoctial wind, a rain of fire was falling on the Kremlin, from tenuous sparks to flaming brands that rattled on the metal-clad roofs of the palace and the copper domes of the churches like hammer strokes on the anvils of invisible blacksmiths. With the shouts and screams that rose on all sides, it made a terrifying and fantastic symphony. The whole city was howling to heaven, a blazing, fiery inferno in which the very air breathed fire.

The green umbrella of the tree overhead gave Marianne a measure of protection from the incandescent shower, but how long would it be before even that refuge caught alight?

By peering through the branches, she could see the parade ground between the palace and the Arsenal. It was crawling with troops, all trying, at the risk of their lives, to transport the casks of powder and bales of tow to a place of safety, unavailingly, since nowhere could be counted safe any longer. More men were stationed on the palace roof and, equipped with buckets and brooms, were sweeping away the burning particles as they fell and endeavouring to cool the scorching metal sheets by pouring water on them. The great Russian citadel, with its sumptuous churches and magnificent buildings was like a threatened island ringed by a sea of flame, a plateau emerging from a volcanic eruption. Everywhere that Marianne looked she saw huge flames leaping up beyond the encircling red walls. They were already menacing the imperial stables, where an army of grooms was struggling to lead out the screaming, panic-stricken horses.

'Merciful heavens,' Marianne murmured, 'help me to get out of this!'

All at once, she saw the Emperor. He was hatless and on foot, his short dark hair and the skirts of his grey redingote blowing in the wind as he strode towards the threatened Arsenal, followed by Berthier, Gourgaud and Prince Eugène, and disregarding the frantic attempts of one of his senior officers, General Lariboisière to deflect him from his dangerous course. But when the general tried to block his way, Napoleon merely brushed him aside with an impatient hand and continued on his way. Next, a party of gunners engaged in moving boxes of ammunition flung themselves across his path, almost going on their knees to prevent him going farther. At the same time, Murat's absurd white plumes could be seen emerging from the stables and were borne towards the Emperor on a heaving sea of men. Marianne, perched in her tree, heard someone shouting: 'Sire! I beg of you!'

'No! Get up on the terrace there with the Prince of Neuchâtel and tell me what you see,' Napoleon roared at Marshall Bessières. 'I'm not leaving here before I have to! Let every man do his duty and we shall hold out safely enough.'

Almost as he finished speaking, there came a sound like a cannon shot and the peculiar clatter of broken glass. The windows on one side of the palace had shattered. Whereupon Napoleon himself made for the terrace previously indicated in order to see for himself how close was the danger. Meanwhile, carried on the wind, there came to Marianne the echoes of the King of Naples' fluent cursing.

She was obliged just then to let go of the branch she was holding and throw herself backwards to avoid a blazing fragment of timber which came straight towards her and struck the tree.

'I can't stay here much longer,' she muttered through her teeth. 'I must find some way out.'

The Saviour's Gate, the only one that lay within her field of vision, was impossible, being obstructed by the guns being brought in from Red Square. But by dint of wriggling round she was able to make out that there was a small postern at the foot of one of the towers whose pointed roof could be seen rising behind a small church in the foreground. A chain of soldiers was using it to pass buckets of water up from the rivers to the men on the Kremlin roof. But they were Engineers and had no connection with the ones she had come up against earlier in the prison tower. None of the officers organizing the chain was known to her and, in any case, she had no choice.

She slid to the ground but was no sooner down than a gust of wind caught her and rolled her over and over down the slope to the bottom, wrenching her injured shoulder so cruelly that the tears came to her eyes. When at last she came to a stop, she lay for a moment or two in a daze, flat on the grass with a ringing in her ears and her bruised head aching again as if it would burst. But in another minute, she found herself miraculously on her feet again, and face to face with the oddest woman she had ever set eyes on: a matronly individual, heavily rouged, with a red handkerchief knotted bravely round her head and on top of that a grenadier's bearskin so covered in scorchmarks that it looked like a badly mown field of corn.

From the cask slung round her neck, Marianne knew her for a *vivandière*. She was probably about forty years of age and her clothes, although bizarre, consisting of a print skirt, grey stuff bodice and leather gaiters in addition to her curious headgear, were at least clean. Having picked Marianne up she set about dusting her down, shaking out her dress and brushing off the bits of grass adhering to it with vigorous sweeps of her hand.

'There,' she said with satisfaction, when she had finished. 'Now you look presentable again, love! My but you came a cropper! Not to mention that great bump on your head – though you must have got that some time since, for it's colouring up nicely now.' She indicated the bruise on Marianne's forehead from contact with the Chinese vase, the instrument of the imperial wrath. 'And where d'you think you're going to in such a hurry, eh?'

Marianne pushed back the strands of hair that were falling across her face and gestured to the blazing sky.

'Who wouldn't be in a hurry at such a time?' she said. 'I want to get out of here. A branch of a tree or something fell on my head and I don't feel very well.'

The woman stared at her.

'And you think it's any better outside there? Well, you poor little thing! Don't you know yet those Russkies've sent the 'ole flamin' town sky high? Seems they must've got tired of it or somethin'. But there, it's true you don't look well. 'Cept for that bruise of yours, you're as pale as a bucket of whitewash! You just wait while I give you a sup of what'll set you up! A drop of my fire-water'd have a dead man dancing!'

Detaching a cup from her belt, she poured a generous measure from her cask and put it to her protégée's lips. Not liking to refuse, especially as she really did feel in great need of some stimulant, Marianne swallowed a mouthful and instantly felt as if she had swallowed the fire itself. Coughing and spluttering and half-choked to death, she was grateful once more for the good offices of the sutler woman who thumped her on the back with enough force to fell an ox, laughing merrily as she did so.

'Anyone can see as you're a young lady, gently bred! You've not got the way of it!'

'It – it is a trifle strong but – but, as you say, it does set one up! Thank you very much, Madame.'

The other only laughed the more, clapping her hands to her sides.

'Well, well! That's the first time anyone ever called me madame! I'm no madame, my poppet! I'm Mère Tambouille, *vivandière* to that lot.' She jerked her thumb at the chain of soldiers. 'I was just taking them a little something to keep their spirits up when you came tumbling right on top of me. And there now, you still haven't told me why you're so set on running out into that oven out there!'

Marianne did not hesitate for an instant. The fire-water seemed to have sharpened her mental faculties astonishingly.

'I am the niece of the Abbé Surugue, the priest of St Louis-des-Français.' The words came out without a pause. 'Someone told me that my uncle had come to the Kremlin to see the Emperor, so I came to look for him, but I could not find him here and so I want to go back home—'

'Well I never! So your uncle's a priest, is he? Trust me to run into something out of the way! But, my poor dearie, how d'you know you've even a home left?'

'Perhaps I haven't – but I must go and see. My uncle is an old man and his legs are bad. I must find him or he will be very frightened.'

Mère Tambouille heaved a sigh that rivalled the efforts of the gale.

'Stubborn little thing, that's what you are! You remind me of my donkey, Lisette! Well, if you want to play Joan of Arc, it's your own affair. It's your skin, ain't it? Not but what you'd do better to stay with us and wait a bit, because the Little Corporal, he's not going to stay here for ever.'

'But I heard that he would not hear of leaving.'

'Moonshine! I know better. It was that sly old Berthier who did the trick, telling him that if he insisted on staying he'd likely find hisself cut off from all the rest of the army as was left outside. I 'eard it all as I was comin' 'ere. An officer chap was tellin' one o' the grooms and sayin' as he'd best be saddlin' Taurus, one of the Emperor's mounts. So wait a bit and we'll go together.'

All this talk was agony to Marianne. She was desperately afraid that one of her pursuers would pick up her trail and find her standing chatting amicably with the *vivandière*. Now that she could regard the cardinal's escape as an accomplished fact, she was terrified by the thought of having to face Napoleon. She knew his uncontrollable temper only too well, and that he would regard the rescue of a man who desired his own death as a personal affront, capable of erasing all else that had ever passed between them. She was, in fact, in very real danger of finding herself arraigned as an accomplice and, as such, a traitor to her country.

However, seeing that she remained firm in her determination to quit the Kremlin without delay, Mère Tambouille gave in.

'Go, then, if you must,' she sighed. 'I'll come with you as far as the gate.'

Together, they reached the postern where the men were still tirelessly passing their buckets of water. They greeted the *vivandière* with a volley of cheerful oaths and coarse jokes about the new assistant she had got herself. Marianne's shape, in particular, excited their interest and Gallic wit, coupled with more explicit invitations, began to flow freely, so freely, indeed, that Mère Tambouille lost her temper with them.

'You stow your gab, my lads,' she bawled at them sternly. 'Where d'you think you are, eh? She's none of your lightskirts but a curé's niece! So if you've no respect for her petticoats, have some for her uncle's! Now step aside there and let the lady out!'

'Out? That's no way to treat a lady,' observed a magnificently bearded, red-haired sapper, who had been winking so hard at Marianne that she began to wonder if it was a nervous tic he had. 'It's blazing like hell out there! She'll be burnt to a frazzle and that would be a shame – and all on account of a curé, too!'

'We've been into all that already. So just you shove over. Out of the way and let her get through the gate. And keep your hands to yourself, what's more. It's a tightish squeeze.'

'Hands? What hands?' panted a perspiring youth. 'Have to drop the buckets, wouldn't we?'

And in fact, for all their joking, the men were wasting no time. All the while they talked they were passing the full buckets of water, not without spilling a good deal over their feet, while the *vivandière* poured generous rations of her famous fire-water down their throats. However, since they still showed no sign of making way for her, the officer in charge of that section of the line, who had so far taken no part in the affair, now came forward and took Marianne by the hand.

'Forgive them, Mademoiselle. They are reluctant to let you go. And indeed, they are right. It is not wise.'

'I am grateful, Monsieur, but it is imperative that I rejoin my uncle. He must be very much alarmed on my account.'

With the officer's solicitous hand to guide her, Marianne negotiated the gateway, no easy task since a miniature landslide had combined with the water slopped from the buckets to turn the passage into a quagmire. When she was through, she thanked him politely, suppressing a sigh of relief at finding herself outside the citadel at last. Not that the view of the burning city which met her eyes was at all reassuring. All round the Kremlin was a ring of fire.

'Over there, there's a gap in the flames,' called Mère Tambouille who had followed her out, still doling out measures of spirits to the men. 'If that's your way, you've a chance.'

It was true. In the direction of St Louis-des-Français, the city was still standing and the fire had not yet become general. Only the Bazaar was burning, but less fiercely than elsewhere.

'Yes, that's it,' Marianne called back, glad to see that there was still a possible avenue of escape. 'Thank you again, Madame Tambouille!'

The *vivandière*'s laughter followed her as she set off along the river and she heard her new friend crying after her through her cupped hands: 'Hey! If you can't find your uncle, come back here! I can do with a pretty girl like you – and so can the lads here, too!'

The next moment, Marianne had plunged into the seething confusion of Red Square. The troops who had been bivouacked there the previous night were doing their utmost to save their guns and their ammunition and some of them were occupying the mansions and other buildings surrounding the square in an attempt to protect them from the fire. There was also a wild assortment of vehicles of every description, from gentlemen's carriages to tradesmen's carts, all of them filled to overflowing with plunder, for, acting on the excuse of saving what property they could, the troops had been pillaging to their hearts' content.

Jostled on all sides and in constant danger of being run down by carriage wheels, Marianne succeeded somehow in reaching the Rostopchin Palace, only to run straight into the arms of Sergeant Bourgogne when literally on the doorstep.

She started violently on recognizing him. Early that morning, when Gauthier de Chazay had launched his attack on the Emperor, Bourgogne had been in the gallery with the party of *boutechniks* he had taken prisoner. He must have witnessed all that passed. But she pulled herself together at once. He had seen what happened, certainly, but if he had come back to the Rostopchin Palace after that he could not be aware of what had followed.

However he was barring her way.

'And where are you off to, little lady?' he inquired with his usual good humour.

'Inside. Have you forgotten that I was living here when you arrived the other evening, with a gentleman with a broken leg – my uncle.'

He beamed on her candidly. 'Indeed I've not! In fact I'm fairly sure I saw you at the palace this morning. But you can't go in here. It may not be burning yet, but it's in danger and has been requisitioned, on his Majesty's orders. Besides, all civilians are to leave the city.'

'But I have to meet my uncle! He should be here already! Have you not seen him?'

'The gentleman with the broken leg? No. I've not seen anyone.'

'But he must have come here. Are you sure he did not go inside when you were not looking?'

'Couldn't have done that, little lady. I've been on guard here with my men now for four hours. If anyone had come I'd have seen them, as sure as my name's Adrien Jean-Baptiste-François Bourgogne of Condé-sur-Escaut! If your uncle was in the Kremlin, he must be there still. So long as the Emperor is there—'

But Marianne, giving him a pale smile of thanks, was already turning away. She made her way towards the church of the Blessed St Basil, meaning to think over her situation. Where could Gracchus and Jolival be? If the sergeant had not seen them, it could only be because they had not been there. 'That much is obvious,' Marianne muttered to herself, 'but what could have kept them? And where shall I find them now?'

She stepped aside just in time to escape being run down by a spring van, piled high with furniture and bales of cloth and far too heavily loaded for its brakes to be of any use, which came plunging without warning down the hill from the church. Instinctively, she flattened herself against the circular, stone-built platform on which the punishments meted out by the Muscovite law were habitually carried out, then, the danger past, climbed on towards the church, thinking to find a few moments' peace and quiet inside, even if the place were overflowing with refugees at their prayers. Never had she felt in such need of divine support as at that moment, knowing that she was lost and alone in the midst of an unfamiliar and hostile city.

But as she climbed the steps leading up to the doors the sound that met her ears was not the murmur of prayers but the neighing of horses and the cursing of their grooms. St Basil the Blessed had become a stable.

This discovery came as such a violent shock to her that she turned on her heels and fled as if the place had been infected with the plague. Her heart was bursting with an anger and indignation that drove out all her private fears and alarms. They had no right to do such things! However little a Catholic like herself might think of the Orthodox faith, still its adherents worshipped the same God, and in a manner not so very different from her own. Moreover, lax though she might be in the practice of it, her faith was none the less deep and what she had just seen had touched her to the quick. So, not content with driving out the cardinals, making the Pope a prisoner and flouting the Church's laws by his divorce and remarriage, Napoleon was actually permitting his troops to profane God's house! For the first time it occurred to Marianne that his cause might after all be doomed to failure. Cardinal de Chazay's passionate words suddenly took on a strange, almost prophetic resonance.

She paused for a moment, wondering what to do. Where, in all this confusion and sea of flames, could she go? The thought of her godfather, and the remembrance of the story she had told to Mère Tambouille a little while before came together in her mind. Why not do as she had said? The cardinal must have gone either to St Louis-des-Français or to Count Sheremetiev's house at Kuskovo, where he had arranged to meet her before. That was the answer, of course. In fact it was the only possible answer since Jolival and Gracchus were not to be found. Perhaps they had not even managed to leave the Kremlin. With only one good leg, the Vicomte was not exactly mobile and if he had failed to reach the Rostopchin Palace, how much less likely the posting house on the road to France, with that great conflagration barring the way on every side.

Having made her decision, Marianne tucked up her skirt and pulled it over her head, like a peasant woman in the rain, to protect her hair from the sparks that were still flying through the air, and then set out to cross the square in the direction of the Lubianka district in which the French church stood.

But in spite of all her efforts, she found it impossible to push her way through the solid mass of vehicles and men, all struggling to get to those few gates which the fire had not yet reached. She heard someone shouting in French that the Tver road was the only one still open but it meant nothing to her. She did not want to go with these people. She only wanted to find her godfather.

Suddenly, she gave a joyful cry. The crowd had parted for a moment, thrust aside by a platoon of soldiers emerging from a side street, and she had caught a lightning glimpse of a figure that made her heart beat faster: a grey-haired man wrapped in a long, dark cloak, just such a cloak as she had thrown round the cardinal's shoulders a short while before. He was there, ahead of her.

After that, instead of fighting against the tide, she let herself be carried along with it. In any case, to have tried to cut across it would have been to court certain death under the wheels of the carriages and the hooves of the maddened horses, many of which were barely under control. Instead, she directed all her efforts to catching up with the man in the black cloak.

All at once, what had been a narrow street seemed to open out. They were crossing a wide boulevard lined with fine, large houses. Just then, the man in front stepped out of the main stream and hurried down the boulevard, although that, too, was blocked by fire at the far end. Marianne darted after him, calling at the top of her voice but without making herself heard above the roaring of the fire and the howling wind. She began to run, oblivious of everything about her and not even aware that all those gracious houses were at that moment given over to plunder by the drunken soldiery.

The man ahead – she was sure that it was the cardinal when the wind blew aside a fold of his cloak and revealed the black soutane – was running now, like a man pursued, so fast that Marianne had the greatest difficulty in following.

She was gaining on him, even so, when all of a sudden he vanished. At the place where she had last seen him there was nothing but a high, gilded iron gate and beyond it a bit of stunted shrubbery. Desperately, she hurled herself against it. It gave out a metallic clang but held as firm as if it had never been made to open. Catching sight of a bell, Marianne hung on to it with all her strength but there was no answer. No one came. The man had vanished as completely as if a trapdoor had opened suddenly and swallowed him up.

Marianne sank down despondently on a stone block that stood beside the gate and looked about her. Everywhere were yelling voices, the crash of broken bottles and the strains of drunken singing. The city was burning, the flames coming closer every minute, and still there were men capable of breaking into cellars and revelling in their contents rather than flying for their lives.

From two or three of the adjacent streets, small groups of scantily clad women and children were running out into the still empty boulevard, weeping and shrieking aloud with terror. It was at this point that Marianne first noticed a big woman, dressed in much the same fashion as the *vivandière* she had met earlier but with the difference that instead of a bearskin this one sported on her head a policeman's cap with a long red silken tassel. This creature's conduct was so revolting that it roused Marianne from her own misery. She was armed with a cavalryman's sabre and was using it to hold up the fugitives who were trying to make their way out of one of the side streets, letting them pass only when she had searched and stripped them of all that they were carrying. Already she had a heap of jewels and valises on the ground beside her, for the wretched people, terrified of the fire at their backs, suffered themselves to be robbed without protest.

The next group to appear consisted of an old man leaning on a stick, a young girl, two children and two men bearing between them a stretcher on which was a woman, evidently very ill. Before any of them could make a move to stop her, the harpy had rushed at the stretcher and begun to search the sick woman with such unfeeling roughness that Marianne could bear it no longer.

She sprang forward, spurred on by a fury that crystallized all her loathing and disgust, and fell upon the woman, grasping her by the grey hair that straggled from under her cap and jerking her backwards with a force that sent her sprawling on the ground, then throwing herself down on her and pummelling her with her fists. Never before had she felt such need to bite and rend and kill. She was ashamed, bitterly ashamed that people like this were her own fellow-countrymen and, somehow or other, she had to show them what she felt.

The woman, meanwhile, was yelling like a stuck pig and in another moment three or four half-drunken soldiers came lurching to her rescue.

'Hold on, Ma!' one of them bawled out. 'We're coming!'

Marianne saw that she was lost. The party to whose aid she had so rashly gone had taken the opportunity to make good their escape as soon as their assailant was laid low. She was alone now, face to face with four angry men who were already dragging her bodily away from her victim. The woman herself had staggered to her feet, cursing venomously, with blood pouring from her nose. Reeling slightly, she made for the sword she had dropped.

'Ta, lads,' she wheezed. 'Now you keep a 'old on 'er, acos I'm a goin' ter carve out one o' them there ogles. Jest to larn 'er!'

Holding the sword unsteadily at arms length, she was advancing on Marianne when she jerked and fell headlong at the feet of the startled girl. A long whiplash had curled around her knees and cut the legs from under her. At the same time a mocking, nasal voice spoke brusquely.

'All right, my lads! That will do! Be off with you, unless you want a taste of my whip – or a noose! And take this doxy with you!'

The men did not wait to be told twice and in another moment Marianne found herself alone with her rescuer, who was even then descending from a kind of open carriage which, at that instant, looked more like a removal van than a respectable conveyance.

'You are not hurt?' the young man asked her as she began automatically brushing down her skirts and pushing back her long, dishevelled hair.

'No, I don't think so. I owe you my thanks, Sir. But for you—'

'Please. It was the least I could do. It is bad enough to have been driven out of every successive refuge by this confounded fire without being forced to realize that one belongs to a race of savages into the bargain. But—' He broke off and, studying Marianne attentively, said suddenly: 'But I know you! Good Lord, this is certainly fated to be the most fantastic night of my whole life! Who would have thought that I should have the luck to run across one of the prettiest women in Paris amid the flames of Moscow?'

'You know me?' Marianne said uneasily, thinking that this was the last thing she wanted after all that had happened at the Kremlin. 'You have the advantage of me, Sir.'

'De Beyle, at your service, Princess. Auditor 1st Class, Council of State, at present attached to the staff of Comte Mathieu Dumas, Assistant Quartermaster-General of the Imperial Army. My name will mean nothing to you, of course, because I have never had the privilege of being introduced to you, but I saw you one night at the Comédie Française. The play was *Britannicus* and you were escorted by that damned scoundrel Chernychev. You were dressed all in red and looked like one of those flames there – only infinitely sweeter! But we must not stay here. The fire is gaining on us. Allow me to offer you – I can hardly call it a seat, but at least a perch in my carriage?'

'The fact is – I don't know where I am going. I was making for St Louis-des-Français—'

'Well, you will never get there. Indeed, one might say that none of us knows where he is going. What matters is to get out of the city through such roads as are still open to us.'

As he spoke, Monsieur de Beyle was assisting Marianne to climb up on to the heap of baggage which included, in addition to a number of bottles, a small cask of wine and a prodigious quantity of books, for the most part very generously bound. Sprawled among all these was also another passenger in the shape of a very fat man of pallid complexion who seemed within an inch of expiring altogether.

This person turned his head and gazed at her with a complete lack of expression. When he had satisfied himself that she was undeniably about to take her place in the vehicle, he uttered a heart-rending sigh and, releasing his clutch upon his stomach, made some effort to shift his ponderous body to one side to enable her to sit down. As he did so, he produced a travesty of a smile.

'Monsieur de Bonnaire de Giff, auditor 2nd class,' Beyle introduced him. 'He is suffering,' he added in a sardonic tone devoid of all trace of sympathy or compassion, 'from a severe attack of dysentery.' It was evident that he found his passenger both irritating and repulsive. Marianne smiled, nevertheless, and murmured a few sympathetic expressions, to which the invalid responded with a groan.

Monsieur de Beyle then climbed in after Marianne and instructed the driver to continue along the boulevard and join the queue of the vehicles at its end. As she watched him, Marianne was aware of a vague recollection stirring deep down in her mind. She did remember having seen his face somewhere. It was a young face, not particularly handsome, even rather coarse, but powerful, with a high forehead made higher still by a receding hairline, lively, observant dark eyes and an ironical, almost bitter twist to the lips. He had spoken of that memorable performance of *Britannicus* and now she realized that that was where she had seen him. Fortunée Hamelin, who knew everybody, had commented somewhat slightingly on his presence among the occupants of Comte Daru's box.

'No one in particular. A provincial young man with literary aspirations, I believe. Some kind of relation of the Comtesse – probably her lover as well. His name is – Beyle. Yes, that's it, Henri Beyle. Rather a ladies' man.'

None of that was much comfort to Marianne. She began to feel that she was dogged by ill-luck. She was trying to find Jolival, her godfather, Gracchus – and instead she had to fall into the hands of someone on the Quartermaster-General's staff, and a man who knew her, at that! She would be lucky if she did not find herself face to face with Napoleon. But then, was there anyone in Moscow at that moment who was not, in some way, connected with him? And she really had no idea of where to go. By this time the only possible place was somewhere out of reach of the flames.

Every bit as much at ease as if they had been conversing in a drawing-room, her companion was explaining to her that he had been obliged to interrupt a most enjoyable dinner in the Apraxin Palace when the flames threatened to engulf it.

'We have already sought refuge in two or three places,' he told her, evidently enjoying himself enormously despite what seemed to be a heavy cold. 'But each time this blessed fire caught us up. That was how we came to visit the Soltikov Palace, an excellent club with a quite outstanding cellar and a library in which I came across a very rare edition of Voltaire's *Facéties*. Let me show you.' He pulled a small, richly bound book out of his pocket and stroked it lovingly. Then, hastily, he thrust it back again and leaning his arms on the wine cask muttered: 'Unhappily, I fear that all that remains to us now is the open country – supposing we can ever reach it. Look, everything seems to have stopped moving.'

This was true and when they tried to edge into the endless procession of vehicles they were immediately thrust back by a cavalcade of horsemen and carriages which came charging out of a side street and literally plunged straight into the crowd.

'The outriders of the King of Naples!' Beyle muttered. 'That is all we need! Where does the great Murat think he's going?' He spoke to the driver. 'Wait, François. I want to see.'

Once again, he jumped down from the carriage and darted into the crowd. Marianne saw him eagerly questioning three men in splendid livery lavishly adorned with gold braid who seemed to be trying to force a way through the traffic for their master's coaches. When he came back, he was white with anger.

'Well, dear lady,' he said acidly. 'We must stay here to be roasted alive, I fear, so that Murat may save his wardrobe. Look there, the fire is creeping forward to overtake us. In a little while it will be threatening the Tver road also. True, the Emperor is coming this way before long.'

Marianne gulped painfully.

'The Emperor? Are you sure?'

He stared at her in some surprise.

'Why yes, the Emperor. Did you think he was going to stay

and burn with the Kremlin? I must say, to judge from what I have just heard, there seems to have been some trouble but in the end his Majesty got out of the confounded place by way of a postern leading on to the river bank. He's going to withdraw to a country house outside the city – Petrovski or some such name. We'll wait for him to pass and then follow on after him – I say, where are you off to?'

For Marianne had scrambled over the cask and slid to the ground.

'I am grateful to you for all your kindness in rescuing me, Sir, but this is where I get down.'

'Here? But this is nowhere near St Louis-des-Français. And I thought you told me you didn't know where to go? Princess, I beg of you—' His face was suddenly very serious. 'Do not do anything rash. This city is doomed and us with it. It may be that we shall not see the day out. Do not leave it on my conscience that I abandoned you in peril. I don't know what has made you change your mind but you are the Emperor's friend and I—'

She fixed her green eyes on him squarely.

'You are mistaken, Monsieur de Beyle. I am no longer the Emperor's friend. I cannot tell you the whole, but you could endanger your own position by helping me. Go to his Majesty. You have a right, even a duty to do so. But let me go my own way.'

She turned and was beginning to walk away but he caught her firmly by the arm.

'Madam,' he said, 'between women and politics I have never known a moment's hesitation. I will serve a lady before I serve the Empire. I have not so far had the privilege of being numbered among your friends. Permit me to take advantage of the unlooked-for opportunity which fate has put in my way today. If you do not wish to see the Emperor, you shall not see him.'

'That is not quite enough, Sir,' Marianne said with the shadow of a smile. 'Neither would I wish the Emperor to see me.'

'Then I will arrange it so, only, I implore you, Princess, do not reject the hand I offer you. Do not deny me the happiness of being, if only briefly, your protector.'

They looked at one another for a moment and Marianne had

a sudden conviction that she could place complete trust in this stranger. There was something solid and rock-like about him, like the mountains of his own native Dauphiné. Impulsively, she put out her hand, partly that he might help her up again on to the pile of baggage and partly, also, in acknowledgement of a kind of pact between them.

'Very well,' she said. 'I trust you. Let us be friends.'

'Wonderful! This must be celebrated! The best way to pass the time when you've nothing else to do is to have a drink, and we've some excellent bottles here . . . Hey, Bonnaire, old fellow! Don't drink all of that!' he cried suddenly becoming aware that his passenger was engaged, with an air of unshakeable gloom, in getting through the contents of an ancient, crusted bottle.

'It's not that I'm enjoying it,' the other returned with a hiccup, releasing the neck of the bottle for an instant. 'But a good wine is the best thing in the world for dysentery.'

'Well I'm damned!' Beyle said indignantly. 'If you can equate Vosne-Romanée with laudanum, then you and I are going to fall out! Hand me a bottle and see if you can find a glass.'

Marianne accepted a glass of wine but after that left her new friend to finish the bottle. Nor was he the only person drinking. All round her she could see people busy draining flasks and bottles, some even as they ran. Beyle himself paused briefly to heap curses on a group of three or four lackeys who came up with their carriage and tried, as well as their tottering legs would allow them, to scramble aboard. The whip was brought into play again, all the more vigorously because the men proved to be the young auditor's own servants.

Then, without warning, they saw the Emperor's party flash past. His black hat emerged briefly from the smoke, hung there for a moment in the gloom and then vanished, borne on a wave of white plumes, down a street in which the houses, one after another, were bursting into flames.

'Our turn next,' Beyle said. 'It's time to go.'

Seeing that his own driver seemed likewise to have passed the interval in drinking, he grasped the lead-horse's bridle and, swearing like a trooper, set about guiding the vehicle into the Tver road. The wind had changed again and was now blowing as fiercely as ever from the south-west. Before long the procession of refugees, buffeted by the gale and blinded by the ash that filled the air and clung to skin and clothes, had almost reached a standstill. The heat grew every moment more intense, exciting the horses until it was all they could do to prevent them bolting. Buildings collapsed with a noise like thunder while others were already reduced to smoking ruin, from which a few charred timbers stuck up desolately.

They were passing a large mansion in the course of construction when Marianne uttered a cry of horror. From the unfinished window sockets of the house, never to be completed now for already it was beginning to burn, hung the bodies of some dozen men who there awaited the last judgement day. They were barefoot, clad only in their shirts and had been shot before being suspended in blood-stained clusters with 'I burned Moscow' written on placards round their necks, flapping dismally in the wind about the bullet-riddled corpses.

'It's horrible!' she choked, almost sobbing. 'Horrible! Have we all gone mad?'

'Perhaps we have,' Beyle said quietly. 'Who is the more mad, he who came here seeking death, or he who seeks to wipe out his defeat in a bath of blood? Either way we are all mad! Look about you! This is a very carnival of madmen!'

A frenzy seemed to have overtaken the long stream of vehicles, all laden with booty and compelled by the pressure all around them to proceed only by fits and starts. The drivers, terrified of being trapped by the flames, were shrieking hideously and belabouring their horses. On both sides of the street a mass of armed men were breaking down the doors of every undamaged house as they went along. Such was their fear of leaving anything behind that they would plunge inside and emerge laden with booty. Some covered themselves with stuffs richly worked in gold; some were enveloped in beautiful and costly furs, while yet others dressed themselves in women's clothes and precious cashmere shawls worn round their waists like sashes. Any who fell were lost, for at once a dozen eager hands reached out, not to help him to rise but to plunder what he had. Everywhere, against the roaring of the flames, were faces distorted by fear, cruelty and lust. The Emperor had gone, he had abandoned Moscow, and now there was nothing to restrain the hundreds of men for whom, all through that endless journey, the great Russian capital had gleamed like the promised land, the cornucopia which was to make them rich.

Marianne buried her head in her hands and tried not to look. She no longer knew which was uppermost in her mind, fear or shame: she only knew that at that moment she was in hell.

When at last they passed outside the walls of Moscow it was black night and a huge, round white moon was rising. The long line of close-packed vehicles burst out and scattered, like the contents of a bottle of champagne when the cork is popped. One highroad and a number of smaller ones led out into the countryside.

Beyle halted the carriage on a little ridge and mopped his brow with his sleeve. He looked exhausted.

'Well, here we are outside,' he murmured. 'I think we owe some thanks to Providence for getting us out of that death-trap.'

'What are we going to do now?' Marianne asked wearily, wiping away the tears the smoke had brought to her eyes.

'Find somewhere to sleep if we can. We are still too close. The heat is like an oven. We could get no rest.' He broke off, interrupted by a fit of coughing, and took a generous draught of brandy to cure it.

Marianne scarcely seemed to notice. Although practically asleep on her feet, she was fascinated by the spectacle, even in spite of the accumulated fatigue of the past three days.

The city looked like a volcano in the course of eruption. It was a titanic crucible, melting down all the riches of the world, bubbling and throwing up great sheets of flame, showers of sparks, with the occasional brilliant flash of an explosion. It was like some monstrous firework display for a mad god, blazing away in the darkness. It was the triumph of a demon whose fiery breath could burn even at a distance and whose long, red arms, reaching out over the walls, were still seeking, like the tentacles of a giant squid, to claw back those that had escaped.

'Can't we rest here?' Marianne asked. 'I can't go any farther.'

It was true enough. Her body, deprived of sleep for too long, would no longer obey her except by an immense effort of will.

'It's very hot here, but must we really follow all those people?' She pointed to the column of refugees, still moving onward into the night. 'Where do they think they are going?'

Beyle laughed cynically, his voice already thickening a little from the drink he had taken. Then he shrugged. 'Where they've all been going inexorably for years – where old Panurge's silly sheep went: to look for a shepherd! They've been told the Emperor is going to Petrov-something, so they, too, are going to Petrov-something, without even asking themselves whether they'll find a place to sleep or anything to eat there. Most of them will stay outside in the wind, in the pouring rain if need be, entranced by the place where their god is, like Tibetan lamas before the face of Buddha. But you're right. There's no need for us to follow them. I can see a small lake just ahead, with a little wood beside it. We'll camp there. What's more, I believe I can see the place they were all talking about.'

At the end of what now developed into a broad, well-kept avenue, lights had begun to spring up, shining out of the darkness, revealing a large, brick-built mansion of a curious architectural style oscillating between Louis XIV and Louis XV with a touch of the classical added on. Several more substantial dwellings were visible in the vicinity and the host of refugees flowed into them, while some kind of guard system seemed to have been established around Petrovskoi itself, in order to protect the Emperor's rest as much as possible, supposing he were able to get any.

Beyle, however, drove his carriage, as he had declared his intention of doing, to the edge of a little lake in which was reflected a small, thickly planted wood of birch and fir. The wretched Bonnaire greeted the sight of the wood with immense relief and vanished into it precipitately as soon as the carriage came to a stop.

With the help of those of his servants who were still on their feet, Beyle set up some kind of a camp. The mountainous clutter of baggage was removed from the carriage so that there was room to lie down and the hood drawn up against the cold night air and the likelihood of insects dropping out of the trees.

Marianne took no part in any of this activity but sat by the lake, her feet among the reeds and her arms about her knees. She was so tired that every separate fibre of her body ached and yet she could not relax. The thoughts continued to go round and round in her head, like a runaway machine, without getting anywhere and without even any logical connection. She stared at the water stretching at her feet, lit by the reflected glow of the fire, and thought that it might be good to bathe in it and find a little coolness after so much heat. She bent down and scooped up some of the water in her hand and splashed it over her burning hot face and neck. But the water was not really cool. It was as if the fire, penetrating deep down into the earth, had imparted some of its heat to the little pool. All the same, it did her good.

From behind her, she heard her new friend laugh.

'Apparently Wittgenstein and his army are not many leagues away from here, guarding the road to St Petersburg. If they only knew that the Emperor was within their grasp, and practically defenceless, they could scarcely resist the temptation.'

Bonnaire, who had re-emerged from the wood, said something in answer, that Marianne could not catch but which the other greeted with a prolonged bout of sneezing, before adding: 'I hope, for all our sakes, we shan't be obliged to remain here for long. I've no desire to find myself a prisoner of war.'

But of all that, Marianne's mind had registered only one, small fact: that this broad, well-made highway that stretched so invitingly before her was the road to St Petersburg. This was the road that, ever since she had first entered the Kremlin – was it really only yesterday, or months ago? – she had been consistently renouncing, although it had never been out of her thoughts. Was it fate that had made them camp beside that tempting route? Perhaps even the fire that had driven her out of Moscow had been part of God's will? It was so easy to see the hand of Providence in everything when it seemed to point to what your heart yearned to do.

'I'm afraid I can't offer you a feast,' said Beyle's voice

pleasantly beside her. 'Our provisions are limited to some raw fish that my driver came by somehow or other, a few figs and some wine.'

'Raw fish? Why not cook it?'

He laughed, with a rather forced heartiness.

'I don't know how you feel, but for my part I've seen enough of fire for one day. The mere thought of lighting one makes me feel a trifle sick. To say nothing of the fact that the wood is full of pine needles and as dry as a bone. We could easily set it alight. I think I'd prefer to eat my fish raw after all. They say the Japanese eat nothing else.'

In spite of these encouraging words, Marianne contented herself with a few figs and a little wine. The bottles had not lasted out the journey and they began on the cask. The white wine it contained was far too young and so sharp that it made the tongue contract and left the throat raw but this did not prevent Beyle, Bonnaire and the servants from consuming a good deal of it and by the time Beyle announced that it was time for bed they were all gloriously drunk and inclined to be hilarious.

Even so, Beyle, as a man of the world and able to hold his liquor, retained just enough lucidity to escort Marianne to the carriage and install her on the back seat. She, however, was reluctant to lie down at once.

'I'm tired,' she said, 'but my nerves are still on edge. I'll just sit under the trees for a while. You go to sleep and don't worry about me. I'll rest later.'

He did not insist but wished her a good night and then, while the unhappy Bonnaire, by this time reduced to a mere shell, took the forward seat, he settled himself on the box, rolled in his coat, and was asleep almost at once. The servants, heavy with wine, were already snoring here and there about the lake.

In an incredibly short time, Marianne found herself alone amid a concert of noisy breathing. The men sprawled about her in the moonlight looked like bodies left lying on a battlefield. Away in the darkness, Petrovskoi blazed with light now from every window.

It was chilly under the trees and Marianne went automatically to collect the horse blanket which Beyle had left on the carriage seat for her. But as she threw it round her shoulders some awkwardness in her movements reawakened the pain in her shoulder. Her forehead, too, felt burning hot. She shivered and drew the rough, heavy, horse-smelling rug more closely round her.

The road running nearby fascinated her. It drew her like a magnet. Her feet hurt, her legs ached and her whole body was trembling with weariness and with the slow onset of fever, yet she went towards the road, reached it and began to walk along it steadily, step by step as though in a dream.

Behind her was the burning city but it meant nothing to her. It was merely a flaming barrier set between her and the road back to Paris. While there, before her, the road lay clear ahead to Petersburg.

'Jason,' she murmured, the tears welling into her eyes. 'Jason! Wait for me – wait for me!'

The last phrase had been a cry, uttered aloud, and, weak as she was, she had begun to run straight ahead, carried by some unknown force she was powerless to oppose. She had to get to the end of the road, the end of the night – to the blue sea and the sun and the fresh, salt breezes.

Something bumped into her, causing her to fall to her knees, something that then clung to her, with heartbroken sobs, crying: 'Mama! Mama! Where are you, Mama?'

Holding it at arms' length, she perceived that it was a small boy with dark curls clustered thickly round a chubby face. He stared back at her with big, frightened eyes and tried to burrow against her.

A flash like lightning went through Marianne's brain and there was a tearing pain in her heart. Her spirit broke free of the hideous present and from all the events of that dreadful day, to reach out after a deeper need. She held the unknown child in her arms and hugged him to her.

'Oh, my darling! Don't be afraid, my darling! I am here. We'll go home together, you and I. We won't go to Petersburg . . .'

Carrying the strange child in her arms, his little arms clasped round her neck, her body burning with fever, Marianne made her way like a sleepwalker back to the carriage to await the dawn.

'We'll go home,' she said, over and over again. 'We'll go home very soon.'

Chapter Seven

Take Hold of Life –

Next day, while Moscow continued to burn like a devastated coal-mine and Napoleon sat in Petrovskoi and contemplated the inferno with what patience he could muster, Marianne lay beside the lake, delirious and in a high fever, much to the alarms of her companions in misfortune.

The child she had found slept peacefully against her breast and this unexpected addition only increased the two auditors' perturbation. Nor were they themselves in the best of health. Bonnaire's dysentery, not at all improved by a period of heavy, drunken slumber, was as bad as ever. Beyle's cold was worse and he was liverish into the bargain.

'It's that filthy white wine. We drank too much of it last night, I must confess,' was all he would say about it and then set about doing what he could to improve their present position. Underneath his nonchalant pose he was, in fact, a man of considerable energy and quite capable of decisive action when it was required of him.

He proved this in the first instance by kicking his servants awake and obliging them, with the assistance of several buckets of water drawn from the lake, to sit up and take notice. Meanwhile the little boy had woken up and started crying and Bonnaire was feeding him with figs. Only Marianne was still in no condition to take any part in what was happening. She lay moaning softly under the horse blanket in which Beyle had hastened to wrap her as soon as he realized that she was ill.

'The two most important things we have to do,' Beyle declared, 'are to try and find this child's mother, who may not be very far away, and to discover some form of shelter for ourselves. It doesn't matter what, as long as it has a bed for this poor girl.'

'A doctor would be no bad thing either,' Bonnaire remarked. 'We could all three do with one.'

'My dear fellow, we must make do with what we have. Trying to find a doctor and medicines in our present situation would be like looking for poppies in a snowfield in midwinter. But good God!' he broke out aiming some perfectly useless but very satisfying kicks at the carriage wheels. 'Why in heaven's name did I ever come to this cursed country! If the devil were to appear to me now and offer to transport me to Italy, to Milan, say, or those exquisite lakes, in exchange for my soul, I'd not simply accept, I'd feel as if I were robbing the poor chap. François!' he yelled at the top of his voice. 'François! Take that child and carry him to the house there and see if anyone claims him. And see if you can't dig up a bed somewhere while you're about it.'

Leaving Bonnaire to take care of Marianne, he set out himself on a tour of exploration, riding one of the horses taken from the carriage. François was the first to return and he was alone. He had found the child's mother without much difficulty. She was the wife of a French confectioner and had been hunting for her little boy all night after losing him in the stampede out of the city. But there was not an empty bed to be had for miles around. All he was able to bring back was some food, biscuits, dried fruit, cheese and smoked ham, given him by the grateful mother.

Beyle was away a long time and in the meanwhile Bonnaire and the driver, François, did what they could for Marianne. François found a spring and brought some water and the fat man did his best to make her swallow a little food, but with no great success. She was shivering violently and muttering incoherent phrases through chattering teeth, echoes of the nightmare phantasms that haunted her mind which threw poor Bonnaire into a dreadful state of agitation. Hearing her rave of the Emperor and a host of other things; conspiracy, Kuskovo, a cardinal, a masked prince, a man called Jason, the Duc de Richelieu, the King of Sweden and the war in America, the poor man began to wonder whether Beyle had not taken up with a notorious female spy. Consequently it was with profound relief that he greeted his superior's return.

'You can't think how glad I am to see you back. What's the position?'

The younger man shrugged eloquently and sighed. Then he turned to his driver.

'Did you find anything, François?'

'Not a thing, Sir, except for the child's mother. All the places round about the big house are full right up and so jam-packed that an invalid would get no peace at all. Here, at least it's quiet.'

'You've windmills in your head, my friend,' Bonnaire protested. 'The lady is burning hot. I'm sure her fever is worse than it was. We can't possibly stay here – though as to knowing where we can go—'

'Oh, as to that, there's no difficulty,' Beyle said calmly. 'We'll go back to Moscow.'

A chorus of protest greeted this apparently nonsensical suggestion, so he went on to explain. It was true, he said, that the town had been two-thirds destroyed but the fire had ceased to spread. In fact it was beginning to die out. The troops left behind by Napoleon had worked miracles in their fight against the conflagration and Beyle had been able to pick his way fairly easily through the smoking ruins until he came to the French quarter. At St Louis, he had found the Abbé Surugue, as cool as ever, saying mass before a large congregation, urging them to keep calm and blessing them energetically.

'The yard behind the church is full of refugees,' Beyle went on, 'but for the most part that district is undamaged. The engineers even managed to save the Marshals' Bridge. And now the wind has changed yet again and is driving the fire away from that part. What's more, if we go back to the city we may be able to obtain some medical help. The main hospital is still standing and I ran into that remarkable fellow Baron Larrey. Neither he nor his assistants have left Moscow since the fires began. It's true he's a good deal to keep him busy.'

'Many people burned?'

'More broken bones. You'd never think how many have thrown themselves out of windows for fear of the flames. You—' He turned to his servants. 'Do your best to load the carriage without disturbing the lady more than you can help and let's be off.'

It did not take long. They left behind some of what they had brought with them, on Beyle's assurance that there was enough food in the city to feed an army for a considerable time. Bonnaire continued to object that they ought to have some idea of where they were going to lodge but on Beyle's retorting peremptorily that the Abbé Surugue would have made arrangements for them he subsided and accompanied them willingly enough, beginning to indulge himself with the idea of a hospital bed.

Thanks to the abbé's ability to point out those houses from which the owners had departed well before the start of the fire, they found themselves a house in the neighbourhood of the old Lubianka prison. Though small, it was comfortable enough, being the property of an Italian dancing master belonging to the household of Prince Galitzine, who had gone with his master into the country, and owing to its modest appearance it had so far escaped pillage.

It was not, however, entirely unoccupied. As he stepped inside, Beyle tripped over the figure of a youngish middle-aged woman lying in a puddle of wine on the hall floor and snoring like a grampus. She was dressed in a court dress of peacock blue satin with a cloth of gold turban on her head and she was quite evidently drunk. She possessed, however, one quality of supreme importance to the young auditors: she was female and he needed a female to attend to Marianne. This one, once brought round, might well answer the purpose.

A bucket of water or two from the well in the yard and a few vigorous slaps worked wonders. It seemed probable that the woman had been there some time and had slept her fill, for she opened one large, bloodshot eye and then the other, then sat up and pushed back her elaborate headgear which by this time was soaking wet and decidedly askew. Finally, she favoured her assailant with an ogling grin.

'And what can I do for you, my lovely?' she inquired in good French, though spoken with a formidable slavonic accent.

The tone of the invitation left the young man in no doubt as to her profession. But, prostitute or not, he had no alternative. Upon interrogation, the woman revealed that her name was Barbe Kaska and she was, as she freely admitted, a member of the oldest profession in the world. She had moved into the house because the one she had been sharing with some others of her kind since their arrival in the wake of the Polish troops had burned to the ground. Her explorations of the house having begun with the cellar, she had no idea yet whether the rest of it would suit her. The cellar had been charming.

When Henri Beyle asked her if she would consent to abandon her usual occupation in order to take care of a sick lady, Barbe put on a virtuous expression and demanded: 'Is she your wife?'

'Yes,' Beyle lied, deciding there was no point in embarking on unnecessary explanations. 'She's outside, in the carriage. She – she's dreadfully ill. A high fever, delirious in fact. I don't know what to do for the best. I'll pay you well if you will help.'

Barbe's only answer was to step over the pool of wine, nonchalantly sweeping aside a broken bottle with one foot, and, picking up the dripping wet folds of peacock satin, march regally to the front door. The sight of Marianne, lying flushed and shivering, with closed eyes, drew from her murmurs of shock and sympathy.

'Jesus Christ! The poor love! What a state she's in!'

This was followed by a spate of oaths and exclamations and invocations of every saint in the Polish calendar. Then, inspired by the age-old feminine instinct that makes every woman at heart a blend of sick-nurse and sister of mercy, Barbe hurried back into the house to look for somewhere the sick woman could be put to bed, at the same time shouting that they must be careful how they lifted her from the carriage so as not to let the rug slip from round her.

Half an hour later Marianne, undressed and put into one of the dancing master's nightshirts, was lying in bed between white sheets and well protected from draughts by huge curtains of mustard-coloured rep. Barbe herself, having shed the fumes of alcohol along with her drenched blue satin, had bundled her hair up in a towel and dug up from somewhere a sort of grey overall, evidently the property of some manservant, and put it on over her wet petticoats.

In the ensuing hours Beyle was to thank heaven again and again for having put this extraordinary woman in his path. She was invaluable. In no time at all she had explored the Italian's house and discovered everything they most needed. She had a fire going in the dark, vaulted kitchen which was situated in the basement next door to the famous cellar, which also contained a variety of useful provisions such as tea, sugar, honey, flour, dried fruit, onions and preserves. Barbe went through it all and decreed that the first thing to be done for the invalid was to make her swallow a big cup of hot tea. Then, when Beyle's servants appeared at the kitchen door, she promptly got rid of them by the simple method of telling them outright that there was no room for them in such a small house and they must shift for themselves elsewhere. Only François, the driver, found favour in her eyes but the new abigail's would-be ingratiating smile was enough to send him hurrying off to join his fellows in their search for lodgings nearby. He was, as it turned out, the only one of them to continue in Beyle's service, the others having found, in addition to new quarters, a more lucrative occupation in plundering the Great Bazaar.

There was, of course, equally no place for Bonnaire in the establishment. He, in any case, was anxious to seek treatment on his own account and directed his steps hopefully towards the main hospital of the city. Beyle, meanwhile, made himself as comfortable as he could in the single living-room of the house.

But when he came to tap on the door of the room in which Barbe had for some moments past been closeted with Marianne, the sight that met his eyes had him rooted to the spot. The Polish woman was sitting on the bed with Marianne's head resting on her bosom. She had the girl's mouth open and was examining her throat by the light of a candle. Beyle sprang forward.

'Here! What do you think you're doing?'

'Trying to discover the cause of her fever. There's such a redness down there, you'd think she was on fire.'

'Well? And what do you propose to do?'

Barbe, quite unmoved by his tone, set the candle on the bedside table, laid Marianne back on her pillows, and came towards him.

'All that may be necessary,' she said simply. 'You must know, I've seen a fair bit of fighting since I've been following the army, and nursed more than one man. I've learned things. More than that, before I – came down in the world I used to be waiting woman to Princess Lubomirska and my father, God rest his soul, was apothecary on the Janowiec estate. I know what I'm about. I've seen fevers of this kind before in plenty. So just you go and rest yourself and leave me be. I daresay that great baby of a man of yours can knock you up something to eat.'

With her flaxen hair ruthlessly swept up into the towel, large, bulbous violet eyes and face not altogether unattractive, despite the massive forehead, too broad for a woman, Barbe was, in her way, a formidable figure. Her references, moreover, seemed to be excellent so that Beyle succumbed and let her have her way. He was not feeling particularly well himself and so retired without further argument, merely asking the nurse if she would be good enough to save a little tea for him if, as she had announced, she was going to make some for Marianne.

'I am feeling a trifle liverish,' he confided, with some idea of enlisting her sympathies on his own account, 'and I'm sure it would do me good.'

'It won't do you any harm, certainly, as long as you don't fill it up with cream.' Barbe gave a sigh. 'Well, well, it seems to me it was high time you found me. You're neither of you what one might call blooming. By the way, what's your name?'

'I am Monsieur de Beyle, auditor to the Council of State,' he told her, with his usual emphasis on what, in his opinion, was his impressive position.

However, it did not appear to satisfy Barbe.

'Yes, but what are you? Count, marquis, baron or what?' she asked, reeling off the list ingratiatingly.

Beyle flushed to the roots of his black hair.

'None of them,' he said, nettled. 'Although my position is at least equivalent to a title.'

'Oh.' said the Polish woman. She said no more but the shrug

with which she shut the bedroom door upon him indicated the measure of her disappointment.

Disappointed or not, Barbe the prostitute worked like a Trojan that night, shut up alone with Marianne. She fought the fever with every means in her power, making the invalid swallow cup after cup of weak tea with plenty of honey in it and a greyish powder, a supply of which she seemed to carry in a metal box in a pocket in one of her petticoats, along with her other valuables – just then consisting of a string of pearls and a few rings acquired from an abandoned house. She even went so far as to bleed Marianne, with the aid of a carefully sharpened kitchen knife, an operation that would have made Beyle shudder if he could have seen it but which she performed with a skill and confidence that any experienced apothecary might have envied.

She laboured to such good effect that by midnight or thereabouts Marianne was sleeping at last, a sleep that was no longer the unconsciousness of delirium. Her kindly physician then settled down in a large elbow chair with plenty of cushions to refresh herself with the remainder of the tea heavily laced with an old Armagnac she had found in the dancing master's cupboard, where he kept his scores and a few Italian books.

It was broad daylight when Marianne struggled slowly back to consciousness again. Finding herself lying in a strange bed, in a strange room, with a strange woman sitting beside her she thought at first that she was still dreaming.

But the room smelled of cold tea, brandy and the smoke which was still creeping in through the drawn curtains. Moreover the grey shape with the human face that lay huddled in the armchair was snoring too loudly to belong to the world of dreams. All this, and the aches and pains in her own body, convinced Marianne that she was wide awake.

She had, besides, a horrid feeling of being stuck to the bed. She must have perspired a great deal when the fever broke because the sheets and the nightshirt she was wearing were soaked with sweat.

She hoisted herself painfully into a sitting position. Even this simple action was enough to tell her that, while her body was wretchedly weak, her mind at least was quite clear again. With that, she began trying to put her thoughts in order and to work out how she came to be in this room, the details of which she could not make out clearly because the drawn curtains left it still in semi-darkness.

Memory returned swiftly enough: her flight through the blazing city, the fight with the drunken harpy in the boulevard, Beyle's carriage and the little wood beside the lake, then her stupid, irrational urge to follow the road to the sea, the way it had seemed to call her, and the child who had run into her arms and calmed that urge. After that, everything was very misty and she could not remember, only she had an impression that she had travelled a long way, tumbling into huge chasms peopled with evil shapes and grinning faces.

Her mouth felt dry and she saw a glass half-filled with water on the table by her bed. She reached out her hand to get it but there seemed to be no strength in her. She would never have believed a glass of water could be so heavy. It slipped out of her clumsy fingers and fell and broke on the floor.

Instantly the grey bundle sprang up like a jack-in-the-box.

'Who goes there! Stand and show yourself!'

'Oh, I'm so sorry! I didn't mean to wake you,' Marianne stammered, startled. 'I was thirsty – I was trying to get a drink.'

The woman's answer was to rush to the curtains and fling them wide open. Sunshine flooded into the room, lighting up the bed and the pale-faced girl, her great dark eyes made even larger by the dark rings under them. Barbe came and stood beside her, hands on hips, and studied her with a beaming smile.

'Eh, but that's better! So you've decided to come back to us, have you, little lady? By St Bronislawa, you've done the right thing! I'll go an' tell your husband this instant.'

'My husband—?'

'Why, yes, your husband. He's sleeping in the next room. You've had a nasty bout of fever but you surely can't have forgotten that you've got a husband, eh?'

If the woman had not spoken with such a strong accent, Marianne might have thought, from her appearance, that she was not unlike her old acquaintance, Mère Tambouille, but clearly this one was a Russian or something not far removed. Marianne wondered if she could also be mad. What was all this about a husband?

She had her answer when the strange creature reappeared, dragging after her Marianne's friend of the day before, still half-asleep and struggling to open his eyes. The woman must have hauled him from his bed.

'See!' she exclaimed triumphantly, pointing to the girl propped on her elbow in the bed. 'What do you say to that? Have I nursed her well or not?'

Beyle finished rubbing his eyes and smiled at her.

'Yes, indeed you have! It's like a miracle. My dear Barbe, I make you my apologies. You certainly are a remarkable woman. I suppose you wouldn't carry your goodness still further and go and make us a hot drink? Coffee, for preference, if you can find any.'

Barbe laughed, shook out her overall and crumpled petticoats flirtatiously, and pushed back the hair that was escaping from the towel and straggling about her face. Then she made for the door.

'I see how it is! You want to make a fuss of her? No need to worry about me, you know. I know all about it.'

She went out, shutting the door firmly behind her and Beyle walked over to the bed.

'Feeling better?'

'As weak as a new-born kitten but certainly better. Tell me, where are we and who is that woman?'

'A kind of fallen angel, incredible as it may seem. I shall always be grateful to Providence for having placed her in our path.'

He told her rapidly all that had happened since she had lapsed into her fever and even managed to make her laugh by describing the manner in which he had made Barbe's acquaintance.

'She asked me if you were my wife and I thought it best not to go into details.'

'You were quite right. It makes things easier. But what are we going to do now?'

He drew the chair in which Barbe had slept up to the bed and sat down.

'The first thing is to have breakfast, just like any respectably married couple. After that we'll put our heads together. This house is not too bad at any rate and I think we may as well stay here for a while. There's not a great deal left standing in Moscow that is not full of troops. You must get well again and, from what I understood you to say, you are anxious to keep out of the way of the Emperor and his suite?'

A faint flush rose to Marianne's cheeks and at the same time she felt a rush of gratitude. This man who was a total stranger to her had behaved with the delicacy and discretion of a true friend.

'That is true. And I think it's time I gave you some explanation—'.

'There's no hurry. Please. You are still so weak. And the little I have done for you does not deserve your confidence.'

She smiled at him, in gentle mockery. 'That is not how it seems to me! I owe you the truth – the whole truth. Are you not my husband? It will not take long.'

As clearly as she could, she described in her turn what had taken place in the Kremlin and why it was that she must avoid coming within Napoleon's reach until she knew what the situation was.

'If you have ever met him,' she finished, 'you must know what I mean. He will not forgive me for having assisted in the escape of a man who, to him, was a dangerous spy. What I want to do now is to find my friends as soon as possible, and then leave Moscow as discreetly as I can.'

'And go back to Italy, I suppose?' He sighed comically. 'How I understand you! And how I wish I might really pass as your husband and go with you! I love Italy more than anything. But I don't think you have any need to worry. For one thing, we have no idea what the Emperor will decide to do as a result of this disaster, and for another, you are perfectly safe here. Ah, here is breakfast at last!' The last words were uttered simultaneously with Barbe's appearance bearing a tray the size of a small table. She made her entry as majestically as a Spanish galleon sailing into harbour.

Although her throat was still very sore, Marianne managed to eat a little boiled ham floating in a sea of cabbage, which was the easiest thing in the world to come by in Russia. Cabbage was the national vegetable and vast acres of it were grown all round Moscow. Marianne was not fond of it but she made herself eat some in the belief that it would help her to get back her strength. Then Beyle went out, saying that he was going to take a look round and see how matters stood and Marianne let Barbe change her sheets and her nightshirt, both of which had become unpleasantly sweaty. As Barbe pulled the nightshirt over her head, Marianne's hand went instinctively to the little wash-leather bag she always carried round her neck, in which was the diamond drop, as though to assure herself that it was safe.

The movement did not escape Barbe and she shot a severe look at the girl, then smiled somewhat grimly.

'I lay no claims to virtue,' she said, 'but I think I am honest. Oh, yes, I picked up a few trifles in the fire, but only because it would have been a shame to leave them to burn. I wouldn't touch your relics.'

Marianne understood from this that Barbe, greatly to her credit, had not investigated the contents of the bag, evidently taking it for the kind of thing in which pious souls liked to carry a little consecrated earth or some relic they regarded as a talisman. She blamed herself the more for having unconsciously wounded her feelings.

'Please don't be offended,' she said gently. 'So much has happened in these last three days that I had forgotten all about this. I was simply making sure I had not lost it.'

With peace restored between them, Marianne drifted back into sleep again. Sleep was still the thing she needed most and she dropped off very quickly while Barbe busied herself in putting the house to rights and coming to terms with Beyle's servant.

When the young auditor returned towards the end of the afternoon, he brought a quiverful of news. First and most important was the fact that the Emperor had returned to the Kremlin at about four o'clock, after making a tour of what remained of the city. His mood had darkened as he traversed the devastated streets where houses, palaces and churches were all reduced to black and smoking ruins. But when he came to the parts that had been saved his grim mood changed to anger at the realization that these were still given over to pillage and that the scum of the city had joined with the still more or less drunken soldiery to carry off everything worth having. A rain of stern commands began to issue forth, accompanied by some harsher sentences.

'It was not the moment to go up to his Majesty and start trying to gauge his intentions towards a mutinous princess,' Beyle concluded. 'Besides, I ran into Dumas, of the Quarter-master-General's staff, and he advised me to stay where I was until he sent for me, which will be tomorrow or the next day. It seems we're going to have the devil of a job to sort out what provisions are left in the city and bring in more from outside if necessary.'

But the provisioning of the army, or even of the city, was of scant interest to Marianne. What she wanted to know more than anything else was what had become of Jolival and Gracchus and to rejoin them as soon as possible. For all Beyle's friendly care, she felt lost without them and she felt as if nothing could be done until they were all three together again. They had travelled the world together for so long now that it had become inconceivable to envisage returning to France without them. She said as much quite frankly to her supposed husband and he did his best to soothe her impatience.

'I know what you are feeling. To tell you the truth,' he added in a burst of confidence, 'when I met you in the avenue, I was searching frantically for an old friend of mine, a Frenchwoman married to a Russian, the Baronne de Barcoff. I have long cherished a great regard for her. She seems to have quite disappeared and I shall not be easy in my mind until I have found her. But I know that, short of a miracle, I shall never do so until order has been re-established. You cannot conceive of the confusion in the city, or what is left of it. You must not expect too much all at once.'

'You mean that we are lucky to have escaped with our lives from one of the greatest disasters of all time?'

'More or less, yes. We must be patient, and allow all those who have fled time to return. Only then will we be able to search for our friends with some hope of success.'

Marianne was too much a woman not to ask what seemed to her the natural question.

'This Madame de Barcoff – are you in love with her?'

He smiled a little sadly and brushed one of his small, white, carefully manicured hands across his brow, as though to drive away a cloud.

'I did love her once,' he said at last. 'So much that surely something must remain. In those days she was called Melanie Guilbert and she was – exquisite. She is married now and I love another but, even so, there is still a great bond of affection between us and I am anxious about her. She is so fragile, so helpless—'

He seemed to be very much disturbed all of a sudden and Marianne held out her hands to him impulsively. Two days before, she had not even met him, and yet now the feelings he inspired in her were so warm that they could readily be called friendship.

'You will find her – and you will see again the woman you love. What is her name?'

'Angelina. Angelina Bereyter. She is an actress.'

'She must be very beautiful. You shall tell me about her. It will help to pass the time. You told me the other day that you would like to be my friend. Would you like us to seal that friendship today – a real friendship, such as you might feel for another man?'

Beyle laughed. 'You are a deal too lovely for that, I fear! I am only a man, after all.'

'Not to me, since you love another. My heart, too, belongs to someone else. You shall be my brother. And my name is Marianne. It's as well for a husband to know his wife's name.'

His answer was to kiss the hands she gave him, one at a time, and then, perhaps in order to conceal an emotion he was ashamed to let her see, he hurried from the room, saying he would send Barbe to her.

The brief respite allowed to Beyle by the Quartermaster-General was over the next morning. A messenger was knocking on the door at the crack of dawn to tell him he was wanted. The Emperor did not mean to waste a moment in bringing Moscow back to life again.

'He's firing off orders in all directions,' the courier said. 'There's work for you.'

There was indeed. They did not set eyes on Beyle again until the evening and by then he was exhausted.

'I don't know who was fool enough to suggest that the Emperor was overcome by the amount of destruction done to this confounded city,' he said privately to Marianne. 'He's as busy as a bee. He's ridden three times round the ruins since this morning and orders are pouring out like hail. The Kremlin is to be put in a defensive state and the same with all the fortified monasteries in the vicinity. There are orders, too, to fortify all the posting houses along the road to France and institute a regular service of couriers. Orders have been dispatched to the Duc de Bassano and General Konopka in Poland to muster a force of six thousand Polish lancers – "those Polish Cossacks", as his Majesty called them – and get them here in double-quick time, since it seems that we have now run short of troops. Orders to station troops all along the way to Paris to guard our rear—'

'But you surely haven't had to do all that yourself? I thought you were concerned with food supplies.'

'I am. Men must be sent out into the country round about to bring in all the cabbages and other vegetables that have not yet been taken. There's the remainder of the hay to be got, and oats for the horses, the potatoes to be dug, the one remaining mill to be got into working order, stocks of oil and biscuit to be laid in, flour to be found from somewhere, for that is getting scarce, and lord knows what besides! At the rate he's going, he's quite capable of sending us off to get in the harvest in the Ukraine!'

'I suppose the fear that the army might run short of food is his greatest anxiety. It's natural enough.'

'Oh, if that were all,' Beyle said furiously, 'I wouldn't really mind. But in the midst of all this, he must needs think of settling his scores as well.'

'What do you mean?'

'This.' Beyle took from his pocket a large sheet of crumpled paper and spread it out on the bed where she could see it. It contained two 'wanted' notices to be displayed on walls about the city. One offered five thousand livres reward to any person giving information leading to the apprehension, dead or alive, of a certain Abbé Gauthier. This was followed by a detailed description of the wanted man. The second notice offered a further thousand livres in return for information leading to the recovery of the Princess Sant'Anna, 'one of His Majesty's personal friends, lost during the fire'. This also included a good description.

Marianne read both notices and then raised a woebegone face to his.

'He's hunting me – like a criminal!'

'No. Not like a criminal. That's just what I've got against him. Anyone at all might give you up without a qualm thanks to that word "friends", put in to deceive the unwary. If you want to know my feelings, I'd say it was – despicable.'

'It must mean that he is very angry with me, that he hates me, even! At all events, you are certainly taking a great risk, my friend, in staying with me. You ought to go away.'

'And leave you all alone? At the mercy of any inquisitive person who might give you up. I'm even beginning to wonder if I ought not to send Barbe about her – er – business.'

'She's a wonderful nurse and she seems quite devoted.'

'Yes, but she's intensely curious, which I don't care for. François caught her listening at the door of this room. What's more, she asks too many questions. Obviously she has a poor opinion of our marital relations.'

'Well, you must do as you think best. In any case, I shall see to it that I leave Moscow as soon as I have found my friend Jolival and my coachman.'

'I'll see if I can pay a visit tomorrow to the first posting house on the Paris road. Probably your friend is there. I'll bring him back with me.'

But when Beyle returned the next evening, covered with dust from his ride, he brought disturbing news. Jolival and Gracchus were nowhere to be found. They had not been seen either at the posting house or at the Rostopchin Palace, where he had also gone in search of news.

'There is one more possible answer,' he went on quickly, seeing Marianne's face crumple and her green eyes fill with tears. 'They may never have left the Kremlin. A good many people stayed there even after the Emperor had left, beginning with the troops left behind to hold the fire in check if that were possible. It's not easy to move a man with a broken leg.'

'I've thought of that. But how can we find out?'

'Tomorrow, the Assistant Quartermaster-General is going to the Kremlin to make his report to the Emperor. He has asked me to go with him. It ought not to be too difficult for me to make my own inquiries and if your friend is there I will find out.'

'You would do that for me?'

'Of course, and much more if you should ask me. For to tell you the truth I did not mean to go with Mathieu Dumas at first.'

'Why not?'

He smiled a little wistfully and indicated the coat he was wearing.

'An audience with the Emperor in my present state—'

In fact this visit to the Kremlin which gave Marianne such pleasure posed considerable sartorial problems to her friend. He had lost all his baggage, having jumped into his carriage right in the middle of his dinner in the Apraxin Palace. He had driven back to his lodgings just in time to see the house burn down and had been obliged to look on, in helpless rage, while his belongings were destroyed. His entire wardrobe now consisted only of what he stood up in: a coat of blue superfine, of an excellent cut but no longer very clean, blue kerseymere pantaloons and a white shirt decidedly the worse for wear.

'We must think of some way to make you look more presentable,' Marianne said. 'The Emperor has a great dislike of slovenliness in dress.'

'I know that well enough. He'll favour me with one of those damned disgusted stares of his.'

All the same, a couple of shirts made of a reasonably fine linen were dug up from somewhere, with the help of Beyle's driver, François, now, by reason of the defection of his fellow servants, promoted to the office of valet. The coat was made fairly presentable by dint of a careful going over, followed by some energetic brushing. This left the elegant kerseymere pantaloons, for which no replacement could be found, and they were badly snagged in several places, one more than a trifle embarrassing. For his day-to-day work in the Quartermaster-General's office, Beyle had managed to discard them in favour of a coarse pair of infantryman's breeches but there could be no question of wearing these in the Emperor's presence.

'There's not so much as a yard of the damned stuff in our stores,' he complained. 'I'll have to resign myself to appearing before the Emperor bundled up in a pair of sergeant major's breeks or else in none at all.'

From this dilemma he was rescued by Barbe who, once she heard of it, promptly saved the situation. François, moved more by a sense of duty than by any real belief in what he was doing, had already washed and dried the offending garment. Barbe now carried them off and darned them with such exquisite neatness that by the time she had done with them they were virtually a work of art and infinitely respectable.

Beyle was so delighted that, quite forgetting his earlier suspicions, he instantly invited this new guardian angel to form a permanent part of his entourage.

'I engaged you for the duration of my – er – my wife's illness,' he said, 'but I should be very happy to keep you on indefinitely, unless, that is, you have some objection to returning with me to France or feel any hankering after your former – profession.'

Barbe, her yellow hair now neatly braided up in a coronet about her head and adding to the natural dignity of her demeanour, raised one haughty eyebrow and quite literally looked the young man up and down.

'I had not looked,' she said stiffly, 'after all that I have done, for your honour to have so little delicacy as to remind me of my youthful indiscretions. At my age, I'd have you know, such a way of life loses its charm. I should be glad to quit it and take service again – in some great house.'

Now it was Beyle's turn to be vexed. His usually even complexion flushed brick red.

'Do I understand you to imply that my household is not good enough for you?'

Barbe inclined her head. 'You have it,' she said coolly. 'I have been tirewoman to Princess Lubomirska, may I remind you. I could not, for the sake of my own self-respect, undertake to serve a lady of lesser degree. My dead father would turn in his grave.'

For a moment, Marianne thought Beyle would choke.

'Ha! I suppose you think you had his blessing when you became a whore!' he yelped.

'Maybe not, 'though I always kept myself for soldiers so in that way I was serving my country. But supposing I were to go back into service for good, I could only do so with a really great lady. Now if your good lady were not merely your good lady – if she were a duchess, say, or even a princess, well, in that case, even supposing she should be homeless and without a penny to bless herself with – even wanted by the law, then I'd not refuse. Oh, by no means! Yes,' Barbe went on dreamily, 'I can see her as a princess. It would suit her down to the ground.'

Beyle and Marianne stared at one another in dismay. It was obvious where Barbe was leading. The woman knew their secret. Going about the city as she did each morning to see what she could pick up in the way of food, she must have seen the bills pasted up everywhere with their accurate descriptions of Marianne. And now, not satisfied with the thousand livres offered as a reward, she was intending to blackmail her employers.

Seeing that Beyle was too much overcome by this blow of fate to answer, Marianne took the matter into her own hands. Going right up to Barbe she looked her straight in the eyes.

'Very well,' she said icily. 'I am completely at your mercy. But, as you yourself have observed, I have no money, only—' She broke off, biting her lips as she realized that, stupidly, she had been on the point of mentioning the diamond. But that did not belong to her. It was hers only in trust and she had no right to use it even to save herself.

'Only what?' Barbe inquired innocently.

'Only the knowledge that I have done nothing to deserve that I should be hunted. But I will not argue with you. Since you have discovered who I am – the door is there! You may run to the nearest soldiers and give me up. The Emperor will be delighted to pay you the thousand livres when you tell him you have found the Princess Sant'Anna.'

She had expected the woman to sneer at her, perhaps utter some coarse words of abuse, and then make a dash for the door, but nothing of the sort occurred. Barbe certainly began to laugh but, to Marianne's immense surprise, her laughter was as candid as it was free of all malice. Then she came to Marianne and took her hand and kissed it, in the best tradition of Polish retainers.

'There,' she said, happily, 'that was all I wanted to know.'

'I don't understand you.'

'It's simple enough. If your highness will allow me to say so, I have known for a long time that you were not the wife of – this gentleman.' Barbe jerked her head in a vaguely contemptuous fashion to indicate Beyle. 'And I was hurt that you did not trust me. It seemed to me I had earned the right to be treated, not as a friend, to be sure, but at least as a loyal servant. I hope your highness will forgive me for having, to some extent, forced the truth from you, but I had to know where I stood and now I am content. I should not care to serve a person of no consequence but I'd regard it as an honour if your highness will allow me to wait on you.'

Marianne began to laugh, relieved and also a little touched, more so perhaps than she cared to admit, by this sudden, unexpected development.

'Oh, my poor Barbe,' she said with a sigh, 'I'd like above all things to keep you with me, but you know my position. I have nothing, I am hunted, threatened with imprisonment—'

'As if that mattered! The great thing is that no great lady can afford to be without an abigail, not even in prison. It is the privilege of those who serve a great house to follow their masters into misfortune. We'll begin with that and maybe the good will follow in its own time.'

'But why choose me? Why not rather go back to your own country?'

Barbe's violet eyes darkened briefly.

'To Janowiec? No, there is nothing for me there any more. No one is waiting for me or wishes to see me again. Besides, for us Poles, France does not seem so very far from home. But most of all, if your highness will allow me to say so, I've taken a fancy to you – and there's no gainsaying that!'

After that, there was nothing more to be said, and so it came about that Barbe Kaska came to occupy the place in Marianne's life left vacant by young Agathe Pinsart, much to the disappointment of Henri Beyle who had already been picturing the Polish woman ruling over his own bachelor establishment in the rue Neuve de Luxembourg. But he was not the man to give in to disappointment and nevertheless gallantly offered to pay the new abigail's wages for as long as her mistress remained in his company.

These matters of domestic economy once settled, Barbe set to with a will to assist François in turning her master out creditably. The young man departed for the Kremlin looking distinctly presentable.

Marianne's heart beat high with hope as she watched him go. All the time he was away, she could hardly sit still. While Barbe settled herself by the window with some sewing – she had undertaken to run up a chemise or two for Marianne out of a length of batiste acquired by Beyle out of the products of the sack – singing to herself one of those lugubrious Polish ballads of which she seemed to have an unending repertoire, Marianne paced up and down, hugging her arms across her chest, unable to control her excitement. The hours dragged on, keeping her suspended between hope and foreboding. At one moment, she would be sure of seeing Beyle come back bringing Gracchus and Jolival with him, the next she would be on the brink of tears, convinced that everything had gone wrong and Beyle too had been flung into prison, if not worse. She had suggested to her friend that he should try and speak to Constant who, she was sure, was still her friend.

It was late before Beyle returned. Marianne ran to meet him when she heard his footsteps on the stairs but hope was snuffed out like a candle when she saw his face. He was looking so unhappy that it could only mean bad news.

The news was certainly not good. The Vicomte de Jolival and his servant had not left the Kremlin where, on Napoleon's orders, they had been kept under guard ever since the cardinal's escape.

'They have never left the Kremlin, do you say?' Marianne demanded incredulously. 'Do you mean to tell me the Emperor left them there when he went to Petrovskoi himself? But that's dreadful! They might have been burned to death!'

'I don't think so. Plenty of people stayed there. A good half of the imperial household and all the troops detailed to try and save it from the fire. Napoleon only left in response to the united entreaties of his whole staff who felt they could not guarantee his safety, that was all.'

'Were you able to speak to them?'

'Lord, no! They're closely confined. No one is allowed to communicate with them on any pretext whatever.'

'Did you see Constant? Does anyone know where they are being held? Are they in their rooms or have they been put in prison?'

'I don't know. Even Constant, who sends you his respects, by the way, knows nothing concerning them. When he dared to mention your name to the Emperor, he was told that he had much too great a weakness for the rebellious Princess Sant'Anna, and that if you wanted to know what had become of them, you had only to give yourself up.'

There was a short silence. Then Marianne shrugged despondently.

'Then that is that. He has won. I know what I must do now.'

Instantly, Beyle was between her and the door, barring the way with outstretched arms.

'You are going to give yourself up?'

'I don't see what else I can do. They may be in danger. How do you know the Emperor isn't planning to have them tried and condemned in order to force me to go back?'

'It has not come to that yet. If their fate had been decided, Constant would have known. He would have been told, if only so that he might try and communicate with you. In any case, it will do no good for you to give yourself up. You did not let me finish what I was saying. If you want to secure the release of your friends, you must not only go yourself but also take with you the man whom you helped to escape. Only then will Napoleon forgive you.'

Marianne sat down abruptly on a chair and stared up at him with drowned eyes.

'Then what can I do, my friend? I don't know where to find my godfather even if I wanted to, which I do not. I've no idea whether he went back to St Louis-des-Français—'

'No,' Beyle told her. 'I went there after I left the Kremlin. The Abbé Surugue has not set eyes on him since the day of the fire. He doesn't even know where he might have gone to.'

'To Kuskovo, I expect, to Count Sheremetiev's house.'

'Kuskovo has been burned and our troops are encamped in what remains of it. No, Marianne, you must not look for anything in that direction. In any case, there is nothing you can do that will satisfy the Emperor and your own heart.'

'But I can't just abandon Jolival and Gracchus! The Emperor must be mad to vent his spleen on them. He is so angry with me that he is quite capable of putting them to death!'

She was crying hopelessly, the tears running down her cheeks. She had so much the look of a trapped doe that Beyle, overcome with pity, came and sat by her, putting a brotherly arm round her.

'There, there, my little one, don't cry! You are making a great to-do about nothing, you know. You've a good friend in the Kremlin, for Constant won't betray you, bless him, neither for love nor money. In his opinion, the Emperor has the whole affair out of proportion. I did not tell him where you were to be found, of course, but if there should be any danger he will send word to me at my office and then it will be time enough to consider what to do.'

'But, you don't understand! The Emperor will be obliged to do something. He can't clutter himself with prisoners on the road back to Paris.'

'And what makes you think he is going back to Paris?'

Marianne was so startled that she stopped crying and stared at her friend with disbelieving eyes.

'Isn't he?'

'Certainly not. His Majesty has decided to winter here. Count Dumas and your humble servant have precise instructions concerning the victualling of the army. General Durosnel has his for the movement of troops and Marshal Mortier is settling into his role as governor. Even the company of actors who were here when we came are to hold themselves in readiness to perform, as a means of maintaining French morale.'

'But he can't! Spend the winter here? I'd like to know what his Majesty's staff think of it.'

'Nothing good. I never saw so many long faces. None of them have ever wintered out of France except during the Polish campaign. According to what I've been told, the Emperor has two opposite ideas in mind. Either Alexander will agree to discuss terms and we'll think about going home as soon as the peace treaty is signed, or else we'll spend the winter here, bring the army up to strength with the reinforcements that have been sent for and then, in the spring, we march on Petersburg.'

'What? Another campaign – after the disasters of this one?'

'It may not happen. An envoy has been sent to the Tsar. He is carrying a letter from General Tutolmin, the director of the Foundling Hospital, witnessing that the French did their utmost to save Moscow, and another from the Emperor to the Tsar, assuring him of his goodwill and brotherly feelings.'

'Brotherly feelings! But this is absurd! It cannot work!'

'That is Caulaincourt's opinion and he knows Alexander. But the Emperor thinks he's being unduly pessimistic and won't speak to him. The fact is that Murat is still flirting with Platov's Cossacks and doing his best to persuade Napoleon that the Tsar will be only too happy to fall into his arms. Oh, it's a bad business altogether! I don't know what the outcome of it all will be, but I do know one thing – I've no hope of seeing Milan this year!'

That night, Marianne could not sleep. She lay searching feverishly for some way of reaching her friends but, short of finding the cardinal and giving herself up, there was none. There could be no thought of entering the Kremlin unofficially. The old fortress had been placed on a war footing. Regiments of the Old Guard, under the command of Generals Michel, Gros and

Tindal, were on duty night and day, with a hundred men at each of the five gates still in use, while the remaining four were stoutly barricaded and watched by a sergeant and eight men. Entry into that stronghold, bristling with arms, was out of the question. She must wait, then, but for how long? Until when? If Napoleon was determined to spend the winter in Moscow, that might mean six months locked up in the house. It was enough to drive her mad.

True, there was also Constant's theory, as reported by Beyle, that they should allow time for the Emperor's anger to calm down and then he, Constant, would undertake gently to plead the rebels' cause. But Marianne put little faith in this. Napoleon's rage might be short-lived, but he was more than capable of bearing a grudge.

The days that followed were gloomy ones for Marianne, in spite of the lovely weather prevailing out of doors. She gazed out at it despairingly, killing time by sharing Barbe's sewing, but she lived entirely for the hour when her companion in misfortune would come home, bringing with him the day's news.

For the most part, it was dismally monotonous. Nothing had come from St Petersburg and preparations were still going ahead for going into winter quarters. The Emperor was delighted with his courier service, which was working wonderfully, thanks to the brilliant organization of the director of Posts, the Comte de la Valette. The mail arrived every day, with the regularity of clockwork, after a journey of fifteen days and fourteen hours. It had reached the point where the Emperor grew anxious and displayed a degree of tetchiness if one of the couriers was an hour after his time. This apart, he was in high good humour, amusing himself frequently at the expense of the wretched Caulaincourt and his dire pictures of the Russian winter, and for ever remarking that, in autumn at any rate, it was finer than at Fontainebleau.

This imperial jollity found no echo in Marianne, nor indeed in Beyle, who was spending exhausting days inventorying the victuals which were still coming to light in the cellars of the ruined houses.

Beyle, too, was depressed. He had met a man in Moscow, one

Auguste Fecel, a harpist by profession, from whom he had at last been able to get news of his old flame, Melanie de Barcoff. What he heard had distressed him greatly. According to the harpist, the lady had left Moscow for St Petersburg some days before the fire, among the last fugitives to leave the city, and against the wishes of her husband, with whom she was on the point of separating, although about to bear his child. She was, moreover, wholly without money.

This unhappy tale sent the young man into something of a frenzy. He was trying desperately to find some way of reaching his former mistress and taking her back to France with him. He talked about her endlessly to Marianne, for comfort, praising her virtues so incessantly that Marianne found herself beginning to take the unknown Melanie in strong dislike. She grew almost as sick of his present mistress, Angelina Bereyter, although what Beyle had to say about her was more concerned with her charms than her virtues, which seemed to be non-existent. Poor Beyle seemed to have an incorrigible predilection for impossible women.

Only his sister, Pauline, won Marianne's approval. When he was not writing interminable letters to her – to be sent by the postal service the Emperor had been in such haste to re-establish – he was talking about her with an affection that touched Marianne because it was completely unselfconscious. Moreover, he would discuss her in French whereas, whenever he mentioned either of his two loves, he felt obliged to dot his conversation with snatches of English or Italian, a trick which Marianne soon found maddening.

It was only with Barbe that she felt able to relax at all. The Polish woman was comfortingly stolid and tranquil, while the plaintive songs she was in the way of singing as she worked seemed to Marianne to form an agreeable echo of her own melancholy mood. There was one she liked particularly:

Pace gently ere you leave these fields of ours,
My own bay steed, you will not come again,
Your hooves are treading our plains for the last time.

The mere mention of a steed was enough to set her pulses

trembling. Oh, to be able to mount a horse and gallop away into the distance until the trees of France came into sight again! She had begun to hate the vastness of Russia. It had closed on her like a fist. She was stifling in the cramped house, with its wood-panelled walls and the ceiling pressing down on her, and in the daily round of life that went on inside it. Soon, she knew, the snow would begin to fall and bury them, herself and Beyle and all the others who were bound in that place by the will of one man only. The will to leave was becoming a palpable thing in all of them – all save Napoleon, who continued to believe that all was well.

By the end of September, however, the news was not so good. Some of the couriers were seriously delayed and one actually failed to arrive at all. Worse still, a convoy of artillery wagons coming from Smolensk with an escort of two squadrons of cavalry was ambushed, only twenty versts from Moscow, by a band of Cossacks and the escort taken prisoner. Two days after that, eight Dragoons of the Guard were taken at Prince Galitzine's estate of Malo Wiasma. But Napoleon continued to review his Guard on the parade ground at the Kremlin, every day precisely at twelve noon.

Beyle grew increasingly depressed as the news continued to come in and, although he did his best, his jokes became fewer and fewer.

'We've enough to feed the army for six months,' he told Marianne, 'but I find these new tactics of the Russians very alarming. How much longer will we be able to keep our line of retreat open? They say there are bands of armed peasants roaming the countryside around Moscow. The Cossacks, too, seem to be getting bolder. If the Emperor continues to be obstinate we shall soon find ourselves cut off, with our communications cut, at the mercy of the Russian army, which is presumably refitting somewhere, since Alexander has not deigned to give a sign of life.'

'But can't anyone make the Emperor see sense?'

'Berthier and Davout have both tried but Napoleon promptly began working out a plan to march on St Petersburg at once, so that they climbed down smartly. As for Caulaincourt, he no longer dares to open his mouth. The rest go to the theatre. A stage has been fitted up in the Pozniakoff Palace and Madame Bursay's company are performing *Le jeu de l'amour et du Hasard* and *L'Amant auteur et valet* – when everyone is not listening to an effeminate fellow called Tarquinio warbling love songs! Really, I can't believe that any army ever committed suicide with a lighter heart.'

Early in October, Beyle fell ill of a bilious fever. Marianne was obliged to nurse him and found herself very soon out of patience with her patient. Like a great many men, he was a horrid invalid, moaning and grumbling, pleased with nothing, least of all his food. He lay in bed, looking as yellow as a quince and never opening his mouth except to complain, either of their treatment of him or his own intolerable sufferings. For in addition to the trouble with his liver, he was also a martyr to toothache. Marianne sat by him, finding it harder and harder to control the urge to dot him over the head with one of the innumerable pots of herb tea that Barbe concocted for him. Beyle's illness tried her hard, for in spite of his temporary absence from duty, news continued to arrive from the Kremlin, brought by the kindly Bonnaire, who was now recovered and came every evening to keep his colleague up to date with events.

In this way, they learned that the couriers were having more trouble than ever in getting through, and that Prince Schwarzenberg, in East Prussia, was complaining that his position was already awkward and threatening to become worse. The Prince of Neufchatel had tried once again to persuade Napoleon to leave Moscow and fall back towards Poland in order to avoid being cut off from his army. He had earned himself an acid rejoinder.

'You want to go to Grosbois, do you, to see the Visconti?'

When he heard that, the invalid was beside himself with fury.

'Mad! He's run mad! He'll get us all killed! It only needs Marshal Victor, Oudinot and Gouvion-Saint-Cyr to suffer a reverse on the Dvina and we are trapped without a hope of getting out alive. The Russians are getting bolder every day.'

The situation in Moscow certainly seemed to be deteriorating.

Count Daru, the Minister in charge of Supplies, came one evening to call on his young relative – obliging Marianne to make herself scarce – and made no secret of his fears.

'The Russians have got to the stage of picking off men and horses foraging for food in the outskirts of the city itself. We have to give them massive escorts. The mails are getting worse every day. Half the couriers never arrive.'

Every night there seemed to be another piece of bad news to listen to, another stone added to the burden that lay on Marianne's heart. She was almost physically aware of the trap that was closing on her and those with her, so that when, one morning, she saw the Emperor himself ride past beneath her window, it was all she could do not to fling herself at this feet, crying to him to go and leave his insane obstinacy before he condemned them all to a lingering death from fear and the endless northern night that would soon descend. But he seemed to be wholly indifferent to his surroundings. He rode on calmly on Turcoman, one of his favourite mounts, one hand thrust into his waistcoat, smiling at the unusual autumnal sunshine that seemed to follow him and justify him in his stubborn determination.

'We'll never get out of here,' Marianne thought desperately. And now her sleep began to be troubled by nightmares.

On the twelfth of October, however, a somewhat better piece of news arrived. It took the form of a letter, addressed to Beyle from the Quartermaster's office and brought by the indefatigable Bonnaire.

Beyle read it and then handed the unfolded sheet to Marianne.

'Here, this concerns you.'

The letter was unsigned but there was no doubt who it came from. It was from Constant.

'There is now thought to be no hope of recovering the vanished lady,' he wrote. 'Consequently, certain persons are no longer useful. They were instructed to join the train of wounded leaving Moscow the day before yesterday, under the command of General Nansouty, although they will not be released until they reach France.'

Marianne screwed the letter into a ball and dropped it into the brick stove which took up a good half of the end wall of the room. Then she came back to where Beyle lay in bed, clasping her hands tightly together to keep them from trembling with excitement.

'Then my mind, too, is made up,' she said. 'There is no need for me to be a burden to you any longer, my friend, or to go on staying here. My friends have left and I must go too. With good horses, I should be able to catch them up. No convoy can travel fast if there are wounded.'

The sick man uttered a croak of laughter that ended in a fit of nervous coughing and a whole series of moans. He wiped his lips with his handkerchief and lay with his chin in his hands for a moment before he explained.

'Without a signed order from the Kremlin it is absolutely impossible to obtain so much as a donkey. The army has barely enough for its own needs, not counting remounts. Moreover, such animals as we have got are virtually on their last legs, however much we nurse them. And you need not tell me we have only to steal a pair because that, too, is impossible – unless you're tired of life!'

'Very well. Then I'll walk, but I'm going to leave somehow.'

'Don't talk such rubbish. It makes you sound like an idiot. You are quite mad! Walk, indeed! Six or seven hundred leagues on foot! Why not on your hands while you're about it? Besides, what would you eat? The convoys and the couriers have to take their own food with them at least as far as Smolensk because, thanks to our friends the Russians' pleasant little habit of burning everything behind them, there's not so much as a cabbage stalk to be found. Lastly,' he reminded her, 'the news from outside is alarming. Bands of furious peasants are attacking small groups of travellers. Alone, you would be in danger.'

He was really angry and had quite forgotten his own physical discomforts, but his anger dropped before Marianne's desperate face.

'But what can I do?' she stammered, almost in tears. 'I want to go so much! I'd give ten years of my life to go home!'

'So would I! Now, listen to me, and above all don't cry. When you cry it makes me stupid and feverish again. There may be some hope – if you will only be a little patient.'

'I will be patient, only tell me quickly.'

'Well then, Bonnaire brought me some news as well as this letter. Our situation is becoming worse every day and the Emperor is beginning to realize it. He has heard rumours that the Russians, far from being exhausted as the King of Naples persists in claiming they are, are concentrating not far away in considerable strength. Now, we are in no condition to face an all-out attack, not even if the regiments that have been sent for should arrive in time. Unless I'm very much mistaken, we'll be leaving here before very much longer.'

'You think so?'

'I'd swear to it. What's more, ill or not, I'm going out to get the news tomorrow. Bonnaire is a good fellow but his understanding is not great. I'll find out in the office what's really happening.'

'But you are not well yet, your fever—'

'Is a good deal better. And it's high time I did something a little heroic. I've been pampering myself. And it's time you stopped lamenting, too. You have to stand up to life, by God! Else it will get the better of you.'

'Stand up to life?' Marianne echoed thoughtfully. 'Oh, my poor friend, I seem to have been doing nothing else for years. Life has treated me like a coconut palm. It's given me plenty of nuts – only it's dropped them all right on my head.'

'Because you were standing in the wrong place. You were born to be happy. If you can't be, it's entirely your own fault. Go and rest now. Something tells me you won't have to frowst indoors much longer.'

It almost seemed to Marianne afterwards that her friend must possess the gift of second sight because the very next day he came home with amazing news.

'We're off in three days' time,' he told her simply.

'In three days?' Marianne cried, feeling all at once as if the heavens had opened. 'But how?'

He bowed extravagantly, like an actor in a play. 'You see before you, fair lady, that most important person, the director of Reserve Supplies. General Dumas has just told me of my new appointment. The mission that goes with it is, unfortunately, no very simple one. I am to assemble supplies of food sufficient for two hundred thousand men in the three regions of Smolensk, Mohilev and Vitebsk. The Emperor is beginning to think of leaving Moscow and wintering in Smolensk or Vitebsk, it seems, so as to be nearer to the army on the Dvina. He can wait there in comfort until his reinforcements arrive and then march on Petersburg in the spring.'

'But when?'

'I don't know that. As far as I can make out, before settling down in winter quarters, his Majesty has some idea of going and chivvying old Kutuzov a bit, just to keep him quiet – and to check the truth of what Murat has to say about the Cossacks. But that need not concern us. The important thing is that we leave in three days' time for Smolensk and I must ask you to let me have the use of this room because I am expecting several secretaries. I've got any number of letters to dictate. Somehow, I've got to get together something like a hundred thousand quintals of flour, oats and beef cattle – and I've not the faintest notion where I'm going to find them.'

Marianne was already rising to leave the room, when he stopped her.

'By the way, should you have any objection to dressing as a man? You could pass as my secretary.'

'None at all. I used to love doing so – once upon a time.'

'Splendid! Good night.'

That night, Beyle's voice droned on endlessly in the next room, dictating a host of letters to three weary secretaries whom he had to nudge awake from time to time. Marianne fell asleep at last and slept the tranquil sleep that came with a heart at ease and a mind freed from all her most pressing anxieties. She was not out of the wood yet but she was beginning to relax a little. All her fears and torments had crystallized into that one, obsessive longing to leave Moscow.

There would be time to think of other things when the road to freedom lay open before her. Only, she had to find Gracchus and Jolival as soon as possible, because she had to face the fact that, even when she reached the end of the journey, Paris was likely to prove as dangerous for her as Moscow as soon as the Emperor returned – the Emperor who was now her implacable enemy.

But even that disturbing thought must wait until another day.

Chapter Eight

The Merchant of Smolensk

They left Moscow on the sixteenth of October, in weather that, while still dry, was beginning to turn cold. The exceptionally mild autumn which had lulled Napoleon into a sense of false security for so long was reverting to more normal temperatures.

As she followed Beyle into the carriage, which had been made more comfortable and weatherproof by the addition of leather aprons, Marianne paid tribute to her friend's talent for organization. Nothing had been left out, from the luncheon basket to extra supplies of warm clothing.

She herself, now dressed as a man and entered into her new career as secretary to the director of Reserve Supplies, had been thoughtfully provided by him with a full, dark green polonaise with silken frogs which reminded her a little of one she had worn in Paris, only that it was much bigger all round. It was trimmed and lined with grey fox and with it went a hat of the same fur, worn crammed down low over her ears to hide the hair which Barbe had plaited tightly round her head.

Barbe was up on the box beside François. She was bundled up in several layers of shawls and wore a thick scarf tied under her chin. Between them they had collected far too many rugs for the mere hundred leagues or so from Moscow to Smolensk but if Beyle's journey officially ended there, it was only a stage in Marianne's. For the auditor of the Council of State believed, with some reason, that in Smolensk he would be sufficiently his own master to be able to arrange for her to travel on quite comfortably to France.

If Marianne had expected that first stage to be accomplished very swiftly, she was singularly disappointed, and that even before they left Moscow. Instead of taking the most direct way over the Marshals' Bridge and through the ruins of the suburb of

Dorogomilov to join the Smolensk road, the carriage turned in the direction of Red Square and took its place in the long convoy that was getting ready to leave: several hundred sick and wounded men and an escort of three hundred more.

Beyle shrugged as he saw Marianne's eyes turn to him questioningly and he said gruffly: 'You were so happy to be going. I didn't want to spoil your pleasure by telling you General Dumas had ordered me to travel with the convoy. The roads are so unsafe that, travelling alone in a European carriage, neither it nor we would probably have got there at all.'

'All the same, I wish you had told me straight out. You'd have done better not to hide it. I learned long ago, you know, not to fight against the inevitable. It's true the journey will take longer but nothing can spoil my happiness in leaving this city!'

All the same, she could not help a shudder of retrospective fear as she saw the Kremlin walls again. The old fortress was still standing amid the ruins that lay all about it, looking redder than ever in the rising sun, as though its very bricks were sweating blood. Marianne felt the bitterness swelling in her again as she recalled how eager she had been to get inside and see Napoleon. Because he had been her lover and she still felt affection and loyalty towards him, she had sacrificed everything, her love and almost her life, for his sake. And her reward had been a nasty bill pasted up on all the walls of Moscow.

'Don't lean out,' Beyle warned her suddenly. 'You could still be recognized, in spite of all our precautions.'

This was true. There were a number of brilliant uniforms to be seen here and there among the incredible collection of spring carts and private carriages that made up the convoy. Eugène de Beauharnais popped up without warning only a few yards away from them. With characteristic kindness, the Viceroy of Italy was personally seeing an old soldier, bundled in blankets and with a face as grey as his beard, put into his wagon.

Marianne sat back hurriedly, making sure the spectacles which Beyle had advised her to wear until they had put several versts between themselves and the Kremlin were firmly settled on her nose. She was praying that they might start soon, for she had just caught sight of Duroc, also going the rounds of the wagons dealing out encouragements and good wishes for the journey. Her heart was beating wildly and to calm it she tried to interest herself in what she could see from underneath the hood. High above them, on the gilded dome of the largest of the Kremlin towers, sappers of the guard were perched on makeshift scaffolding, engaged, at some risk to their lives, in taking down the great gold cross of St Ivan. A flock of blackbirds, crows or rooks, wheeled thickly round them, squawking so dismally that Marianne shivered, seeing an evil omen in their sinister cries.

She touched her companion lightly on the arm. 'Why are they doing that?' she asked.

'Oh, on his Majesty's orders. It's his idea that the great golden cross will make a handsome ornament for the dome of the Invalides.[1] As a prize of war, it will remind old soldiers of the miseries they endured and of the laurels they won on the banks of the Moskva.'

'I should have said they'd have been better allowed to forget them,' Marianne murmured. Then, remembering what Constant had said to her, she added: 'Their laurels are crowns of fire and when they are burned out nothing will be left but a little grey ash.'

The convoy moved off at last, to the accompaniment of cries of goodwill from those left behind. Men ran along on either side of the line of vehicles, waving hats and arms and shouting out: 'Goodbye! We'll be catching you up soon!' and 'Watch out for the Cossacks!' They all sounded cheerful enough.

'Is it known how soon the Emperor means to leave Moscow?' Marianne asked.

'Very soon. In two or three days. He intends to march on Kuluga first.'

By this time the carriage had crossed the bridge and Beyle leaned out and looked back across the Moskva. He stayed hanging out of the door for so long that Marianne inquired whether he had forgotten something, or was really so sorry to be leaving Moscow.

'Neither,' he told her. 'I simply wanted to have one last look

[1] In fact it disappeared during the retreat from Moscow, possibly sunk in the Beresina.

to take away with me. Because that is a sight I shall never see again, even if I come back ten times over. The Emperor has determined that when he quits Moscow, the Kremlin is to be blown up. I suppose it's one way to be revenged.'

Marianne said nothing. The behaviour of men in general and of Napoleon in particular was becoming increasingly alien and incomprehensible to her. Hadn't he told her that he was not a man to leave ruins behind him? Apparently he had changed his mind again. Those changes of mind were happening more and more often, and with less and less reason. But after all, who could say what his feelings towards herself might be when, if God willed it so, they met again in Paris?

The journey dragged on for eighteen long days and very rapidly became a nightmare. The weather turned wet and freezing cold and this had its effect on the tempers of the sick men. All day long it was nothing but quarrelling, cursing and abuse, flying back and forth between the wagons which were continually having to be manhandled out of ruts or across streams, with or without fords, where the bridges had been broken down. Each time it meant another three or even four hours' wasted time.

A little way short of Mojaisk, they passed a camp of Russian prisoners. Hideous yells came from it, with a stench of rotting cabbage and other decaying matter. Marianne was appalled and shut her eyes tightly so as not to see the bearded, demoniacal faces pressed to the fence, pouring out a stream of filth which she, mercifully, could not understand but which had Barbe crossing herself almost continuously.

At Mojaisk itself, where the Westphalian troops of the Eighth Corps, under the Duke of Abrantes, were encamped, they found the main ambulance unit and took on a fresh batch of wounded, many of them with amputated limbs. Junot had succeeded in getting together a number of vehicles, peasant carts for the most part, but they were not nearly enough and the wagons that had come from Moscow were more crowded even than before. The sky was grey and the men's spirits no brighter.

The crossing of the battlefield of Borodino and its village was another ordeal. Even Beyle's habitual pose of elegant, slightly cynical scepticism deserted him at the sight that met the travellers' eyes and he sat staring speechlessly. For all the dead of that great battle were still lying where they fell. No effort had been made to bury them. The field was thick with them. Only the frost, covering them with a thin coat of rime, had arrested the processes of decomposition sufficiently to make them still recognizable. Everywhere lay the bodies of horses, half-eaten by dogs and carrion birds, and all round them the remains of drums, helmets, breastplates and weapons, while the fat, black crows were all about. In spite of the cold, the smell was abominable.

But while Marianne, half-fainting, muttered prayers under her breath and Beyle, stiff with revulsion, held a pouch of tobacco to his nose, the wounded with the convoy seemed to revive at the sight. They forgot their troubles, their disputes and bad tempers and pointed out to one another with pride the places where they had fought, recalling great feats of arms and acts of heroism and the fierce scent of victory. Some were pointing out the cottage that had served as General Kutuzov's headquarters, others gazing at the celebrated redoubt which brooded over the tragic landscape like some Aztec temple.

'They must be mad,' Marianne murmured incredulously. 'It's not possible! They must be mad!'

A great roar of laughter answered her.

'No, lad! They're not mad. But what can a green youth like you know of soldiers? All of us here have toiled and suffered on this field. It's true that there are plenty of our own good fellows lying there, but there are many more Russians. It was a great day and a great victory, and it made Ney a prince!'

The man who had spoken was one of the two occupants of the carriage ahead of theirs. He was a big, splendidly bewhiskered fellow, with a general officer's greatcoat slung negligently over an empty sleeve. The legion of honour glowed on his breast and a long scar, still not quite healed, ran down one cheek and vanished under his high, braided collar. He was eyeing Marianne as if he could cheerfully have hacked her in pieces there and then. Beyle deemed it prudent to come to her rescue.

'Come now, General,' he said laughing. 'Don't be too hard on my young secretary here! He's Italian and his French is not good. Besides, he's only seventeen.'

'I was already a subaltern at his age! The boy should be capable of sitting a horse and handling a sabre, for all his girlish features and those great staring eyes of his. I'll remind you of what poor Lassalle said, that a hussar who's not dead at thirty isn't worth his salt!'

'That's as may be. Anyone who gave this lad a sabre would be taking a lot on himself. He's as blind as a bat! Put on your spectacles, Fabrice,' he added in Italian. 'You know you can't see a thing without them.'

Angry and annoyed, Marianne obeyed. She found herself hating the arrogant officer who was watching her with such open contempt. Indeed, it cost her a considerable effort to refrain from telling him just what she thought of him and his like. To them, a battlefield even one covered with dead men, was, if not precisely paradise at least a very special place. It was the gigantic board on which they played out their favourite game, the heady sport of war. They did not care if they left various portions of their anatomy on the field, what mattered to them was the game itself, its frenzy, its intoxication and its dreadful glory. And to the devil with the cost!

When the convoy moved on again and the general had got back into his own vehicle, Marianne tore off the spectacles, which were making her nose sore, and vented her rage on her companion.

'Who is that bloodthirsty imbecile? Do you know him?'

'Yes, of course. He is General the Baron Pierre Mourier, commanding the 9th brigade of cavalry of the 3rd Corps, which is Ney's own. He was wounded on this very field. Nor, let me add, is he in the least imbecile. He merely said what any experienced soldier would have said at the sight of a good-looking young man with nothing apparently wrong with him and all his limbs intact, sitting comfortably in a well-sprung carriage.'

'Oh. Well, you need not go on about it. It was not my idea to dress as a man.'

'No, it was mine. It was the only way you would be acceptable in a military convoy.'

'What about Barbe, then?'

'She is my servant. I said she was my cook. Come now, Marianne, try to keep your spirits up in spite of everything. You are likely to encounter many more incidents of the same kind. It is simply one of the necessary evils of your disguise. Be patient. And you may tell yourself, if it's any comfort to you, that the general thinks much the same of me. He doesn't think much of an auditor of the Council of State, especially one my age. He'd call me a shirker. Just keep your mind on playing your part properly and we'll be all right.'

Marianne glared at him but he had already ceased to pay much attention to her. He had taken a small book, elegantly bound in brown calf from his pocket and plunged into it with such evident enjoyment that Marianne could not resist the urge to disturb him a little.

'What are you reading?' she asked.

'Madame du Deffand's letters,' he said, without taking his eyes from the page. 'She was blind but so intelligent! Far too intelligent ever to interrupt someone else's concentration.'

There was no mistaking his meaning and Marianne subsided indignantly rather than engage in further argument. She flung herself back sulkily into her corner and did her best to sleep.

Progressing at the rate of three or four leagues a day, the journey became depressingly monotonous. The cold set in so bitterly that Beyle and Marianne formed the habit of walking a little way each day to stretch their legs and to ease the horses. The road was broad and quite good, winding in a serpentine fashion through thick forests of dark firs and pale birches. It was all up and down and in the early stages some of the more heavily laden wagons had to be pushed very often. In all this time, they did not see a living soul. Such villages as they came across were deserted and more than half ruined.

They bivouacked at night round huge fires, for which there was never any shortage of wood, and slept as well as they could wrapped in blankets which, by morning, had turned into crackling, icy shells.

At each of these halts, Marianne did her best to keep as far from General Mourier as possible. It was not that he was openly unpleasant, but he seemed to take a mischievous pleasure in teasing the supposed secretary, subjecting him to a spate of humorous pleasantries of a military kind and so broad that for all her self-control Marianne could not help blushing to the roots of her hair, to the great delight of her tormentor. Beyle, meanwhile, was obliged to resort to the most devious methods to enable her to escape by herself from time to time to satisfy the needs of nature. Moreover, however often he repeated that Fabrice, as he called him, did not understand much French, Mourier would still persist in trying to acquaint him with the finer points of military slang, assuring him that this was an excellent way to learn. Having served in Italy, Mourier had some rudiments of Italian, which he could use with fiendish cunning.

One thing that particularly exercised his wit was the fact that Fabrice was never seen to remove his hat. The fur cap had remained firmly pulled down over his ears ever since leaving Moscow, and the general's witticisms rained down on the unfortunate headgear. If he was not hinting that the wretched Fabrice, besides his lack of physical endowments and courage, was also as bald as a coot, he was promising him a fine crop of lice as a result unless he took it off. Poor Marianne could only wish with all her heart that she had listened to Beyle's advice and had her hair cut short before she set out. She had not been able to bring herself to do it, and in this she had been upheld by Barbe's loud indignation at the very idea of parting with her crowning glory. Now she could only suffer in silence, for the sacrifice was no longer possible.

They were almost halfway to Smolensk when the first attack came. It was the evening of the twenty-fourth of October, the cooking fires had been lighted and the meagre daily ration of bacon and dried peas, for food was growing scarce, was stewing over them. The convoy had become a single, great encampment in a clearing in the forest, where the men huddled together, quarrels and bad temper forgotten, seeking only a little warmth and human comfort from one another. The camp was a little patch of France set down in the vast immensity of Russia and the men clung together for company. They had gained a few more leagues that day. It would not be long now before they were safe again behind the thick walls of Smolensk, where supplies of food were pouring in daily – or so Beyle hoped.

Then grey figures loomed up, without warning, under the trees. Simultaneously, there was a crackle of gunfire. A man dropped, headlong, just beside Marianne and was dragged back hastily before his hair caught fire, but he was already dead. She was staring down at him in horrified fascination when she heard General Mourier's voice bellowing: 'To arms! We are attacked! Each man take his weapon and fire at will—'

'Who is it?' Beyle asked, peering into the half-light. 'The Cossacks?'

'No. Cossacks would have rushed up before now. These are on foot – and I've an idea there are peasants among them. I'm almost sure I saw the gleam of a pitchfork.'

With amazing speed, he succeeded in putting the camp in a posture of defence, running up and down the line, bent almost double, handing out ammunition and making sure that everyone had as much cover as possible, especially those of the wounded who could not move from where they lay. He had used his rank to take command automatically, the officer nominally in charge of the convoy being no more than a colonel, and Dutch to boot.

'Try to hold your fire unless you're sure of a hit,' he counselled them. 'Better not waste your powder. We're not at Smolensk yet.'

'If we ever get there at all.' Beyle muttered, drawing a long pistol from one of his valises. 'If the Russians attack in force, we'll never hold them.'

'Don't be so defeatist,' Marianne retorted sharply. 'You must have known we were likely to meet some of them. Or have you forgotten what you were always saying in Moscow, that we were practically surrounded?'

He mumbled something indistinct in answer and then devoted himself earnestly to the business of loading his pistol. Everything was very quiet now but Marianne, crouching behind the carriage and peering out into the gathering dusk, was able to make out stealthy figures creeping nearer. The grey-clad Russians melted into the twilight and it was not easy to distinguish them from the trees they were using as cover. They advanced in short dashes from one trunk to the next but the girl's sharp eyes soon learned to pick them out. All at once, without quite knowing why, she found herself eager to take part in the deadly game.

In the old days, when she was growing up at Selton, Dobs had seen to it that his 'tomboy pupil', as he called her, had acquired a pretty skill with firearms as well as with the foils. Consequently, when Mourier came back to take up a position behind his own carriage, she spoke to him outright, but still remembering to do it in Italian.

'Give me a pistol!'

He did not understand at first and said something coarse in answer. Then Beyle intervened.

'The boy is asking you for a weapon, a pistol,' he translated coldly, but the general only gave a shout of laughter.

'A pistol? What for? Those dainty hands of his could never hold it steady. Oh, no, my friend, just you tell your young fire-eater that guns are for men. This is no time to be playing games. I don't know what the Russians are waiting for, but it won't be long now. I think they're coming. When they're close enough, every shot must go home.'

Some odd impulse of bravado made Beyle hand his own weapon to Marianne.

'Here you are, then,' he said, shrugging. 'It can't make a difference anyhow – we'll all die in the end.'

She took the gun without a word and studied it briefly. It was a duelling pistol and a magnificent piece of work.

'It's loaded,' Beyle said. Lowering his voice, he whispered a little anxiously: 'Are you sure you know how to use it? I don't want to make a fool of myself.'

Marianne's only answer was to draw herself up a little. As confidently as any experienced duellist, she laid the barrel on her forearm, took aim at one of the grey figures and fired. The grey shape dropped among the fallen leaves. The second shot followed almost instantaneously, with the same result.

There was a silence while Marianne returned the weapon coolly to its owner, conscious of the respect mingled with the startled amusement in his eyes.

'Good God! I'll think twice before I send my friends to wait upon you, my dear Fabrice.'

Marianne was turning away with a smile when another weapon was thrust at her. The hand that held it ended in a braided sleeve and the general's voice, sounding oddly hoarse, muttered in her ear: 'I apologize. I think I have been much mistaken in you.'

Then, before Marianne could stop him, he had expressed his contrition by grasping her impulsively by the shoulders and kissing her soundly on both cheeks. Marianne was conscious first of a strong smell of tobacco and then that his sudden action had been the ruin of her disguise. Under Mourier's brusque assault, the fur hat had tilted wildly and then falled to the ground, revealing the plait of long hair wound about her head.

For an instant, Marianne and the general stared at one another, still half-kneeling on the muddy ground. She saw his eyes widen in amazement as they took in the head before him, but only for a moment, for he made a swift recovery. Quickly scooping up the hat, he placed it on her head again, as carefully as Barbe could have done, then glanced hurriedly round them, but every man was at his post and watching the wood beyond the camp.

'No one saw you,' he said softly. 'And no one shall know. Oh, you, translate, can't you?' he added impatiently, speaking to Beyle who was still too stunned by what had happened to open his mouth. Marianne laughed.

'It's not necessary now that you know my secret. You have found out so much that I may as well tell you the whole. I do speak French.'

She broke off then because a volley of musket fire rang out from the other side of the camp. Absorbed by the general's discovery, she had temporarily forgotten the danger they were in. Fortunately the Russians, shocked by the sudden death of two of their number, seemed to have halted their advance. Possibly they meant to withdraw now that they had lost the advantage of surprise.

All the same, as he knelt down at his post again, next to Marianne, Mourier could not help demanding, in an agonized whisper that made Marianne's lips twitch: 'Did you really understand all the time?'

For a moment, her better nature prompted her to say no, but the idea of that small vengeance at least was too seductive. She let her face break into a sudden, dazzling smile which completely rolled him up.

'Oh, everything,' she assured him. 'It was most amusing.'

The Russians attacked just then and saved Mourier from the necessity of a reply. For a few seconds, the sound of musket fire dominated everything. Then, almost as suddenly, it died away. The engagement had been short-lived, probably owing to the energetic defence put up by the convoy, unless, as Beyle suggested, the Russians had found their numbers insufficient. Mourier, however, was still uneasy. He did not like this sudden withdrawal, or the young auditor's hypothesis. When the last of the moving figures had vanished into the undergrowth, he got up and slipped off his greatcoat and his hat.

'I'm going to have a look round. We had better know what we're in for tomorrow. Tell the colonel in command of the escort. I'll be back in a moment.'

'Take care,' Marianne whispered. 'If anything were to happen to you, I think we should all panic. You are the only one able to keep order amongst us.'

'Don't worry. I can take care of myself.'

He vanished as silently as a shadow while the commander of the escort party was placing sentries and arranging watches. When he returned they could all see that he was looking very grim.

'Have they gone?' Marianne asked, without much hope.

'No. They have made camp some distance away. The forest ends a little farther north.'

The escort commander came up to them. He was a Dutchman, a Colonel Van Caulaert who, until the previous September, had belonged to the 2nd Hussars. He had been wounded, not seriously but enough to send him home, and had been given charge of the convoy on the way.

'Are there many of them?' he asked.

Mourier shrugged. 'Hard to say. The mist has got up. I saw

several parties of infantry and round one of the fires was a group of peasants armed with scythes and pitchforks. I think they have us surrounded.'

While he went on to describe as well as he could what he had been able to discover of the enemy's position, Marianne felt a shiver run down her spine. There was something terrifying about the thought of those primitive weapons, especially the scythe, that emblem of death. They were so much more frightening than guns. They filled her imagination with horrible visions of hamstrung horses and men dying in pools of blood. It crossed her mind that her own hour might come, either that night or at dawn and she was suddenly afraid, afraid of dying there, in that enemy forest, among so many people who were strangers to her and far from all she loved. It was impossible, surely it must be impossible! Her whole being rebelled against the horrible idea that all her youth and love of life could – Instinctively, she moved closer to the one-armed general who, until that moment, had seemed so detestable to her but whom she now thought of as the only man able to save them in this present peril. What he had to say, however, was not reassuring.

'I don't think we've very much to fear tonight. Even so, we must keep a strict watch. Tomorrow, at first light, we'll form a square with the wounded – and the weakest—' this with a flickering glance at the girl devouring him with her eyes, 'in the middle in the wagons. Then we'll try to make a breakthrough. If, as I fear is the case, we are surrounded, our one chance is to attack first.'

'And – if we don't get through?' the Dutchman said.

'Then we'll have to consider abandoning the wagons and forming a smaller square – and so on until some of us do get through or we are all killed in the attempt.'

'All—?' Marianne said faintly.

'Yes, my – er – my young friend. All. Believe me, it's a deal better to die fighting than to wait to have your throat cut by the peasants – or worse.'

'I'm with you there,' Beyle sighed, checking the charge in his pistol with a frown. 'Trust me to see to it that neither I nor this young man here fall into their hands alive.'

It was a strange night in which no one was able to sleep very well. They were all, in their own ways, preparing for what lay ahead. Some were busy removing every ounce of unnecessary weight from the wagons and stripping down the ones that were to be left behind to make the convoy more compact. Some were giving each other messages to take back if they should escape. Others again were writing, a letter or a will, although with little hope that it would ever reach its destination. But they did it more to occupy their minds than because they really believed in it. Some, who happened to have money, were sharing it with others who had none. Some of the carts carried wine and that was shared out equally. Beyle had discovered a party of Belgian soldiers among the wounded and was chatting to them about Liège and the countryside around, which he knew well, having numerous friends there. He even went so far as to exchange addresses and messages with them, facing the prospect of death with perfect sang-froid.

Marianne sat by a fire with her back against a tree stump and watched them all with astonishment and envy. The probability of imminent death had produced a curious feeling of equality, had brought them all down to one level. Officers of all ranks, private soldiers and civilians like Beyle, they were all one in a strange brotherhood. Faced with a common end, they realized that they were all equally poor and naked. But they were together, while she was alone, shut out, as it were, from all this warmth.

There was Barbe of course, but the Polish woman had shown herself as brave as any man. A little while before, Beyle had advised her to escape.

'You speak the language and are dressed in the same fashion as the women hereabouts. You could easily slip through their lines, especially in this mist. Why don't you go?'

But Barbe had only shrugged and answered: 'We must all die some day. Like this or in some other way. You shall see that I, too, know how to fire a gun. Besides, didn't I tell you that when you take service with someone you share all their fortunes, good and bad?'

She had said no more but had gone calmly off to roll herself in a blanket and lie down under a tree. She had been sleeping ever since with as much tranquillity as if she expected to have many years before her.

Towards dawn Marianne, exhausted, fell asleep herself for a while. It was Beyle who woke her, shaking her gently.

'Come,' he said. 'We are going now. We must make the most of what God sends us.'

In fact, the forest was enveloped in a thick mist. They were moving in the heart of a damp, white cloud that made the men look like ghosts, the more so as they had orders to move with as little noise as possible. Like a machine, Marianne did as she was told and took her place in the convoy.

The wounded were loaded into as few of the wagons as could possibly hold them. The rest of the vehicles were abandoned, giving them extra horses for a last flight if the worst came to the worst. All the able-bodied men were on the outside, armed to the teeth, and so they set off through the mist.

Marianne, a pistol thrust through her belt, walked behind Beyle, with Barbe at her heels. She was praying with all her heart, convinced that death was going to strike at any moment.

The silence in the forest was oppressive. The wheels of the wagons had been greased during the night and the horse's hooves muffled with cloths. In the thick fog they might indeed have been a procession of spirits moving endlessly through a ghostly world. The mist was so thick that it was impossible to see more than three paces ahead. As Beyle said, it could be a gift from heaven.

Mourier had vanished. He was now at the head of the column with Van Caulaert, guiding them all. The minutes crept by slowly, one by one, and each, to Marianne, seemed like a miracle. Keeping her eyes fixed on Beyle's back, she followed him blindly, her mind concentrating on all those whom she would probably never see again . . . her beautiful baby boy . . . Corrado, so noble and generous and yet so sad . . . Her dear Jolival . . . young Gracchus with his mop of red hair . . . Adelaide in Paris, who had probably given her up for dead long ago . . . The thought of Paris made her smile. Here in the midst of this wild, dangerous forest, in the choking mist, it seemed impossible that there could really be such a place as Paris . . . Suddenly, she had a desperate longing to see Paris again. She thought of Jason, too, but, oddly, her mind refused to dwell on him. It was as if he had chosen deliberately to leave her and she did not want to mar her last moments with thinking of him. In the end, she made up her mind to give those minutes to Sebastiano and she clung to that with a desperate intensity of love and tenderness that she had never felt before. At least her useless life would have served some purpose if it had produced that fine boy to be the heir of a great name.

Between her prayers and these bitter thoughts, she ceased to notice the passage of time. Only after they had been marching for four hours and the mist parted suddenly as they came to the end of the forest did she realize that the danger was past. The convoy was now in an open plain, empty except for an occasional clump of trees. They had made it! A great shout of joy went up from every throat. Beyle turned round and Marianne saw that he was as white as a sheet and his lower jaw was quivering uncontrollably, but he was smiling.

'It seems it wasn't to be this time, after all,' he said simply. She smiled back at him.

'It's a miracle! I can't believe it!'

'Perhaps it is. Let's hope we have a few more miracles between here and Smolensk. This time, the enemy can't have thought us worth pursuing.'

Certainly they were not seen again. They went on for two more days and saw nothing of them. But another problem arose, which was the lack of food. They had brought from Moscow only sufficient for a ten days' march, for no one could have imagined that the journey would take so long. In addition, the weather became much worse. Snow began to fall, thickly and continuously, hindering their progress. They had to slaughter some of the horses, partly because there was no fodder for them and partly to feed the men. Every night it was a little harder to find shelter and each morning, when they broke camp, they found a few men missing. Men who had gone looking for food in the unharvested fields or ruined villages about.

One night a few Cossacks attacked them. Uttering their shrill war-cries, they charged like thunderbolts at the rearguard, transfixed several men with their lances and then disappeared as quickly as they had come. The dead were buried and fear crept slowly and insidiously into the hearts of the weakening convoy.

Ignoring all Mourier's efforts to persuade her, Marianne steadfastly refused to take a place in one of the wagons reserved for the wounded, although he was much distressed by her pinched cheeks. With Beyle on one side of her and Barbe, as tireless as a machine, on the other, she marched on with blistered feet, gritting her teeth and trying not to listen to the groans and screams of the most severely injured men. And always there was the same lowering, yellowish-grey sky with, now and then, a flight of black birds like a presage of misfortune.

Beyle did his best to cheer her and the men. He was always saying that Smolensk was not far now, that they would be safe there and find everything they needed. The wounded would be fed and cared for. They need only be brave a little longer.

'I may reach Smolensk,' Marianne told him one evening when they had managed to find shelter in a huge barn that was still standing, 'but I shall never see Paris again. I can't. It's too far. There's the cold and the snow – and the country's so vast! I shall never do it.'

'Then you had better spend the winter in Smolensk with me. The Emperor will be at Kaluga, so you will have nothing to fear. In the spring, as soon as it is possible, you can resume your journey.'

Weary and depressed after a painful day's march, in the course of which they had suffered another attack by Cossacks, Marianne shrugged.

'How can you be sure the Emperor will stay at Kaluga? You know as well as I do that he wants to be nearer to Poland. If he winters in Russia at all, it will be at Smolensk or Vitebsk. Kaluga is nearly as far from the Niemen as Moscow itself. Sooner or later we shall see him come. So I must go on, and the sooner the better if I want to avoid the worst of the winter.'

'Very well, then, you shall go on. After all, this convoy is bound for Poland. Why should you not stay with it? I'll ask Mourier to take care of you.'

'Upon what pretext? Everyone thinks I'm your secretary – all except Mourier and he thinks I'm your mistress. What would they say if we were to part company?'

'You might be ill, unable to endure the climate, frightened of the snow – or something of that sort. Our gallant general is more than half in love with you already. He'd be delighted to be rid of me.'

'That is precisely what I wish to avoid,' Marianne answered uncommunicatively. She had not been unaware of the alteration in Mourier's feelings towards her and she did not like it, for she was not at all attracted to him. She had found him an annoyance from the beginning but she had come to regret the bluff, soldierly manners and the coarse pleasantries because now he had taken to hovering close to her at every possible opportunity, especially when there was no one else at hand. Consciously or unconsciously, he had begun to treat the supposed secretary with something perilously close to gallantry, stroking her hand furtively whenever it came within reach and trying to slip his arm round her waist when an alarm obliged them to stand close together. His barrack-room jokes had at least had the advantage of making the men laugh and so helping to lull their suspicions. Now, whenever they were together, men followed them with their eyes, wondering.

More than once, already, Marianne had warned him tactfully. He would apologize and promise to take more care but almost at once the glowing look would be back in his eyes and, to an attentive observer, it looked odd to say the least. No, it was quite simply impossible for her to continue the journey under those conditions, and especially without Beyle! Marianne felt that she would a hundred times rather go on alone and on foot than have to defend herself against continual pressure to which, sooner or later, she would be bound to yield.

Barbe had listened to the conversation with Beyle but she said nothing then. That night, however, she watched until she saw Marianne turn away to go to the fire and then came up to her.

'Don't worry,' she whispered. 'I'll think of something else. I don't want to go on like this either.'

'Why not, Barbe? Is something troubling you?'

Barbe's broad shoulders were seen to shrug under her mass of shawls.

'I'm the only woman in this convoy,' she said shortly, 'and I've no intention of going back to my old ways.'

'Then what do you suggest?'

'Nothing for the moment. The first thing is to reach Smolensk. After that, we shall see.'

To reach Smolensk! That had become the unbearable refrain. None of them could ever have dreamed that it could be so far. It seemed to be drawing away from them as they went on, like places in nightmares. Some were even beginning to murmur that they must have taken the wrong road and would never get there. And so it was with a mixture of surprise and incredulity that, on the evening of the second of November, they heard the news that was flying down the convoy.

'We are there! There is Smolensk!'

The army had been there before and the men recognized the place with delight, Beyle most of all.

'Yes,' he said, with a deep sigh of relief, 'there is Smolensk. And not before time!'

They had come to the edge of a deep valley with the quicksilver gleam of the River Dnieper flowing through it and the town was before them. It stood dreaming within its circle of high walls on the right bank of the river, amid a landscape of wooded ravines, firs, pines and birches standing out starkly against the fresh snow. That great fortress town with its thirty-eight towers and great smooth walls which for three hundred years had defied all that time and men could do would have presented a picture both archaic and beautiful, but for the fresh scars of war that were so clearly visible in the form of trees felled and burned by gunfire, ruined and fire-blackened houses there had not been time enough yet to rebuild, and a temporary bridge made of logs. Of the outlying suburbs practically nothing remained.

Above the walls, they could see the domes of the churches and smoking chimneys, waking thoughts of evening meals in well-warmed rooms. A bell began to ring and was followed by the clarion call of a trumpet and a roll of drums, indicating the presence of troops behind those antique walls that gave the place such a secretive air.

The city had such an air of reassurance and refuge that a great shout of joy went up simultaneously from every throat capable of uttering. At last they would be able to rest, eat, warm themselves and sleep under a roof again. It was almost unbelievable.

Beyle, however, only shrugged and muttered: 'Like the crusaders arriving before Jerusalem, isn't it? You can't see from here, because the walls are too high, but half the town is gone. All the same, I daresay we shall all find a lodging – and I hope to see the results of all that frenzied letter-writing I did in Moscow.'

He was making an effort to seem unconcerned but his dark eyes were shining with happiness and Marianne could tell that he was just as excited as the rest of them, for all his supercilious airs.

They covered the distance to the city gates in record time in spite of the snow and the difficulties encountered by the horses – which no one had thought to shoe for icy conditions – on the steep sides of the valley. Moreover they had been seen by the watch inside the city and men came running out with welcoming cries to help to lead the wagons in.

As they passed through the great gate bearing the arms of the city, a cannon supporting the mythical bird Gamayun, symbol of power, Marianne, despite her weariness, could not help smiling at her companion.

'You may think what you like, but I am just like all the others – very happy to be here. I hope you're going to provide me with something other than raw, frosted potatoes for my dinner?'

She was not the only one to be dreaming of food. All round them, the soldiers were talking of nothing but the good meal they were going to have and their entry into Smolensk was as gay as if they were going to a fair. But their gaiety and the eagerness subsided a little once they were inside the gates and could see the damage that had been hidden before. The snow threw a merciful covering over the ruins but it could not hide the tragic gaps in the streets as the tapers were lit behind the squares of waxed paper that replaced shattered window panes.

As the convoy made its way along the street, people came out from such houses as were still standing and stood in groups on both sides of the road, watching the new arrivals silently. They were all like so many bundles of shawls and old rags, except for their eyes, which glittered with a hostile light, and now and then there came from them a murmur that had nothing friendly in it. All Marianne's happiness fell away from her. Here, even more than in Moscow, she felt that she was in enemy territory.

Mourier had paused by the gate to exchange a word with a captain of carabiniers, but now he rejoined them, looking worried.

'It seems that our three hundred men are a welcome addition. I was thinking we'd find Marshal Victor's 9th Corps here, but there's only a remnant of them left. The Marshal's gone off with the bulk of his force to Polotsk, where Gouvion St Cyr is said to be in difficulties. Even the governor has gone.'

'Who is it?' Beyle asked.

'General Baraguey d'Illiers. He ought to be here with the Illyrian Division which should have left Danzig on the first of August. He's gone to take up a position on the Yelnia road, leaving Smolensk to General Charpentier, chief of staff to the 4th Corps and before that governor of Vitebsk. I'm wondering what we are going to find here with so slender a garrison and all this chopping and changing in the command.'

Beyle, listening, was growing visibly gloomier, evidently worrying about his famous supplies. When they came out into a square, he suddenly left his companions and darted towards a private house, from the doorway of which two figures had just emerged. They proved to be the temporary Governor of Smolensk in person and, with him, none other than the Intendant of the province, Monsieur de Villeblanche, with whom Beyle promptly entered into a brief and clearly acrimonious dialogue. By the time he came back to Marianne, the unhappy Director of Reserve Supplies was in something approaching a state of collapse.

'This is appalling! They haven't got a quarter of what I asked for! I hope to God the Emperor doesn't show up here or I'm a ruined man! Come on, we can't stay here. This is where we leave the convoy and rejoin the Supply Corps. I must see for myself. We'll easily find a lodging here somewhere.'

In fact, it was less easy than he imagined because, although the Quartermaster's staff had managed to acquire an undamaged house for their own use, this was already so full that they could offer the director of Reserve Supplies nothing more than a mattress squeezed into a small room already occupied by two of his colleagues. There could be no question of Marianne's inclusion in this offer, much less Barbe, whose ample dimensions required no less ample space to house them. They would have to find somewhere else.

Beyle deposited what remained of his baggage and then set out with one of the young men on the staff in search of a lodging for his 'secretary' and his cook.

They found one, in the end, in the house of an elderly German Jew, not far from the New Market. It was little more than an attic, but provided with a stove which made it seem to the two women the very height of comfort. In order to move in there with Barbe, Marianne was obliged to reveal herself as a woman but this scarcely signified since she was leaving the military convoy and the usefulness of her disguise was at an end. Nor did she have cause to regret discarding it. Solomon Levin and his wife Rachel were good souls and full of compassion for the girls white face and pinched cheeks. They were tactful, too, and neither showed any surprise at her unusual garb. Concluding that questions would be out of place, they asked none, merely assuring the gentleman that he might go about his business with an easy mind for the ladies would be safe with them. Good relations, moreover, were very quickly established when it emerged that Marianne's German was as fluent as their own. Satisfied as to his friends' welfare, Beyle left them, promising to return next morning.

Solomon Levin, as a trader in furs and other such essential commodities as dried herring, was on terms with the invader which, if not precisely cordial, were at least very correct and had therefore been permitted to pursue his business in a city where most things had come to a standstill. Which is to say that no one in his house was actually starving.

Solomon's big wife Rachel went to work busily and Marianne found her attic provided with mattress, blankets, sheets and, most rapturous of all, a great bearskin rug. But she almost burst into tears of joy when Rachel and her little servant maid brought in a big washing copper and two huge jugs of hot water, with towels, rough but clean, and a bar of soap. In the twenty-eight days since leaving Moscow, she had not had her boots off once and her linen was the same that she had set out in. Never had she felt so dirty, and the smell that clung about her was a far cry from her favourite scent of tuberoses.

The sight of the copper full of steaming hot water filled her with such joy that she flung both arms round the old woman and kissed her impulsively.

'I'll bless you as long as I live for this, Madame Levin,' she said. 'You can't think what that bath means to me!'

'I think I can. Our house is not large or handsome, or even very comfortable, but we set great store by cleanliness, for that is the way of all those of our faith who would follow closely the law of Moses. Give me your clothes and those of your maid and I will see that they are washed.'

Up to that point, Rachel's reply had been made with great dignity, but there she broke off and added, smiling very shyly: 'I, too, shall remember you always, my lady, for I would never have believed that a European lady would ever do what you have just done. Had you forgotten that I belong to a despised race?'

The sudden sadness in the old woman's voice went to Marianne's heart. She went to her quickly and took both her hands in hers.

'To me, a stranger, you have been more than hospitable, you have been friendship itself and I always kiss my friends. Have *you* forgotten that I belong to a nation of invaders?' And she kissed Rachel again, never for a moment suspecting what was to come of those two kisses prompted by nothing more than gratitude and liking. Then Solomon's wife withdrew, telling Barbe that she might, if she wished, come down and wash herself in her kitchen. Marianne was left alone to the delights of her tub.

When Barbe returned, well-scrubbed, she brought a big tray with her. On it were a number of dishes: kasha, a thick buckwheat porridge, a kind of stew made with cabbage and blinis, little stubby pancakes eaten with sour cream. There was also a steaming pot of tea.

It was a long time since Marianne and Barbe had seen such a feast. They ate like the starving people they were, too intent on their food to utter a single word. Then, as though the act of eating had taken all their strength, they lay down on the mattresses and, heavy with food, fell into a deep sleep which, for Marianne at least, lasted until well into the following afternoon.

She woke to the contented realization that her long sleep had done her good. She had not felt such a sense of well-being for a long time because she had gone straight from a life of total seclusion indoors to an exhausting outdoor one. After another meal she felt full of energy again and equal to anything, a state of affairs which expressed itself in an acute impatience to continue her journey to France as soon as possible. Her brief sight of Smolensk, or what was left of it, had cured her of any wish to linger there, even in the warmth and simple friendliness of the Levins' house.

Beyle came again at nightfall, just as she was finishing dressing. She had found it a relief to put on the women's clothes that she had brought with her in her bundle.

Beyle had clearly not been enjoying the same measure of comfort as Marianne. He was pale and his face was puffy with fatigue and his nerves were so much on edge that it was evident he was deeply worried. He seemed quite offended to see Marianne looking so fresh and clean and rested. He himself was still almost as dirty and complained of a night tormented by fleas. After that, however, he ceased to dwell on his own sufferings and reverted to a subject which, although less personal, was equally on his mind.

'The convoy leaves again tomorrow,' he began without preamble. 'Do you want to go with it or not?'

'You know I do not. The pretence that I was your secretary ended here and I've no wish to face the prospect of several hundred leagues as the only woman, apart from Barbe, among a thousand or more men, all of them practically reverting to the condition of savages. Ask Barbe what she thinks of it. Even she will not do it.'

'This is silly and stupid! You know quite well that Mourier will look after you—'

'Oh, will he? And on what conditions? No, my friend, don't talk to me about chivalry and gallantry and such drawing-room niceties. They do not hold in a situation of this kind. Not to beat about the bush, I've no desire to be raped I don't know how often before we reach civilization. In any case, have you forgotten what you promised me in Moscow? You said that, once here, it would be easy for you to help me to continue my journey.'

Beyle literally exploded. 'How do you expect me to do that? You've seen what's left of the city on which we had all based such hopes! No garrison to speak of, no supplies, no communication with other cities, and a hostile population only waiting for the word to turn and rend us.'

'Well, you might have expected all that.'

'I might not! Smolensk was our main supply depot. Only it seems that since Marshal Victor left, all our reserves have mysteriously disappeared. As for the things I sent for from Mohilev and Vitebsk, scarcely any of it has arrived. And I was told nothing, nothing! They let me come here without saying a word. Poor Villeblanche almost died of fright when he got my letters and dared not tell me. But now, I must admit, I'm just as frightened and as desperate as he is. Do you know that in a fortnight from now we shall have something like a hundred thousand men descending on us and all we've got to feed them is a few quintals of flour, a little flour and buckwheat, a handful or so of hay and oats, a few dozen scrawny hens, a mountain of cabbages – oh yes, and casks and casks of brandy! How the devil do you expect me to find the time or means to do anything for you when I'm within an ace of going raving mad!'

'A hundred thousand men? What do you mean?'

He smiled bitterly. 'That instead of the modest title I'd been looking forward to as the reward of my labours I'm likely to find myself wholly and irrevocably disgraced. The Emperor will never forgive me – or Count Dumas, either, or my cousin Daru. I'm finished, ruined utterly!'

'Oh, do stop moaning,' Marianne cried impatiently, 'and explain! Where are these hundred thousand men to come from?'

'With the Emperor! A courier arrived this afternoon, on foot because his horse had broken it's neck on the ice coming down the valley. The Emperor is falling back on us.'

The gloom in his voice told how little he relished Napoleon's imminent arrival. Like a man getting a burden off his chest, he went on to pour out all his news in a rush. He said that on October 24th Prince Eugène had defeated General Dokhtourov's Russian troops at Malo-Yaroslavetz but it had been no more than a partial victory as a result of which Napoleon had learned that the Russian army was re-forming behind Dokhtourov in incalculable numbers. Aware of his own dwindling resouces, he had decided to return to the main road and when the courier set out the French army's headquarters had been at Borovsk.

The Emperor's orders were precise. Everything was to be made ready at Smolensk to receive the hundred thousand or so men that remained with him, along with several thousand civilians who had left Moscow in his train.

'But that's not all,' Beyle went on tensely. 'The Emperor is expecting to find massive reinforcements awaiting him here – the 9th Corps, which has gone off to assist Gouvion St Cyr. The Marshal has been wounded and is no longer able to hold the line of the Dvina. And Oudinot's 2nd Corps, which included, among others, four stout Swiss regiments, has suffered heavy losses. Consequently Victor can't hurry back to Smolensk, not if he wants to continue to keep watch on the Vilna road, and without him it's by no means sure that Napoleon could withstand an all-out Russian attack if Kutuzov took it into his head to launch one ...'

Marianne listened, appalled and at the same time vaguely irritated by the flat expressionless voice. Beyle might have been reciting a lesson – a lesson he had not learned very well. Then, quite suddenly, a dark flush mounted to his cheeks and he began to shout in uncontrollable anger:

'So this is not the moment for you to be talking of your finer feelings, Marianne! Can't you understand that you've no choice! If you won't go with the convoy, then you'll fall into the Emperor's hands before very much longer. Therefore I have decided that you're going with the wounded, whether you like it or not.'

Marianne jibbed at that, stung by his angry tone.

'*You* have decided, did you say?'

'Yes, I! Mourier will come for you at dawn tomorrow with a carriage – yes, I've even managed to work that miracle for you! You won't have to go on foot. You ought to thank me.'

'Thank you? Who gave you the right to order me about?'

She, too, was beginning to lose her temper. By what right did this young man who, after all, was nothing to her, dare to take that tone with her? He had helped her during the fire but had she not returned his kindness a hundredfold? Forcing herself to remain calm, she said, with awful clarity: 'I refuse absolutely to submit to your dictation, my friend. I have said that I am not going and there is an end of it.'

'And I tell you that you are going because I say you shall. You may think you would prefer to face Napoleon. Your previous intimacy may give you the right to hope for some lessening of his displeasure, but I am in no such happy position and I've no wish to make matters worse for myself than they are. If he finds out, at the very moment when I'm having to confess my failure to produce those damned reserve supplies, that I've been hiding you and helping you to escape from his anger my position will be intolerable! I'll be court-martialled, perhaps even shot!'

'Don't talk such nonsense! Why should the Emperor find out all that now? We're not living together any more, are we? And I can't see the Emperor taking a Jewish house for his headquarters. Mourier is the only person who knows that I am a woman and once the convoy has gone no one will ever guess that you helped me.'

'And what of the people here? Believe me, your disguise was transparent enough to the fellows at the commissariat. Then there are the people of this house.'

'Exactly. And it may surprise you to learn that I've nothing to fear from them. I'm sure of that. Far from it, indeed. There's no reason why I shouldn't stay hidden in this house until the time comes when I can get away.'

Beyle shrugged angrily. 'Hide here for months, is it? You really are mad. Anywhere is safer in these days than a Jew's house. Suppose the Russians retake Smolensk! These people you trust so much will throw you out into the street at the first hint of danger. And I'll wager you'd not stay here long if they found out the terms you'd been on with Napoleon. They could find themselves in serious trouble if you were discovered in their house. Enough of that! You'll be fetched tomorrow at dawn – and you will go. I shall get an expulsion order from the governor tonight. It won't be hard to drum up some pretext. Then the house will be searched from top to bottom should you fail to appear. Now do you understand–?'

For a moment they stood facing one another like a pair of fighting cocks. Marianne was white and Beyle red with anger, and both pairs of fists were clenched. The girl was trembling with indignation at the discovery of what changes fear and selfishness could work in a man who at the outset had shown himself good and kind, with a mind and heart not merely better than average but even with a kind of greatness. She had learned enough during the time of their enforced proximity to know that there was the stuff of a great literary genius in this young man. But he had been prised out of his cosy elegancies of life and thrust into the hell of ice and fire by turns that was war. He had been tired and hungry and dirty, and frightened, too, almost certainly. And now to that was added the fear of disgrace, because in his pride and his innocence he was taking on himself all the responsibility for this – by no means unforeseeable – shortage of provisions. If he were not quite himself there might certainly be said to be some excuse for him, but she, Marianne, was not going to allow herself to be infected by his panic.

'This is a great change in you,' was all she said, her anger subsiding all at once, like a ship in a storm. Her calmness acted on Beyle like a shower of cold water. Gradually, his natural colour returned and he shook his head, opened his mouth as if to say something, shut it again and made a helpless gesture with his hands. Then, abruptly, he shrugged and turned away.

'I'll come and say goodbye tomorrow – before you leave,' he said. Then he was gone.

Marianne stood motionless in the middle of the room, listening to the echoes of their quarrel dying away in the quiet house. Then she turned slowly and looked at Barbe.

Barbe was standing by the stove, her arms folded low over her stomach and her breathing sounding strangely loud in the silence of the room. The green eyes and the violet met but Marianne's were beginning to glisten with unshed tears while the Polish woman's showed only a quiet contentment.

'Well,' Marianne said with a sigh, 'it seems we have no choice, Barbe. We must resign ourselves to going with the convoy. We'll defend ourselves as long as we can.'

'No,' Barbe said.

'What do you mean, no? Are you saying we shan't have to defend ourselves?'

'No – because we're not going with the soldiers.'

And before the startled Marianne could say another word, she had marched to the door and opened it.

'Come my lady,' she said. 'There is no time to lose. Our host awaits us in the parlour.'

'The parlour?'

Barbe smiled briefly. 'Why yes,' she said. 'There is a parlour in the house. Although it may not be quite what you are accustomed to.'

Solomon Levin's house, although the largest and handsomest in the long narrow street that constituted the ghetto of Smolensk, was a cramped building with no more than two rooms on each floor. Downstairs was the shop, dark with age and, opening directly out of it, the kitchen, a cavernous, vaulted place, lit by a single narrow window but containing the unheard-of luxury of a pump. On the first floor (the second consisting of a corn loft and the attic occupied by Marianne and Barbe) was the Levins' bedchamber, over the kitchen, and the parlour, which was directly above the shop. It was a dark room, hung with faded green tapestry, but it was scrupulously clean. The principal piece of furniture was a table covered with a carpet worked in a floral design on which was a large book, bound in black, and a brass candlestick. A number of straight-backed wooden chairs stood guard around the walls.

When Rachel ushered Marianne and Barbe into the room, the candles were alight and old Solomon, a black silk skull cap on his head and a thing like a striped shawl over his shoulders, his spectacles on his nose, was reading from the book – it was the Talmud – with an expression of pious concentration. He closed it as the women entered and as he did so let his hands, which were pale and thin, yet curiously beautiful, caress the binding lovingly. He rose and, bowing slightly, indicated that they should be seated. Then he took off his spectacles and studied Marianne attentively for some time in perfect silence.

She thought that he looked like a weary prophet, with the grey skin of his face sagging a little on the firm bone structure. His beard, which he wore long, seemed made of the same stuff as his skin and the hair under the black cap, which might once have been curly, now hung in sad, wispy corkscrews. But the glance of the dark eyes was still young and steadfast.

'Young woman,' he said, 'your companion tells me that you are here against your wishes and in danger and that it is your earnest desire to return to your own place by some other way than in the company of soldiers. Is that so?'

'It is.'

'Then I may be able to help you. But I must know who you are. In these evil times we live in, faces are often not what they seem, souls even more so, and an innocent gaze may hide an unclean heart. If you want me to trust you, you must trust me first. You are a woman, yet you came here in man's clothing.'

'How will it help you to know my name?' Marianne asked gently. 'We belong to such different worlds. My name can mean nothing to you – nor is there any way for you to know that I am telling the truth.'

'Tell me, nevertheless. Why should you greet a friendly offer with suspicion? It says in this book,' he patted the dark cover softly, 'that a goose may walk with bent head but yet his eyes miss nothing. We Jews are like geese – and we know a great many more things than you might expect. Amongst others, I am familiar with many names – even in your world.'

'Very well,' Marianne said. 'I am the Princess Sant'Anna and I have incurred the Emperor's displeasure because I helped to secure the escape from prison of a man who had been as a father to me and who was then under sentence of death. And now it is for me to warn you. You are taking a grave risk in helping me.'

The old man's only answer was to take from the pocket of his long, grey gown a sheet of paper which he unfolded and laid before Marianne. To her amazement, she saw that it was one of the bills that had been posted on the walls of Moscow concerning her.

'You see,' Solomon remarked. 'I had the means of knowing whether you spoke truth.'

'Where did you get this?' she asked in an altered voice, not taking her eyes from the soiled sheet of paper.

'From outside the posting house. It seems that the men carrying the mail have left them at every place of any size all along the road to the Niemen. I make a point of picking up printed sheets. They can be interesting.'

Marianne said nothing. She felt as if she were sliding into a bottomless pit. She could never have believed that Napoleon would carry his resentment so far. Because she had been mistaken in her first impression that this was the same bill as before. The text was different. There was no longer any mention of the Emperor's friend. This time it called purely and simply for the apprehension of the Princess Sant'Anna, and the reward had been doubled.

Something snapped inside Marianne. Her world had fallen in ruins. If Napoleon's hatred was so bitter, what respite could she ever hope for? Wherever she went, his anger would pursue her and, sooner or later, he would catch up with her. She was alone and utterly helpless in a vast empire where no one was safe from the imperial wrath. Her thoughts flashed to her house in Paris, where Adelaide might already be suffering persecution from the police, and then to Corrado himself! In his determination to capture Marianne, Napoleon was capable of harrying him in his own house, or even of forcing him to appear in public or stripping him of his possessions.

The touch of Solomon's hand on her shoulder made her start. She had been so lost in her own bleak thoughts that she had not seen him rise and come round the table to her. When he spoke, she realized that he had read much of what was in her mind.

'You must go home,' he said gently. 'You have risked everything to save your kinsman and the Almighty will not forsake you. In our law it is said also that it is more blessed to be cursed than to curse and it was the Lord's hand that led you to this house. You are a great lady and yet you kissed my old wife. We are your friends – and it may be that the great emperor will never leave Russia.'

'What do you mean?'

'That it is a long road to France and the Russian winter is a fearful thing. Ataman Platov's Cossacks are like locusts, they descend in their thousands and when those are destroyed they are reborn miraculously. You did well to refuse to travel with the convoy, for that, too, may never arrive.'

'But what am I going to do? What will become of me?'

'One hour before dawn, I will take you to our cemetery. It lies in a quiet spot outside the city and few Christians go there. There is a ruined synagogue where you will find a conveyance waiting, with a good horse and food enough to last you as far as Kovno. Only you must be prepared to pass as one of us. If you do as I say, you will be able to continue your journey without hindrance – and without danger.'

'Without danger!' Barbe had so far taken no part in the conversation, but now she broke in loudly. 'Say, rather, that we'll be in danger from both French and Russians. We'll be robbed at the very least!'

'No you will not. Listen.'

Then Solomon Levin explained to them the laws passed by Tsar Alexander I concerning the Jews and how these would help them. Alexander had not been blind to the profit to be had from the commercial efficiency of the Jewish people and at his coronation had conferred notable advantages on them, reserving only the trade in alcoholic beverages, but these had been counterbalanced by a number of restrictions, including that of being obliged to live in the towns, in areas called ghettoes, varying in size from a whole district down to a single street and never in the country villages. But it was on these restrictions that Solomon based his plan. For, since they were not allowed to stay in the villages, Jewish merchants, when they travelled, as they must from time to time, were given permits to go from one town to another, and these were generally respected by the authorities. The only danger might come from occasional bands of Cossacks, but they had no respect for anyone, not even the Tsar's own officials.

'But you are women,' Solomon went on. 'You will pass as my sister and my niece and that will give you some protection, for the Cossacks do not care to soil themselves by contact with Jewish women. Moreover, the young lady will be unwell – with a contagious infection. I will give you letters to my brothers in Orcha, Borisov, Smorgoni and Vilna and so you will travel from town to town until you reach the Niemen. At Kovno, you will find my cousin, Ishak Levin. You may leave the horse and the vehicle with him and they will be returned to me in due course. At Kovno, you will be in Poland and will have nothing more to fear from the Cossacks. Ishak will provide you with the means to reach Danzig. There, with a little money, you may choose what you wish to do. Danzig is a port and ships trading in contraband goods are more numerous than honest traders. The Emperor's power, too, is more theoretical than actual. His troops pass through it and it is a depot for them, but the people do not love them. What you do then is for you to decide.'

A port! Marianne started at the word. A port meant the sea, the best possible way of escape. She had been trapped in this vast country for so long that she had almost forgotten the sea existed. In an instant the old dream, so painfully buried beneath the rocks of reason and the promise that had been extracted from her, shivered and tried to raise itself again. Danzig. It was there that she had tried to make Jason go, there that she had hoped to take ship, with Napoleon's blessing, bound for the high seas and the land of liberty. It was there, perhaps, that the great vice that was crushing her would loose its hold.

All of a sudden she felt a wild, irresistible longing to reach that city and its port. The small amount of gold that she had managed to save, sewn into her chemise, might be enough to buy her a passage on one of those contraband ships of which Solomon had spoken and after that would come the cold seas and the perilous shores of all those countries where the Emperor ruled, but there might be another port also, and another ship . . . Then the vast ocean, spread like a giant sail from pole to pole, and beyond the ocean – America, and another war, and that special American of Marianne's, whose name was Jason Beaufort.

She was so lost in her own dreams that she did not notice that Solomon had stopped speaking and was looking at her, obviously expecting her to say something.

'Well?' he asked, when she still gave no sign.

Marianne started and stared at him blinking like someone only half-awake. Then she smiled.

'It's wonderful,' she breathed. 'How can I ever thank you for what you are doing for us? Why are you so generous?'

The old Jew's shoulders lifted a little under his faded robe. He went to the far end of the room and a small panel in the wall, perfectly concealed by the pattern of the hanging, opened as if by magic under his agile fingers. He took out a package wrapped in a dirty cloth and, after first shutting the cupboard again with the same conjuring trick as before, brought it to the table. A second later, the package had passed from his hands to Marianne's. She stared at it without understanding.

'Give that to Ishak. Tell him to lay out half of it as he knows and return the remainder to me in the form of merchandise, of which he also knows.

Automatically, Marianne undid the cloth and looked, with Barbe craning over her shoulder. They uttered a simultaneous gasp of amazement. There, nestling in the folds, gleamed six flawless pearls as big as quails' eggs.

As Marianne looked up at him with a question in her eyes, the old man coughed a little and pulled vaguely at his wispy grey beard. His eyes twinkled suddenly as he murmured: 'I – er – found them, during the fighting, in the Church of the Assumption. If they were found here, I should hang for it.'

'And if they're found on us?' Marianne asked.

'Ah, well – then I suppose you would be likely to hang too, but it will at least release you from the intolerable burden of gratitude. If those things get to Ishak, we shall be quits.'

There was nothing particularly funny in it, yet Marianne was beset by a sudden urge to laugh, as she thought of the brilliant still lying on her breast. The diamond taken from a notorious thief – and now these pearls got from a Virgin who, in Russia, must amount to much the same! If she died in this adventure, those who came to strip her corpse would surely make their fortunes. But she had never been afraid of danger, especially when she saw beyond it the way out of a desperate situation.

'Very well,' she said gaily. 'I'll undertake this commission for you. And in spite of it, I'll still say thank you!'

An hour later, when Marianne and Barbe were up in their attic sleeping the sleep of the just, Solomon Levin, enveloped in an immense furred gown that made him look as broad as he was long, slipped cautiously out of his house and through the snowy streets to the city wall. He passed through, by way of a breach made earlier by the French guns, and made his way swiftly to the Jewish cemetery. As he walked, he smiled into his beard and now and then he rubbed his hands together, perhaps to warm them.

Chapter Nine
The Last Bridges

There were a dozen of them barring the road where the snow was trodden hard by horses' hooves. But more could be seen, patrolling in small groups, among the trees that clothed the sides of the valley. Cossacks! Straight-legged in their long stirrups, they looked like barbaric statues, no different, except in the colour of their clothes, from those that Marianne had seen on the banks of the Kodyma: bearded men with fierce eyes, dressed in coarse red or blue wool. They wore shaggy fur hats or flat caps and carried long, red lances and their little spirited horses seemed swamped under the high painted wooden saddles.

Motionless, in spite of the fierce wind from the north that drove the powdery snow at them in great gusts, they watched the approaching vehicle. Barbe, who was driving, gritted her teeth so hard that the line of her jaw showed clearly through the white skin but she said nothing, and went on. Only the snowlight reflected back from her eyes with a harder brightness. Sensing danger, Marianne coughed to hide her anxiety and jerked her head at the river whose grey and swollen waters, flecked with fragments of ice, hurried past to the left of them.

'The bridge? Is it far?'

'Three or four versts,' Barbe answered, her eyes still on the riders ahead. 'We want to get over quickly. There's a storm coming up. But with those—'

The weather was certainly threatening. Thick, black clouds were rolling up at frightening speed, driven by the north wind that froze the skin and brought tears to the eyes.

It was an hour since the two of them had left the little town of Borisov, on the right bank of the Berezina, where they had found shelter for the night in the home of a dealer in second-hand clothes. For the first time in the ten days since they had left Smolensk they had had some trouble in finding a lodging, for the troops of the Russian Admiral Chichakov were billeted there, moving into position to deal the final blow to Napoleon.

The whole town was overrun with soldiers and even the second-hand clothes dealer, Jew though he was, had little more than his shop for himself. If it had not been for Solomon Levin's letter, he would probably have rejected his unwanted visitors out of hand, since they were not even of his own race, but the merchant of Smolensk seemed to possess great influence among those of his faith. Out of deference to him, the second-hand clothes dealer had allowed the travellers to spend the night in his woodshed, along with their horse and cart. They had slept badly but at least they had been sheltered from the cold.

As far as Borisov, things had gone better than they could possibly have hoped. The cold had not been unbearable, two or three degrees below zero at most, and thanks to Solomon their travelling arrangements were both sound and unremarkable. Their little kibitka, although it needed a coat of paint and looked shabby enough to attract no covetous eyes, was equal to the worst roads, while the little, shaggy horse that drew it was strong and sturdy and well shod for going on ice. What was more, they carried with them oats, food and blankets and even weapons, a gun and two hunting knives, intended chiefly for defence against wolves, made bolder by the winter and the snow.

On those nights when there was no town for them to stay in, Barbe made sure that they pulled up to sleep in a wood, where they were sheltered from the wind. Then she would light a fire, to keep off wild animals. She was used to camping and her knowledge was precious to them now. She had the strength and courage of a man, and with it a placidity that was a great comfort. What was more, ever since officially entering Marianne's service in Moscow, she seemed to have given up drinking. It was true that little opportunity to do so had come her way, but it was she who had insisted on the careful rationing of the little cask of brandy Solomon had placed in the cart: a thimbleful for each of them every night for warmth. And so, little by little, a kind of friendship was growing, with no word spoken and no outward sign, between the one-time camp follower and her aristocratic mistress.

Until now, they had encountered no serious unpleasantness. The worst moment had been when they were leaving Orcha and some stones had been thrown at them by Christians in the town as they came out of the house of the money-changer, Zabulon. But neither had been hit.

Now and then they had caught a glimpse of a line of Cossack horsemen etched against the clear line of the sky. Then the wind sweeping over the plain had brought to them the disturbing strains of a wild singing, matched to the beat of the horse's hooves, quickening as they passed from a walk to a trot and swelling tempestuously at the gallop. For all their terror at the sight, Marianne and Barbe could not help listening with an involuntary stir of pleasure to the beauty of those voices, their harmonies as deep and solemn as the age-old Russian earth, but it was a pleasure that only showed itself when they were sure that they themselves had not been seen. Then the bearded horsemen would vanish like a dream beneath the lowering sky as the echo of their warlike singing died away.

But there was nothing dreamlike about these waiting here by the river. Silent and still as statues, they looked menacing and very far from poetic.

'Get ready,' Barbe said softly.

Marianne was already doing so. Rachel Levin had taught her how to cover her face and hands swiftly with the fine, alarmingly coloured membranes which had once formed part of the stock in trade of many a cunning beggar. Marianne had become adept at the horrid game and within seconds she was lying flat on her back in the bottom of the cart, wrapped from head to foot in a grubby blanket and with her eyes closed and her face dramatically covered with dark, purplish-red blotches. The effect was positively frightening. As the cart drew up she uttered a groan worthy of any actress.

One of the Cossacks had the horse by the bridle and Barbe launched immediately into a flood of cringing speech. Marianne naturally understood not a word of this, but she did catch the sound of the borrowed names Solomon had bestowed on them. They were Sara and Rebecca Louria of Kovno, going home so that Rebecca might die in peace.

Rebecca, of course, was Marianne. She had chosen that name for herself in memory of the woman in Constantinople who had saved her life when her son was born. It had seemed to her that it would bring her luck.

Just at that moment, however, she was beginning to have doubts about this because the voice that alternated with Barbe's sounded very violent and aggressive. Things did not seem to be going according to plan.

'Watch out!' Barbe's whisper came suddenly in French.

The supposed invalid caught her meaning and moaned industriously, letting her head roll from side to side on the sack of oats that served her as a pillow. All at once, she saw through half-closed eyes a hairy head thrust into the body of the wagon an inch or two from her face. The kibitka was filled with a reek of stale tobacco and rancid fat, so nauseating that it made her retch most convincingly. Then the man poked the butt of his gun inside and jabbed her in the ribs with it so that she screamed aloud, while Barbe broke into a fresh spate of tears and entreaties.

The Cossack withdrew almost at once, muttering what was evidently a stream of fierce profanities. The next moment, the vehicle was moving again and Marianne was on the point of sitting up to nurse her aching ribs when Barbe hissed at her: 'Don't move! They're coming with us.'

'What for?'

'They say this is a military area and we are breaking the law. They say we must go with them.'

'Oh my God! Where to?'

'How should I know? To their camp, I expect.'

'But – but what about our permit?'

'They don't care for that. Or for your sickness either. All that interests them is the horse and what's inside the wagon. I think – they're going to kill us.'

Barbe did not sound in the least frightened as she said it. It was a simple statement of fact, a little sad but resigned. Marianne gulped and shut her eyes. Even the sight of the way Barbe's broad shoulders had drooped suddenly was depressing. And once again Marianne was determined not to die.

She felt with an icy hand for the hunting knife at her belt, hidden under her many shawls, and made up her mind to use it to sell her life dearly at least. The wind rose in a sudden squall, roaring along the valley and sending a wet, snowy blast into the kibitka. Crows lifted their harsh voices from somewhere near at hand and the sudden dreadful feeling came to Marianne that she was lying in a hearse and it was bearing her inexorably to her grave. It was then that she began to pray under her breath.

Escorted by four Cossacks, the kibitka continued on its way along the Berezina until it came to a primitive bridge made of tree trunks and beaten earth and, looking down on it, the hamlet and little castle of Studianka. Barbe let out a groan.

'Saint Casimir! There are more Cossacks there, hacking the bridge down. We'll never get across, even if these should let us go.'

Meanwhile, the men with the kibitka had begun shouting.

'What are they saying?' Marianne whispered.

'It's very strange. They're telling them to stop a moment as they want to get the wagon across before the bridge is down. I don't understand it at all.'

She was not given long to wonder. Both the Cossacks and the wagon had come to a standstill and in an instant two huge, bearded giants had snatched Barbe from her seat, ignoring her screams of protest. Two more took hold of the supposedly sick woman by her head and feet and pulled her out of the back. Playing her part to the end, she made no attempt to resist but only groaned more loudly, thinking they would lay her down in the snow.

Then she saw that they were close by the bridge. The Cossacks had dismounted and Barbe was struggling like a fury in the grip of three of them. They were carrying her towards the river. In sudden terror at the sight of that dirty grey water and the big, yellowish-coloured lumps of ice in it, Marianne began to scream and tried to struggle, but in vain. The men's grasp held firm and she felt paralysed with fear.

Forgetting where she was, she began to scream aloud in French: 'Help! Help! Save me!'

She was answered by such a roar that it seemed as if the earth itself had burst asunder. At the same time she felt herself swung up and tossed into the cold air. Then the river waters closed over her cries.

The water was freezing cold and fast-moving, made still more dangerous by the floating ice and the fact that it was in spate. Marianne felt that she was falling into a bottomless abyss, a cold hell that ate into her bones. Instinctively she tried to swim. Letting go the blanket round her and her enveloping shawls, she managed to struggle to the surface. Arms and legs were already numbed with cold but she forced them to the proper motions for swimming. Then, suddenly, her foot struck against something solid. She stood up and found that there was firm ground under her feet. There must be a ford, and the bridge overhung the ford because when she wiped the water out of her eyes she saw that she was quite close to one of the wooden piles. She reached out and clung to it.

To her surprise, the bank from which she had been thrown was empty. The kibitka was still there but there was no one with it. At that point it occurred to her that Barbe must have suffered the same fate as herself and she began searching the river with her eyes. She saw nothing and her heart contracted. Whether from the cold or because she could not swim, poor Barbe must have perished.

Frozen to the marrow, her teeth chattering, Marianne let go of her pile and staggered to the bank where she dropped on to the frosted grass. Her heart was thudding like a bass drum in her breast, filling her ears with a noise like thunder. She knew that she must get up and move about if she did not want to die of cold instead of drowning. The instinct of self-preservation was so strong that she did not give a thought to the fact that by coming out of the water she was likely to fall into the hands of her former persecutors again.

She dragged herself up the gently sloping bank and as her eyes came level with the road she understood at last that the thundering had not been only in her head. A short way off, between the river and the village, the Cossacks were engaged with some other horsemen – horsemen who could only belong to the Grand Army.

Marianne felt as if the heavens had opened for her. Her fingers twined into the frozen grass were insensible to cold or pain as she followed the combat with her eyes. It was an unequal fight: some fifty Cossacks to half a score of French who, though fighting like lions, were evidently getting the worst of it. Already three men were down and two horses lay dead in the snow.

'Oh God,' she prayed. 'Save them! Save us all!'

A great shout came in answer. Another little troop of horses had emerged beside a clump of trees at the top of the slope. This time there were perhaps a dozen of them. An officer in a plumed hat, evidently a general, broke away from the group and rode forward a little way, observing the skirmish by the river. He sat on his horse for a moment, the feathers in his hat streaming in the wind, then suddenly he pulled it off, drew his sword and, pointing to the fight, cried: 'Forward!' in unmistakable French.

What followed was magnificent. The handful of horses swept down on the Cossacks in a furious charge, smashing into them like a tornado. Man after man went down before them as they rode to the relief of their friends, the murderous flash of their sabres whirling like sickles in a harvest field, spreading death around them.

It was quickly over. In a few minutes the surviving Russians had turned tail and were fleeing back towards the trees, pursued by the solitary figure of the general. The sound of his laughter was borne on the wind.

Then, quite suddenly, Marianne almost sang for joy. She had seen Barbe emerge from behind a fir tree and go running towards the wagon. Marianne stood up and tried to run after her but her frozen limbs refused to bear her. She fell heavily to the ground and called as loudly as she could: 'Barbe! Barbe! I'm here, Barbe! Come to me!'

Barbe heard her. In another moment she had reached her and

was hugging her in her arms, laughing and crying at once, calling on every saint in the Polish calendar and swearing to light a forest of candles to every one of them at the first opportunity.

'Barbe,' Marianne wailed, 'I'm so cold I can't even walk!'

'Never mind about that!' And with that Barbe lifted Marianne as easily as if she had been a child and carried her, shivering, to the kibitka. Only then did they see that a man had forestalled them and recognized the general who had led the charge. He had his hand on the horse's bridle.

'My apologies to you, my good woman, but I've two wounded men here.'

Marianne had closed her eyes, as though in an effort to keep in what bodily heat she had left, but at the sound of his voice she opened them and saw to her amazement that the dashing rider of a moment ago was indeed none other than the man who had rescued her from Chernychev and fought with him for her sake in the garden in the rue de Lille,[1] Fortunée Hamelin's favourite lover, Fournier-Sarlovèze.

'François!' she said weakly, finding his name spring as naturally to her lips as if they had been brought up together.

He turned and gaped at her, rubbed his eyes and then looked more closely.

'I've been drinking too much of their damned vodka again!'

'No, you're not seeing things, my friend. It really is me, Marianne. You've just rescued me for the second time, although you did not know it.'

For a moment he was speechless, then he burst out with a loud: 'Good God! But what the devil are you doing here? And soaking wet at that!'

'The Cossacks threw me in the river – it would take too long to explain. Oh, my goodness, but I'm cold! I'm so dreadfully cold!'

'Threw you in the river? My God, I could kill another hundred of 'em for that! Wait a moment— Here, you, woman, take those wet clothes off her.'

He hurried to his horse, unfastened the big cloak that was

[1] See *Marianne and the Privateer.*

rolled at the saddle and ran back again to fling it hastily round her as she stood in her soaking petticoat. Marianne tried to stop him.

'But you? Surely you'll need it?'

'Don't you worry about me. I'll pick up another from some Cossack. Did you say this cart belongs to you? Where were you going with it?'

'I was trying to go home. François, for pity's sake, if you should see the Emperor, don't tell him you've seen me. Matters between us could not well be worse.'

He laughed, not without a touch of bitterness.

'Why should you think I'll be saying anything to him? You know he hates me – almost as much as I hate him. And this harebrained escapade isn't going to make us better friends. He's destroying the finest army in the world. But tell me, what was it happened between you to put you on such bad terms?'

'A friend of mine had given him some offence and I helped him to escape. Oh, François, I am being sought for! Haven't you been in Smolensk lately, or in Orcha, or any other town on the road to France? My description is pasted up everywhere.'

'I never read their damned notices. I'm not interested.'

Briskly he threw his arms round her, picked her up and carried her to the wagon and set her down inside it, tucking the cloak carefully round her feet which were blue with cold. Then he studied her intently for a moment, his face suddenly grave, bent down and set his mouth to her cold lips, hugging her to him with a kind of passionate fury.

'I've been wanting to do that for years,' he muttered gruffly. 'Ever since the night of Napoleon's marriage to be precise. Are you going to slap my face again?'

She shook her head, too much moved for speech. That burning kiss had been just what she needed to bring back the raw taste of life and make her herself again. She wanted to cling for a moment to that manly form and to the passionate lust for life that was in this unrepentant duellist. And she told him as much.

'Where are you going? I wish I could come with you.'

He shook his head and his handsome face twisted sardonically.

'Come with me? I thought you wanted to get out of this hell hole? All I could offer you would be a worse one, because we don't know what is coming to us. We've lost two-thirds of our force and the Cossacks are everywhere. And now, instead of going on to Poland we've got to fall back with what troops we have left to join up with Napoleon. So you be off! And as quick as you can, while there is still time. Take a look at that river and the bridge. You must get across at once because as soon as our backs are turned I dare swear there'll be another lot of Cossacks here to break it down. And I can't stop them. I've too few men.'

'But if the Emperor is retreating into Poland, how will you manage? The bridges at Borisov have been destroyed already.'

He made a tired, angry movement.

'I know. Well, we shall see. Go now, off with you! I'll see you in Paris – God willing.'

'And supposing I'm permitted to live. But what about your wounded?'

'We'll hoist them on to a horse. There's a medical unit not far off. Goodbye, Marianne. If you should happen to see Fortunée before I do, tell her not to start looking for consolation yet awhile because I'll be back. Do you hear that, I'll be back. Russia shall not have my bones.'

Was he saying that to reassure himself, she wondered? No, he was too sure of himself. It was not even a boast. If there were to be only one man left out of all the *Grande Armée*, Fournier would be that man. And, one way and another, it was good to know. Marianne smiled. And this time it was she who drew the general down to her and kissed him – in a very sisterly fashion.

'I'll tell her. Goodbye, François.'

After piling on top of Marianne everything they possessed in the way of clothes and blankets, Barbe clambered back on to the driving seat and took up the reins. A click of her tongue and they were off, lumbering towards the bridge. The wind had brought the snow with it and it was falling thickly now. Fournier stood by the road and watched the heavy wagon lurching over the uneven surface of trampled earth that covered the logs. He made a trumpet of his hands and shouted through them into the gales.

'Go carefully! Beyond the bridge the road goes through some nasty boggy ground, and the wind is very strong. Keep to the path! And try to avoid Smorgoni! There was some fighting there yesterday!'

Barbe waved her whip to show that she had understood and the kibitka rolled on into the white whirlwind on the road to Vilna, some fifty leagues farther on. When it was no longer visible, Fournier-Sarlovèze gave an angry shrug and put up his sleeve to brush away a drop of moisture from his cheek. Then he turned and walked back to his horse and springing lightly into the saddle trotted back to the head of his troop. The last bridge across the Berezina was left alone in the rising storm with only the dead for company. By next day, it was gone.

In the snow, the road to Vilna proved to be a terrible ordeal for the two women. On the day after her enforced bathe in the Berezina, Marianne was coughing her lungs out and shivering with fever. By now she had no need to feign illness. She lay in the back of the kibitka, muffled up in blankets and in Fournier's great cloak, enduring the agonizing jolting without a murmur of complaint because she would not add to Barbe's difficulties.

Barbe's courage and fortitude were quite incredible. She slept for no more than three hours a night and she saw to everything. When they halted for the night she would make a fire and cook the invalid a soup of flour, rice and such few vegetables as they had left, concoct hot possets out of melted snow and heat up large stones that could be slipped inside Marianne's blankets at night to keep her warm. Nor did she neglect the horse but curried him at every halt, fed him, even put a blanket over him and saw that he was tethered out of the wind. By day, she sat stolidly in the driving seat, her eyes fixed on the line of the road, which was inclined to be haphazard except where it ran through trees. She had even used the gun against a pack of wolves, handling it with a skill denoting long practice. Her whole being was concentrated on a single thought: to get to Vilna, where the house where they were to put up belonged to a Jewish apothecary who was also a physician.

It was not more than a week after their adventure at Studianka that they caught their first sight of Vilna. Nestling in a line of hills, between the arms of two rivers, the Wilia and the Wilenka, it was built around an impressive mound, the long-ago tomb of the earliest Lithuanian princes, and surmounted by a red brick citadel. Streaming from its highest point was the imperial eagle of France on its tricolour ground, and beside it the personal standard of the Duke of Bassano, who governed the city for Napoleon. Here there was no longer any fear of Cossacks. The town was undamaged, well-provisioned and well-defended.

In summer weather, the Lithuanian capital, set amid rolling hills, with its white walls, red roofs, dome and baroque, Italianate palaces and its magnificent churches, presented a gay and colourful appearance but now the colours were dulled by the universal covering of snow. Even so, the sight of the lovely city drew a great sigh of relief from Barbe.

'Here we are at last! Now we'll be able to take proper care of you. All we have to do now is to find out where Moïse Chakhna lives. And we'll stay there for as long as it takes to get you well again.'

'No!' Marianne protested, making painful efforts to sit up. 'I don't want to stay – not more than two or three days, so that you can have a rest, Barbe. Then we'll go on.'

'But it's madness! You are ill – very ill, I think. Do you want to die?'

'I – shan't – die! We must go on. I want – to get to Danzig as soon as possible – do you understand? As soon as possible!'

A violent fit of coughing shook her and she fell back, bathed in sweat. Realizing that it was better not to persist, Barbe shrugged and set out to look for their host in the city.

Moïse Chakhna's house was in the suburb of Antokol, not far from the bank of the Wilia and next door to a pretty, half-ruined Italianate palace which had belonged to the powerful Radziwill family. Unlike the Jewish houses they had seen before, it was a place of some style, for the Jewish community in Vilna was both rich and influential. The majority lived in the centre of the city, in a jumble of dark and tortuous alleyways bounded by the three principal streets, but some of the most eminent dwelt on the outskirts, in houses befitting their wealth and abilities.

Marianne and Barbe were welcomed there with an almost biblical hospitality. As in the other places where they had stayed, no one asked them any questions, although it must have been apparent that they were not of the people of Israel. Solomon's letters clearly worked as a powerful charm. Moïse Chakhna and his wife Esther did everything necessary for the invalid but when she told them of her wish to continue her journey in two days' time, the apothecary frowned.

'You cannot do it. You are suffering from severe bronchitis. You must stay in bed and, what is most important, you must avoid all risk of catching cold again, for you would be risking your life.'

Even then she persisted, with the obstinacy of the very sick. Her determination was strengthened now by fear of these vast, inhospitable wastes of country with their endless snows and sunless, hopeless skies. She wanted to escape from them as soon as she could. The thought had become an obsession with her, fixed in her head like the barbed arrow of some demon archer. To tear it out now might be to tip her over into madness.

What she longed for was to see the sea again, even in a port so northerly as Danzig.

The sea was her friend, a friend that had always spared her life, even though it had more than once put it in danger. The sound of the sea washing the shores of England had lulled her through most of her childhood and for years now it had carried all her dreams, her hopes, her love. In the depths of her illness, Marianne was convinced that somehow everything would be miraculously all right, her health restored and her sufferings at an end, as soon as she came safe to a harbour.

Barbe, worried as she was, could still understand the sick girl's overriding longing to be gone.

'Do what you can for her,' she said to Moïse. 'I will try to make her stay another two or three days by telling her how tired I am, but I don't think it will be any good.'

In fact it was five days before Marianne declared that she would wait no longer and by that time the fever had almost left her.

'I must go to Danzig,' she kept repeating. 'I know I shall be strong enough for that. But I must go quickly – as quickly as I can. Something is waiting there for me.'

She could not for the life of her have explained just why it was that she felt so certain. Barbe, in any case, put it down to her illness. But as she had lain there with the fever on her, her mind wandering in vague feverish dreams, Marianne had gradually convinced herself that her fate was waiting for her there, in that Baltic port where she had so longed to go with Jason. Perhaps, after all, that fate would take the form of a ship . . .

Barbe was no actress but she was still trying manfully, and with no success at all, to portray a woman in the last stages of exhaustion, when she received the first direct order she had ever had from her mistress. She was to have the kibitka ready to leave tomorrow, Marianne told her, and when Barbe tried to argue she was told that Kovno, the next and final stage of the kibitka's journey, was no more than twenty leagues ahead of them. Marianne was in haste, too, to hand over the precious package entrusted to her to Solomon's cousin. It was beginning to weigh on her mind. In her weakened state, her mind had begun to play superstitiously with the belief that those jewels, taken from a church, might be a cause, if not the only one, of all her sufferings. Moreover, those pearls had only narrowly escaped ending in the Berezina along with herself.

Barbe found her orders all the more distressing because they were interrupted by frequent fits of coughing. As a last resort it seemed to her that the physician's voice might be more effective than her own, but much to her surprise she found, when she went in search of Moïse, that his eagerness to detain them in his house had waned considerably. Unless, that was, they were willing to remain there alone and exposed to possible unpleasantness.

'I am leaving,' he explained. 'I and my family. We shall quit Vilna very soon for Riga where we have a house and kinsfolk. It is unwise for us to remain longer here if we care for our possessions – and even for our lives.'

When Barbe expressed astonishment, he told her of the latest news which was going about the country. It was disastrous news for the French, because it said that Napoleon's army, broken and starving after a series of catastrophic engagements, was now falling back on Vilna as its one port in a storm. It was said also that there had been some kind of battle that was more like a massacre when the fleeing army had tried to cross the Berezina at the very spot where Barbe and Marianne had made the crossing. The bridges were all destroyed and but for the heroism of the Engineers, who had succeeded in erecting makeshift ones, the whole army might by then have been destroyed or taken prisoner. Many had got across, including a host of civilians following the army, but since then repeated attacks by the Cossacks had caused more tragic gaps in the ranks.

'As far as I can gather,' Moïse said, 'all this took place on about the day that you reached here. Since then, Napoleon has been making for Vilna as fast as he can, dragging in his train a host of desperate and starving men to descend on us like locusts. They will want houses and huge quantities of food and we shall be ravaged to supply them. And we Jews most of all, for we are always the first to suffer when there is looting or requisitioning. Therefore I would rather take my family and my most precious possessions out of harm's way while there is still time. They can burn my house after that if they please. It will be no more than an empty shell. So that is why,' he went on gravely, 'I must, for my own sake, so far fail in hospitality as to beg you to resume your journey. All I can suggest is that you follow us to Riga—'

'No, no. We may as well continue on our own road. But can you give us some protection for my mistress, to save her as far as possible from the dangers of a relapse. In this cold weather it is still to be feared.'

'Of course, of course! You shall have furs, and lined boots, even a stove which you may keep alight in the kibitka, and food, of course.'

'Thank you. But what of you, will you be permitted to leave? The French governor—'

Then Moïse Chakhna did something very odd for one of his quiet, even rather reserved, disposition. He shook his fist, as though at some invisible third person present in the room.

'The governor? His grace the Duke of Bassano does not believe the rumours of disaster. He is threatening imprisonment for anyone who spreads them. He himself is thinking of giving a ball. But I, I know that every word of it is true and I am going!'

The next day, the kibitka resumed its journey to Kovno and the crossing of the Niemen. True to his promise, the physician had provided the two travellers generously with everything they needed against the cold, nor were his provisions at all unnecessary because now, at the beginning of December, temperatures dropped, suddenly and dramatically. The thermometer fell to 20 degrees below zero, the rivers froze and the carriage wheels no longer sank into the soft snow. The horse, too, moved surefootedly over the hard surface, although they dared not travel very fast because of the danger of overturning the top-heavy vehicle altogether.

To help maintain its balance, Barbe wrapped woollen rags about her boots and resigned herself to walking beside it, for she was desperately afraid of seeing it capsize and throw Marianne out on to the ice.

Fortunately, quite contrary to her fears, Marianne seemed to be rather better than otherwise. The fever had not returned and her cough had loosened and the fits were not so long. But to be on the safe side, Barbe made her stay wrapped up in her furs, so that only her eyes showed, bright and feverish.

In this way they travelled for three days and nights before they came within reach of the Niemen. On the evening of the third day, Barbe was so worried by the increasing cold that she refused to stop at all, especially since by this time they were in the midst of an exposed plain with no possible shelter anywhere.

'We may as well go on now,' she declared, when they stopped as they had to for something hot to eat and drink. Scattering the remains of their fire with her foot, she added: 'Tomorrow morning we shall be in Kovno.'

And so all that night Barbe walked on, carrying a lantern to light the way. She walked on doggedly until the devil sent a new ordeal to try her. Two hours before dawn, when they were actually within sight of Kovno, one of the rear wheels of the kibitka struck some unseen obstacle and broke. The kibitka lurched violently and ground to a halt.

Marianne, who had been dozing, was woken by the shock. She poked her head outside and saw Barbe's face, white and shining with mutton fat, loom up, moon-like, in the light of the lantern. In spite of the grease, which was designed to prevent her skin from chapping, little crystals of ice had formed in her eyebrows and under her nose, where her breath had frozen. Her whole face was a picture of despair.

'We've broken a wheel,' she wailed. 'We can't go on! No, no—' as she saw Marianne preparing to descend. 'Don't get out! It's much too cold. You'll catch your death.'

'I'll catch it either way if we have to stay here very much longer. Are we very far from Kovno?'

'Two or three versts at most. You can see from here where the Wilia runs into the Niemen. The best thing might be—'

She had no time to say what the best thing might be, however, for just then a horseman swept round a bend in the road and bore down on them. He just managed to avoid the kibitka, which was occupying the crown of the road, but was no sooner past than he struck the bank and fell. He was up again almost at once and helping his horse back on its feet. Then, cursing volubly in French, he made his way back to the vehicle.

'Thunder of God! What in hell's going on here? You damned—' He had drawn his pistol and seemed inclined to use it. Barbe cried out quickly before he could take aim.

'It will do you no good to kill us. We've broken a wheel and we've troubles enough of our own!'

Startled at hearing his own language coming from this unrecognizable being that looked as if it were part and parcel of the country around, the man came closer.

'Oh, you're women. I'm sorry, but I could not know that and I came the very devil of a cropper. What's more, I'm in a hurry.'

As he came into the lantern light, Marianne saw to her astonishment that the man was not a soldier but an outrider of the Emperor's household. So shatteringly unexpected was his presence here, in this icy wilderness, that before she could stop herself she had demanded to know his business. Whereupon he introduced himself.

'Amodru, Madame, Outrider to his Majesty the Emperor and King. I am riding to command fresh horses. The Emperor is behind me.'

'What's that? The Emperor, do you say?'

'Will be here at any moment! So forgive me if I desert you. I'll send someone to you from Kovno. And in the meanwhile, I'll give you a hand to get this cart to one side, or else his Majesty will be obliged to stop – though I should hope less violently than I did! Make haste. I'm late already on account of having to fight off a pack of wolves.'

As he spoke, he took hold of the horse's bridle, calling out to Barbe to push as hard as she could. But Barbe did not hear him. At the mention of Napoleon's approach Marianne's first impulse had been to run wildly to hide herself in the open country and Barbe had her hands full to prevent her.

'Please! Don't be a fool! Stay here. He may not even see you. And even if he does, what have you to fear? There is no prison here, no court of law—'

'Give me some help, for God's sake!' the outrider yelled, finding the horse would not obey him.

'What do you expect me to do? Rupture myself lifting the thing? If the Emperor comes, he'll just have to stop, that's all. There'll be soldiers to move the wagon, won't there?'

'I said the Emperor, not the army,' Amodru snapped back angrily. 'His Majesty is obliged to travel on ahead. He must be in Paris as soon as possible. It seems that there's bad trouble there. So are you going to help me— Oh, my God! Here they come'!

Three vehicles had emerged from the clump of trees that marked the bend in the road. They were the Emperor's sleeping coach and two closed carriages, all three white with frozen snow. They were followed by a dozen or so mounted men.

There was no time for Marianne to scramble back into the kibitka and hide. She gave a little moan and clung to Barbe, pressing her face into her shoulder. She was ashamed of the fear which suddenly possessed her, she who had faced so many perils far worse than an Emperor's wrath, even with the full force of the law behind it. Yet what frightened her was not so much Napoleon himself as the ill-luck which dogged her so relentlessly, raising one obstacle after another in her path. It almost seemed as if she were fated never to reach Danzig.

The outrider, meanwhile, was hurrying up to the leading vehicle where a head was already poking out of the window. Marianne heard a well-known voice demanding impatiently: 'Well? What is the matter here? What is this vehicle?'

'It belongs to two women, Majesty. They've broken a wheel and I haven't yet managed to clear the road.'

'Two women? What are two women doing at this hour of night on such a road as this?'

'I don't know, Sire. One of them speaks French with a local accent and the other with no accent at all. I think that she is French.'

'Wretched fugitives like ourselves, I daresay. Someone see what can be done for them. I will wait.'

So saying, Napoleon opened the door and sprang out on to the frozen snow. In spite of her terror, Marianne could not help stealing a glance at him as he wriggled out of the great bearskin that enveloped him and came towards her, walking with some difficulty on account of the thickness of his garments and the huge fur boots he wore. Then he was beside them and Marianne's heart was thudding in her breast as he addressed them pleasantly.

'You have suffered an accident, ladies?'

'Yes, Sire,' Barbe answered him hesitantly. 'We were hoping to reach Kovno before daybreak but then this mishap occurred – and my companion is barely recovered from a grave illness. I am afraid for her in this terrible cold.'

'I see. She must have shelter. May I inquire who you are?'

Barbe was opening her mouth to say something when all of a sudden something gave way inside Marianne. Perhaps it was the will to fight. She was tired of struggling against the whole world, mankind and the elements alike. She was tired and she was ill, and it seemed to her that any prison would be preferable to what she had endured. She thrust Barbe aside and, turning so that he could see her face, sank to her knees.

'It is I, Sire! Only I! Do with me what you will.'

He uttered a muffled exclamation and then, without turning, called out sharply: 'Rustan! A light!'

The mameluke hurried forward, looking like a mountain of furs with a turban perched incongruously on top. He carried a lantern and by its fitful light Napoleon studied her face, sunken with illness, and the tears that welled from her eyes and rolled freezing down her wan cheeks. A light flashed briefly on his own eyes and was as quickly extinguished. Then he was bending over her with so stern a look that she could only moan helplessly: 'Sire – will you never forgive me?'

He did not answer but took the lantern from the mameluke's hand.

'Take her,' he said. 'Put her in the coach. Her companion may travel with Constant. The horse can be unhitched and led but don't waste time on the cart. Push the wretched thing into the ditch and let's be on our way. We could all catch our death standing here.'

Rustan lifted Marianne without a word and set her down inside the coach. There was a man there already and Marianne's lips twitched involuntarily when she saw that it was Caulaincourt. He was staring at her in blank astonishment.

'We two seem fated to meet in unusual circumstances, my lord Duke,' she murmured, but then a violent fit of coughing shook her and she could say no more. At once, the Duke of Vicenza slipped a hot brick under her feet and reached for a travelling case from which he took a bottle of wine and a gilt cup. He poured some and held it to the girl's lips.

'You are ill,' he said sympathetically. 'This is no climate for women—'

He broke off as Napoleon climbed back into the coach and settled himself inside his bearskin once more. He appeared to be in a very bad temper. His movements were brusque and he was frowning heavily, but Marianne was feeling somewhat restored by the wine and she risked saying softly: 'How can I thank you, Sire? Your Majesty—'

'Be quiet.' He cut her off short. 'You'll make yourself cough again. Wait until we get to the inn.'

They reached Kovno in no time and drew up outside a house on the outskirts. It bore evidence of having been badly damaged at some time and only half of it was left standing. The rest of the town offered a similar picture, for Kovno had been largely destroyed in a disastrous fire some ten years before and had not yet recovered. Nor had the arrival of the French on this side of the Niemen improved matters. Except for the old castle, some of the churches and about half the dwelling houses, the whole place was in ruins.

The building in front of which the three carriages had stopped was an inn of a sort, kept by a young Italian, a cook who had come there with the army the previous summer. He seemed to be making a success of it because, although he had received no more than a few minutes' warning from the outrider Amodru, who had already ridden on again, he had worked miracles in the time. When Marianne entered the coffee room on Caulaincourt's arm there was a bright fire burning and she saw a table laid ready with a white cloth, white bread, roast chickens, cheese, preserves and wine and she felt as if she had walked into paradise. The room was warm and bright as a new pin and there was a delicious smell of omelettes in the air.

To Guglielmo Grandi, as he came forward bowing, cap in hand, Napoleon said bluntly: 'Have you a good bedchamber?'

'I have three, Imperial Majesty. Three good bedchambers. Does your Majesty wish to honour my house by staying to rest here?'

'Not me, I've no time. But this lady needs a bed. Have a room made ready. I see you've maidservants there. Have them light a fire and make some supper for her.'

He beckoned curtly to Barbe who had just come in, along with the occupants of the other carriages. These proved to be Duroc, General Mouton, Baron Fain and Constant. The latter, recognizing Marianne, came hurrying towards her, his face alight with joy.

'Princess! Good God! This is a miracle!'

Napoleon checked him sternly.

'That will do, Constant. See to it that the lady has everything she needs. And you,' he added, speaking to Barbe who had been staring at him with big, anxious eyes, 'go with her and help her to bed.'

'Sire!' Marianne begged. 'At least let me speak to you, explain—'

'No. Get to bed. You can scarcely stand. I will come up in a little while and tell you what I have decided.'

With that he turned away, as though she had ceased to exist, and began divesting himself of his great overcoat and peeling off numerous woollen garments that enveloped him like the layers of an onion. That done, he went to the table, sat down and began without further ado to demolish the omelette set piping hot before him.

As was his way, the Emperor did not dawdle over his meal. Only about ten minutes after packing Marianne off upstairs, Napoleon followed her. She had just got into the bed, which was so heaped with mattresses that it looked like a ship on the high seas, and was sipping with cautious enjoyment at the first cup of scalding hot milk she had seen for a long time.

She paused when the Emperor appeared and would have handed the cup to Barbe but he stopped her.

'Finish it,' he said, in his most peremptory tone.

Not daring to disobey him or risk trying a temper she knew to be short, Marianne swallowed it down heroically, then, flushed to the roots of her hair, she handed the empty cup to Barbe who curtsied and withdrew. Marianne waited with unaccustomed humility for what the Emperor might have to say to her. It was not long in coming.

'I had given up hope of finding you again, Madame. Indeed, I can scarcely believe even now that it was really you I found shivering in the snow beside the wreck of that pathetic cart.'

'Sire,' Marianne ventured timidly, 'will your Majesty permit me to tell you now—'

'Tell me nothing. I've no time for your story, or your thanks. My coming to your assistance was a matter of common humanity. Thank God for it.'

'Then – may I ask what your Majesty means to do with me?'

'What do you expect me to do with you?'

'I don't know, only – since your Majesty went to the trouble of having me sought for – and even of putting a price on my head—'

Napoleon laughed shortly. 'A price on your head? Don't exaggerate. If I did offer to pay for news of your whereabouts it was not in order that I might have the pleasure of shooting you, nor did I expect you to imagine anything of the kind! I am not, let me tell you, either a tyrant or a madman, nor is my memory so short. I have not forgotten what service you have rendered, or that it was for my sake alone that you thrust yourself into this hornet's nest of a country.'

'But I helped your prisoner to escape—'

'Allow me to finish. I have not forgotten that you once loved me and that, when your heart is involved, you are capable of behaving with the utmost folly, like this escapade of yours in rescuing that contumacious cardinal. And finally, I have not forgotten that I have loved you and that you will never be indifferent to me.'

'Sire—'

'Be quiet. I told you I was in haste. If I sought for you, it was because I hoped to save you first of all from yourself, by preventing you from running after your American's coat-tails, and then from the unbelievable perils of that country – perils which I have been able to measure fully since your disappearance and in comparison with which you seem to me very frail. Has it never occurred to you that I might have been afraid – God, how afraid, that you had perished in the fire? No, I'm very sure you did not give a thought to it!'

'How could I have guessed that? I thought—'

'It was not for you to think. Your duty was to obey. Of course I should have been angry with you – but I have been angry before and you have taken no harm, I think? Then I should have sent you back to your own house in France as soon and as expeditiously as possible.'

Moved to tears by this, Marianne murmured huskily: 'Do you mean, Sire, that – that you are not going to punish me for my disobedience?'

'By no means. But the very fact that you are here, and in this condition, is the best possible proof that you have not betrayed the promise you made me, by which I mean that you did not take the road to St Petersburg, easy as that would have been for you. Because of that, I shall inflict no worse penalty on you than I have done.'

'And – that is?'

'Your house in Paris is yours no more. Just as you have long ceased to be Mademoiselle d'Asselnat de Villeneuve. Your family's mansion shall belong henceforth, as of right, to your cousin, Mademoiselle Adelaide d'Asselnat.'

There was a lump in Marianne's throat and she lowered her eyes so that he should not see the sudden pain in them.

'Does that mean – that Paris is closed to me? That I must live in exile?'

'That's a funny word for an *émigrée* brought up in England. But don't imagine I'm sending you back to Selton Hall. No, you are not exiled, only you may no longer make your home in Paris. You will not be forbidden to visit it, but you will live henceforth where you belong.'

'And where is that?'

'Don't play the simpleton with me. You are Princess Sant'Anna, Madame, and you will live with your husband and your son. No other home within the Empire is permitted to you.'

'Sire!'

'No argument. What I have said is no more than you have already promised. Go back to Prince Corrado. He is worthy of your love, even if – the colour of his skin is not what might be looked for in such a man.'

'The – colour of his skin? Then your Majesty knows—'

'Yes, madame, I know. In the hope of sparing you my displeasure at the news of a divorce, Prince Sant'Anna has confided his secret to me, trusting to my honour. I had his letter in Moscow. His hope in writing to me was to make me understand you better and forgive you for blindly following your heart to America. I know now what manner of man you have married.'

He moved slowly to the bed and laid his hand on her shoulder as she sat listening with bent head, overwhelmed by feelings she could not control.

'Try to love him, Marianne. No man could deserve it more. If you want me to forgive you wholly and completely, be a good wife to him – and bring him back with you to my court. A man of his quality should not live apart from the world. Tell him that. And tell him also that after the welcome he will receive from me, no one will dare to look askance at him.'

The tears were streaming down Marianne's cheeks now, but they were blessed tears of relief and gladness. Turning her head quickly, she pressed her moist lips to the pale hand that gripped her shoulder, but she could not utter a single word. They remained thus for a moment, then Napoleon gently withdrew his hand and walked to the half-open door.

'Constant!' he called. 'You have it ready?'

The Emperor's valet appeared almost at once and placed a folder and some loose papers in Marianne's hands.

The Emperor explained.

'Here is a passport, a requisition order for a vehicle, a permit to obtain post horses and, finally, money. Go to sleep now. Rest here for a few days and then go on to France by easy stages. When you leave here, take a sledge if you can. It's what I'm going to do.'

'You are going now, Sire?' Marianne asked timidly.

'Yes. I must get back as soon as possible. I've had word that in my absence a crazy fool named Malet, by declaring that I was dead, has come within an ace of succeeding in a *coup d'état*, thanks to the stupidity and carelessness of those I left in charge in Paris. I'm off again almost at once.' He turned to Constant, who was standing on one side, awaiting orders. 'Has it been decided yet which route we are to take? Königsberg or Warsaw?'

'The Duke of Vicenza has just dispatched a man to Gumbinnen to see what the road is like to Königsberg, since that is the most direct.'

'Good. Let's go. We may be able to make a detour if the going is bad. It might be better to avoid going through Prussia. Farewell, Madame. I hope that we may meet again in less tragic circumstances.'

For the first time for a long while, Marianne found herself able to smile.

'Farewell, Sire. If God answers my prayers for you, your journey will be a safe one. But before you go, Sire, tell me – about the army. Is it as terrible as I have heard?'

The Emperor's tired, handsome face tautened suddenly, as though at a blow. The hard eyes filled with a grief such as Marianne could never have suspected him of feeling.

'It is worse,' he said heavily. 'My poor children – they have slaughtered them, and the fault is mine! I should never have stayed so long in Moscow. I was deceived by that damned sunshine – and now I must leave them, leave them just when they still need me so badly.'

Marianne thought that he was going to weep but Constant came softly to his master and deferentially touched his arm.

'They have men to lead them, Sire. They will never be quite abandoned as long as they have men like Ney and Poniatowski, Oudinot, Davout and Murat to command them.'

'Constant is right, Sire,' Marianne said eagerly. 'And the Empire needs you – we all need you. Forgive me for reminding you of your grief.'

He shook his head as if to say that it was nothing and passed a shaking hand across his face. Then, with the shadow of a smile for her, he left the room and Constant closed the door softly after him. Very soon, the morning streets were echoing to the sound of departing vehicles. It was broad daylight by now and the weather was clearing.

Marianne and Barbe left Kovno three days later in a travelling coach mounted on runners, drawn by a pair of horses, and took the steep hill that led out of the town in the direction of Mariampol. While Marianne lay in bed at the inn, Barbe had gone in search of Ishak Levin and handed over to him his cousin's letter and the pearls, as well as the little horse that had brought them. She had also told him where to find the damaged kibitka. She had returned from this visit with new clothes that were not merely warm but also more in keeping with her mistress's proper station in life. Barbe could not help remarking with deep satisfaction as she took her place in the coach beside Marianne: 'I was quite right in thinking our luck would turn one day, but I'd no idea it would be so soon. Now your Highness has no more need to worry. All our adventures are at an end.'

Marianne glanced at her and behind the big muff of black fox that she was holding before her face, her lips twitched with something of their old irony.

'Do you think so? Oh, my poor Barbe, I'm very much afraid I'm one of those women who go on having adventures until the day they die. But I hope you won't have to suffer again as you did on that appalling journey.'

At Mariampol they learned that the Emperor had abandoned the idea of travelling by the direct route, by way of Königsberg and Danzig and had elected instead to go by Warsaw, so as to revive the waning enthusiasm of his Polish allies, chilled by the news of the reverses he had suffered. But Marianne had no reason to alter her own route and they pressed on towards the Baltic despite the difficulties of the road, where snowdrifts often made the going painful. More than once in the course of that long journey, Marianne blessed the encounter with Napoleon which had made it possible for her to travel in this unlooked-for luxury.

'In our kibitka, I don't think we should ever have got there,' she confided to Barbe.

'Oh, we'd have got somewhere right enough, only there's a good chance it would have been to heaven.'

Even so, with regular changes of horses and stopping at inns for no longer than they needed to snatch a bite of food, it took them nearly a week to reach Danzig. The cold was intense and as they drew nearer to the sea they ran into such a storm as wrought havoc in the countryside and sent the sea storming against the shore.

They caught their first sight of Danzig one evening through the raging wind that swept across the flat, low-lying plain whipping up flakes of frozen snow. Built on a marshy site between two rivers and the estuary of another, the Vistula, it loomed up beneath a darkening of ragged cloud like a ghost city among the massive white shapes that were the military earthworks ordered by Napoleon and discontinued when the first frosts came.

The land hereabouts was so low that it might have been Holland but for the high hills to the south-west. But beyond the dark mass of the ancient Teutonic city was the boiling whiteness of the sea, making a roar like gunfire as it bombarded the dykes.

Marianne had spoken little during the journey. She sat huddled in her furs, her face turned to the window, staring out at the snow-covered world through which their sledge was gliding smoothly now on its great wooden runners. She seemed, if not perfectly restored to health, at least a great deal better and Barbe could not understand why, as they drew nearer to Danzig, her mood seemed to grow more dark and sad.

She could not know that in this city by the sea, Marianne was to face a great decision in which no one could help her but herself. What lay before them in the drear light of that late afternoon was, for her, the crossroads, the point of no return. It was there that she must make the ultimate decision, on which all the remainder of her life would depend.

Either she would continue on the road mapped out for her by the Emperor, with a wisdom it did not even occur to her to dispute, or she must disobey him once again, for the last time, perform her final act of rebellion and burn her boats once and for all. If she did that she would go down to the harbour in Danzig and try to find a ship to carry her out through the bay, dotted with low-lying islands on which the sea broke in foam, and through the perilous Nordic straits to some Atlantic port where she could take passage at last for America. But what would she find there? That was the question she was asking herself, sitting silently in the sledge, throughout that long journey.

And the answer had been: the unknown, waiting for someone to come to her, for the end of the war, for love, yes, and happiness, perhaps. That it could be at most a partial happiness was certain. It could not be otherwise because Marianne knew herself too well now to be unaware that, even married to Jason and the mother of more children, there would always be one corner of her heart that would mourn for little Sebastiano, for the child who would grow up without her and who might one day, grown a man, meet with no feeling whatsoever, a woman who would be his mother.

Only in Danzig could that heart-rending choice be made. Easy as it looked, it would be impossible to return to France and sail from Bordeaux, Nantes or Lorient. If she wanted to vanish, she must do it now, once and for all, because only then would it seem feasible. It was a long way from Danzig to Paris and the weather so bad that an accident was always possible. Her friends would believe her dead and it would not occur to Napoleon to revenge himself on her family. They would mourn her for a little while and then forget her. Yes, the thought of such an escape was tempting because it would effectively wipe out all trace of Marianne d'Asselnat de Villeneuve, Princess Sant'Anna. She would be born again and one fine day a new woman, without ties, without a past, would step out on to the quay at Charleston and start to breathe a new air . . .

A cough from Barbe brought her back to earth.

'Are we stopping here, my lady?' she asked. 'Or are we simply changing horses and going on?'

'We'll stop, Barbe. I'm tired out. I need a rest and so do you.'

They entered the city just as the courier bearing the mails was leaving it in a miniature whirlwind of flying snow after changing horses, clattering over a wooden bridge above the white and frozen waters of a moat. And as the sledge glided through the narrow streets of the old Hanseatic town it seemed to Marianne that she was being carried back into the Middle Ages. It was a medieval world of tall, gabled houses, timbered walls and upper storeys overhanging narrow alleys, dark as mountain chasms.

Here and there, round the corner of a street, a soaring red church would rise in gothic splendour, as though out of the mists of time, or it might be a mansion, a period gem bearing witness to the city's wealth in the fifteenth or the seventeenth century. Yet those few people they saw who were not soldiers of the mixed French, Dutch, German and Polish garrison commanded, since General Rapp's departure for Russia, by General Campredon, were plainly dressed and their cheerless looks were out of keeping with the beauty of this queen of northern cities. There was an atmosphere of constraint, of suppressed anger and an obstinate reserve.

The carillon in the imposing town hall, its belfry reminiscent of the Flemish towns, was striking four as the sledge made its way along the waterfront, lined with tall houses buffeted by the howling wind. Just opposite the Krantor, the corn exchange, was an inn. The snow lay thick on its gilded signboard and the lights that twinkled behind its small, bottle-glass windows were bright and welcoming. There was a continual coming and going through the low doorway, sailors in sealskin boots and soldiers muffled to the eyebrows, and those coming out were noticeably redder in the face than those who went in.

The sound of the sledge brought out the innkeeper attended by a beanpole of an ostler with heavy clogs on his feet, both bowing low at the sight of such evidently well-to-do travellers. Marianne had just descended and was about to enter the inn when she was jostled aside by a tall, red-headed individual coming out. He was singing loudly, evidently the worse for drink, and the song he was singing was an Irish air.

'Hic! Pardon me!' this person remarked, gently removing the human obstacle from his path.

Marianne would have known him anywhere.

'Craig!' she cried with amazement. 'Craig O'Flaherty! What in heaven's name are you doing here?'

He had been on the point of walking on, but at the sound of his name he paused and screwed up his eyes like someone peering through a fog.

'Craig!' she repeated rapturously. 'It's me! Marianne!'

He bent down at that and picking up a handful of snow rubbed it energetically over his face and head. Then he looked again.

'So it is, by St Patrick!'

Uttering a joyful bellow, he swept her bodily up off the ground and held her, like a little girl, at arms' length before setting her down, none too gently, and depositing a couple of smacking kisses on either cheek.

'Glory be! It can't be true! Sure and if this doesn't beat all! You! You here, me darlin', I can scarce believe it! But come away with you, into this thieves' kitchen here. You'll be perished with cold – and we have to celebrate this!'

In another moment, while Barbe went with the landlord to take possession of a well-appointed bedchamber looking out over the harbour, Marianne, regardless of the soldiers and sailors drinking and smoking their clay pipes all around them, was sitting with Craig beside the big white porcelain stove that was roaring like a furnace. The Irishman was calling loudly for brandy.

'I'd rather have tea,' Marianne said hastily. 'But tell me, Craig, tell me quickly – are you here alone, or did you find Jason?'

He shot her a swift glance that suddenly held no trace of inebriation in it.

'I found him,' he said briefly. 'He's on board just now. But tell me about yourself. I want to know—'

But Marianne was not listening. Her heart was banging like a demented gong within her and her cheeks were flushed with excitement. So she had been right! Her premonitions had not been deceiving her, nor those dreams which had so often seemed like nightmares: something had been waiting for her at Danzig, and that something was Jason! She clasped Craig's hand with both hers where it lay on the table while he rummaged with the other for his pipe.

'I want to see him. At once! Tell me where he is. What ship is this?'

'There, there! Keep calm! You'll see him, but for God's sake don't get excited. I'll tell you all about it. Sure, it won't take long.'

Nor did it, for there was little enough to tell. Craig had reached St Petersburg without much difficulty, thanks to the name of Krilov which he brandished like a passport whenever he fell in with Russian troops. In this way he had accomplished the entire journey on horseback, with an official escort into the bargain, since he had been obliged to pass through the lines of Wittgenstein's defending army to reach the capital. Once there it had been a simple matter to find the Krilovs' house and Beaufort.

The two of them had stayed in the little palace on the bank of the Neva until they were able to find a ship to take them out of Russia. This was no easy matter because Russian ships no longer plied through the Denmark Straits since the beginning of the war with France, and there could, of course, be no question of an American citizen taking a passage on one of the occasional English ships that dropped anchor in the roadstead since those two countries were also at war.

In the end, they had found berths on a Swedish vessel which, owing to the double game played by the Swedish crown prince, Bernadotte, was equally immune from the effects of the continental blockade and from difficulties with the Tsar. The master of the *Smaaland* had agreed to carry Beaufort and O'Flaherty as far as Anvers, from which port they should find it comparatively simple, despite the French occupation, to get a ship for America.

'We ought not to be here at all by rights,' the Irishman concluded. 'We only called at Danzig to make good the storm damage we suffered after leaving Königsberg. Our vessel broke a mast and we were forced to run for port. We've been here three days now and while she's refitting—'

'You are making a study of the local hostelries,' Marianne finished for him merrily. 'I see it all! But now, please won't you take me to Jason? I can't wait to see him.'

'Sure, you can spare a moment yet. Tell me what became of yourself.'

'That can wait, but I cannot! Oh, Craig, can't you see what this means to me? It's like a miracle finding him again when I had thought him gone for ever! Have mercy on me and take me to him. You can see I'm dying of impatience.'

It was quite true. Incapable of sitting still a moment longer, she had jumped up, forgetting all about the hot tea that a maidservant had just set before her, and was already halfway to the door. O'Flaherty was obliged to follow. Tossing a few coins on to the table, he followed her outside but the look on his face might have done something to cool her ardour had she paused to look at him. But Marianne was carried away by an emotion stronger than herself, by a joy so delirious that it came close to madness. Regardless of the freezing wind in her face and of the foreign city all about her, she had eyes for nothing but that one familiar figure that was dearer than all else to her. The doubts, the half-promises wrung from her by Napoleon were all gone and all that mattered was that she had found her love again.

Hardly knowing even where she was going, she ran on, skidding perilously over patches of frozen snow, hurrying down the long waterfront in the gathering purple dusk. The *Smaaland*, Craig had said, and she was searching for a vessel with that name and a broken mast. She wanted to shout out loud and call to Jason, to proclaim in triumph that the moment had come when they could be together for always. Meanwhile, Craig pounded breathlessly after her, shouting: 'Marianne! Marianne, for God's sake, wait for me! Let me explain!'

But she neither heard nor saw. She was all instinct and joy and passionate eagerness and with the sureness of a compass needle swinging magnetically to the north, she went straight to that ship that she had never seen.

Then, all at once, he was there, the man she had loved more than her own life. She saw him walking easily, with his long, loose-limbed stride, down the gangway connecting a big, swag-bellied vessel with the quay. The cry that burst out of her then rang like a paean of victory.

'Jason!'

He heard and gave a start of surprise. One glance was enough to tell him and they met at the foot of the gangway. Laughing and crying at once, Marianne flung herself into his arms with such enthusiasm that she all but tumbled into the water. Jason caught her in a strong grip and as she clung to him on the verge of hysteria led her gently away from the edge, but without letting go his hold.

'You!' he uttered. 'Is it really you?'

A trickle of icy water came to damp down the blaze of joy. There had been amazement in his voice and something very close to disbelief, but no real gladness. It was not the welcome she had hoped for.

'Yes,' she said, in what was almost an undertone. 'It's really me . . . Did you – did you think I was dead?'

'No, of course not. Craig told me you were safe and had managed to reach Napoleon. I'm only surprised because I'd not thought to see you here. It's so unexpected—'

Marianne released herself then and stepped back to look at him. Could he really be just the same as she remembered him? There was still the same tall, lean, active figure, the same strongly marked features, the same face, too deeply tanned ever to revert to its natural whiteness, the same hawk-like profile, the same brilliant eyes – and yet it suddenly seemed to her that she was looking at another man, a man she did not know.

What was it? Was it in the hard twist to the mouth, a certain weariness in the eyes or something distant in his whole attitude? It was as if he had suddenly removed himself into another world. Still gazing at him intently, she nodded slowly.

'So unexpected?' she repeated after him. 'Yes, you are right. It's quite incredible that we should meet like this! Especially since you have really done nothing at all to make it happen.'

There was a flash of the old, mocking smile that she had always loved.

'Don't talk nonsense. How could I have done? There were armies between us, and a whole vast country.'

'You knew I was in Moscow. Why didn't you come back? Why didn't you look for me? That woman who tried to kill me, Shankala, she told us before she died that you had gone with your friend Krilov, without a thought for me! I was alone, lost in a doomed city, and you could not know what would become of me, and yet you left me.'

He shrugged a little wearily and the light that had come into his blue eyes a moment before died suddenly.

'I had no choice, but you had! I thought you would have followed me when the Cossacks took me.'

'Haven't you heard what prevented me?' She turned her head sharply to where Craig O'Flaherty, seeing them together, had paused beside a stack of empty casks a few yards off and was watching them.

'Yes, when O'Flaherty joined me, I heard then. But when I left Moscow I did not know. I thought – that Napoleon was near and you had made your choice.'

'Made my choice!' Marianne said bitterly. 'Is there any choice to be made when everything is burning and collapsing and dying all round you? I had to think of survival before I could start making any choices! While you—'

'Come. We can't stand here. It's too cold.'

He would have taken her arm to lead her back to the inn but once again she moved away, leaving the remainder of her sentence unspoken. For a moment or two they walked side by side in silence, each lost in their own thoughts, and Marianne's throat contracted as the conviction came to her that never again would they be reunited, even in spirit.

As they came level with the Irishman, Jason paused for an instant.

'All's ready now,' he said shortly. 'We sail with the tide. Weather's fairing up.'

Craig nodded and with a smile for Marianne in which she seemed to read both sorrow and a hint of compassion, he went on without a word to where the *Smaaland* lay.

Silence fell again between them, broken only by the drunken singing of three sailors reeling gloriously from a waterside tavern. Marianne was struggling to still the frantic beating of her heart beneath her furs. It seemed to have got colder all at once, although the wind had dropped, but then she realized that the cold was inside herself. It was spreading from the numbness round her heart.

'You are going?' she asked after a moment.

'Yes. Our ship is fit to sail again – and we have wasted too much time already.'

She gave a tiny laugh. 'Yes, you're right. You have wasted a deal of time to be sure.'

Did he sense the bitterness in her tone? Abruptly, he seized her by the arm and drew her into the deep shadow of a doorway where they were comparatively sheltered from the wind.

'Marianne,' he begged, 'why do you say that? You know very well how things stand with us just now! You know I'm going to the war, that I'm no longer my own man, that I have no future to look forward to. It's true. I have wasted too much time, for my time is my country's and my country is at war. We agreed that you should join me later on, remember? Have you forgotten that?'

'No. I think it's you who have forgotten – forgotten even me!'

'This is madness!'

'Very well then. There is one thing that has not even occurred to you. Ever since we met just now, it has not once crossed your mind to ask what I am doing here, how I escaped from Moscow and what has happened to me since. No! It does not interest you. Craig asked me, and I didn't tell him because I was in too much haste to see you. But then Craig is my friend!'

'And what am I?'

'You?' She uttered a tiny laugh, full of infinite sadness, and shrugged her shoulders faintly. 'You – are a man who loved me once – and who loves me no longer.'

'I do! I swear I do – I love you still!'

All at once he was again the passionate lover of their nights on the hard beds of those posting houses in the empty steppe and the forest. His arms went round her, drawing her to him, and his breath was warm on her face, but she did not return his embrace. Something inside her remained frozen.

'Marianne,' he implored her, 'listen to me! I swear to you as I hope for salvation that I've not stopped loving you. Only – I no longer have the right.'

'The right? Oh yes, the war – I see,' she said wearily.

'No! Listen! Anyone who says that we can ever escape our destiny is a fool or a dreamer! We can never break free from the mistakes that we have made. We must carry them with us for as long as it pleases God to make us! Because we loved each other, you and I, we have done everything we could to bend fate to our will. We've run to the ends of the earth – but however far we've gone, fate has caught up with us. It is stronger than we are.'

'But – what do you mean? What fate?'

'Mine, Marianne. The fate that in my stupidity I forged for myself, out of disappointment, anger, jealousy, call it what you will. Crazy as it seems, it caught up with me back there in St Petersburg, in a city that for us Americans might almost as well be in the middle of Africa. I thought, you know, that I might have some trouble making myself known to the Krilovs, who were my father's friends. I thought that they might well have forgotten the very existence of the last of the Beauforts. Do you know what I found when I reached their house?'

Marianne shook her head. There was something rather frightening about the way he was leading up to this and she was beyond speech. She knew that he was concealing something terrible, something that was going to hurt her very much. It might have been some attempt to soften the blow that made him lower his voice almost to a whisper.

'I found the Krilovs' youngest son – Dimitri – just returned from a voyage to America. His father had sent him to try and find out what had become of us and to renew the old ties, which might lead to some commercial advantage nowadays. He was in Charleston.'

'Yes – well?'

'My – Pilar, whom we thought locked up for good in a Spanish convent, Pilar has come back to me.'

Marianne was conscious of a sudden surge of anger. So this was his destiny? That wretched woman who had done her utmost to send her husband to his death on the scaffold? Who had come near to killing her, Marianne, also! Was this what was worrying him?

'Well?' she cried fiercely. 'What does it matter if she has come back? You can send her packing!'

'No. I can't. Not any more. I have no right to do it. She – she has come back with a child, my child. My son.'

'Oh—!'

Marianne said nothing more, nothing but that one tiny sound, but it held all the cruel anguish of a dying breath. Jason was right. Fate, that fell and cunning sergeant, had caught up with them. Their long, unremitting struggle against it was over at last.

Feeling her body suddenly lifeless against his, Jason tightened his hold and bent his head and tried to kiss her ice-cold cheeks, her closed lips, but she laid her hands flat against that breast where she had dreamed of laying her head all the nights of her life and thrust him gently away without a word. Like a child whose favourite toy is broken, he tried to snatch her back to him, crying out in his sudden grief and terror: 'Say something!

Speak to me! Please! Don't just look at me like that. I know I have hurt you, only speak to me! It's true I love you, you know it is! You are all I love and I'd give anything in the world to be able to live out my dreams with you. Listen – there's no need for us to part yet. Surely we can still snatch a little happiness, a little joy from life? I may die in this war, die far away from you – so come with me! Let me take you aboard this ship. It sails at dawn and it is still many days to Anvers – and many nights. Let me go on loving you to the end! Let us not refuse this last miraculous gift—'

She felt the fever that possessed him. She knew that he was speaking the truth, that he meant what he said, he really did want her to go with him. As he said, it would mean many more days, many more nights for loving, forging a chain of passion which at the last moment he might not have the courage to break. Then, at Anvers, he might ask her again to follow him across the seas to his own land where she might still live a life of secrecy and sacrifice as his mistress. That too would mean many more nights of love – and she did love him so! It was a terrible temptation . . .

In the depths of her misery she might have yielded, might have let him persuade her. But then all at once three faces came into her mind: her father's, proud and sardonic, Corrado's, splendid and sad, and then the tiny, soft face of a sleeping brown-haired baby . . . And with that the weak, desperate and desperately loving Marianne shrank away, driven out by the Marianne d'Asselnat who, on her wedding night and for her honour's sake, had fought the man she loved and left him lying wounded on the floor of Selton Hall, and that same night had sent Jason Beaufort from her. It was no longer possible for her to be any other.

Firmly, now, she pushed him from her and stepped out of the doorway into the icy wind that billowed out her clothes and stung her body like a whiplash. Gripping her hands together tightly inside her muff of black fox fur, she threw her head back proudly and looked for the last time into the pleading eyes of the man she was leaving and who did not deserve that she should abase herself for him.

'No, Jason,' she said gravely. 'I too have a son. I am Princess Sant'Anna.'

Night had fallen. Without looking back, Marianne walked towards the inn which shone through the darkness like a great ship's lantern, or like a beacon through the storm in which her love was foundering.

Epilogue

Journey's End
May 1813

Epilogue

As before, the black and gold iron gates between the pair of stone giants seemed to open of their own accord at the horses' approach. As before, the magical tranquillity of the park descended like a caress upon those who entered.

There was still the same pale, sanded avenue running like a river between the black plumes of cypresses and round, fragrant orange trees to lose itself in the misty spray of the fountains. And yet Marianne was instantly aware of a feeling that something had altered, that these gardens were not quite as they had been three years ago, almost to the day, when she had come there for the first time at the cardinal's side, as one entering an unknown world.

It was a sudden exclamation from Adelaide that gave her the clue to the difference.

'But it's beautiful!' she breathed. 'All those flowers!'

That was it! The flowers! There used not to be any flowers in the gardens, except when the orange and lemon trees were in bloom. Its beauty had derived solely from the contrasting shades of trees and turf and the tossing waters of the fountains where the statues stood unmoving, with an air of infinite boredom. Now there were flowers everywhere, as though a magician in a moment of madness had scattered all the colours of the rainbow over the whole garden. There were pale, fragrant laurels, huge silvery-pink peonies, great purple rhododendrons, pure white lilies and roses, above all roses – an orgy of flowers! Their splendour had brought the great gardens to life. They rioted everywhere, competing with the shining jets of water from the fountains whose refreshing murmur formed a background to the voices of the songbirds. For there were birds, too, as there had not been before, as though the sadness that had weighed on the whole of the enchanted demesne had frightened them away. Now they were singing with all their hearts.

Amused by Marianne's evident surprise, Jolival bent forward and touched her hand.

'Are you awake, Marianne, or are you dreaming? Anyone would think you had never seen these wonderful gardens before.'

She gave a little shiver, as if she were indeed just waking from a dream.

'In a way that's true. I have never seen them like this. There never used to be any flowers, or birds, or any real life at all, I think . . . It was all like a strange dream.'

'You were very frightened then. You can't have looked properly.' And Jolival laughed and turned to his newly wedded bride for confirmation. But Adelaide shook her head at him and slipped her arm through Marianne's.

'You don't understand at all, my dear. For my part, I think this change has come about because there is a child here now. A child can make even a graveyard burst into blossom.'

Adelaide and Arcadius had been married for a month now. On her return to Paris in the previous January, Marianne had found the two of them living a cloistered life together in the Hôtel d'Asselnat, locked in their shared grief and it was that, little by little, had brought them together. They were both sure that Marianne was dead and they mourned for her with all their loving hearts.

The arrival of official documents confirming Adelaide as the lawful owner of the family mansion in place of Marianne had not helped matters. Quite the reverse, in fact. This unexpected inheritance had finally convinced them that Marianne was really gone, especially as no one had been able to give them the slightest news of her. After that they had suddenly felt very lonely and unwanted, no longer knowing what to do with their lives. The house had become a mausoleum and the two of them settled down behind its drawn curtains to wait for the end, with only Gracchus to wait on them, but a Gracchus who no longer sang.

On the night when the mud-bespattered coach bearing Marianne and Barbe had drawn up below the steps, the travellers had been met by two very old people dressed in deepest mourning and leaning on each other's arms, both of whom had, in good earnest, very nearly died of joy.

That unexpected homecoming had truly been a great and wonderful moment. They had clung to each other for minutes on end, unable to tear themselves away, while Gracchus, having kissed his mistress in his turn, sat down on the front steps and sobbed as if he could never stop.

After that, they had sat up all night telling one another their adventures, Arcadius and Gracchus with the convoy led by General Nansouty and Marianne and Barbe on the long road to Danzig. There had been eating and drinking, too, and Adelaide, who for a month had scarcely touched a morsel, had suddenly recovered her old voracious appetite. On that memorable night she had accounted all by herself for a whole chicken, a pâté, an entire dish of prunes and two bottles of champagne.

By daylight, she was slightly grey about the face, but as happy as a queen. And it was then, while she went off to seek her bed with steps that tottered a little, that Jolival turned to Marianne as she stood in the middle of the yellow salon, gazing up at her father's portrait.

'What are you going to do now?'

Without taking her eyes from that proud face whose faintly ironic stare seemed to follow every move she made, she lifted her shoulders in a little shrug.

'My duty. It is time I – for me to grow up, Jolival. And besides – I'm tired of adventuring. You wear yourself out and tear yourself to pieces, and all to no avail. There's Sebastiano – I want to think of him now.'

'Of him alone? There is someone else with him, remember.'

'I've not forgotten. It must be possible to find some sort of happiness in making another person happy. And he more than deserves it, Jolival!'

He nodded, paused for a moment and then said tentatively: 'And – you'll have no regrets?'

She gave him the same proud glance as she had given Jason Beaufort at the moment of parting. But now there was no anger in it. It was as calm and limpid as sunlight on the sea.

'Regrets? I don't know. All I do know is that for the first time for a long while I feel at peace with myself.'

The interminable journey had left her very tired and so she decided to rest for a little while before going on to Italy. The house, needless to say, was still hers to stay in for as long as she pleased. They saw a few friends, among them Fortunée Hamelin, who cried like a schoolgirl when Marianne told her of her meeting with François Fournier. Talleyrand, too, as biting and affectionate by turns as he had ever been, but visibly suffering from a good deal of nervous strain, like Paris itself, which Marianne scarcely recognized.

The city was very grim. The Emperor had come back almost furtively and then, after him, week by week, the survivors of what had been the finest army in the world. Sick and wounded men, dragging frostbitten limbs. Many would never rise again from the beds they had gone through so much to reach. And yet it was said that the Emperor was already trying to assemble a new army. The recruiting sergeants were hard at work. For Prussia was raising its head again, encouraged by the disastrous Russian campaign, fostering small rebellions here and there, mustering arms and allies. In the spring, Napoleon would be off again with fresh troops, and Paris was beginning to murmur.

Yet, one piece of good news there was in these dark days. It came to Jolival through his lawyer, and it was good news in keeping with the times, for it, too, told of a death. Jolival's estranged wife was dead. Septimanie, Vicomtesse de Jolival, had succumbed to a severe inflammation of the lungs, contracted while accompanying the Duchess of Angoulême on charitable errands in the vicinity of Hartwell in the chill of the English winter.

Jolival was not hypocrite enough to weep for her. He had never loved her and she had played little part in his tempestuous life, but he was too fine a gentleman to betray any ill-timed rejoicing.

Marianne did it for him. She had not failed to notice, with pleasure and affection, the bond that had developed between her cousin and the Vicomte de Jolival. Jolival's behaviour to Adelaide held a tenderness and consideration that revealed his feeling for her. And so, on the day that she announced to them her intention of leaving for Lucca almost at once, she went on to say point-blank: 'Now that you are free, Jolival, why don't you marry Adelaide? The two of you get on so well together and it would at least give you some proper status in the family, instead of being merely a sort of adopted uncle.'

Jolival and Adelaide both blushed as red as each other. Then Jolival said quietly, and with evident emotion: 'My dear Marianne, it would give me the greatest happiness – but I am not the most eligible of husbands. I've no money, no estates, still less any expectations. A carcass that's seen better days—'

'Well, I'm not precisely the Queen of Sheba,' Adelaide murmured, fluttering like a schoolgirl. 'But I do think I might make a good wife if I were to be asked.'

'That's settled then,' Marianne told them, smiling. 'You shall be married and then come with me to Italy. It shall be your honeymoon.'

And so, on a late afternoon in April, when the air still had a nip in it, Adelaide d'Asselnat and Arcadius de Jolival were married in the lady chapel of the church of St Thomas Aquinas, with Prince Talleyrand and Madame Hamelin as witnesses. The Vicomte stood straight as an arrow, his dress a symphony of exquisite pearly grey, while Adelaide at his side was radiant in heavy Parma violet silk with a bouquet of violets in her hand, and looking ten years younger in a matching silk bonnet with feathers in it. Afterwards there was a delicious supper at the magnificent Hôtel de Talleyrand in the rue St Florentin, where the Vice Grand Elector had been living for the past year and more, since selling Matignon to the Emperor, at which the great Carême deigned to display the full fruits of his genius.

It was just before midnight on the same night that a man in black came knocking on the door of the house in the rue de Lille. He was heavily cloaked and his face was hidden by a mask, but he bowed to Marianne as to a queen. He extended his black-gloved hand without a word, showing her a gold disc engraved with the four letters: A.M.D.G.

Then Marianne knew that this was the messenger of whom Cardinal de Chazay had told her in Odessa. Hurrying to her bedchamber, she took from her desk the diamond drop that she had carried with her faithfully through so many perils. She did not even pause to take it from its leather bag for one last time, but went straight down again and placed it in the messenger's hand. He bowed once more, then turned and went away. She had not even heard his voice. Nor, indeed, had he heard her, for neither of them had uttered a single word. But when the heavy front door had closed behind the man in black, Marianne sent for Gracchus.

'You can be ready to leave now,' she told him. 'I have nothing more to do here.'

The post-chaise bowled on through the park, with Gracchus sitting on the box in all his former dignity. It reached the vast spreading lawn where the white peacocks were wont to parade majestically, came in sight of the house and drew up at last at the foot of the broad sweep of stone steps lined with white and gold footmen, one of whom stepped forward quickly to throw open the door.

Marianne sprang out, disregarding Jolival's proffered hand, her eyes looking instinctively for the turbanned figure of Turhan Bey. She was followed by Adelaide and by Barbe, and Barbe it was who suddenly clasped her hands together with a soft exclamation.

'Oh! What a little darling!'

Marianne turned. A strange little procession was coming along the driveway from the stables. Rinaldo, the head groom and formidable ruler of the magnificent Sant'Anna stables, was leading a minute grey donkey by the bridle and, perched on its back, held upright by Dona Lavinia's careful hand, was a laughing, black-haired baby boy. And Marianne thought that Rinaldo could not have looked more proud and happy if he had been leading the Prince's favourite stallion, the splendid Ilderim himself.

Dona Lavinia, meanwhile, had caught sight of the travellers and started so violently that she all but let go of the child. But it was only for an instant and then Marianne, standing rooted to the spot by the emotion that swept over her, heard her cry out incredulously.

'Her Highness! Oh God, it is her Highness!'

The next moment she had lifted the protesting boy out of the saddle and was running forward with him bouncing in her arms.

'Hush, my treasure,' she told him, laughing and crying at once, when he objected to this cavalier treatment. 'It's your Mama!'

'Mama – Mama—' At the sound of the baby voice Marianne's heart melted in her breast.

In that instant all the shyness that had paralysed her a moment before suddenly vanished and she leapt forward in her turn, to reach Lavinia only just in time to prevent her from attempting the impossible feat of curtsying with Sebastiano in her arms. Her own arms had gone out to take the child, but then she paused.

His head resting on Lavinia's shoulder, he was looking at her with the mixture of curiosity and alarm that children frequently accord to strangers and Marianne found herself powerless to move. She stood with her hands clasped before her, just as Barbe had done a few seconds before, her eyes devouring this child of hers and her heart turned upside down at the beauty of him.

Sebastiano was big for his fifteen months. His little round face was illumined by a pair of huge green eyes, the very image of his mother's. The white suit he wore showed up the warm golden colour of his neck and his plump little arms. His curly head was black and shining and when all at once he smiled, Marianne caught the gleam of three or four white teeth in the tiny mouth.

Meanwhile, Lavinia was gently detaching the baby's arms from round her neck.

'Well?' she said softly. 'Take him, my lady. He is yours.'

The child made no resistance, as Marianne, in the flurry of heart, had feared he might. He simply went from one pair of arms to the other as if it were something he did every day of his life. Marianne felt the touch of the little bare arm against her neck.

'Mama—' the baby said crooningly. 'Mama.'

Then and only then, holding back her tears for fear of frightening him, did she dare to kiss him. A tide of love rolled over her and drowned her, a torrent that swept away the last doubts, the last hint of regret, while a voice within her whispered in terror as it died away: 'You might never have seen him . . . You might never have held him in your arms . . . You might never . . .'

Carrying her son as proudly as any empress, and with Lavinia at her side, Marianne walked back to the little group at the foot of the steps. They, too, had been moved to tears by the little scene which they had looked forward to, ever since leaving Paris, with an impatience not unmixed with apprehension. Jolival greeted Lavinia as an old acquaintance and introduced his wife. Then, as they were all about to go inside, Marianne plucked up courage to ask the question which had been on the tip of her tongue all along.

'The Prince – my husband— Shall I be permitted to see him?'

The housekeeper's face broke into a beaming smile which left her utterly confused.

'But of course you shall see him, my lady,' Lavinia cried, 'just as soon as he returns.'

'Returns? Is he not at the villa? Oh my God! Do you mean he is away—?'

She had a sudden sense of disappointment, a disappointment so sharp that she herself could not understand it. For months now she had been living with the thought of meeting this strange, attractive man once more, of being with him and sharing the inhuman life that he had chosen for himself, and now she was finding that she must wait longer yet to offer him the gift of herself that she had come to make.

She was so disappointed that it came as something of a shock to hear Lavinia laugh and she did not take in immediately what she was saying.

'No, your Highness, he is not away from home. He is not here at the moment, that is all. But he'll not be long. He has only gone out to the fields.'

'Oh, he has gone—' And then, abruptly, she understood. 'Dona Lavinia, do you mean he has gone out? Outside – in broad daylight?'

'Yes, my lady. The nightmare and the curse are all done with now. You see, he wanted there to be flowers everywhere and all the old, bad memories to be wiped away – for the child's sake. He could not go on living secluded as he had done. The child loves him and would not have understood. It was not easy, but I managed to convince him at last, with Father Amundi's help. And then, when we came back here, we gathered all the servants together, and all the tenants on the estate as well. They were all here, at the foot of these very steps. Father Amundi spoke to them, and then I said a few words, for they all know me and I am one of them, and then at last the Prince came and he burned the white leather mask in the sight of them all.'

'And what then?' Marianne asked anxiously.

'Then? Why then they knelt, every one of them, as though in church, and after that they cheered and cheered until the echoes rang. And they made a feast for two whole days because their prince had shown them his face at last. Listen! Here he comes!'

The sound of galloping hoofbeats made itself heard, waking memories for Marianne. That thunderous beat had haunted her nights in the dark days after her marriage, beating time to the wild gallop of a snow-white stallion. The noise grew louder, nearer, and then in a moment Ilderim and his rider were soaring like white lightning over a tall hedge. The horse came on, leapt again and sailed over the basin of a fountain as lightly as a swallow. Sebastiano, in Marianne's arms, was shouting joyfully: 'Papa! Papapapa!'

Marianne kissed him gently on his little nose and handed him to Lavinia. Then, slowly and steadily, she walked back down the steps and across the lawn to meet the man on the horse. He was on her like a thunderbolt. It seemed likely that he had not even seen her. Yet even then she did not flinch, held spellbound by the wild beauty of that gallop, and in imminent danger of being ridden down if Corrado could not master Ilderim in time.

But there was no question of his mastery of that kingly animal who for so long had been his only friend. Only a few yards away from Marianne, who still had not made the slightest move to avoid him, the great horse reared back, slender legs pawing the air, then dropped on all four feet and stood quietly while his rider sprang lightly to the ground.

Marianne saw then that the bronzed god of her recollection had indeed become a man. He was dressed like any country gentleman going about his land on a summer's day, in well-cut dark breeches, soft leather boots and a white shirt, open at the neck to reveal the dark, smooth muscles of his throat. But his blue eyes were smiling and there was a light in them that she had not seen before.

She was gazing at him so intently that it did not even occur to her to speak. She felt as if she were waking from a dream when he gently took her hand and brushed it with his lips.

'You are welcome,' he said in the low, deep voice that had always moved her so strangely. 'Have you come – to pay us a visit?'

She guessed that even now he could not quite believe that she had come back and that, chivalrously, he was offering her this one last avenue of escape. Yet it seemed to her that in his voice she caught a note of anguish that smote her heart.

'No. I have come to stay, if you still want me to. I have come to be your wife, Corrado, wholly and entirely. I do not ask you to forgive me for all that you have suffered on my account but I am offering myself to you. Will you have me?'

For a moment they stood without speaking. The Prince's blue eyes gazed into hers as though seeking to plumb their uttermost depths, and Marianne was overwhelmed at the passionate desire she read in them, yet the green eyes did not flinch or turn away.

Then, gently, almost timidly, he drew her into his arms.

'What man ever turned his back on the dream of a lifetime?' he murmured.

Marianne knew that night that this was not the first time Corrado Sant'Anna had made her his own, and that the mysterious lover of Corfu had returned to her.

Jean Plaidy

The Regent's Daughter 95p

The Ninth book in the Georgian Saga

The marriage of The Prince of Wales to Caroline of Brunswick was strewn with private skirmish and public scandal yet it did bear a daughter – Princess Charlotte, heiress presumptive to the English throne. Ever bewildered by her bizarre collection of royal relatives, Charlotte grew up honest, forthright and always sure of her destiny . . .

The Goddess of the Green Room 90p

The Tenth book in the Georgian Saga

In the glittering world of scandal and celebrity that was the Georgian theatre Dorothy Jordan reigned as a comic actress of genius. From Dublin's Smock Alley Theatre, her great talent brought her to Sheridan's Drury Lane in the heyday of Regency London. Here she met William, Duke of Clarence. Their liaison was the talk of London and the delight of the cartoonists. Everyone's attention was locked on to The Sailor Duke and his Goddess of the Green Room . . .